Marching With Caesar – Praetorian

By R.W. Peake

Also by R.W Peake

Marching With Caesar® – Birth of the 10th
Marching With Caesar – Conquest of Gaul
Marching With Caesar – Civil War
Marching With Caesar – Antony and Cleopatra, Parts I & II
Marching With Caesar – Rise of Augustus
Marching With Caesar – Last Campaign
Marching With Caesar – Rebellion
Marching With Caesar – A New Era
Marching With Caesar – Pax Romana
Marching With Caesar – Fraternitas
Marching With Caesar – Vengeance
Marching With Caesar – Rise of Germanicus
Marching With Caesar – Revolt of the Legions
Marching With Caesar – Avenging Varus, Part I
Marching With Caesar – Avenging Varus, Part II
Marching With Caesar – Hostage to Fortuna

The Titus Chronicles – Eagle and Wyvern

Caesar Triumphant
Caesar Ascending – Invasion of Parthia
Caesar Ascending – Conquest of Parthia
Caesar Ascending – India
Caesar Ascending – Pandya

Foreword

A common question I get from readers is what level of advance planning I do as I tell the story of the Pullus family, and it's true that way back when I started what is now the *Marching With Caesar* series, I made a vow that my characters would remain in the ranks, and the story would be from a "grunt's-eye view" of the Roman Legions.

However, one of the things I enjoy about what I do is that it's a never-ending learning process, and one of the first things I learned is that a story takes on a life of its own, and while I can plot out the major moments and ensure that characters end up where I want them to end up, *how* they get there can be as much of a surprise to me as it is to the readers. It is, when all is said and done, one of the things that makes me so prolific, because I'm just as interested and excited to find out what happens next as you readers.

I offer this as an explanation of how, despite that early vow, and as the title indicates, Gnaeus Volusenianus Pullus finds himself serving in the Praetorian Guard. In simple terms, he's in the Praetorians because it made sense in context of the story. One thing that the Pullus men have had in their favor (and this was always by design) is something that was absolutely crucial in the Roman world for any man who aspired to a level of greatness; within, of course, the limits imposed by the Roman class system, and that was having a patron. Roman society was famous, and rightly so, for its system of patronage, which is why it made sense to me that, given all that Germanicus has done for Gnaeus, it was time for a bit of *quid pro quo*, and it also made sense that it would concern Lucius Aelius Sejanus, who was just beginning his ascent to become one of the most powerful and second most dangerous man in Rome.

This also fits into a larger issue that has been part of the story since the very beginning, and that's the growing politicization of the Roman military, and I would argue that the shift of power from the Legions to the Praetorian Guard was a direct result of the consequences that confronted Augustus in the aftermath of the second civil war, after the Legions had tasted from the cup of power and found they liked it a great deal. While the army would still be a potent force, it would be the Praetorian Guard that emerged as the true Imperator maker, and it began with Sejanus (and his father), and it's his growing power and influence over Tiberius that concerns Germanicus to the point he feels he needs a pair of eyes that he can trust, inside the Praetorian Guard, which is why we find Gnaeus wearing the Praetorian colors.

On a separate and more personal note, I would be remiss if I didn't acknowledge what an utter shitshow the year 2020 has been, and it's my sincerest hope that, as difficult as it's been, each of y'all have weathered it with the least amount of disruption and pain possible. Very early on, I had a scare where I ran a fever and had a lingering cough for almost two weeks. Since this was also back when getting a test was next to impossible, and with my age and health issues (a couple of autoimmune diseases), it was a stressful time, one that I know others have undergone as well. If we were only dealing with COVID 19, it would be bad enough, but while I have very strong political opinions, I have never, nor will I ever express those beliefs in the world of *Marching With Caesar*. After all, there's more than enough political intrigue going on in Gnaeus Pullus' world, and all I will say is that I hope that we can find our way back towards each other again and start focusing on what we share rather than our differences.

Thanks as always to Beth Lynne for what is now our 22nd collaboration, and to Laura Prevost for the cover (that I'll talk more about in the Historical Notes), but even more than normal, my real thanks goes to y'all, my readers. Over the last few months, dozens of you have reached out personally because of my relative quiet on social media through the MWC Facebook page, and your concern has been, quite simply, overwhelming, and very important to me personally. Thank you isn't enough, so I hope that this story will go some way towards expressing my gratitude.

Semper Fidelis (and to a better 2021)

R.W. Peake

November 27, 2020

Historical Notes

For an organization that had such an outsize impact on Roman history from the early First Century CE until its disbandment by Constantine, precious little is known about the early days of the Praetorian Guard, especially during the early period under the rule of Sejanus. Longtime readers will know that I trace the evolution of the Guard back to Marcus Antonius, when he formed what were known as the Brundisium Cohorts, which was how Titus the Elder and his contemporaries knew them. This story covers the year of 17 CE, when Sejanus becomes the sole power over the Praetorians, after his father is named *Praefectus Augustalis*, and I suspect that there will be some sharp-eyed readers who notice that I actually have Sejanus the Elder assuming that post a bit earlier than the historical record for the purposes of the story, for which I ask their forgiveness.

Otherwise, as always, I tried to hew to the primary record as much as possible, and for this, Tacitus and Dio have the most to say about the Praetorian Guard; it's from them that we know the most about Praetorian pay, for example...but only for men of the ranks, and only Tacitus for the period of time close to the year in the story. Otherwise, the evidence is fragmentary, and from a wide number of sources that range from bronze discharge tablets, funerary monuments, and the odd comments made by other contemporaries like Suetonius. With that in mind, for example, I decided to be a bit vague in describing what Gnaeus got paid as a Centurion, mainly because it has no real bearing on the story.

Along with primary sources, I relied on a couple of works, one more heavily than the other. *Praetorian-The Rise And Fall Of Rome's Imperial Bodyguard* by Guy de la Bédoyère by Yale University Press (2017) is a *very* well researched work, although he expresses the same frustration that I experienced about how little we actually know about the Praetorian Guard, at least when it comes to the kind of details that someone like Gnaeus Pullus would relate to his readers. The second work is *The Praetorian Guard-A History of Rome's Elite Special Forces*, by Sandra Bingham and published by Baylor University Press (2013), and while I found myself turning to de la Bédoyère more often, it's from Bingham, for example, that I learned that the Guard, especially during its early period, relied almost completely on men from the home provinces of Italia.

What we *do* know is that, under Augustus, there were a total of nine Cohorts, and that only three of those Cohorts were permanently stationed in Rome, at least until 23 CE after the construction of the Castra Praetoria, when all nine were brought to Rome. There's no record of which I'm aware or could find that indicates that the three permanently stationed Cohorts shared a barracks prior to that, and which is why I have them housed separately. The fact that they *are* separated, and the location of each barracks, with the First on the Palatine, and the Second on the Esquiline is strictly my own invention, but it's based on the idea of even coverage of the city, and while I never mention the Third's location, it would have been on the Viminal, creating a triangle of sorts with the Forum more or less in the middle. In terms of the landmarks I use, they are accurate; the Temple of Isis, for example, was located on the Esquiline, but aside from well-known examples like the Via Sacra, the Vicus Iugaris, etc., my street names are invented as well.

That brings us to, if experience is any guide, what might be the one thing that will generate the most negative comment from readers, and that is the absolutely crucial question...what color uniforms did Praetorians wear?

The answer, the *real* answer, is that nobody knows to a degree of certainty, at least when it comes to the men of the ranks. Yes, we're fairly certain that Centurions wore togas when on duty, and while I've seen references about rankers going togate, it wasn't in the early days of Sejanus' time as Prefect. I did think about making the tunics white, but in the end, I decided to make them blue as a way of differentiating them from not just the Legions, but the men of the Urban Cohorts, and blue dye, being more expensive back then, seemed to be an appropriate expenditure to make on the men who were, if not the truly elite warriors of the Roman army as they have been portrayed, were at the very least the most prestigious. Consequently, the Praetorians in *Marching With Caesar-Praetorian* wear blue tunics, while the senior Centurions' crests were blue; hopefully, this won't be enough to ruin the story.

One area where I suppose my personal feelings might show through is in my depiction of the Praetorian Guard of this era being more focused on appearance and not on their fighting prowess, and this gets back to my belief about Sejanus. While there's no way to tell, my suspicion is that Sejanus set his sights on ultimate power very early in his career, where the appearance of an ultimate loyalty to Tiberius was far more important at this point than anything else. And, given what appears to be Tiberius' naturally suspicious nature, I believe that Sejanus would have been careful to avoid arousing that suspicion that might stem from having his Praetorians focused on their fighting skills, for the simple reason that Rome's enemies were hundreds or thousands of miles away, with tens of thousands of men of the Legions and auxiliaries, formed into groups like Gnaeus' Army of the Rhenus, in between them. The reality was that the Praetorians didn't *need* to know how to fight, but they *did* need to make Tiberius, and to a lesser extent the citizens of the city, feel secure while the Prefect worked on his larger plan by slowly eliminating or isolating those men who posed a threat. For Sejanus' purposes, the Praetorian Guard looking the part of elite warriors was what mattered more than the reality.

The description of the triumph comes from a number of sources, not least of which is Mary Beard's *The Roman Triumph*, by The Belknap Press of Harvard University (2007), including the route the triumph took. My depiction of Thusnelda originates with Tacitus, and to a lesser degree, Strabo, but while there is no record of the dioramas I describe in Germanicus' triumph, they were a known feature of previous triumphs, including those held by Caesar during his four successive triumphs, which Titus the Elder describes in his own account.

Finally, a word about the cover image. This is the first cover for which I can take any kind of credit, because the base image that my stellar cover artist Laura Prevost turned into this cover was one that I took during one of my months in Rome. It's a fragment of a pediment that has essentially been discarded and is lying behind the Portico of Octavia, at the Portico d'Ottavia, 29, 0186 in an alley, in pieces and with vegetation growing up around it. Although its provenance hasn't been established beyond doubt, it's considered to be a representation of the Castra Praetoria, and despite the fact that the Castra hadn't been constructed yet, I thought it was a perfect choice. I hope readers agree.

Table of Contents

Chapter 1

It seems that, almost with every passing day, I am learning just how wise both my father and my great-grandfather were. Specifically, when I began following in their footsteps by recording the events through which yet another Roman under the standard bearing the Pullus name is living, I resolved that I would do so during the relatively quiet winter months, immediately after a campaign season, when events were still fresh in my mind. However, I suppose that it is possible that the gods, having already adopted me as their plaything, decided to have some more fun at my expense by placing me in a position for a period of time where there is no such thing as a campaign season.

I offer this as explanation for why I am now sitting in our apartment in Ubiorum, two years after my time in Rome, and am now back with the 1ˢᵗ Legion. I am now the father of a healthy, sturdy son six months away from his third birthday, and it should not be a surprise that his name is Titus Volusenianus Pullus, and he is now an older brother to his sister Giulia, who is six months old, and already a picture of her mother, with a head of red curls that are a brighter shade of red than Bronwen's burnished copper tresses. Bronwen is now legally my wife, thanks to a dispensation by Germanicus Julius Caesar, although it was certainly not a given that I was still in his favor after my excursion to Alexandria to salvage at least some of the remaining fortune of my real family that they used to obtain my release from the Parisii king Cogidubnus, after my First and Second Centuries were marooned in Britannia. It was a trying time, but I have never regretted it, given that I returned to Ubiorum with a prize in Bronwen that is even greater than the money I recovered, a statement that is absolutely true, but has still caused Alex to roll his eyes as he writes my words.

Speaking of Alex, he is still with me, serving in the same function as the clerk of my Century, the Fifth of the First Cohort, although this time, it did not take a healthy bribe to secure his position as it did when I served as the Pilus Posterior of the Second Praetorian Cohort. In fact, as we learned very quickly, while there is, and always has been a level of corruption in the Legions, what is practiced in the Praetorians makes that look like petty thievery. As we both quickly learned, *everything* is for sale in the Praetorian Guard, and as we just as quickly discovered, Rome is an expensive place to live. Granted, the pay for a Praetorian Centurion was several times what I made, even when I was the Quartus Pilus Prior but while Rome may not be several times more expensive, it is close. However, what all this means is something that I will describe later. First, I need to pick up this account where I left off, when Bronwen, Alex, his woman Algaia, their daughter Iras, and I, answering what can only be described as a curt summons from Germanicus back in Rome, departed Ubiorum on a frosty winter day.

Mainly because of Bronwen's condition, I insisted that we hire a small wagon, not a full *carpentum*, but larger than a *cisium*, and more importantly, it had a canvas top, although the sides were open. Fortunately, thanks to the shopping trip she had taken with Birgit, Gisela, and Miriam in Arelate, she was sufficiently bundled up. It also had a small cargo space for baggage, which meant that we only needed one pack animal for myself, while Alex's, Algaia's, and Iras' belongings were carried by another. Unfortunately for our party, this was all that I was willing to do in order to make my companions comfortable, but thankfully, they all understood. I was carrying a scroll that gave us priority at every Imperial relay station for fresh animals, but when I suggested that we hire a man to drive the wagon, neither Algaia nor Bronwen would hear of it.

"That is a waste of money," Algaia scoffed, but I noticed that Bronwen was standing behind her and nodding almost as emphatically. "Both of us are perfectly capable of driving a wagon that small!"

A glance at Alex told me that he had already yielded the ground, and while I was skeptical, I congratulated myself for recognizing that this was one of those battles that it was better to lose when it comes to the relationship between a man and a woman. We departed two days after I met with my comrades, the men of the Fourth Cohort, at the Dancing Faun, which I still own thanks to my father, although I appointed Titus, Alex's younger brother and a smith whose business is in Ubiorum, to keep an eye on things, for a portion of the proceeds, of course. The decision not to depart the day after I reported back to Ubiorum was actually because of a "suggestion" by Primus Pilus Sacrovir, which surprised me a great deal, but he proved to be wise in knowing that I would be in no condition to travel after the night celebrating the brief reunion with my men. And, if I am completely honest, I probably could have done with yet another day, so I was not particularly good company our first day of travel. Since anyone traveling south from Ubiorum has essentially one road to take, it meant that we passed through Mogontiacum again, but while we stopped, it was only long enough for me to apprise my mother of what had awaited me in Ubiorum. Even as I did it, I knew I was violating regulations by allowing her to read the scroll that had been waiting for me, written in Germanicus' own hand, which Alex had confirmed.

Knowing that even if I tried, it would be impossible, so I did not attempt to hide my keen interest, and anxiety, as I asked my mother, "Well? What do you make of this? What do you think it means? What kind of 'new assignment' do you think he's referring to?"

Now, I know that if I do not do so, Alex will point out that we had already deduced that I would be reporting to the Praetorian Guard, but my mother Giulia is one of the cleverest people I know, and I did not want to taint her opinion with my own.

She did not hesitate, saying flatly, "I think he wants you in the Praetorian Guard."

Even though this confirmed our belief, it was still sobering, but I also informed her of one thing I had learned from Sacrovir. "The Primus Pilus received a dispatch from Rome that arrived after Germanicus wrote that, and while he said his orders were the same, he told Sacrovir that it wasn't a permanent assignment."

My goal had been to assure her, but she shook her head, and I saw the tiny flare of nostrils that I had long before learned her temper was roused.

"I don't care if it's only a day," she snapped. "Rome is a nest of vipers!" Surprising me, she reached out and grasped, or tried to grasp my upper arm, but her grip was as strong as ever as she spoke urgently. "Gnaeus, you're going to have to watch *everything* that you say, and I mean at every moment. Even," she insisted, "when you think you're in private. You *cannot* trust anyone." She released my arm to indicate the other three people in the room. "Only them, Gnaeus; they're the only ones you can be honest with." When she turned back to look up at me, the intensity in her eyes was, frankly, unsettling, as she continued, "Swear it to me, Gnaeus! Swear that you will guard your tongue, and even if you *think* you're alone, watch what you say!"

"I swear, Mama," I began, but she cut me off with an impatient shake of her head.

"No," she countered, "I wasn't through. I want you to swear on the standard of your Legion that you'll do as I say!"

For the briefest of instants, I thought about pointing out that I was technically no longer part of the 1st Legion, but as soon as the thought came, I drove it out of my mind.

"I swear, Mama," I assured her with as much sincerity as I could muster. "I swear on the eagle of the 1st that I'll watch everything I say and will always assume someone is listening that shouldn't be."

Only then was she satisfied, but as usual, it was Alex who discerned that this was more than just a mother's worry.

"Mistress Giulia? What is it? What do you know?"

The look she gave Alex made me feel slightly better, but her scorn was for something else.

"Don't you call me that, Alex!" she snapped, but then I saw the slight lifting of the corner of her mouth. "It makes me sound old!" He laughed as he bowed his head, but she was completely serious as she answered, "I don't know anything specific, but the talk among the wives here is that the Praetorian Prefect Sejanus has completely fooled our new Imperator into believing that *he* is the only man in Rome that Tiberius can trust, and that he's been utterly ruthless in removing anyone he sees as a rival with him for Tiberius' favor."

For the first time, Bronwen spoke up, asking hesitantly, "Remove? What does this mean?"

"He's having men killed or exiled on trumped-up charges that they're plotting against Tiberius, and Tiberius has believed him, at least so far," my mother answered her, and I had to swallow my stab of anger at her blunt words, because I saw Bronwen go pale, but I said nothing because I understood that she was speaking the truth, and most importantly, why she was saying it.

Fortunately, my mother is very perceptive, because she saw the same thing I did and quickly moved to embrace Bronwen, then whispered something in my love's ear that I could not hear, but clearly made her feel better.

"Is there anything...*solid* that you can tell us before we leave?" he asked my mother, and she thought for a moment, but then shook her head.

"Just that the Praetorian Guard is wholly loyal to Sejanus," she said softly.

We departed shortly thereafter, and I do not believe it should surprise anyone to know that we were mostly silent after our departure.

This, I thought with some amusement, albeit with a bitter edge, is becoming a habit. For the fourth time in a relatively short period, I was standing at the stern of a riverboat, brushing the snow off Latobius as we were rowed upstream from Augusta Raurica, with Brigantium being where we would resume riding for a time. Not that this interlude was necessarily bad; it gave me an opportunity to continue Bronwen's education, and both Algaia and Alex were experienced at this form of travel as well. Seemingly every day during this relatively peaceful period, I caught myself marveling at how quickly Bronwen's mind worked, and how easily she seemed to absorb new information. Oh, I was aware that she was clever; I had learned that when we were still in Britannia, and I understood why her father Prausetaugas, a merchant who traveled to Gaul frequently, relied on her so heavily, yet it was still quite pleasing to see how hungry she was to learn. Iras was initially fascinated by the newness of everything, but she quickly grew bored and restless onboard since her mother would not let her go anywhere around the boat without a firm grasp of her tiny hand, which Iras did not appreciate in the least. It was amusing, at least at first.

"I wonder where she got her independent and stubborn streak from?" I teased Alex, who brought me low with one well-aimed shot, delivered with a smug smile.

"Oh, you'll be finding out what it's like soon enough."

Hearing Bronwen and Algaia snickering did not help matters,

but I managed to keep my mouth closed, if only because I knew that he was speaking truly. Bronwen had just begun to show the signs of her pregnancy, and as she had on the journey to Ubiorum, she took frequent naps, except this time, I at least knew why, and which Algaia assured me was completely normal. Returning to our normal mode of travel at Curia, we rode south to the Via Postumia before turning east, heading for my place of birth, Mediolanum. Honestly, I was caught by surprise at the turbulent feelings I began experiencing as we drew closer to what is now a decent-sized city. Naturally, it was Alex who divined the cause of my agitation, which even as I tried to hide it, I knew that my companions were not fooled, but when Bronwen asked me why I was bothered, I insisted that I was fine.

"When's the last time you've been to Mediolanum? And why are you worried about it?"

Alex's question was like a thunderbolt from a clear sky, and I instantly understood this was his intent, since I tend to blurt out the real answer when caught by surprise, something that he had either been told by my mother or learned on his own.

"The day I left for Ubiorum," I replied, hoping this would suffice but knowing that it would not. The silence, which I am uncomfortable with, went on for several heartbeats before I continued, "I didn't come back for my father…for my stepfather's funeral."

For this was the source of my guilt, that when I got the news that Quintus Claudius Volusenus had died, I had made no real attempt to take leave to return home to honor the man who, while I never would have admitted it at the time, I had already begun to doubt was my real father. When my mother sent the message that he had died suddenly of a bilious fever, I am still somewhat ashamed to say that my initial, and sadly, strongest emotion was one of irritation because of the timing of his death. As I dictate this and Alex writes the words, I cringe at them, knowing how callous that was of me, because while I cannot say that Quintus Volusenus was affectionate towards me, given what I know now about how he was aware of who my real father was, he did treat me well, all things considered. Frankly, I cannot imagine how he managed to keep himself from being overtly hostile towards me, although now that I am aware of how he treated my mother Giulia, essentially saving his hostility and hatred for her, I do not look at him nearly as kindly as I did.

Nevertheless, I do not regret my decision to turn down the full *nomen* Porcinianus Pullus and use Volusenianus instead.

My hope that we would arrive in Mediolanum early enough to press on, switching back to river travel by floating down the Ticinus (Ticino) River to Placentia, which is about forty-five miles south of Mediolanum, where we would catch another barge on the Padus (Po), was dashed when it became clear that we would be arriving in the city relatively early in the afternoon, but not early enough to keep going. It was, I thought miserably, the worst possible result, because Bronwen, having learned this was my birthplace and where I grew up, was demanding that I show her around the city. Certainly this was a product of her intense curiosity, but I was acutely aware that because of its importance in my life, that natural inquisitiveness was magnified as she tried to learn more about me. I had never really thought of myself as a private person, yet I now realize that I am, which I understand can seem to be a contradiction since neither am I shy about talking about myself.

However, it was Alex who pointed out, "You talk a lot about the things you do, but you hardly ever talk about who you are."

It was true when he said it, and it is still true today, although Bronwen has forced me to lower my defenses, as it were.

We rode up to the western gate, where we were naturally allowed in with a simple display of my *vitus*, accompanied by a stern glare at the pair of *vigiles* that have become essentially standard in every Roman city that does not have an auxiliary Cohort. The first thing I noticed was that the walls had been replaced and not simply added to as in so many towns and cities, while the gateway was much larger than when I left. Entering into the city of my youth, as we rode down the Via Principalis, heading in the direction of the forum, I realized that the reason the walls had been replaced was because they had been extended more than two hundred paces, with the foundation of the old wall already overgrown with grass in spots, at least where some new structure had not been constructed. The street was busy, and it was easy to see that the population had grown in the eight years since I had left at nineteen, but there was still much that was familiar. The temple to Jupiter Optimus Maximus was still the tallest building, and visible from several blocks away from the forum, but I was more concerned with finding rooms at the one inn inside the walls that catered to the Equestrian and higher orders. It was where I remembered it, on my daily route to the Campus Martius where I performed my exercises, and it looked essentially unchanged, although I cannot say why I expected it to, but when I dismounted Latobius and handed the reins to Alex to stride through the gated archway, the last thing I was expecting was to see a familiar face.

"*Gerrae*! It can't be!"

He had managed to spot me before I him, but I instantly recognized the voice, and my stomach clenched in an unconscious reflex caused by one of the people from my past, who, if I had known this would happen, would have caused me to refuse to enter Mediolanum, no matter what time of day.

Because he had been standing tucked in a corner of the small outer courtyard, he was essentially behind me, and I turned very slowly, both to give him the impression of my indifference, and to prepare myself for what might be coming.

"*Salve,* Nasica. It's been a long time."

As I hoped, using the *cognomen* that I knew he despised, a reminder of his nose that was no longer all there made him flush with anger, and for a moment, I thought I might have erred and angered him to the point that he would order his two companions, both former gladiators, although I only recognized one of them, to come after me.

If I had to guess, a good five heartbeats passed before, suddenly, he relaxed, a bit, and chuckled. "You always were a haughty bastard, Volusenus."

I knew that he was repaying me in kind with his slur against my mother, but I still felt the flare of anger, although I managed to smother it enough to counter evenly, "You're a bit behind, Nasica. I'm now Gnaeus Volusenianus Pullus..." I cannot say why it came to me, but it seemed like a good idea as I added, "...of the Praetorian Guard."

This obviously startled him enough that I used it as the opportunity to turn away, but for a reason I still do not really understand, it was not to return to Bronwen and the others to find another spot, but into the inn to secure rooms. Given what occurred, both Bronwen and Alex are convinced that I had something like this planned all along, but I swear on the black stone I did not; he clearly still does not believe me.

His full name was Publius Sempronius, but after he had gotten the tip of his nose bitten off in a brawl long before I met him, in typical mocking fashion, he had been given the *cognomen* Nasica. It is what he represented from my past that warrants a brief explanation. I know that I am not the first, nor will I be the last man who went through a rebellious phase as a teenager, especially once we don the *toga virilis,* the traditional sign of Roman manhood. However, not many fifteen-year-olds are already six feet tall and, while I had not fully filled out, I was close to two hundred pounds. And, in all honesty, I was not rebelling against Quintus Volusenus, if only because he was largely indifferent to what I was doing; by this point in their marriage, my mother and stepfather mostly ignored each other, and what little contact they had between them was through me, which was an acutely uncomfortable position to be in. At the time, I told myself this was partially the reason I was rebelling, but even in the moment, I also understood much of my anger was directed at my mother Giulia, though I could not have articulated why this was the case. Looking back, now I know that I had already begun to suspect that she was hiding something from me, and that the man I still thought of as my father was involved in some way, not in the sense they were sharing something as much as that he was aware of whatever it was, meaning that I was the only person left in the proverbial dark. So, in the manner of all rebellious children who are angry at one or both of their parents, I began doing things that I knew my mother would disapprove of; namely, I began debauching and gambling, which was how I met Publius Sempronius Nasica.

He ran the *collegia* that controlled Mediolanum east of the forum, while his rival, Numerius Blaesus, ran all of the vice and protection west of the forum. As might be expected, the two men hated each other, and when I was about twelve, there was about a month where I was not allowed to leave the villa because the two were fighting each other over control of the entire city. Neither was strong enough to defeat the other, and after a couple dozen deaths, they had settled into an uneasy peace that was still in place the first time I sneaked out of the villa to visit Proserpina's Lair, which I thought was very imaginatively named, given her role as the goddess that Pluto kidnapped and made her his wife, where she ruled the underworld with him. To the fevered mind of an adolescent, it hinted at all manner of lascivious and, most importantly, forbidden delights. I did learn very quickly that its main distinction was that it was both a *taverna* and a brothel, although it was two buildings that were connected by an enclosed walkway, thereby taking up an entire block. This, I would be told, was because the men who frequented Nasica's establishment were the type who wanted their fleshly pleasures to be discreet. In my purse, I carried part of my name day gift, five hundred *sesterces*, a sum that would not last long, although I did not lose it all gambling…or drinking. As self-confident as I was for my age, thanks to my size, I still did not possess the boldness of spirit to swagger up to the entrance that led directly to the brothel part of Proserpina's, so I entered on the opposite street into the *taverna*. It was about a watch before midnight, so the place was almost full, but when heads turned at my entry, I barely noticed since this had been happening, and still happens, on almost a daily basis. I told myself that I was standing there to let my eyes adjust, which was a fiction; I was only slightly less nervous being in the *taverna* part of the place than if I had entered on the brothel side. Spotting a table that was partially unoccupied, I started towards it, my intention being to behave as if I had done so many times before, just another customer who wanted to wet his throat.

"*Oy*! You! Young Master!"

This was the first time I laid eyes on Publius Nasica, who had called me from what I would learn was his customary spot behind the bar where trays of wine were set for the four female slaves who served as both servers and cut-rate whores for the poorer clientele who picked them up. Fortunately for me, there was enough distance between us that it was not obvious that my eyes went to his distinguishing feature. To be fair, since the entire nose was not missing, just the tip to about halfway down his nostrils, I could see that it made wearing a false nose, as I've seen some men do, problematic. In appearance, he looked something like a pig, but for whatever reason, he had not been given a *cognomen* that made a play on that. Regardless, he *was* big, only an inch shorter than I was, although his muscles were encased in a layer of fat that, as I would come to learn, did not detract from his strength. He was smiling at me, and at first, I thought he was just greeting me as a new customer, but when I nodded in acknowledgement of his call, I learned differently.

"It's a rare day when someone my size enters here," he said as he stepped from around the counter, "so let me welcome you personally to Proserpina's Lair!" He reached me as he finished and offered his arm, which I took, and he introduced himself. "*Salve,* I'm Publius Sempronius and," he extended his free arm as he crushed my forearm, "this is my establishment. So," he grinned at me, and he seemed genuine enough, "what does young Master...?"

"Volusenus," I supplied. "Gnaeus Volusenus."

"Ah." He nodded, which I thought he was doing out of politeness, but he surprised me. "Yes, of course! You're Quintus Claudius Volusenus' son."

"How did you know that?" I asked, not trying to disguise my startlement.

"Your father and I have...done business on occasion," he replied, but before I could press him further, he went on, "But men our size aren't very common around here, and I recall seeing you with your father once perhaps a year ago. Although," he added offhandedly, "you obviously favor your mother. Now," his tone turned, if not brisk, then more businesslike, "if you've come for good wine, companionship, and perhaps a game or two of dice, just let me know. But," he nudged me with his elbow and gave me a grin that even in my inexperience I saw was more of a leer, "if you're here for *another* form of companionship, I can escort you to the brothel without having to leave the premises!"

The brutal truth was that I had acted impulsively, without having a firm plan of what I wanted to do, although being with a prostitute was certainly high on the list. But I was also acutely aware that even with my size, my youth was obvious, and I desperately wanted to give this man, and the other patrons, the impression that this was not my first foray into debauching.

Trying to sound as cool and collected as I could, I offered an elaborate shrug, and I said, "I think I'll start with a cup of wine, Publius Sempronius. Then," I gave him what I considered a manly wink, "let's see where Bacchus takes me, eh?"

I cringe as I dictate this, and all I can offer in my defense is that it would not be much longer before I understood that Sempronius had instantly seen me for what I was: a callow, green as grass wealthy equestrian boy desperately wanting to be a man. For some time afterward, I often wondered what would have happened if I had been caught by my parents when I came skulking back to our villa that was two blocks north of the forum, but the gods had deemed that, for a time, I would be the plaything of Publius Sempronius Nasica.

After I procured the rooms, I brought Bronwen, Algaia, and Iras into the inn and led them there, for which I had to pay extra since, even with establishments that cater to equestrians and higher orders, space is at a premium.

"The proprietor said that they begin serving at the beginning of first evening watch," I informed them. "Why don't you get some rest until then? I'm going to go help Alex and rub down Latobius."

When I descended, I used the rear entrance, briefly entertaining the idea of going out into the courtyard to see if Nasica was still about, but I quickly dismissed it, assuming that he had some sort of business here and was long gone. I found Alex in the stable, where the horses were unsaddled, and he was beginning to care for them, but we switched off and he took the baggage inside, leaving me to attend to Latobius and the other horses, including Alex's Lightning, although I naturally spent more time with Latobius, who searched for his apple, then munched it as I brushed him.

"I didn't expect to see Nasica." I heard my voice, so I knew I was not thinking silently, but it was not the first nor will it be the last that I talked to my horse about a problem. "I doubt I'll see him again, but he brought back some…memories."

As always, Latobius' reaction was blowing through his huge nostrils in the signal that I had learned was his way of telling me that he had consumed his apple and was, in fact, expecting another.

"You're no help," I grumbled, but after a few more swipes with the brush, I strapped on his feed bag and put Nasica out of my mind.

I did notice the slave pitching hay into the stalls of some mounts that I assumed belonged to other guests, but I gave him no thought; he was just another of the faceless, nameless people who actually are everywhere around us. Still, even if I *had* noticed him, I doubt that I would have made any connection or gotten suspicious about what was in my immediate future.

I lay down with Bronwen, having become accustomed to her

frequent napping, and I dozed off myself, because when the time slave struck the gong signaling the change of watch, I almost jumped out of my skin. Bronwen was already awake, and my reaction made her laugh.

"What a fierce Centurion of Rome you are," she teased. "You jumped up like you thought Arminius was after you!"

That earned her a glare, and I grumbled, "You know, I recall being told that Parisii men beat their women because they have a bad habit of talking too much."

"Who told you that?" she shot back scornfully. "Cogidubnus?"

Actually, it had been his brother Ivomagus who had told me this, but I actually had come to like Ivomagus, despite his treachery on behalf of his brother the king, so I said nothing and let her assume she was correct.

"Ha!" She nodded emphatically, her deep red tresses flying about her face, making me wonder if perhaps we should delay going downstairs for the meal. "I know his wife, Queen Cartimandua. If Cogidubnus lifted a hand to her, she would wait until he was asleep. Then," she smiled, but it was not a particularly sweet one as she mimed a slicing motion, "she would slice his balls off!"

I do not think that I am unique among men in that my first reflexive action was to drop my hand to my crotch, which amused Bronwen even more, while I reminded myself that if I ever strayed from our bed, I needed to make sure that it was far, far away and she never find out about it. We left our room, and Bronwen knocked on Alex's door, and a moment later, the five of us were descending to the main room of the inn where, to my relief, the dining area was far from crowded. I had insisted that we eat at the first opportunity since we would be retiring early in order to leave at first light; at least, that was my stated reason, but of equal importance to me at all times is my stomach, and I am always concerned that, when eating in a strange place that was not familiar with my appetite, they would try and restrict the amount of food I ate. After all, my eating habits had become something of a spectator sport during my captivity with the Parisii, and I had gotten accustomed to a small audience, usually but not always the kitchen slaves, as they watched me consume what, to me, is the normal amount of food to sate my appetite.

And, I should have known better than to think this escaped

notice, because as we occupied an empty table, Alex said to Bronwen, "You know that he's afraid there won't be enough for him to eat if we came later, don't you?"

I did not ask, but I was certain they had concocted this beforehand given how, without hesitation, Bronwen agreed, "I know! He always thinks with his stomach!"

It was bad enough that the three adults laughed, but even little Iras thought this was funny.

"Uncle Gnaeus, you're not supposed to think with your stomach!"

I could not help myself.

"I don't always think with my stomach!" I triumphantly pointed down to Bronwen's belly. "See?"

Bronwen responded by giving me a playful slap on my arm, while Alex and Algaia laughed, exchanging knowing looks, but Iras broke in to demand, "Mama, what did Uncle Gnaeus mean? Why did he point to Aunt Bronwen's belly?"

"I'll explain later, *meum mel*," Algaia answered quickly, shooting me a mock glare, which I returned with a completely unrepentant grin.

The serving slave arrived then to inform us of the choices available to us, and because of the class of clientele, as one might expect, there was a larger array, including some delicacies that you will never find in a roadside inn.

"I'll take one of each," I informed the server, a girl of about sixteen who strongly resembled the man who I had procured the rooms from, down to the wart on the side of the nose, although I think it was on the opposite side of her father's.

"Yes, Master." She nodded, but then she turned away before taking the others' orders.

"Girl!" I did not raise my voice, but I hardened it enough that she spun about, and I could easily see that she was, if not afraid, then concerned. "You," I pointed to the others, "forgot to find out what they wanted to eat."

Her eyes went wide, and I should have anticipated her gasped question. "You mean all of this," she waved the wax tablet, "is for *you*, Master? You're not sharing?"

Before I could say anything, her query elicited an amused reaction from my companions, but it was Bronwen who said kindly, "No, girl. He doesn't share his food, ever."

"That's not true!" I protested, but she simply raised an eyebrow, and I could see Alex was grinning broadly. Nevertheless, I insisted, "If you were starving, I'd share. Not," I admitted with exaggerated reluctance, "that I'd be happy about it."

Now that the girl knew what was expected, she took their orders, but I noticed the expression on her face, so before she turned to head for the kitchen, I called out to her, "Is there a problem, girl?"

"I...I...I need to speak to someone, Master," she said, but before I could press her, she turned and practically ran out of the room.

"You terrified that girl, Gnaeus," Bronwen scolded me.

"I did not! At least, I didn't mean to," I answered.

"I think she's worried what might happen if whoever runs this inn says that you can't have that much food," Alex put in wryly. Then, after a heartbeat, he added with a laugh, "And she's right to be worried. Getting between you and your food is always a deadly business."

Our banter was cut short when we heard a male voice coming from the kitchen, but while it was raised, it was impossible to make out what he was saying. However, there was something about the voice that gave me just an instant of warning, in the form of the hair on the back of my neck sticking up, so that I was not completely surprised to see Nasica emerging from the kitchen.

"Ha! I *knew* when Clodia here gave the cook that order that there was only one man who could eat that much!" Before I could stop him, Nasica made his way to our table, his eyes taking in both Algaia and Bronwen, although Bronwen was facing him sitting next to me, as we were with our backs to the wall, something that my real father ingrained in me as a habit. Nasica's expression changed, while Bronwen, completely unaware that there was an extra dimension to his obvious interest in her, offered him the kind of smile that she always offers men who are clearly attracted to her. With an obvious effort, Nasica tore his eyes from her to address me, "And who is *this*...vision, Gnaeus Volusenus?"

"I see that you've gotten forgetful in your old age, Nasica," I replied, trying to sound cool and disinterested. "I told you less than a watch ago that my name is Gnaeus Pullus now."

Oh, he did not like that, that was plain to see, although I could not tell whether it was because I used the *cognomen* I knew he hated, or my jibe about his age, but I will give him this much: the look of rage that flashed across his face was gone so quickly, I could almost have imagined it.

"Why, yes, yes you did," Nasica nodded, then gave me a mocking bow, "and I *beg* your forgiveness, Gnaeus *Pullus*. We go back a long way, *neh*? Old habits and all that." Returning his attention to Bronwen, he kept his eyes on her as he continued, "Now that I've made amends, you didn't answer my question, Pullus. Lady, may I say that you are a rare beauty!"

I have said it before: Bronwen has a very quick mind, and she had instantly determined that there was some sort of animosity between us, so while she answered, there was no missing the coldness in her tone.

"My name is Bronwen, daughter of Prausetaugas, a wealthy merchant of the Parisii tribe who live on the island you Romans call Britannia."

"A *Briton*!" His eyes went wide, and I did not get the sense that he was feigning surprise, which seemed to be confirmed when he exclaimed, "I've never met anyone from Britannia!" He turned back to me, and he gave me the same kind of leering grin that he had offered the first time we met when I was fifteen. "So, Pullus. Are these Britons as...wild as I've heard? Eh?"

Bronwen's hand, which had been under the table, grabbed my arm, squeezing it with sufficient pressure to let me know she was aware of my likely response, which was to leap across the table.

"Nasica," I spoke slowly, which I do when I am struggling to control my temper, "you always had a big mouth. But," I stood, but slowly, "I'm not fifteen anymore. Now," I pointed down to Bronwen, "apologize for your rude comment."

For an instant, I thought he might refuse, but I was certain that he knew that the man he was looking at now bore only a passing resemblance to the overgrown Equestrian boy who bore no scars of battle as does the man I am today. Our eyes were locked on each other, but after no more than a heartbeat, he broke his gaze from me to turn back to Bronwen.

"I apologize, Lady Bronwen. Your beauty made me forget myself, so please accept my apology if I gave any offense."

Bronwen noticeably hesitated, as if she was considering a refusal, but then she gave a nod of her head as she answered, "Your apology is accepted, Nasica."

I had to struggle to keep a grin from my face at Nasica's reaction, but he managed to reply evenly, "Actually, Lady, my proper name is Publius Sempronius. 'Nasica' is what *some* people call me. Although," he smiled, not at Bronwen but at me, "not many men have the courage to call me that to my face."

"Oh, Gnaeus is *very* brave," Bronwen assured him cheerfully. Then, before he could reply, she added, "I have seen him kill a man your size with his bare hands."

Frankly, I was as surprised as Nasica obviously was; we had only discussed what happened with Berdic once, and this was the first time she ever made any reference to that moment, in my hearing at least.

When I was a teenager, I had observed that Nasica was the type who needs to have the last word, but standing there now, I could see that he was completely nonplussed, not that I could blame him all that much.

"Yes, well," he cleared his throat, "that's very impressive. But," I supposed the sound of his voice helped him restore his equilibrium, because he smiled his false proprietor's smile that I witnessed my first time at Proserpina's Lair, "there's no need for such talk. Pullus and I are old...acquaintances." He was wise enough to not say "friend." "Besides, my real reason for coming out here was to assure you that we're more than happy to provide everything our kitchen has to offer for our guests...even if it's going to empty our larder and cost us money!"

He said this laughingly, and I could feel the others relax, but

Alex and Algaia had their backs turned, while Bronwen had just met the man, so I was certain that she accepted his words at face value, which was confirmed when she answered for us, "Thank you, Publius Sempronius, that is very kind of you."

I was only partially listening, because my ears had picked up something, and I spoke up. "You said 'us.' What does that mean? You didn't have any stake in this place when I left."

It was slightly disappointing that Nasica not only did not seem surprised by the question, he actually liked it.

"Clodius ran into some...difficulties a couple of years back," he replied with a shrug. "He needed some cash to handle them, and I stepped in."

"Oh? What kind of...difficulties did he run into?"

"He had some damages. And," he added this with a grin that I understood was meaningful, "he had a bad fire. The stables were completely destroyed. So," he held out his hands as if he had no other choice, "not wanting poor Clodius be ruined, I offered to help."

"Of course you did," I shot back. "And now you're...what? Owner in all but name? So Clodius is the one who has to pay the taxes?"

"Something like that," he answered placidly.

This time, when he turned away, I did not stop him.

Once he was out of earshot, Alex broke the silence. "I take it that you two have a history?"

"You could say that," I answered shortly, not wanting to go into any more detail. "But," I waved a hand at Nasica's back, "we're leaving in the morning and I'll never see him again. Now," I forced myself to sound jovial, "let's get ready to eat."

Somewhere, the gods laughed.

Nasica is a clever man, and he had sized me up perfectly that first night in Proserpina's Lair, because rather than take all of my money, he patiently baited his hook, certain that I would develop a taste for the kind of living that he offered. That first night, when I sneaked back into my villa, I had every *sestertius* that I had left with, but not because I had not spent any money; I most certainly had, yet Nasica allowed me to "win" it all back dicing. Indeed, I did not lose, at least substantially, the first three or four times I visited, which were initially spaced a few days apart because of my fear of being caught, but my appearances quickly grew in frequency until I was visiting every other night. It was not only because I was gaining confidence, but because Nasica appeared to take me under his wing, as it were, commiserating with me based on the one thing we had in common: our size and all the attention that stemmed from it. He lent a sympathetic ear as I guzzled unwatered wine, rattled the cup and threw the dice, asking me questions that only in hindsight did I realize was for two purposes: to pump me for information about Quintus Volusenus' business dealings, and to win my trust by stroking my budding *dignitas*, which was already sizable enough, something that I have only come to recognize relatively recently.

The night he hooked his fish had started like any other when I visited; I had foregone loitering in the *taverna* to begin my night, choosing to visit the brothel first, where my infatuation Niobe was waiting. For a brief period, I was certain that I was in love with her; she was only two years older than I was, and she was from Syria, which made her quite exotic. But she was born a slave, so that even if she had not been a whore, any kind of permanent arrangement was out of the question. She professed her love for me as well, and I believed her at the time because I wanted to believe her; now I laugh at myself about my innocence back then. Nevertheless, she had put me into a state of post-coital bliss, which was reinforced by the wine, and as I had become accustomed to, I won my first couple of throws, losing on my third. Now it is so glaringly obvious that there was a pattern involved, where I won more than I lost, the former being two-thirds of the time. Naturally, there were other men besides Nasica, and I was aware that two of them worked for him, but they had always been friendly towards me. There was another regular there, his name Manius Pedo, and he was decidedly *not* friendly towards me, although up to this point, he had been largely indifferent, preferring to mutter comments to whoever was sitting next to him while looking in my direction. This night was different, because it quickly became apparent that he was openly hostile towards me, and he began speaking loudly enough for me to hear him.

"Volusenus bets like an old woman, Spurius!" He changed his voice to what I suppose was his idea of an old woman's quaver. "Oh,

I don't want to risk more than a *sestertius* or I might not be able to buy my loaf!"

The words were bad enough; the fact that the other men around the table burst into laughter, a couple of them slapping the table in their appreciation of Pedo's wit only exacerbated it. I blame the wine for not noticing how counterfeit it all was, or how suddenly the men I had thought of as, if not friends perhaps, then at least friendly were eyeing me coldly, despite their seeming amusement. And, naturally, I took the bait, immediately shoving more coins in front of me when it was my turn with the cup, congratulating myself on my cunning in refusing to take the bait when one of them was throwing, maintaining my habit of no more than two coins when the cup was in their hands. It took a bit of time for me to notice that, while I had begun losing more money on my own throws, if I had risked more when it was one of the others' turn, I would have more than covered what I was losing on my throws. Which, of course, was exactly the plan. Nasica was not there for this part of it, claiming that he had some important business to attend to in the room behind the bar that he used as his office. This had happened before, so I thought nothing of it at the time. Honestly, I cannot remember many of the details, other than the fact that, shortly before dawn, I was sitting at what had become my accustomed spot, the only difference being that I was now in massive debt, far more than my name day gift, which meant that I would have to approach my parents. However, when I got up to leave, suddenly, any trace of friendship vanished, and one of the men I knew worked for Nasica, Vibius Cordus, leapt to his feet and blocked my path, while the other man, Gnaeus Stator, produced a cudgel from under the table. He did not wave it at me but just put it on the table.

What surprised me was that it was Pedo who demanded, "And where do you think you're going, *boy*?"

"I...I need to get home," I said lamely. Thinking this would help, I added, "I'm good for the money! Vibius," I turned to face him, but I saw nothing friendly in his face, "you know me! I'm..."

"You're a pup who owes us five thousand *sesterces*," he said coldly. "And I don't give a fuck who your Tata is."

I was angry, certainly, but I was also frightened; I had seen what Cordus and Stator had done to a man who was unable to produce the money at the end of his night, and while they did not kill him, it was a savage beating.

"Where's Publius Sempronius?" I blurted out. "Go ask him! I'm sure he'll tell you that I'm good for the money."

Cordus and Stator exchanged a glance, and since I was facing Cordus, I was certain I saw the doubt, completely unaware that this was exactly what they wanted me to do.

"What do you think, Gnaeus?" Cordus asked. "You know Sempronius doesn't like being bothered when he's conducting business. Still," he rubbed his chin thoughtfully, "we both know he likes the boy."

I was sufficiently distracted not to bristle at being called a boy, and I was unable to hide my relief when Stator said only, "I'll go get him."

Not that I appreciated it, but this would be my first experience in one of the little games some superiors in the Legions like to play with their subordinates by keeping them waiting for an inordinately long period of time, although under the standard, you are generally standing in front of the man who is snubbing you. Compounding my fear was that the crack at the bottom of the door leading outside was becoming more distinct, the sign that dawn was not just approaching, but was essentially here. I could make it back into my room, but it would be extremely close, provided that Nasica arrived in the next span of heartbeats. He did not, so that by the time he had appeared, any chance of returning home undiscovered was gone. Like the others, the Nasica who emerged from his office was quite different than the one who had been such a convivial host; if anything, his eyes were even colder than the others'.

"Stator tells me that you've gotten yourself into trouble," he said, "and you owe us a lot of money."

I had to swallow once before I could answer, "I do. But," I held out my hands in a gesture that Nasica would use on me more than a decade later, "I don't have that much money on me."

"Then you shouldn't have gambled what you didn't have," he shot back coldly.

Which, of course, was true, although this was exactly what he wanted, but I was unaware of that, so I decided that some humility was in order.

"I know that, and I humbly beg your pardon, Publius Sempronius. But," I insisted, "you *do* know who I am! You know who my father is!" Suddenly, I was inspired to add, "Didn't you tell me that you'd done some business with him in the past?"

I was encouraged by the manner in which he seemed to hesitate, nodding thoughtfully.

"That *is* true. But," he shook his head, seemingly dashing my hopes, "you know the rules, Volusenus. Nobody leaves Proserpina's Lair without paying what they owe. Now," he pointed a finger at me, "if I was to make an exception for you, how long do you think it would take to get out that other men could expect special treatment like that? How long would I be in business?"

"I swear on Jupiter's stone that I won't say a word about it," I assured him, and I was completely sincere.

Nasica pursed his lips, then asked suddenly, "How long do you think it would take you to pay me what you owe?"

Now I had absolutely no idea how long it would take for my father to come up with five thousand *sesterces*, but that did not stop me from answering immediately, "No more than two days, Publius Sempronius."

He said nothing to this, choosing to cup his chin in one hand with the elbow of that arm in his other, tapping his lips with one finger as he stared at me. Somehow, I understood that I could not break this silence and had to wait for his decision.

"Very well," he said finally, and I could not help slumping in relief, releasing the breath I had been holding in an explosive gasp. I would come to regret that deeply, because when he added, "Two days and six thousand *sesterces*," I had no air in my lungs, and for a moment, I was sure I would faint, the room actually starting to spin a bit.

I finally sucked in enough air to gasp, "*Six* thousand! But I only lost five thousand!"

"Actually," Cordus cut in, "you lost five thousand and fifty *sesterces*."

"See?" I nodded emphatically. "It wasn't six thousand!"

"I didn't say it was, Volusenus," Nasica replied calmly. "But it's still six thousand because of the interest."

"For two *days*?"

"I'm not running a fucking charity, I'm running a business." Nasica snarled this, and this time, he actually crossed to stand in front of me.

Yes, I was already his height, and while he outweighed me, it was not by much, but he was a full-grown man who had clearly battered and beaten his way into a position where he ran the *collegia*, and even if he was not missing part of his nose, I would have been intimidated.

"All right." I closed my eyes, hoping it would lessen the humiliation. "Six thousand *sesterces*, delivered here in two days' time."

It did not lessen the humiliation, but when Nasica gestured with his head to Stator to stand aside, I beat a hasty retreat, ignoring the roars of laughter as soon as the door slammed behind me. Gone was any thought of hurrying home; frankly, the idea of being scolded for coming in so late, or early, was suddenly the least of my concerns.

My decision to approach my mother instead of my father was not based in my fear of Quintus Volusenus, but in my knowledge that it was my mother who managed the finances of the Volusenus house. For the most part, my father was about as indifferent about money as he was about me; however, I was as certain as it was possible to be without experiencing it that he would be enraged that I had lost what was, and is for most people, a staggering sum of money. I can also attest that his attitude about money was perhaps the one thing that he imparted to me, but as I have learned, this is not only not unusual, it is practically expected for people higher up the Equestrian Order, and more than once, I had heard Quintus Volusenus say that it was beneath a man at the upper crust of our order to concern himself with such matters.

"That's for the merchants to worry about, not us."

If I had a *denarius* for every time that I had heard him say this or something like it, while it might not have been enough to cover the debt, it would have made a good start. Still, I also knew that his rage, while not being about the money, would still be very real and, I assured myself, even more potent because it involved loss of his *dignitas*, because it was a practical impossibility that word of this would not become known among his circle of friends. After all, the reason I knew about Proserpina's Lair in the first place was hearing my father and some of his friends talking about it in glowing terms. Now that I think about it, perhaps this was one time the gods decided to favor me, because I was completely ignorant of the truth, that I was not really the natural son of Quintus Volusenus, and it was almost a certainty he would have taken out his ire on my mother. Regardless, I was still extremely nervous as I approached the villa, trying to come up with a way to evade my father, who would be on his way to the baths if he followed his normal routine, and get to my mother first. As it turned out, things worked out perfectly for me, because just as I turned the corner, I saw my father exit the villa, with his body slave following behind him and carrying his portable game board, which made me recall this was his day to spend playing tables with some of his friends and gossip about their social equals, and betters. I had actually been invited to join him in honor of my name day when I donned the *toga virilis*, and naturally, I accepted. Within less than a third of a watch after the bath, I was bored almost to distraction; thankfully, he only made that offer once. Any relief I felt about my father was swept away like a twig in a torrent when, going to my window to climb in, my mother was standing there, arms crossed and nostrils flaring, but it was the expression on her face that told me she was truly enraged.

"I have no excuse, Mama." I congratulated myself for starting like that after I clambered through the window.

"Oh, I know that," she replied tersely. Her tone softened, just a fraction, as she added, "But I do appreciate that you didn't even try. Now," she folded her arms, "tell me where you've been going for the last three weeks?"

How, I wondered with dismay, did she know that?

Quickly realizing that this was not important, I essentially confessed everything, then and there; well, *almost* everything. I did not mention Niobe's name, but I could see she was not fooled that I had visited both parts of the Lair. When I got to the events of the night before, my stomach began churning, even more than what I had become accustomed to from drinking heavily, but I plunged ahead, except that while I told her how it happened, I still had not mentioned the amount.

When I paused, she stood there for a moment, then sighed. "So, you were played for a fool by no less than Publius Sempronius Nasica."

Before I could stop myself, I mumbled, "He doesn't like being called Nasica, Mama."

"Well, that's too bad for him," my mother snapped, her cheeks flushing with anger that I could only recall seeing a handful of times in my life, "because he not only looks like a pig with that *snout,* he acts like one!"

I know that she did not mean it humorously, but I could not stop myself from snickering, which earned a glare from her that quickly dissolved into a soft laugh of her own.

"I will say that Nasica has done something like this to men much older than you," she went on. "So I suppose it's less shaming since you're just fifteen." Despite knowing this was the truth, I could not help bristling, yet I managed to keep my mouth shut. And I could not stop the feeling of a huge weight lifting from my shoulders as the thought came: Perhaps this won't be so bad. That lasted for the time it took for her to ask briskly, "How much do you owe him?"

It took me two tries to get the words out. "I lost five thousand *sesterces,* but he wants six thousand in payment."

My mother went white, and she actually took a staggering step backward as one hand flew to her mouth; I should have been paying attention to notice that it was her left hand. I did not even see the blow coming, and it is still the hardest she has ever slapped me, sending me reeling back myself, my ear ringing and face feeling as if it was on fire.

"You stupid, stupid *boy!*" she shouted, and for an instant, I thought she would hit me again; I am happy that she did not, because despite understanding that I deserved it, I also felt the anger coming, of the kind that I had to that point only experienced once before. That rage dissolved when her eyes filled with tears, and in almost a normal tone, she cut me deeply. "Gnaeus, how could you do something like this? How could you be so foolish?"

"I know!" I felt mortified as my own eyes began to fill with tears, but my mother had never spoken to me in this manner, and I think that this was when it really hit me just how badly I had erred. "I'm sorry, Mama! I am! I just…I just…got carried away!"

"No," she sighed again, which seemed to decrease her anger, "you were taken advantage of by a horrible, evil man." She stopped suddenly, regarding me for a long moment, and I had the feeling she was considering something. Evidently, she decided, "And the thing is, this isn't even really about you, Gnaeus. That's what makes it even more horrible."

"What do you mean?" A thought occurred to me, prompting me to ask, "Is this about my father?"

Only now as I recall this do I understand why my mother stiffened at the mention of Quintus; clearly for an instant, she feared I had somehow divined the truth, but that was years in the future.

It was not much of a reaction, nor did she hesitate to reply, "Yes, although it's not only about him." She finally stepped away from the window to sit on the edge of my bed, while I was still sufficiently cowed that I remained standing…out of arm's reach. "While I can't say with any real certainty, I strongly suspect that this is about a contract for grain that was put up for auction by the *duumviri*. Your father was a partner. A *minor* partner," she modified. Then she sighed and continued, "But he was also the most vocal partner of the group, and I was told by Tiberius Lentulus' wife that there was a rumor that Nasica was bidding on it. And," she gave a grim smile, "that he had paid a hefty bribe to get it."

I listened with interest; it was exceedingly rare for me to be given a glimpse into the inner workings of not just my own family's business dealings, but the labyrinthine world of relationships, partnerships, and the betrayals that are part and parcel of life with the Roman upper classes.

This was what prompted me to interject, "But why would Nasica be angry with Father? He should be angry at whichever *duumvir* took the bribe then awarded the contract to Father's group."

"Oh, I don't doubt that Nasica is livid," my mother agreed. Then she pointed out the obvious. "But he's not powerful enough to do anything about the *Duumvir*, so he has to look elsewhere to vent his rage. And," she finished quietly, "because of your father's…enthusiasm for this venture, he's an easier target."

She fell silent, and I did not feel it wise to say anything more, so the quiet stretched out as she looked down at her hands in her lap. Finally, she looked back up at me and broke the silence.

"I think I know what to do. I'll take care of it," she said in a tone I had never heard from her before, and if she had been a man, I would have said that it sounded like someone who has made a decision that involves some form of action that extended beyond handing over a sack of money. I did not have time to ruminate on this because she continued, "And, Gnaeus, hear me now and heed my words." She stood back up and moved in front of me and took both of my hands, which she squeezed with enough pressure that I had to bite my lip to keep from crying out. "Your father must *never* know about *any* of this. Not that you've gone to Proserpina's Lair, not that Nasica gulled you, and *definitely* not that I'm the one who's taking care of this. Give me your solemn oath, before the gods and on Jupiter's black stone that you will never tell him, Gnaeus. And we will *never* speak of this again, and you will never ask me what I did. The gods know that I owe your father this much."

Naturally, I gave my oath, completely ignorant to the fact that when my mother invoked my father's name, she was not referring to Quintus Volusenus. I lived up to that oath, and never set foot in Proserpina's Lair ever again, but there was one last message coming my way, and while the message itself was positive, the manner in which it was delivered left me shaking. The messenger arrived just before dawn of the second day, the day I was supposed to hand over Nasica's money, but I received it in my bed, when a rough hand on my shoulder woke me up. Just as my eyes opened, an even harder hand clamped itself over my mouth, but despite being fifteen, I was still very strong, and in a reflex action, I grabbed at his wrist and was able to wrench it from my mouth.

I was just opening my mouth to shout when the figure hissed in my ear, "Volusenus! I'm not here to hurt you, I swear it!"

Even at a whisper, I thought I recognized the voice, and asked, "Cordus? Is that you?"

"Yes." He nodded his head, which I could barely make out moving in the darkness. "It's Cordus, and Publius Sempronius sent me to tell you that the…matter between you has been resolved."

I did not even try to hide my relief, but I managed to gasp, "I understand."

Then, without another word, he turned and slipped through the window, the same one I had been using for my comings and goings, and I remember thinking, Maybe I should keep them shuttered at night. Once the cock crowed and our daily routine began, which included a visit from a slave who, for all intents and purposes, was my body slave, I hurried through my ablutions so that I could catch my mother, who liked to break her fast in the *triclinium*, sipping *posca* and eating bread with honey, alone. Unfortunately, she was not, but the instant I laid eyes on her, I saw her silent warning to me, which I understood well enough, but I did think that she needed to know of my visitor, at least what he said. Unfortunately, my father entered the room, barely glancing at me or my mother, snapping his fingers to the kitchen slave to bring him something to eat. We ate in silence, but this was not unusual, and finally, I got up to leave the room, but just as I reached the doorway, my mother called to me.

"Gnaeus, I was hoping that we could spend some time together today. Will you accompany me? I'm taking a pair of shoes to Cornelius' to have them repaired, then I was thinking that we might look at a couple of new tunics for you." She smiled and said laughingly, "You're growing so fast that I think it's a waste of time..."

"...And money," my father interrupted, but he was reading from a scroll and did not look up; this was not unusual, nor was his sour comment, so we both did what we normally did and pretended that we did not hear him.

"Of course, Mama," I replied, and I saw her wince slightly, while my father did lift his eyes briefly, an eyebrow slightly raised.

"He must want something to agree that readily," he said to my mother, but then he dropped his eyes back to his scroll and I heaved a sigh of relief, because he was clearly done with me.

As soon as we were well away from the villa, I told my mother about Cordus' visit; that was the last we spoke of it for the rest of my time in Mediolanum, and I never heard anything more.

We finished our meal, and by this time, the dining area was full, and our party attracted the normal amount of attention because of me and the number of dishes stacked in front of me.

I saw Iras whisper something to Algaia, and I got the idea it had to do with me because of the way her mother glanced over at me, but she nudged Iras and said encouragingly, "Go ahead, ask him."

"Uncle Gnaeus, may I give Latobius…" she was at the age where she pronounced our "L" like we pronounce our "V," which I found absolutely charming, "…his apple tonight?"

Of course I was going to say yes, but I did decide to have a bit of fun, so I drew up in mock indignation. "And who says that Latobius gets *two* apples a day?" Suddenly, I frowned, then gave Alex a mock glare as I demanded, "Who's been talking? Is it you?"

Alex, instantly understanding the game, held up both hands, saying, "Of course not, Gnaeus! I would never betray that secret!"

Switching my gaze to Algaia, I pointed at her and said accusingly, "Then it must have been *you!*"

"No!" She shook her head vigorously. "I haven't said a word, I swear it!"

Before I got to Bronwen, who was trying her best not to laugh at this point, Iras shouted, "I know who did it!"

"Who? Tell me now, and I swear that I'll…"

"It was *you*, Uncle Gnaeus!" She was pointing up at me, her baby teeth showing and perfect, still about a year away from losing them. "I *sawl* you do it!"

"Me?" I made my eyes as wide as I could. "That couldn't be! You must have seen someone else!"

"There's nobody else who looks like you," Iras retorted, and I heard a ripple of chuckles from the other diners.

I had forgotten that Iras still mispronounced some words, one of them being the word "saw," which she added an "L" to for some reason, despite how many times her parents corrected her, but it was just another thing I adored about her.

"Well," I drew the word out, rubbing my chin, "*maybe* I might have forgotten that I did that. Still," I lowered my voice to just above a whisper to lean towards her, "this isn't something I want known. What's the price for your silence?"

Knowing perfectly well the answer that was coming, I was rewarded with, "I want to give Latobius one of his apples every day for the rest of the trip!"

"By the gods," I groaned, "you drive a hard bargain!" Sighing, I said, "I suppose I have no choice." I thrust my hand across the table. "This is how we seal an agreement."

As I expected, she eagerly put her tiny hand in mine, so soft and slightly moist, and I do not know why, since I had held Iras' hand before as I led her to Latobius' stall, but the reality that, in the near future, I would be doing this with my own child hit me particularly hard.

I did my best to appear unaffected, but when I glanced over at Bronwen, her eyes were shining, and she pulled me down to whisper, "You are going to be a good father, Gnaeus."

"I hope so," I replied.

With this important matter settled, we got up to leave the dining room when Nasica, as if summoned by some form of sorcery, suddenly appeared. I cannot say that he was blocking our path, exactly, but there was no way to avoid him if we were to reach our rooms, which I am certain was his intent.

I should have been warned when Nasica, making no attempt at any false affability, said, "Centurion Pullus, may I have a private word with you?"

The others stopped, but while I was annoyed, I was not worried, so I bent down to drop the apple I had picked up from the table and proffered it to Iras, telling her, "Go with your parents and Bronwen. I'll be along shortly."

Alex lingered for a moment, but I gave him faint shake of the head; again, I was not worried about Nasica being a physical threat to me.

"Yes, what is it, Nasica?"

As I hoped, this irritated him, but I supposed he had become accustomed to the name, and he did not hesitate to reply, "I think some privacy is in order."

Before I could comment one way or another, he turned about and led me from the dining area, passing through the kitchen. This was when I began to have reservations, but while I did not have my *gladius*, I was wearing my *pugio*, which would do if necessary. Exiting through the only other entrance to the kitchen, he stopped at a door that he opened, without knocking, and I got my real answer about who was running this inn by the manner in which the purported owner Clodius came scurrying out, refusing to meet my gaze as he turned sideways to pass me in the opposite direction. Now, I was alert, but when I peered cautiously through the doorway, I saw that it was nothing more than an office, and that given our size, there would have barely been enough room for a third person of average size if they wanted any freedom of movement.

Moving behind a wooden table that appeared to operate as a desk, Nasica dropped into the chair behind it as he extended his hand towards the one on the opposite side. "Please, Centurion. Take a seat."

"I'm not sitting down, and you have to the count of ten to tell me what this is about before I leave."

Honestly, I could not tell whether his expression, which was one of pain, was genuine, nor did I care, but he said, "I had hoped that we could conduct this business amicably."

"What business? We don't have any business together," I snapped.

And in doing so, I gave him the opening he needed.

"I'm afraid we do," Nasica countered. "It concerns the matter of a debt for which I have yet to be repaid. Now," he extended his hand again, "please sit down and hear me out."

By the time Publius Sempronius Nasica was finished, I was certain of two things: that somehow he was lying, and that we should have never stayed in Mediolanum. When I left his office, Latobius had gotten his apple, and the rest of my party were up in their rooms, although only Iras was now asleep. Knocking before I entered my room, when I opened the door, I was not particularly surprised to see the three adults sitting there: Bronwen and Algaia on the edge of the bed, with Alex occupying the lone chair.

"What," Bronwen spoke first, "did that man want, Gnaeus?"

I considered the question for a moment, but while it was straightforward enough, the answer was quite a bit different.

"Supposedly," I began, "a debt that I thought had been paid by my family years ago hadn't been."

"A debt?" Alex spoke. "What kind of debt?"

"It's...complicated," I answered, but in that moment, I did not believe that the reason for it was of paramount importance, and I still believe it was the right decision. "But what matters is that he has a document, that as far as I can tell, is authentic, signed by one of the *Duumviri* that attests that when my father died, he still owed Nasica."

"Then, if it's authentic, doesn't that mean that you *do* owe him, my love?" Bronwen asked this, and it was a good thing that it was her.

Nevertheless, my tone was short with her as I replied, "But it's not authentic. I know it isn't."

"How?" Alex asked, another reasonable question, and once again, the answer was not as straightforward as it should have been.

"I just do," I said sourly, unwilling to say aloud that if Nasica was right, my mother had deceived me about paying off the debt, which prompted me to add, "And I need you to accept that."

There was no hesitation that I saw when the others all nodded their agreement.

"How much is it?" Alex asked, and I could not stop from a bitter laugh from escaping my lips.

"Part of the reason I was gone so long was because of the lengths Nasica went to assure me how much more it would be if he were to go by the law, so I suppose he wanted me to be grateful when he told me it was just for five thousand *sesterces*, the...principal amount and not the interest."

There was a silence at this; from Bronwen because she was still learning our system of coinage and finance, so she was unable to immediately translate the sum in her head, and from Alex and Algaia because they were both stunned.

Finally, Alex asked, "What are you going to do?"

"I don't know," I answered honestly. "But I suspect it means that we're going to be here for an extra day."

"Or," Alex offered calmly, "we could leave at dawn as we planned." This startled me, if only because Alex is generally the voice of caution, while I tend to go charging in. Sensing my hesitance, he pressed, "What does he have, really, Gnaeus? He's got a document that you're certain is a fake, and you're under orders from Germanicus Julius Caesar. If he's *really* that concerned, then he can follow us to Rome and make his case directly to Tiberius. Or Germanicus."

I immediately realized that, as he usually is, Alex was right. Tiberius had continued the tradition of citizens pleading their case directly to the Imperator, although in practice, the chances that Tiberius would sit and listen to the pleadings of an unsavory character like Publius Nasica were practically nonexistent. What, I thought with some excitement, can he really do?

"You're right," I announced. "This is a nuisance and nothing more. I'm not delaying even an extra day for Nasica."

I could tell by the reactions of the others that this was expected, and we retired for the night, and I for one was completely unaware that Publius Nasica had been paying attention to us the entire night.

When we arose the next morning, I felt refreshed, and I felt at peace with my decision not to countenance what Nasica had told me, that my mother, while promising to repay the debt, had reneged on it, using her influence with the wife of one of the *Duumviri* that year to issue a citywide edict that all debts under a certain amount that had been incurred for that year were canceled. While I had no recollection of this event, even if it was true, I would not have cared, not only because it was more than a decade earlier, but like my mother, I understood that Nasica's intentions from the very beginning had been corrupt; whether it was as my mother feared, that he was trying to get revenge for losing a contract, or this was simply what a criminal like Publius Nasica did, did not really matter all that much to me. I gathered up our belongings for the first trip to load the packhorse, with Alex carrying their baggage, and it was still dark, not surprising given the time of year, but I almost immediately sensed something was wrong, not because of what I saw, or heard, but what I did not. From the first day I was introduced to him, Latobius would thrust his head out of whatever stall he was in, blowing and sucking in air because my scent had warned him of my approach, yet when I entered the stable, nothing happened. Oh, there were the sounds of hooves pawing at the straw and some soft nickering, but nothing from the private stall that stallions like my horse required. I do not remember doing so, but I must have dropped the packs I was carrying to hurry down the run between stalls to learn that my ears, and now my eyes, were not deceiving me; his stall was empty.

"Nasica," I breathed more than said the name.

I sensed Alex was not far behind me, and he was standing off my right shoulder, sharing the same disbelief that I did.

"What was he thinking?" He broke the silence, and it was reassuring that he had instantly reached the same conclusion I had. "What could he possibly hope to gain by doing this?"

"I don't know," I was already stalking back towards the inn, "but I'm going to find out."

Truly, the only real sticking point was whether I donned my *hamata*, helmet, and greaves; naturally, I argued for this, but the other three were adamantly opposed.

"If you go stomping up the street wearing your armor as if you're going into battle, you're going to instantly draw attention from the *vigiles*," Alex had argued, "and this isn't a military town."

He was right, yet I was still reluctant to forego both the protection and the announcement of my status, but I finally demurred, strapping on my *baltea* and attaching the sheath to my great-grandfather's *gladius*. When Alex moved to my other piece of baggage and withdrew the *gladius* I had had made by Decimus Scrofa, the best smith in Ubiorum when it came to forging *gladii* but had become my spare with my father's death, my initial instinct was to forbid him from accompanying me. For the first time, however, I kept that thought to myself, although I did worry about what Algaia would do to me if he got hurt, or worse. I just have to make sure that doesn't happen, I told myself as I watched him strap on the blade.

"Ready," he said quietly. "I assume you know where we're going?"

The truth of the matter was that I did not, at least not with any real certainty. As Nasica's takeover of Clodius' inn had shown me, he had not been idle in the years I had been away from here, so it was certainly possible that he had purchased more property.

Nevertheless, I tried to sound confident when I explained, "Knowing Nasica and how we met, and given how long I've been gone, I'm betting that he's going to be at Proserpina's Lair, waiting for me."

Bronwen had been sitting on the bed, and she was joined by Algaia and Iras, who was still sleeping on her mother's shoulder.

"We'll be back as soon as we can," I promised, keeping my voice low to avoid disturbing the child's slumber.

"I know," Bronwen said simply. "Go get Latobius so that we can leave this place."

I kissed her, but before I could leave the room, Alex pointed to the leather pouch, in which were my orders.

"Let's take that with us," he suggested, but I did not see the point, so he explained, "You've got a scroll with Germanicus Julius Caesar' seal on it. If Nasica has one of the *duumviri* in his coin purse, waving that might be just what you need to shove into his face."

It was, I recognized immediately, a good idea, so I grabbed it and slung it over my shoulder, then stepped out into the hallway while Alex and Algaia exchanged a few words; I had been somewhat heartened to see that Algaia was not glaring daggers at me when she came into our room, taking this as the sign she at least understood why Alex was coming along. He joined me, and we descended the stairs and I led him out of the inn, reminding myself to shorten my stride so that he could keep up. The sky was pinkening, and there was a smattering of people about, but I ignored the stares as always, my *sagum* and Alex's cloak hiding the fact that we were armed. It was quite strange, honestly, walking these streets that I once knew so well, and it brought back many memories, a good portion of them unpleasant. Not, I would add, because of what had happened to me, but because of who I was back then, when men of the lowest order were beneath my attention, so sure was I that they had absolutely nothing to offer me of any value. Now I would gladly lay down my life for my men and comrades like Saloninus, Gillo, and Marcus Macer, my first Pilus Prior and my father's best friend. It seemed as if every corner I turned as we walked across the city forced me to confront another memory of something that I had said or done that shamed the man I am now, but this seemed to have an unexpected benefit, because with every pace closer to Proserpina's Lair, I was becoming angrier.

Following behind me, something in my body language must have alerted Alex, because when we were a block away, he called out, "Gnaeus. Let's stop for a moment."

"Why?" I asked over my shoulder but did not slow.

"So that you don't go walking into an ambush, that's why."

As he knew it would, this got me to stop dead in my tracks, because I knew that he was right. Nasica was nothing if not cunning, and while it had been more than ten years since we last saw each other, he was undoubtedly aware of at least some aspects of my time in the Legions. He would know that I was not the rawboned, callow youth any longer, and he would assess that I posed a threat to him; to what degree was the question.

"What are you suggesting?"

"How well do you know the place we're going to?"

I thought for a moment, then answered, "I know it well enough, but that was more than ten years ago. I have no idea if he's changed anything about the layout."

"There's really only one way to find that out, but if he hasn't changed anything, didn't you say there are essentially two ways to get in?"

"Yes. *If* he hasn't changed anything."

"Let's get closer to find out." Alex resumed moving, but I was not satisfied.

"What are you thinking about?" I demanded.

"That we show up where they don't expect us to." This time, he was the one calling over his shoulder, which I immediately understood he had done on purpose, forcing me to a trot to catch up as I muttered curses at him.

Only with retrospect can I say that the gods, for their own reasons, saw fit to favor us by Nasica leaving Proserpina's Lair unchanged, and my gamble that Nasica used the same room in the rear of the *taverna* as his office also turned out to be correct. It also helped that, unlike the *taverna*, a brothel never closes because there are always customers who are willing to pay for an entire night before they have to rise and hurry off to their jobs or families. Best of all, however, was that the woman who ran the place when I was a youth was still there, her name Plotina, and I had learned during my time with Niobe that she was no admirer of Nasica, although I warned myself that this might have changed. We found her dozing behind the low desk from where she ran things, and while she was grayer, she was essentially unchanged. As most brothels have, there was a little bell attached to the door, so by the time I had fully opened it, she had jerked awake and was favoring us with the kind of smile that is as false as any merchant who smells a profit arriving at their doorstep.

"*Salve,* citizens, and welcome..." She stopped abruptly, her eyes narrowing as she took me in, and while the smile remained, I thought that it softened slightly as she moved out from behind the desk. "Well, if it's not young Gnaeus Volusenus! I heard you joined the Legions, so I never thought I would see you again!"

One of the things my real father had changed in me, mainly by his example, was in how I treated women like Plotina, so when I bowed and took her hand to kiss it, it could have been done for Agrippina herself, and she beamed up at me, minus a tooth from the last time I had seen her.

"I see you learned manners," she said with a chuckle. "I would never have believed that being under the standard would do that."

"I learned from the best," I told her, and it was my way of introducing just how much things had changed. "I learned from my father," her smile vanished, understandably so, but I hurried to add,

"I mean my *real* father. I'm not Gnaeus Volusenus anymore, Plotina. I'm Gnaeus Volusenianus Pullus."

"Pullus?" She frowned, though not in a manner that suggested that she was displeased. "Where have I heard that name before?"

"Probably from another man under the standard," I told her. "It's a famous name in the Legions. And," I added, hoping this would forestall a lengthy explanation, "how all that came to be is a long story, and we're pressed for time. I'm actually on orders to report to Rome as quickly as possible."

She surprised me then, both by seeming to accept this without further question, and because she asked suddenly, "You're not here to see Niobe, are you?"

It would be a lie for me to say that the thought of her had not crossed my mind, and more than once, essentially from the moment we rode through the gates, but I was about to assure her this was not the case when my mind caught up to the sudden change in her.

"No," I answered, "but why do you ask? What is it?"

"Niobe died three years ago, Master...Pullus," Plotina answered soberly, and she blinked rapidly, but while it is easy to be cynical at the idea that there is much sentiment among the purveyors of vice, I have seen whores weeping when one of their friends succumbed to some ailment...or worse, so I believe she was sincere. "We had a bilious fever sweep through the city, and Niobe was one of the ones the gods took."

"That's very sad," I replied, and I meant it; none of the memories I have of her are sorrowful or angry.

"So," she went immediately back to the practical mistress of a brothel, "why are you here?"

I hesitated, then glanced at Alex, deciding to let the dice fly.

"Nasica says that I owe him a debt from more than ten years ago," I began, but I got no further because she cut me off with a snort.

"Oh, *that*," she scoffed. "He's been talking about that for years." She looked up at me, her eyes narrowed as she asked sharply, "You don't believe him, do you? Because I know that it's a lie."

"Is there any proof of that, Mistress?" Alex broke in, but as always, he did it in such a way that Plotina absolutely beamed at him, but her words were not much comfort.

"Not that I'm aware of, young Master," she answered him. "I mean," she shrugged, "aside from the fact that I was there when your mother paid him off."

I do not believe that it was her intent to do so, because there was no reason for her to assume that I did not know what had taken place, but I actually thought about taking a seat to catch my breath.

"Wait," I gasped. "Are you saying that my mother actually paid him the money?"

Plotina turned and pointed to her desk. "Yes, right there. I was sitting there when she came in."

Suddenly, she looked acutely uncomfortable and began looking everywhere but up at me.

"Plotina," I urged her, "you can tell me, I won't be angry. Or…upset, I swear it."

This clearly relieved her, but she still did not seem eager to speak, although she said, "It's just that when your mother came in…she's very beautiful, by the way…" I nodded my thanks, trying not to snap at her for stalling, "…but I thought that she had followed your father…" She looked confused for a moment, which was explained when she said with a self-conscious laugh, "I mean the man I thought was your father here to the Lair."

"You mean Quintus Volusenus?" I thought I was beginning to understand, and she nodded.

"Yes, he had arrived earlier that evening, so when she identified herself, I assumed it was because she had followed him there. It is," she assured us, "a common occurrence in this business." That made sense, of course, although I only nodded at her to continue. "But then she told me she was here because she had business with Publius Sempronius…" she lowered her voice despite the fact it was just the three of us, "…I have to be careful about that. He's beaten more than one of the girls who slipped and called him Nasica."

While I was curious to hear about this exchange between my mother and Nasica, I was also aware that time was of the essence, so

I essentially finished for her, "And you saw her hand the money over."

"Oh, it wasn't money." Plotina shook her head, sending my own head spinning again. "It was a tablet, but while I don't know *exactly* what it said, I know that when Nasica looked at it, he snapped it shut and said that the debt was forgiven." She snapped her fingers. "Just like that. Then," she waved one hand towards the entrance, "your mother left and I never saw her again."

Now I was dying of curiosity to find out more, temporarily forgetting that I was the one worried about time, but thankfully, Alex kept his head, confirming, "So we know that there is no debt, but we don't really have any way to prove it."

"You said you were passing through on your way to Rome," Plotina said, and when I nodded, she asked, "Then why don't you just leave? Oh," she allowed, "he'll be angry, but not enough to get men together to come after you. Besides," Plotina smiled again, but it was a grim one, and she swept one hand up and down, "you were big as a young sprout, and the gods know you're even bigger. But," she shook her head, "I've seen my share of men in my day, and you're the kind of man Publius wants no part of, I know that much."

"The reason we haven't left is because he stole my horse, Latobius," I explained.

Saying this made it occur to both of us, but Alex beat me to it, asking her, "Plotina, do you have a stable here?"

"We do." She nodded. "But there's no new horses in it."

"How do you know that?"

She flushed slightly. "Because that's the shortest path to the public toilet, and I had to go not long before you arrived."

"That actually makes sense," I said aloud as I thought about it. "If he thought I'd come here, he'd anticipate I'd look for him in the stable." Turning back to Plotina, I asked, "Does he still have the same office? In the *taverna*?"

"Yes, the same," she replied, then warned, "but he enlarged it by about a third."

"Any idea who's with him?"

"Cordus, Stator, and Vitellius," she answered. I suppose she either correctly read my expression or she just had a good memory because she said, "Vitellius came to work in the *collegia* after you left, about five years ago. And," she warned, "he's a veteran from one of the Pannonian Legions, I think. He's the man who does all of Publius'…unpleasant tasks," was how she phrased it, but I knew exactly what she meant.

"He's the one Nasica sends to maim or kill his enemies."

"Them," she nodded, "and men who have fallen so far behind in their payment that he decides there's no more profit to be had from them."

I was about to ask if that was the usual practice for a man who ran a *collegia*, but I realized it did not matter.

"Mistress Plotina, would you be willing to help us?" Alex asked.

"I thought I was helping you," she replied, not angrily, but I saw that she was becoming suspicious that we were about to ask her to do something she had no intention of doing.

"You've been a huge help," I assured her. "But could you go to the *taverna* and make sure Nasica is there, and with those men you say he's with. And," I hurried to add, "I'll make it worth your while."

"Are you going to kill him?" she asked me bluntly, although I have no idea whether she did this deliberately to catch me by surprise.

My mind raced as I wondered, What does she want me to do? What answer is she looking for?

Aloud, I said, "Not if I can avoid it."

"Then," she replied flatly, "I've given you all the help I'm willing to offer." Her voice dropped almost to a whisper, "Master Pullus, he's going to beat me if he thinks I had anything to do with helping you do whatever you're about to do…at the very least."

I certainly had not thought of that, and a glance at Alex confirmed that he had not either, but as usual, he had a solution, and once he explained it, I saw Plotina relax slightly.

"That could work," she allowed.

Like most of the best solutions, this one was simple. Scrounging up some leather thongs, we bound Plotina's hands and feet, and at her suggestion, we tore some material from her gown to stuff in her mouth.

"I might even get a new dress out of this," she said cheerfully as we were lowering her to the ground behind the desk and just before we stuffed the rag in her mouth.

"Ready?" I asked Alex, and he gave a nod.

"Thank you, Plotina," I said, then felt foolish because she mumbled something since her mouth was full of her own dress. On an impulse, I added, "When we get Latobius back, we'll be leaving. Wait until tomorrow, then go see Clodius at his inn. He'll have something there for you."

Then, there was no more reason to delay.

Exiting the brothel, I had my *gladius* out, thinking that Nasica might have had a man stationed at what was essentially the back entrance to the *taverna*, but once we moved down the walkway as silently as possible, we found that, while the door was pushed shut, it was not latched, and after listening for the sounds of breathing, I slowly pushed it open. The small passageway was deserted, and we continued to tiptoe down it to Nasica's office as I chided myself for not thinking to wrap our feet in rags, because walking in this manner with soldier's *caligae* is extremely uncomfortable, but hobnails against a stone floor are impossible to misinterpret. There were no lamps lit to illuminate the passageway, and while it was now early daylight, the windows were still shuttered, but we could tell the office door was open because there was a rectangle of light on the floor. I paused, mainly to slow my breathing, but to listen as well, and we were rewarded by the muffled sound of voices. Most importantly, while I could not make out what was being said, I could tell by the tone that they were alert but not alarmed. What I could not tell was how many men were in there, so I glanced over my shoulder at Alex, who nodded his readiness, knowing there was only one way to find out. I took off my *sagum* and laid it on the floor, then strode the two paces to the door to stand in it, but with my left side angled inward with my *gladius* down and partially hidden by my body, but they were not the only ones surprised at my sudden appearance.

While I had heard Plotina when she told us he had the office enlarged, I realized that I had made the assumption that the desk he sat behind would be in the same spot, directly across from the doorway. It was not; instead, he had moved it so that his back was to the left wall of the office, aided by the fact that the extra space had been created by moving the left wall. Instead of facing Nasica, I was facing a man I did not recognize, except that I did in a sense, instantly knowing this was Vitellius, the former Legionary. Additionally, there were not four men in the office but five, although I also instantly dismissed the extra man as a threat, at least physically, because of the red stripe on his tunic. It was not all against my favor, however, because all of them had frozen in place, obviously surprised by my appearance, which was my goal.

I had prepared what I was going to say, but the presence of Vitellius, and most importantly what he held in his hand prompted me to instead point to it and ask pleasantly, "Are you planning on using that?"

To his credit, he did not appear flustered, replying coolly, "That depends on you, doesn't it?"

"It does!" I agreed cheerfully, then without taking my eyes off Vitellius, I addressed Nasica. "Where's my horse, Nasica? I'm leaving today, and I don't plan on walking."

I had seen Nasica was seated behind his desk, while Cordus was sitting next to the desk with his back to the passageway wall, while Stator was standing, leaning more accurately, against the opposite wall but also next to the desk. The fifth man was standing just behind Nasica's chair, and he was the only one who looked decidedly nervous.

"Centurion Volusenus," Nasica began, my guess being that his use of my former name was calculated and perhaps a form of payback for my using the name he hated, "I attempted to conclude our business amicably, but you refused to listen to reason. And," I saw his arm lift as he indicated the nervous man behind him, "I'm doing everything according to our laws, which is why the *Duumvir* is here, to verify that what I'm saying is true."

"You've been under the standard." I ignored Nasica to address Vitellius.

"I have," he said cautiously.

I was about to bring up that I knew he had been in one of the Pannonian Legions; fortunately, I remembered who I had learned that from, and it would be a betrayal of Plotina, so instead, I asked, "Which Legion?"

I cannot say that I was all that hopeful, but once again, the gods smiled on me when he said, "The 8th Legion, Centurion. Why?"

"Ah." I nodded, trying not to sound excited at this stroke of good fortune. "So you must know Titus Domitius then."

As I hoped, this had an effect on the man, his eyes going wide as he exclaimed, "Of course I do! He was my Pilus Prior! I served in the Second of the Third! But," he frowned, "how do you know him?"

"I don't," I replied casually. "I mean, not personally. But he was my father's best friend."

"Who was your father?" Vitellius asked, and I got my answer about Nasica's use of my old name when he cut in abruptly.

"Yes, yes, you two can talk about your old acquaintances some other time." I could hear that Nasica was trying to sound irritated, but I also heard the worry there, and I knew what his real purpose was, that somehow he had found out my father's connection to Vitellius' old Legion.

Which was why I again pointedly ignored Nasica to answer, "Titus Porcinianus Pullus."

The effect was even more dramatic on the old Legionary, who gasped, "But Sempronius said your name was Volusenus! He didn't say anything about you being a Pullus!"

"My full name," I did look over to Nasica to give him a smile, "is actually Gnaeus Volusenianus Pullus." I knew that our naming convention would inform Vitellius of part of the story, specifically about my adoption, but I also made sure to add, "But I'm actually Titus Pullus' natural son, which I didn't know until after he died last year, when he revealed it in his will with an offer of posthumous adoption."

Given who this is for, the reader will know this was not *exactly* how things transpired, but it was close enough, and most importantly, it caused Vitellius to whirl about to face Nasica, pointing directly at the man with his *gladius*, which might have been simply because of our habit of pointing with our dominant hand, but I do not think so in this case.

"You didn't tell me that I might be facing the son of *Titus Pullus*!" He did not yell, exactly, but it was the pointing of the blade that got Cordus on his feet, his hand on the hilt of his own *gladius*, while Stator stopped leaning.

I had no idea how Nasica would answer this, thinking that perhaps he might want to placate a clearly disturbed former Legionary with a *gladius* in his hand in an enclosed space; I was wrong.

"Because it's none of your fucking business," Nasica snarled, having gotten to his feet himself. "You're paid to do what you're fucking told, Vitellius, and I tell you exactly what you need to know and nothing more!"

It was quite tense, and I could see that Cordus and Stator, who was now missing most of one ear, seemed to be equally torn about who posed the bigger threat at the moment, me or Vitellius, who, when I looked back at him, seemed to be as confused because his eyes kept darting over to me. Honestly, I was not inclined to move, at least at this moment; I was secretly hoping that Vitellius might solve my problem. He did no such thing, but he also took himself out of whatever was coming, dropping his arm to his side.

"You don't pay me nearly enough to go at the Centurion here, and even if you did, I'd never raise my blade to a man of the Pullus line." His mouth twisted into a sneer. "It's something that men like you will *never* understand, what that name means to any misbegotten bastard who's served under the standard." He showed that he was paying attention to the atmosphere in the room by the slow, deliberate manner in which he dropped his arm, then sheathed his *gladius*, but he surprised me by turning to address me. "Centurion Pullus, I won't draw my blade against you. But…" He hesitated.

"But you work for Nasica here, and since you're a man of honor, you're essentially fucked if things turn to vinegar," I finished for him, and he was clearly relieved, nodding his head, but I was turning to Nasica to address him. "All I want is my horse, Nasica. This can all end right now."

"Would that I could, Centurion," Nasica's transformation back to the polite and sober man of business was instantaneous, and as false as it had been at first, "but I'm afraid that it's out of my hands now. And I didn't take your horse. He," for the first time, he indicated the man in the red-striped tunic, "is the one responsible for that."

The gaze I turned on this man was as cold as I could make it, and it pleased me a great deal to see him not only go pale but start to visibly shake.

"Is this true? Did you take my horse? And," I pointed to the stripe, "I take it you're one of the *duumviri*?"

For a moment, I was certain he would be unable to summon a word, but he finally managed to squeak, "Y-yes." Hearing his own voice seemed to help, because in a firmer tone, though it still was not sufficient to get a Century of whores moving even if he had been dangling a purse in front of them, he introduced himself. "I'm the senior *Duumvir* for Mediolanum, appointed by the Senate. My name is Servius Junius Lentulus, and," he indicated Nasica, "Citizen Sempronius reported to me that he was unable to gain your cooperation in settling an outstanding matter that exists between Sempronius and your family. The," he hurried to add, "Volusenus family, not the Pullus family." I do not know if it was intended as a rebuke, but seeing how he looked down at Nasica with a disapproving frown as he said it, I tend to believe it was. "Even *I* know about the great Prefect Titus Pullus and his descendants, and I didn't have to serve under the standard to know about it." He returned his gaze to me, and I sensed that he was trying very hard to find a way out of what he saw as a predicament he wanted nothing to do with as he continued, "That being said, the proof that Citizen Sempronius has provided is quite conclusive, I'm afraid. So," the shrug he gave I knew was intended to send the signal that he was helpless, "until this matter is resolved, I can't allow you to leave. Your party, however," he acted as if this was some sort of favor, "is free to go whenever they please, and you can catch up with them."

I heard the scrape of Alex's sole, but since I had not moved and was still half-in the doorway, I gestured with my *gladius*, sending a signal I hoped he interpreted correctly, and given that he did not make himself known, it told me that he did.

Addressing Lentulus, I asked politely, "What is this evidence? And may I see it?"

Lentulus clearly expected this, because he leaned over to pick up a tablet on the desk, but in order to give it to me, he would have to move from behind the desk, which he was clearly reluctant to do, so he turned and handed it to Stator. Who, if I was any judge, was no more enthusiastic about coming within arm's reach of me, but he looked at Nasica, who had resumed his seat, and he nodded. Walking slowly, I saw his eyes flickering down to where my right hand, still partially hidden because of the angle of my body, was holding my great-grandfather's *gladius*.

Feeling a bit mischievous, once Stator reached a point where he could extend the tablet so I could take it with my left hand, I asked, "What happened to your ear? Did you lose it somewhere?"

There was a muted snicker that came from the general area of the three men around the desk, and I was satisfied to see his face flush, and he answered sulkily, "I lost it in a fight, Volusenus."

"Call me that again and I'll gut you like a fish." I said this conversationally, but I was fumbling to open the tablet with just one hand, making me realize how there are things we do so often we do not think about how we do it until we cannot.

Stator was angry, but he was wise enough to keep his mouth shut, and even wiser to step back away from me as I frowned down at what, to my eye, were nothing but a series of figures incised next to a list of names, one of which was Quintus Volusenus, except that there was a blank space next to it, unlike the others.

"So?" I shook my head. "This is meaningless. And," I looked over at Nasica, "if that's the only proof you have…"

Even before I finished, I could tell that they were not through, and for this Lentulus withdrew a scroll from the leather satchel that I had missed because it was sitting at his feet. He handed it to Stator, but when he returned to me, I was faced with a dilemma because my one free hand was still full, and I was not about to sheathe my blade. So I snapped the tablet shut and tossed it in the general direction of Nasica's desk, but I missed, it hitting the edge and clattering to the floor, which was the loudest sound to that point. Nasica growled at Cordus to pick it up, and for the briefest instant, I thought about ending this right then, when, for a fraction of time, I had Cordus bent over with his back exposed, and Stator holding the scroll in his right hand, a mistake that could have cost him his life. I did not, and perhaps it was because of the voice in my head that sounded like my father, reminding me how there were times where killing the problem was not the best way to solve it.

When Stator thrust it out to me, I shook my head, saying flatly, "I can't unroll it with two hands, and I'm not going to take the risk that's your goal, to get me to sheathe my *gladius*. So unroll it for me and hold it up for me to read it."

Judging by Nasica's reaction, this was not exactly what he had been hoping for, but he said sourly, "Do as he says."

Stator did so, then turned the written side towards me, and I immediately recognized the signature affixed to the bottom of the document, which Lentulus clearly saw by my expression, but he should have waited an instant longer.

"As you can see," Lentulus explained, "this is a contract that was drawn up between your father and Citizen Sempronius concerning the awarding of a contract by a consortium your father was the representative of that agreed to pay Citizen Sempronius for a service. It was deposited at the office of the City Quaestor as is the requirement until the contract is discharged. And," he pointed out, "the fact that it was still there is proof that the contract hadn't been fulfilled."

"And what was this service?" I directed my question at Nasica, but while he looked uncomfortable, he answered quickly, "I provided your father and his consortium with labor for the new *insulae* that was part of the expansion of the city."

I did not have to feign surprise at this. "And? That's what that," I pointed to the scroll, "is about? It's not about...anything else?"

I cannot say why I was reluctant to say aloud why I was certain we were there, that I had been gulled by an experienced criminal when I was a raw youth.

For the first time, it seemed as if Nasica's reaction was genuine, because he asked in surprise, "Did you think this was about the money *you* owed me?" When I nodded, he laughed, and I believe it was also sincere, and he assured me, "By the gods, no. That debt was taken care of by your mother." I could see the instant the words came out of his mouth he understood how I might interpret it; while the gods had favored me, they were also protecting Publius Nasica, thanks to what I had learned from Plotina just moments before, but he did not know that. Thrusting both hands out, he said quickly, "Not in an unseemly way, I swear it!" Seeing my reaction, or lack thereof, he went on, "In fact, that," he pointed to the scroll, "is how she discharged that original debt, by arranging it between your father's consortium and me for this contract. She brought me your father's pledge to give me the contract. Which," Nasica tried to make it sound as if this was an afterthought, "was my goal all along with you, Pullus. I needed leverage."

Will anything in my past be simple? That was the initial thought that ran through my mind. I had already spent a significant amount of the previous two years trying to unravel and understand all of the events and the people who were responsible for me standing here in Proserpina's Lair. But hard on the heels of that was another, and more unpleasant thought: What if Publius Nasica was telling the truth? Something deep inside me told me that, in all likelihood, he was, and that for one reason or another, Quintus Volusenus had reneged on the terms of this contract that, at least to the naked eye, appeared to be legitimate. It was also for a much larger sum than my original debt, which explained why Nasica was willing to go to such extremes. I was assailed by a cascade of thoughts and memories, remembering, for example, how indifferent Quintus was to the actual details when it came to managing our money, a job that fell to my mother. Beyond that, however, were other things, like the recognition that between the man who I thought was my father and my real father, Quintus Volusenus was not anywhere nearly as intelligent as my real father, but also how, even worse and much like the late and not mourned Gaius Porcinianus Pullus, he thought that he was cleverer than he actually was. And, I recalled, this would not have been the first time where my mother had stepped in and saved Quintus from himself and his arrogant belief that, because of his status, this somehow meant that he was endowed with a greater intellect and acumen than anyone in the lower orders…like Publius Nasica. It was all of this that prompted me to sheathe my *gladius* to reach into the shoulder bag.

"I," I told them, "have something to show you as well."

"You know," Alex commented me as we rode out of Mediolanum, "if you had just pulled that scroll out first, we wouldn't have gotten such a late start."

"Oh, go piss on your boots," I muttered, irritated because he was right, but I was not ready to capitulate. "I needed to see exactly what Nasica had, and my way was the only way to do it."

"You did it your way because you were hoping you could kill him."

I shot an irritated look over my shoulder at Bronwen, who had said this from her spot on the cart, but I was beginning to see the humor, as perverse as it was, in the situation.

Nevertheless, I shot back, "You don't know that for sure."

"Yes, I do," Bronwen replied placidly, probably because she knew the best way to get under my skin. "I know you better than anyone else." Before I could interject anything, she allowed, "Except for your mother...perhaps."

When all was said and done, it had been deceptively simple, and as my traveling companions liked to remind me for the rest of our journey to Rome, I should have understood that carrying anything with the seal of Germanicus Julius Caesar would have overridden any sense of duty or allegiance of an official appointed by Tiberius, through the Senate, of course, towards a strongman running a *collegia* in a provincial city. Not that it was completely unrewarding, although I had harbored the idea that killing Publius Nasica would be quite satisfying; watching his face go pale, then turn to a shade very close to purple as Lentulus fell over himself to assure me that the matter was settled and I was free to leave at any time was fairly satisfying in itself. And, if I am being honest, I was quite pleased with myself for thinking of something witty to say.

"You know," I told Nasica as we left the Lair, after Lentulus had Latobius led to the entrance, "the best part of this is that I believe you. I think Quintus Volusenus cheated you." I was leaping astride Latobius as I said this, and I could not resist saying over my shoulder, "And he got away with it."

Chapter 2

Despite our relatively late start, we made good progress, or perhaps it was just that talking about what had transpired made the miles seem to go by faster, but while I laughed at the jokes, and made some myself, in the back of my mind was the nagging thought: did I really know Quintus Volusenus at all? Truly, I had stopped thinking of him as my father, yet I was not about to, nor will I deny now that he had an enormous impact on my life, and while it was mostly more of a negative, such as his attitude towards the Head Count that he passed to me, it was not all bad. He had taught me the importance of *dignitas* to any Roman man who aspires to perform noble deeds and make a name for himself, how a man's reputation could be shattered by one careless move. Like, I thought bitterly, cheating Nasica out of what, I was certain by that point, was a legitimate contract that, if Lentulus was to be believed, he had actually delivered. Why I felt this was the likely truth was because of how, despite my lack of contact with him before I left Mediolanum four years later, I had heard from multiple sources how desperate Publius Sempronius Nasica was to become seen as a legitimate businessman and a pillar of Mediolanum society. That contract was worth far more than the ten thousand *sesterces* that it stipulated would be paid to Nasica for providing the laborers who built a series of three-story *insulae* in the recently enlarged area inside the city walls, because it was his path to legitimacy, at least in his eyes. I could have assured him that, even if Quintus Volusenus had honored the terms of the contract, and that led to other legitimate business dealings, the men of the higher orders would never forget how Publius Sempronius got his start, or why he had earned the *cognomen* Nasica, and they would have reminded him on a regular basis of that fact.

By the time we arrived in Placentia, well after dark, where I used the Germanicus scroll to have the gates opened for us, it took us three tries before we found an inn, but more importantly, what had happened in Mediolanum had been exhausted as a topic of conversation, for which I was grateful. We were forced to share one room, but that was not why I had trouble falling asleep. While the others had stopped talking about Nasica, my mind still wrestled with the implications of what it all meant, and I realized that, at this point, there would only be one person who knew the truth about Quintus Volusenus, and that was my mother. For a stretch of time, as I listened to the soft snoring of my companions, I composed a letter in my head that I would send as soon as we arrived in Rome, to my mother in Mogontiacum, demanding to be told the truth. Then, somewhere in there, I mentally tore the letter to pieces and discarded it, deciding that, finally, it was time to put my past to rest, all of it. It is a decision that I do not regret, and to this day, I have never asked my mother anything about the affairs of Quintus Volusenus and Publius Sempronius Nasica, and have no plans to do so. Which, I say with some rueful amusement, was a good thing, because I soon had far larger problems confronting me.

The closer we got to Rome, it is probably not surprising that the tension increased, but there was an added element that made this unlike anything I had ever experienced before, and when we discussed it the night before we were arriving in the city over our meal, I learned I was not alone.

"I am so excited to see Rome," Bronwen said it first, then gave me an apologetic glance, "but I feel badly that I am because we do not know what you will be facing."

I was about to assure her that I understood, but Alex spoke up, clearly relieved. "Thank the gods I'm not the only one! We," he indicated Algaia "were talking about it last night. We know that you might be in some sort of trouble when you meet Germanicus…but it's *Rome!*"

"And you think I don't feel the same way?" I did not say this in a challenging manner, but more to assure them that, not only did I know how they felt, I shared their sentiments. "I've waited my entire life to see Rome. I just wish I had some idea of what lies ahead of us."

I used the word "us" intentionally; it was my way of letting my companions know that I was acutely aware that they had chosen to attach themselves to me, and while, if there was some form of punishment coming my way, I would bear the brunt of it, they would be suffering some sort of consequence as well, the only difference being a matter of degree. I thought about making a joke to Bronwen about how she might regret leaving Britannia with me, but I quickly realized this was something she would not find humorous in the slightest, and for perhaps the hundredth time that day alone, I felt my eyes drawn downward to the sight of her swelling belly. We were staying at an inn near Veii that last night, which is only about ten miles north of the city, and meant that we would arrive before midday, more than enough time for us to find a place to stay for my three companions, while I would go on to report directly to Germanicus, although at that moment, I did not know exactly where that would be. I assumed that it would be somewhere on the Palatine, and Alex had raised the possibility that he might actually be in what has become the palace for the Imperator himself, although it still is referred to as the *Domus Augusti*. We could see Rome's location before we got close enough to see its walls with what looked like a single, dirty brownish-gray cloud that just squatted on the horizon.

"How many people do you think it takes to make that much smoke?" Alex commented, which I found curious because I was certain that he knew the answer, but I saw that he had actually aimed his question at Algaia and Bronwen.

They put their heads together, literally, but I could not hear them from where I sat on Latobius, then after a few moments, Algaia spoke for them. "We don't know, other than it must be a lot of people." She cocked her head, then ventured, "One hundred thousand people?"

Alex looked surprised, but he shook his head and said, "Much more than that."

"Then...five hundred thousand people," Bronwen spoke up, and this time, Alex looked to me to inform her that she was still very low on their estimate.

"Think," I said, "*much* bigger. Think twice as big."

That confused them even more, and I realized that, while I knew that more than a million people live in Rome, I had no idea what that looked like, and while Bronwen has an excellent mind when it comes to numbers, she had never had any reason to contemplate just how huge a number one million actually is. And, I must admit, that even when I tried to explain it as a concept, I could see that I was getting nowhere with either of them, but not because they are not clever, but because I had no way to envision that large a number myself.

Finally, I said, "We're going to find out shortly."

We were traveling south on the Via Cassia, and by mid-morning, on either side of the road, there were a variety of inns, *tavernae,* and at least two brothels in what I suppose could be called the suburbs of Rome. Farther off the road, and connected by long driveways, there were opulent estates, and I assumed that many of the people who lived outside the walls did something involving these estates. Not surprisingly, traffic grew heavier, but finally, up ahead in the distance, we saw the red brick structures of the Campus Martius, where I would have normally reported immediately, as this is where all Legion officers are housed when they are in Rome. However, the orders given to me by Primus Pilus Sacrovir had specifically forbidden me from doing so, which was one reason I had worried that there was something coming from Germanicus that I would not like. There was a bottleneck at the Milvian Bridge, but from what we could gather, this was normal, judging from the manner in which people were behaving, and it quickly became apparent that the bridge simply was not wide enough to accommodate all of the traffic. Bronwen's eyes were shining with excitement, while I was happy with my decision to don my uniform, although I had my helmet strapped to my saddle, because it meant that when I caught a man ogling her, all I had to do was guide Latobius in his direction to stare down at the man...with one hand on the hilt of my *gladius* of course. Because of the cart, I resigned myself to move with the flow of the traffic rather than force our way through the people on foot, which was by far the majority of the traffic, small groups of people traveling together, their purpose revealed by what they carried with them; some were carrying leather bags that are used to hold clothing and other items travelers use, while others had sacks or boxes on their shoulders that I assumed they intended to deliver or sell inside the city.

Once past the bridge, we passed through the Campus Martius, and I did not even have to ask if Alex was thinking the same thing that I was, that my father had stayed in one of those buildings, while my great-grandfather had been there as well, although Augustus had ordered the entire complex of buildings to be rebuilt and enlarged. This was almost instantly forgotten as we came to the next large structure, and I cheerfully admit that we immediately came to a stop in the street, blocking the people behind us as we gawked like the provincials that we were. Towering up into the sky was a semicircular building, but with another section jutting out from the semicircle, which was three stories high, with the first story composed of arches about ten feet high, while the second story was essentially the same, but the third level was actually much taller, with inset columns, topped by a red tile roof. It was massive, more than a hundred paces wide, and we could not even see where it ended because of our position.

"That has to be Pompey's Theater," Alex commented, which confirmed my guess.

I had drawn Latobius up next to the cart so that I could talk to Bronwen, and I leaned down to tell her, "This is where Divus Julius was assassinated." This only drew a blank stare, and I added, "Julius Caesar."

"Ah!" Her face lit up, reminding me of her avid interest in our history. "Can we go inside?"

"Not now," I told her, "but we will." I did not say aloud "I hope," but I saw by the expression on her face she understood it was there.

We also passed the Theater of Marcellus, which I only recognized because of my father's account when he went to meet some old comrades of my great-grandfather at a nearby *taverna*, and I pointed it out to the others, telling them how I knew.

The traffic thinned out a bit, but then we reached the Porta Carmentalis, where the old Servian wall abuts the base of the Capitoline to the north and the Tiber to the south. This time, however, I was unwilling to wait, and I decided it was time to strap on my helmet so that my red transverse crest was clearly visible.

"Follow me," I called over my shoulder, then nudged Latobius forward.

I did not intend for him to move as quickly as he did, but I immediately realized that I should have anticipated that he would be excited by the presence of so many people, other horses, mules, and oxen pulling the handful of wagons. This did not help the man that he slammed into and sent sprawling forward, where he collided with the people ahead of him in line. They did serve to break his fall, but two people, a man and a woman, were not as lucky and fell to the paving stones, but the man Latobius struck whirled about, his face contorted with rage as he clenched a fist.

"You *mentula*! You..." He managed to stop himself as his brain caught up with his eyes, which went wide as he looked up to see a very large, uniformed Centurion staring down at him, cutting him off in mid-curse. I was more amused than angry, mainly because watching his mouth opening and closing reminded me of a fish out of water.

"I apologize for my horse striking you, Citizen," I said. Then, shifting my attention to the pair of people who were being helped to their feet, I called out more loudly, "And to you as well. I didn't intend for him to knock anyone down. He's just," I patted Latobius' neck, "as excited to be in Rome for the first time as I am."

I saw that the man was still angry, but he was also clever enough to know that pressing the matter would not end well for him.

"All right, Centurion," he muttered. "It was an accident, and I accept your apology."

But then he did not move, and in fact stood in such a way that it seemed as if he intended to block our path. The problem was that I had bent as far as I was willing, but just before I kicked Latobius to send him flying again, Alex pulled up alongside of me, and I felt him reach over and stick his hand in my leather bag. I instantly knew what he was doing, and I thought ruefully, of course.

"Citizens, the Centurion here is under orders from Germanicus Julius Caesar himself," Alex waved the scroll. Then he lied, "And we were supposed to be here just after dawn, but we've been delayed, and now we're trying to get to him as quickly as possible."

The effect was dramatic, and immediate, with the man Latobius had struck going from antagonist to champion in the span of a heartbeat, as he turned to bellow, "*Oy!* The Centurion here is reporting to Germanicus, and he's late! Step aside, make a path!"

"Thank you, Citizen." I reached down to my coin purse, but he held up a hand, and assured me, "No need, Centurion. It's an honor to help anyone serving Germanicus."

And, just that quickly, we were at the gate, where there were four *Vigiles*, in uniform but holding cudgels instead of javelins, and I let Alex do the honors of presenting the scroll so that they could see the seal. The tunics worn by these men under their boiled leather armor were white, and one of them had a red patch sewn on his sleeve, but when they all straightened to *intente* and saluted, I returned it, more bemused than anything else, wondering if this was some regulation. Emerging out of the gateway, I did think to draw us to the side so that this time when we gaped at the sight before us, we were not impeding people. It was not the size of the throng of people moving in several directions; now that three of us had visited Alexandria, we had seen a city that rivals Rome in size, nor was it the exotic mixture of people, although the combination of people was decidedly different than in Alexandria. There were many more people from the Gallic tribes, for example, although it was somewhat jarring to see men dressed in the Roman style but still wearing the full beards favored by those tribes. More than the people, though, it was the sight of the Temple of Jupiter Optimus Maximus that towered above us atop the Capitoline, although because of where we entered, it was the back of the temple that we saw.

"I think," Alex spoke up, pointing to where the street we were on curved to the left, and we would learn is the Via Sacra, "the Forum is that way."

Judging from the heavy traffic heading in that direction and the time of day, this seemed like a good wager, and we had reached the point where I had to make a decision. The Palatine was directly ahead of us, and we were where the Via Sacra curved, while there was a street that continued directly ahead. Our initial plan had been to find someplace for the others to stay, but frankly, I knew the instant we entered the city this had been an unrealistic proposition because there did not seem to be any inns or even *tavernae* in sight. There were three small temples to our direct right, and directly across the street we were on, to our left were rows of stalls selling vegetables. As I sat there, I saw a familiar face, and I called out to the man who had been our helper in getting into the city, having just made it through the gateway himself.

"Citizen! Citizen!" I actually had to bellow as if I was ordering my Century to do something to get his attention, because he was heading in the direction of the Forum. Fortunately, he did turn, and he came at a quick walk, and I decided it would be the right thing to do to dismount so that I could offer him my arm. "I wanted to thank you for helping us, Citizen…"

"Marcus Sempronius," he correctly interpreted my tone.

"*Salve*, Marcus Sempronius," I offered my arm, which startled him, but he quickly grasped my forearm while I ignored the sudden widening of his eyes, which is the usual reaction men have when they feel the size and firmness of my forearm, "but I'm afraid that I don't have much time, and we need your help."

"Of course, Centurion..." And this time, it was me who understood.

"Pullus. Gnaeus Volusenianus Pullus."

This time, the sudden widening of his eyes was accompanied by a gasp of surprise. "Pullus? Are you related to the Camp Prefect Pullus?"

"He was my great-grandfather," I confirmed, and now he offered a smile, and he replied, "My grandfather marched for your great-grandfather in Pannonia, Centurion! I grew up listening to his stories about how huge he was. And," he laughed, "I always thought he was exaggerating, but I can see now that he wasn't."

This was flattering, but it was also useful, so I wasted no time. "Can you help my clerk and our family so that I can report to Germanicus?"

He did not hesitate, saying, "Anything I can do to help, I will."

"It's not much," I assured him. "I just need to send them to an inn or even a *taverna* where they can wait for me."

"You're in the wrong part of the city for that, Centurion," Sempronius answered immediately, confirming my fear. "But," he thought for a moment, "I can escort them to the Porta Tiburtina side of the city. There are inns there that cater to men like you."

While I was not certain that what he meant and what I thought he meant were the same, neither could I afford to be choosy.

"But don't you have some business of your own to attend to?" I asked, more to be polite than from any real concern, but to my relief, he gave a dismissive wave.

"It wasn't anything important," he assured me. I glanced over at Alex, who nodded, and I reached into my purse, but this time when he said it was not necessary, I insisted. "I won't take no for an answer, Marcus Sempronius. Your time is valuable, and you're doing me a great service." I dropped two *denarii* into his hands, then I asked, "I also wonder if you might know something." When he nodded, I grinned and asked, "Where exactly is Germanicus living?"

Sempronius turned out to be an extremely valuable person to know; in fact, we still have a relationship, although it did not start out smoothly, but that is for later. He gave me the name of the inn where he was taking the others, but even more importantly, he told me that Germanicus was not living in the *Domus Augusti* with the Imperator but was in the villa directly across the street on the northern side. Sempronius also gave me directions for the quickest way there, which was when we learned that it in fact *was* the Via Sacra that curved in between the Capitoline and Palatine on the way to the Forum. I caught a glimpse of the Forum, but the street that ascends the Palatine is between the gate and the Forum, and the view is obscured because of all the villas that begin at the base of the hill. I had to fight the urge to put Latobius to the trot, but the foot traffic was too heavy, although it seemed to be mostly slaves and freedmen servants, all of whom were in a hurry in both directions. There were also several litters, which further hampered any urge to speed up, so I contented myself with plodding along at the same pace as everyone else, looking at the houses as I passed. Not surprisingly, the higher up the hill, the more ornate they are, some of them with statues flanking the gate, and there were at least three residences where the gate was open, and I glimpsed fountains. The climb to the top of the Palatine is not long, but it is steep, except that I was the one sweating heavily and not Latobius, despite it being cool. I tried to tell myself it was just that I was not accustomed to the warmer temperatures this far south from my normal posting, but I knew I was lying to myself. One thing I learned immediately; the *Domus Augusti* is impossible to miss, being two stories and extending for perhaps seventy-five paces, although on the street that I used, the Temple of Apollo and the one to Bellona was in between where I was and the Imperator's palace. This was not my destination, however, and I turned Latobius and rode past the temples, drawing up in dismay once I got past them.

Sempronius had said that Germanicus was staying in a residence directly across the street from the northern side of the Imperator's palace, but he had forgotten to mention that there were three choices, and it was impossible for me to tell at a glance which one was the right one. Resigning myself to essentially knocking on perhaps three gates, I was saved from this embarrassment when I saw a pair of men emerging out onto the street, both of them wearing the distinct blue tunic of the Praetorians. I realized that it was possible that there was more than one personage who might rate this level of protection, namely Tiberius' natural son Drusus, but I assumed that he was sharing his father's palace. Nudging Latobius back into motion, I drew myself up straight as I approached the pair who, while not wearing their armor, were wearing their *baltea*, with both *gladius* and *pugio*, and I saw one of them look in my direction, then nudge his comrade, who moved to stand next to the first Praetorian, facing me as I approached.

When I drew up again, the Praetorian who had spotted me and who looked about my age said abruptly, "What's your business here?"

The flare of anger was immediate, and I snarled, "Why aren't you saluting your superior officer, Gregarius?"

This clearly surprised him, but he also licked his lips, then glanced over his shoulder to his comrade, and while the second man did not say anything, whatever passed between them seemed to stiffen his spine, because he said, "I'm in the Praetorian Guard, Centurion. That means…"

"That means that you're just an overpaid, pampered *cunnus* who probably doesn't know which end of the *gladius* to hold!" I believe that was what I said, although I was truly angered, so it may have been even more colorful, but I do know that I was dismounting Latobius as I said it, and I stalked over to the Praetorians, who I was pleased to see did not look nearly as defiant. When I got within a pace of the man, I saw he desperately wanted to retreat, but whether it was his pride or the fact his comrade was there, he stood there, one hand on the hilt of his *gladius*. "What's your name, Cohort, and Century, and what's the name of your Centurion, Gregarius?" He opened his mouth, but before he could say anything, I bellowed, *"Stand at intente when a Centurion is addressing you, Gregarius!"*

By the time I finished, I had moved so that I was towering over him with barely a hand's width between us, close enough to smell his breath and to see that he was truly terrified, which was exactly what I wanted.

"G-Gregarius Spurius Cocles, Fifth Century, Second Praetorian Cohort, Centurion!"

Ignoring for the moment that he had neglected to provide the name of his Centurion, I pointed to my crest with my *vitus*.

"Don't they teach you Praetorians anything about the *real* Legions, Gregarius? See this? Do you know what a red crest means?"

"It means that you're a Pilus Prior," he answered nervously, but I nodded in seeming approval.

"Well done, Gregarius! Perhaps you're not completely useless! But," I did not raise my voice, though I did lean closer so that his eyes were on my chest, "if you knew that, why didn't you address me by my proper rank, Gregarius?"

He signaled me that he understood he was not going to win this by closing his eyes, then sighing, "I have no excuse, Pilus Prior."

"No, you don't," I agreed, but I was not through, and this time, I poked my *vitus* in his chest hard enough to send him staggering back a step, "and you didn't give me the name of your Secundus Hastatus Prior, Cocles."

"My Hastatus Prior is Gaius Valerius Phillipus, Pilus Prior."

"Good," I nodded. Deciding I had made my point, I extracted the scroll from my bag and held it out for him to see the seal. "You asked what my business was, Cocles. Here it is. I'm reporting to Germanicus Julius Caesar as *he* ordered me, from my post in Ubiorum." He went pale to a satisfying degree as I asked, "Am I correct in assuming that that's who you're supposed to be protecting? I was told that his residence is on this side of the palace."

It appeared that he had to swallow at least twice, although he nodded before he finally managed, "You're correct, Pilus Prior. This is the residence of the *Propraetor*."

For the first time, the second man, who to my eyes just looked happy that it was his comrade who was bearing the brunt of my anger, spoke up.

"May I ask your name, Pilus Prior? So that I can announce your arrival to the *Propraetor*'s staff?"

It was a completely reasonable question, which I answered readily enough. "Yes, you may, Gregarius. I'm Gnaeus Volusenianus Pullus, Quartus Pilus Prior of the 1st Legion, detached from the Legion by order of the *Propraetor*."

At the time, I did not think much of the sudden change in the expressions of both men as they exchanged a glance, because I assumed that whoever was guarding Germanicus' residence had been warned that I was supposed to be showing up. As I would learn in the not-too-distant future, they had been warned, but not by anyone on Germanicus' staff, and it would serve as my first lesson about what life would be like in the Praetorian Guard. In the moment, however, I did not take it amiss, and the second man immediately disappeared, leaving me with Cocles, who had at least deduced that dropping from his *intente* would be a mistake. The second Praetorian was not gone long; when he returned, he was not alone, and I felt myself relaxing slightly at the sight of a familiar face.

"*Salve*, Pilus Prior Pullus," Lysander, one of Germanicus' freedmen scribes greeted me, but while he was smiling, I thought I detected a hint of strain in it, as if he was forcing himself to do so. "It's good to see you again!" Beckoning to me, he turned to head back through the gateway, and before I could say anything, he snapped to Cocles, "Praetorian, take care of the Pilus Prior's horse."

One did not need to have experience in reading men to see that a freedman addressing Cocles in such a manner infuriated him, while I caught his comrade shooting him a sympathetic glance at what they undoubtedly viewed as an insult. And I was fair and honest enough with myself to acknowledge that Gnaeus Volusenus would have had much the same reaction. That is why I did not say anything as I handed Latobius' reins to Cocles, but I did give him a brief nod that he might have interpreted as thanks. Then I hurried to catch up with Lysander, who had crossed the outer courtyard, which had not one but two fountains, along with an even half-dozen statues of gods, goddesses, and nymphs, arranged in a visually pleasing manner, reaching him just as he opened the door.

"We've heard that you had quite the adventure, Pullus," Lysander said over his shoulder as he led me down a long hallway with a series of frescoes denoting outdoor scenes. "Britannia, yes?"

"Yes, Britannia...and a couple other places," I said vaguely, unsure just how much the scribe would know.

Fortunately, we reached a closed door before I was forced to elaborate, and he said, "Please wait here while I inform the

Propraetor that you've arrived, Pullus."

He opened the door and entered the room before I could respond, and I stood there, my helmet under my left arm, my *vitus* clutched in my left hand, and my heart pounding almost as rapidly as it does just before battle. The sweat was now soaking my tunic, making me thankful for my *hamata,* but just as importantly, I did not have to wait more than a dozen heartbeats before the door opened, and Lysander reemerged.

"The *Propraetor* will see you now, Pilus Prior Pullus," he said formally.

I took a deep breath, then I strode to the door, executed the turn to walk into the room, and marched in to learn my fate.

The first surprise in store for me was that Germanicus was not alone, and I am not referring to his small army of clerks and scribes like Lysander. Reclining on a couch in the corner was a woman, one who I had last seen when she was waiting for us as we returned from across the Rhenus, the first year of the campaign against Arminius. She had been reading a scroll, using the light from an open window, and the sunlight fully illuminated her delicate, fine features, but I made sure my gaze was straight ahead as I approached Germanicus seated at his desk, although I saw her head lift to watch me enter. For some reason, I was surprised that he seemed unchanged; I suppose that my own adventures colored my idea that he would look different, despite it only being a few months since we had last seen each other. Keeping my eyes above him, I saw his head lift, then he sat back in his chair as I approached, where I stopped the traditional pace from the edge of his desk.

"Quartus Pilus Prior Pullus, reporting to the *Propraetor* as ordered, sir!"

I made sure to flex my arm rendering my salute, but this time, he actually delayed a moment before returning it, which is a trick many men of superior rank like to play, although he had never done it to me before, and my stomach twisted slightly at the thought that this might mean something.

Then he returned it, and while he was not smiling, his tone was not hostile, but neither was it as warm as it usually was. "Well,

Pullus. It seems as if you had an…adventure on your voyage back to Ubiorum."

"That," I spoke carefully, although I still was looking above his head, "is one way to put it, sir."

Rather than address me, he turned to Agrippina, saying, "This is the Centurion I was telling you about, my love. You remember his father, of course."

"Of course," Agrippina said, but since I was still looking straight ahead, I only saw her come to her feet out of the corner of my vision. "And I remember seeing the Centurion when his Legion returned. He is quite unforgettable…just like his father was."

She's coming towards me! I came perilously close to panic as I wondered what to do; should I break out of my *intente* and turn to face her? What was she going to do?

I got my answer when she extended her hand, palm down in the manner of upper-class ladies, and I had my mother to thank for drilling into me the proper response as I turned in time to lean down to brush my lips against her hand.

"Women don't really want you to *kiss* their hand, Gnaeus," she had lectured me when I was about fourteen, and I had slobbered all over the back of one of her friend's hands. "Just a touch with the lips is all that's necessary. It's a sign of respect."

I apparently did it correctly, because she smiled up at me as I straightened back up, but then the smile vanished, and she said softly, "I never had the opportunity to offer my condolences on the loss of your father, Pilus Prior Pullus. My husband still talks of him often, and he was a true hero of Rome. I know you must be very proud."

Don't cry, don't you dare cry like a little girl; aloud, I managed to sound normal. "Thank you, lady. And he was very proud to have served the *Propraetor* to the best of his abilities."

"And now," Germanicus broke in, gently but firmly, "it's time for us to discuss some matters on that very subject, my dear. If you'll excuse us?"

"Of course," Agrippina replied immediately. "It was nice seeing you again, Pilus Prior Pullus."

We both watched as she left, but immediately after the door closed, Germanicus turned to Lysander and the others, his tone much more peremptory. "Leave us. I'll call for you when we're done."

Before I could have counted to ten, the room was empty except for the two of us, and only then did Germanicus rise and beckon me to follow him to a table with a pitcher and two cups.

"We have a lot to discuss, Pullus. But," for the first time, he seemed to be his old self, offering me a smile as he said, "first, I want to hear about your adventures. And," he added mischievously, "if what I heard is true, that you've abducted a Parisii princess."

I relaxed, slightly, but I warned myself to keep alert.

"She's not a princess," I answered, but then I amended, "but she's certainly beautiful enough to be one."

"So I've heard." He said this blandly, but my expression of surprise made him laugh. "Did you really think that showing back up in Ubiorum with a woman as beautiful as her would stay a secret?"

"Well," I allowed, "when you put it like that, no, sir, I suppose not. Although I'm surprised that we're sitting in Rome talking about her."

"I don't see why," he countered, but he was pouring out two cups as he did so, "given the promise I made to your father." With both cups filled, he lifted his and said quietly, "To the memory of your father, who served Rome as faithfully as any man I've ever met." Once again, my throat tightened, but I also heard a quiet voice in the back of my mind warning me to be careful, that Germanicus clearly wanted something. Still, we touched our cups, and both took a swallow, then Germanicus continued soberly, "In fact, I've been thinking about your father a great deal lately, which is why you're here." He paused, staring down into his cup with a frown that made me think he was trying to decide about something, but he clearly came to his decision because he asked bluntly, "Are you aware of the things that your father did for my father? I mean," he added, unnecessarily, "my adoptive father?"

Any sense of comfort I was feeling evaporated instantly, and I suddenly wished I was anywhere else, but at the same time, I forced myself to think it through; he knew about Bronwen, and he clearly knew that my father had done *something* for Tiberius. Maybe, I thought, he doesn't know the specifics; of course, neither did I, nor do I now know with any real certainty, and it was the one thing I had refused, and still refuse to ask Alex, who is the only other person alive who would know any details on the matter.

"Yes," I answered, surprising myself immensely, although I quickly added, "not to any level of detail. But," I shrugged, "I think I can guess."

"The first thing I want to tell you is that I *don't* want you doing...that," he said. "Not unless it's absolutely necessary."

He stopped, staring at me intently, and I assumed that he was waiting for some sort of response, so I replied, "All right. But," I added, "what *do* you need me to do?"

"I need someone I can trust with my life," Germanicus answered without hesitation. Again I must have shown my surprise, because he went on, "Your father is the only man, of any order, who I knew I could absolutely trust, not just with my life, but to do whatever I deemed necessary to do. Although," he laughed softly, "if he thought I was wrong, he let me know about it. But his objections were always based in what he thought was best, not just for me personally, but for Rome. And now," his tone turned grim, "I need someone like that again. Rome is a nest of vipers," Germanicus leapt to his feet to begin pacing, rubbing the back of his neck, "and I don't know who to trust here. There are...things going on that I don't know enough about, and I need to learn more." He had walked away from the table, then he spun about to face me, and I saw something more than intensity in his gaze; I saw fear. "Can I count on you, Pullus? Before I tell you what it is, I need to know that. And," he held up a hand, "if you say no, then I give you my word that you'll be back with the 1st in your old post, and I won't hold it against you in any way. Because," he finished gravely, "it's not without risk."

"Absolutely," I said before my mind even really registered what he was asking; at least, that was what I told myself. "I'm yours to the death, *Propraetor*."

If he tried to hide his relief, he did a poor job of it, but he did laugh as he said, "Well, let's try and make sure it doesn't come to that."

It was a full watch later before I arrived at the inn Marcus Sempronius had taken the others to, and I relaxed slightly when I saw that his remark about it being for men like me meant that it was an establishment for Equestrians and higher. Rather than hand Latobius' reins to the stable slave, I took him myself to a stall, unsaddled him, and then rubbed him down as I realized that I was simply delaying the inevitable. Part of my quandary was how much to share, particularly with Bronwen, and Algaia as well, because it was inevitable that I would tell Alex most, if not all of what Germanicus discussed with me, mainly because he would be sharing the danger with me. Realizing I could not forestall it any longer, I entered the inn, and the owner escorted me upstairs, where I learned they had only obtained one room, which I corrected by telling him that we would need another. He was very apologetic, but he informed me that this was the only available room, at least for that night, although he said that there would be vacancies the next day. I entered without knocking, where I got a surprise; the room was actually very large and not nearly as cramped as I feared it would be, although I was not at all surprised at the expressions on the faces of the adults, all of whom were seated, either on the bed or on one of the two couches. They did not speak, but neither did I, although in my case, it was because I realized I had no idea where to start.

"Well?" Bronwen broke the silence, coming to her feet as she asked crossly, "Are you going to make us guess?"

"No, *meum mel.*" I held my hands out and I heard the defensiveness in my voice. "It's just that there are…things I need to decide. And," I was suddenly inspired as I recalled one specific warning that Germanicus had given me, so I lowered my voice, "there are…mice in the walls here." Alex and Algaia instantly understood my meaning, but Bronwen did not, so Algaia walked over to her and whispered in her ear, her expression immediately changing, and Bronwen gave me a nod to signal that. I decided that it would be better if I did not stand in the middle of the room, so I went to the couch, taking off my harness so that I could sit, and placed it on the floor next to my helmet before I resumed, my voice just above a whisper. "First," I began, "we were right. I'm being transferred to the Praetorian Guard, to the Second Cohort, but I won't be the Pilus Prior, I'm back to being a Pilus Posterior."

"That's not surprising." Alex's voice was at the same volume I was using, and I agreed; I had not really believed that I would retain my Legion rank, if only because I was still new in the post.

"Why the Second Cohort?" Bronwen asked, and I felt a deep stab of admiration, because I could tell by her tone that she sensed that this was not a random choice.

"Because the Second is one of the three Cohorts who are permanently here in Rome. The other six are stationed in other cities in Latium, although they're all no more than a day's march away. And," I added, "they do rotate one of those Cohorts to be here in Rome, so there are always four Cohorts in the city."

My throat was dry, so I stopped long enough to get up and pour myself a cup of water then came and sat back down, whereupon Alex asked, "What does this have to do with Germanicus, and why does he feel like he needs you here with him?"

I glared at him, since the way he posed the question meant that I had to address the part of what Germanicus had told me that I was still unsure I wanted to share, at least with Bronwen and Algaia. Thinking about this made me think about the fifth member of our party, and I glanced over at Iras, who was playing quietly in the corner with her favorite doll and wooden Legionary, which had been a gift from me. Do I have to worry about Iras overhearing something and innocently repeating it at some point where malicious ears are listening? I forced that thought to the back of my mind, dismissing it as being overly cautious; by the time a month had passed, I know I would have decided differently, not because we were betrayed by a toddler, but I had learned enough to realize there is no such thing as being too cautious in Rome.

Aloud, I said, "Germanicus is concerned that there is a...faction here in Rome that's determined to undermine Tiberius and loosen his hold on his Imperium."

"To what end?" Alex asked, but on this, I was not much help, admitting, "Germanicus doesn't know exactly why. Oh," I waved a dismissive hand, "he told me that there are Senators who want to return to the old way of doing things with the Republic, where the Consuls actually have authority, but..."

"There's always been that kind of talk since before we were born," Alex interjected, and he was right.

"This...whatever it is, is different," I resumed. "At least,

Germanicus is certain of that much. He *thinks* that someone who otherwise wouldn't be considered a threat to Tiberius' authority is working behind the scenes to elevate themselves to the position of a challenger."

"Does he think he knows who it is, at least?" Bronwen asked, and my heart sank, because I did *not* want to utter the name that Germanicus had provided me, which I instantly knew was likely to be true, thanks to the late Tiberius Dolabella, who had warned my father during the Legions' revolt when he had been sent to Pannonia to help with his old Legion, the 8th, about this very man.

Knowing I had to answer, I still hesitated, but I finally answered, "Yes, he knows. But," I warned, "I don't want to tell you because it might be dangerous for you to know."

I did not hold out much hope that this would have any effect on her, but I was not expecting her to ask, "How long are you going to be with the Praetorians, Gnaeus?"

"I'm not sure," I said slowly, trying to divine where she was going with a seemingly innocuous question; while she was right in how well she knew me, I was actually still learning about Bronwen and how her mind worked, but I knew enough by that time to understand that there was more behind the question, although I answered honestly, "Germanicus said he didn't honestly know, but that it will be at least a year."

"And," she asked sweetly, "do you think that I will not find out one way or another, well, before a year goes by?"

Her words were barely out of her mouth when I realized, with an inward groan, that she was absolutely correct; the idea that I would be able to keep it from her for a week, let alone a year, was nonexistent. And even if I did not slip, she would undoubtedly hear it from someone, given how much Romans of all classes love to gossip about their social betters and all the various plots and plans they are supposedly hatching to advance one rung up our ladder.

Alex chose to step in and save me from myself, telling Bronwen, "I actually think I know already, because of what happened with Uncle Titus in Pannonia. It's Sejanus, isn't it?"

I nodded, but said nothing for a moment.

"What does he want you to do about Sejanus?"

There was no mistaking the concern in Alex's tone, and I immediately realized that he was making an assumption, that Germanicus was going to use me in the same manner as Tiberius used my father, and I hurriedly assured him, "Not that. He just wants me to keep my eyes and ears open and gather what information I can."

"When are you supposed to report?"

"Tomorrow morning," I told Alex. Then, deciding I had said enough, I stood up and announced, "I'm getting out of this and going to the bath. I passed one just a block away."

"You don't need to go that far," Alex informed me. "This inn has a private bath, although it doesn't have an *apodyterium* or a *frigidarium*, but you can get scraped and soak for a bit."

I turned to Bronwen with a grin, and she understood me perfectly, but she shook her head. "I already used the bath here."

"You can never be too clean," I insisted, and thankfully, she did not argue the point.

Since we would be sharing the room this night, I thought some privacy could be found in the bath instead.

While I had been forthcoming to a point, there was one thing that I had not divulged, and I am only divulging it now because, while it took longer, my companions worked it out.

"I'm using you as bait, Pullus," Germanicus had told me bluntly. "Sejanus is already suspicious whenever someone joins the Guard from the Legions. In fact, he's trying to put a stop to it altogether."

This offended me, and I could not stop myself from demanding, "On what grounds?"

Germanicus offered a sour smile. "Do you want to know what he *says*? Or the real reason?"

"Both," I answered instantly, and he laughed.

"Good answer." He paused to take a sip from his cup, then said, "He *says* that it's because the Legions simply don't maintain the same kind of standards when it comes to appearance, that too many Primi Pili don't think proper discipline includes things like varnished leathers."

"Well," I said grudgingly, "he's not wrong about that, but that's because we only have so much time before campaign season starts, and we've never killed a barbarian by having our leathers varnished and our bosses polished."

This amused him, and he assured me, "Oh, I agree completely." His smile vanished. "But the real reason is that he's worried that men from the Legions will be loyal to Rome first, and not to him as Prefect."

I reminded myself to read the scroll, one of the last ones written by my father before he died, about his encounter with Sejanus, but I did not feel it was out of place to ask, "What about Sejanus himself? What kind of man is he?"

"He's a treacherous snake!" Germanicus spat, and he seemed as if he was working up to a diatribe, but he caught himself, confirming with a chuckle, "Oh, you mean you'd like to learn something useful about him?" I nodded, and he thought for a moment. "Obviously, he's very clever, but he's also very sly. And, he's obsequious to men of my class. Actually," he amended, "he's obsequious to anyone he thinks can help him in some way, and now that I think about it, he might actually try to be that way with you since he knows we're connected somehow."

This sounded logical, but while I did not have any basis for doing so, I nonetheless shook my head and said flatly, "I don't think so, sir. I think he's going to see my father standing in front of him, and that's all. And," I added hesitantly because I was worried he would ask how I knew, "I know that they had…problems when my father was in Pannonia."

He surprised me, not so much in what he said but in who provided him the information.

"I heard as much from my brother." He nodded. "He actually wrote me a few months afterward about it."

This was when I was reminded of something from my father's

account, about how Germanicus' relationship with Tiberius' natural son had been strained during that period. Happily, I learned very quickly during my time in Rome that whatever tensions there were between them were resolved.

"Either way, you'll find out tomorrow when you report to him first," Germanicus commented.

"What should I be looking for, sir?"

"Anything that will give me an idea of what he's up to, especially as it concerns the Imperator," he answered immediately.

This was still quite vague to me, but I sensed this was all the specifics I would be getting, at least in this first meeting. Thinking about this led my mind to another concern.

"How will I communicate with you if I find something out?"

Frankly, it did not make me feel better that he clearly had not thought it through that far, but after thinking about it for a moment, he said, "I'll use Lysander, but it's better if you don't do it yourself. Coming here will be a problem for you, unless your Century has duty on the Palatine."

"I'll let Alex figure out the best way," I mused aloud, to which Germanicus gave his approval with a nod.

"That's a good idea. I haven't dealt with him all that much, but going back to the Batonian Revolt, everything I've seen of him has impressed me a great deal, and I know your father trusted him implicitly."

"As do I," I put in, slightly offended by what I took as his implication that I did not, although when I thought about it later, I realized I was being overly sensitive.

"Now," Germanicus sat back, and his posture subtly but noticeably altered as he became more relaxed, "tell me about Britannia. And," he gave me a grin of the type that bridges the sometimes vast gulf between our classes and we were just two Roman men talking, "tell me about this Parisii princess."

That was what filled up the rest of the time I was with Germanicus, and when I left, I had the very strong impression that the questions, specifically about Britannia and what I had witnessed between the Parisii and Brigantes, were not asked out of idle curiosity. If anything, it sounded to my ears like someone who was entertaining the idea of making a foray across the channel between Gaul and the island, not as an ambassador or emissary, but as a conqueror. And, as an aside, I will say that ever since Divus Julius' two campaigns in Britannia, Romans have been fascinated with the island kingdom, and I believe that, even if it is not Germanicus doing it, a Roman general will subdue that island in the future. While his main topic of interest was Britannia, he also essentially had me tell the entire story, all the way to Alexandria, which in turn reminded me of something, although it came to me at an inopportune moment, and I am afraid that I actually slapped my forehead in mid-sentence.

"Gods, what an idiot I am! I forgot!"

Not surprisingly, this mystified and intrigued Germanicus, but when I asked his leave for a few moments, he gave it, whereupon I hurried out to where Latobius was tied to the hitching post in the courtyard, where this time both Cocles and the other Praetorian immediately came to *intente* and saluted me, which I returned promptly, without any gloating...at least externally. When I returned to his office, I dropped the two sacks on the table.

"I brought you these gifts, *Propraetor*," I explained. "But it's easier for you to find out what they are just by opening them and taking a sniff."

For an instant, I thought I had made a horrible mistake, because his eyes suddenly narrowed and I was struck by the thought; he thinks I'm going to poison him! Gnaeus, you *are* an idiot! I actually opened my mouth to stop him, but he was already leaning forward and taking a sniff.

His eyes lit up, and I tried not to collapse onto my chair in relief as he exclaimed, "By the gods, this is *kinammon*! And these," he leaned over the second sack, "are peppercorns! Agrippina loves peppercorns, but they're very hard to get. And," he added with the kind of thoughtlessness that comes from being born into a level of wealth that none of us can truly fathom, "not many people can afford them, but when they do show up in Rome, there's a bidding war between the same people."

"Well, the next time it happens, you won't need to participate," I said jokingly, and it pleased me that he laughed.

"That's right, I won't! But, Pullus," he shook his head, "having said that, these are worth a great deal of money. The *kinammon* is not as expensive, but it's still quite dear to buy. Are you certain?"

With any other Roman patrician, I would have immediately dismissed this as just the kind of formality he would feel he needed to go through, with every intention of accepting the gift on offer, but that is not the case with Germanicus.

"Absolutely," I assured him. "We brought back more than enough. In fact," I did not feel as if I was betraying a confidence, "I think that my uncle Septimus is going to change his mind about not becoming a merchant once he sees how much money can be made with this."

"I can see it would be lucrative," he agreed.

He thanked me again, and our time together ended, whereupon I made my way to the inn by the Tiburtina gate.

The next morning, I was back on the Palatine, once again in full uniform, except this time, I went directly to the *Domus Augusti*, because this is where Prefect Lucius Sejanus has his office, which Germanicus had warned me about, and offered as a sign that Sejanus was up to something. His father had been appointed as governor of Egypt earlier that year; apparently, we had been in Alexandria about a month before his arrival to replace Gaius Gallerius as the *Praefectus Augustalis*, the only position of *Praetor* that must be held by a member of the Equestrian Order and not of the Senate. This left Sejanus as the only Praetorian Prefect, which was yet another area of concern for Germanicus, because his adoptive father Tiberius seemed disinclined to name a second Prefect. Somewhat surprisingly, I was more nervous about this meeting than the one with Germanicus, and it is only in hindsight that I can see that, despite the mystery and the manner in which Primus Pilus Sacrovir had delivered the news of my summons, deep down, I did not think Germanicus would be harsh or unjust in his dealings with me. And, as I learned very quickly, I was right to be worried, although things began normally enough. I had decided to walk from the inn instead of riding Latobius, and thankfully, it was quite brisk, though not so much that I needed my fur-lined *sagum*, although I would not have worn it anyway because of what Germanicus had told me about

Sejanus. This was also why Alex was up later than usual, paying particular attention to the varnish job on every piece of leather that is part of our uniform. I even took the time to clean my *vitus* of the stains and shaved the slivers off so that it appeared as if it had been freshly issued from the *Quaestorium*, and I bring this up to show just how determined I was that Sejanus not find any fault in my appearance, at least.

The game began almost immediately, when I was directed to the entrance to the part of *Domus Augusti* that is designated as what is essentially the headquarters for not just the Praetorian Guard, but the entire Roman Army. As expected, there were Praetorians on guard, but this time, it was an Optio who, to my eyes, looked barely old enough to shave, but I could not fault his demeanor, saluting me immediately and escorting me inside, although it was only to the vestibule.

"I'll inform the Prefect that you're reporting, Pilus Prior."

I just appreciated that he had seen my red crest, but whatever charitable feelings I may have held evaporated, because I never saw the Optio again, at least on that day. After perhaps two hundred heartbeats of time, I deduced that, after presumably alerting Sejanus of my arrival, he had chosen to either remain inside or used another exit. I was left standing there for a full third of a watch, and despite knowing what was happening, it was a struggle to maintain my composure. That's exactly what he wants, Gnaeus; he wants you to be flustered, and angry, and embarrassed. I kept repeating this to myself over and over, which helped somewhat. Finally, I heard footsteps, but I could tell by the lack of hobnails that it would not be the Optio, so I was prepared to see a freedman clerk turn the corner and approach me with a smile, which did not help my mood.

"Pilus Prior Pullus, Prefect Sejanus apologizes for the delay, but an important matter came up that he had to deal with first." The manner in which the clerk said it betrayed the fact that this was clearly a lie the clerk had told numerous times before, but I said nothing about it, which seemed to disappoint him for some reason. "If you'll follow me, please."

I still said nothing, but I did nod, and he turned and began walking quickly back down the hallway, which amused me a bit thinking that his fast pace meant I could saunter behind him. We made two more turns into another long hallway with two doorways on one side and, at the very end, another doorway blocking further passage, and my guess was that this was where the official part of Rome ended and the private quarters of the Imperator began. It was the second doorway where the clerk stopped, and I could tell that he had expected me to be farther behind him than I was, so that I was immediately behind him when he rapped on the door, then opened it and stepped aside. In outward appearance, the office used by Sejanus was not that different than the one Germanicus used, but I instantly sensed a very different atmosphere in the room. Nevertheless, I strode across the room to stand in front of his desk, which was directly across the room from the doorway, and made my formal announcement of reporting as I offered my salute, which Sejanus completely ignored as he pretended to read a scroll. I am sure it was not his intent, but this actually settled my nerves a bit, because this was not the first, nor will it be the last time a superior does this to me, and like those before him, he clearly forgot that with my height, I could see that the scroll contained nothing more than a few scratches of what appeared to be figures of some sort, hardly worth such steady scrutiny. I will confess my arm was getting tired by the time that, with a sigh, he dropped the scroll and returned the salute, but it did give me time to examine Prefect Sejanus, and I confess that my initial impression was, This man is dangerous?

Since he was seated, I could not tell exactly how tall he was, but he was a bit pudgy, with a receding hairline and what I would call a weak chin. Don't judge him as you would if he was holding a *gladius*, I chided myself. You're in his world now, and if Germanicus is worried about him, you should be as well. It was when he actually deigned to raise his head and look me in the eyes that everything changed, and my worst fears seemed to be confirmed, because while I had told Germanicus the bare bones of my father's encounter with Sejanus in Pannonia during our meeting, over our evening meal, which I had ordered brought to our room, I reread the scroll of my father's that described the details of it. Consequently, I was not altogether surprised at the sudden glitter of hatred in the man's eyes as he took his first good look at me. It was a visceral, unthinking reflex on his part, and it also served to remind me of what I had gone through when my identity as the natural son of Titus Pullus became known, where I heard on more occasions than I could count that the resemblance was so obvious now that the person would chide themselves for missing the connection.

"So," he finally spoke, and I was surprised at his relatively deep voice, "you're the Centurion from the Legions Germanicus has foisted on me, eh?" When I did not respond to what I was certain was a provocation, he shrugged as if it did not bother him, but he was not done, and he sneered, "And now that I see who it is with my own two eyes, it all makes sense now. The son of Germanicus' pet ranker."

I knew I was taking a desperate gamble when I opened my mouth, but I just could not bring myself to let all of this pass without saying anything.

"The Imperator valued my father's service as well, Prefect." I tried to sound as if I was simply informing of something about which he was unaware. "In fact, Titus Porcinianus Pullus served Tiberius long before he met Germanicus."

At first, I thought I had thrown Dogs, because this caused him to almost come up out of his chair, and I braced myself for him to order the Praetorians I knew were lurking nearby to come and seize me. I also noticed that his face became mottled instead of turning a uniform red, so that he had red and white patches that made me think of something I had read about Lucius Cornelius Sulla. However, he stopped himself, sat slowly back down, and I saw his chest rise as he took a deep breath.

"I was...unaware of that," he admitted, and I was struck by the thought that this was probably what bothered him more than anything else. "You should know, however," he added severely, "that I will check to see if you're speaking truthfully. And if you're not..." He did not finish, verbally at least, giving me a shrug that I supposed he meant to say, "If you lie about the Imperator, your fate is out of my hands."

This would be one of the several times I would thank the gods for my father's account of his life, because it reminded me of his description about Tiberius, how he is a scrupulous but unforgiving Roman. And now, he is the absolute power in most of the known world.

Of course, this meant that I decided to make another throw, saying, "You could check with Tiberius Dolabella. I'm sure he can verify what I'm saying is true."

For the second time, I had the satisfaction of catching Sejanus on the back foot, but it also showed how quickly his mind worked, because after the initial look of surprise, he actually smiled for the first time.

"Ah, you clearly weren't told," he tried to sound regretful, I suppose, "but Tiberius Dolabella crossed the river more than two years ago now."

I knew this perfectly well, but I tried to sound surprised as I lied, "I didn't know that, Prefect."

"Yes, it was very sad." Sejanus did not appear to be sad in the slightest as he gazed down at his desk. "And," he looked back up, "it was very sudden."

"Didn't Divus Julius say that was the best way to die?" I countered, but this did not impress Sejanus.

"So at least you're educated enough to know what every ten-year-old Equestrian boy does," he scoffed.

"I'm educated about many things, Prefect."

This gave me some satisfaction, because he was clearly startled by the fact that I had said this in Greek. Suddenly, he turned his attention away from me to look at a small pile of scrolls on his desk, which puzzled me. He poked through them, then found one, and when he opened it, because of my height, I saw what it was, and my heart dropped down to my *caligae*; it was my official record, the copy of which is sent from every Legion of Rome back to the Tabularium, one of Divus Augustus' many reforms. He didn't bother reading it! He thought he knew all about me based on only knowing about my father! He thinks I'm born and raised from the Head Count! Gnaeus, what have you done to yourself? Now, and actually not long after I left his presence, I realized that it was foolish of me to think that, if he had not already done so, Sejanus would not examine my record. And, thanks to Alex and his connections to the staff in Ubiorum, I had seen what my record contained, and while it is a straightforward document, listing postings, promotions, reports by superiors, campaigns and decorations, mine also records my formal adoption by Titus Porcinianus Pullus...and my original name and status as an Equestrian. I was certain I could track his progress as he read, in complete silence, while the four clerks and two slaves remained busily at work, or pretended to be, when Sejanus' eyes suddenly went wide. He looked up at me for the first time in several moments, and this time, I am sure his smile was genuine because it contained nothing but malice.

"Well, this is…informative." He indicated the scroll, which he had tossed onto the desk. "You weren't born a Pullus, eh? And it says here that you are, what do the rankers in the Legion call it? A paid man? Which," he pointed out needlessly, "is something only a man of the Equestrian Order can do."

"Yes, Prefect, I am aware of that," I answered as dryly as I could manage.

"But," he pretended to be puzzled, "Titus Porcinianus Pullus was a member of the Head Count, after Divus Augustus learned of his grandfather's treachery and barred his descendants from Equestrian status."

"Treachery?" I gasped, then realized what he was doing, trying to bait me into an intemperate response, yet it was still difficult to keep my tone under control. "I'm not sure where you got that information, but I can assure you that it's incorrect, Prefect."

"Of course you would say that." Sejanus shrugged.

"Then where did you get it from?" I challenged, and I was rewarded by a flicker of uneasiness crossing his face, and I recalled something I had read the night before. I knew it was reckless, but I sensed an opportunity. "I do remember one thing," I said. "My father, my *real* father told me that you insulted him when you were in Pannonia, and he offered you a challenge of single combat…which you declined. Could that be why you're trying to insult my family name now?"

I knew immediately that I had scored, and oh, the look he gave me was valuable in itself, because I saw the real Lucius Sejanus in that moment, and suddenly, things began to make more sense. It was the look of a man who had grown up as the weakest, the slowest, and who had developed a natural hatred for men like me who were bigger, stronger, faster, and better at all of the things that Roman men value. For several heartbeats, we stared at each other, and I believe that both of us were being honest in the gaze we were giving the other man.

Finally, he took another deep breath to gather himself, then smiled, or at least tried to as he said, "I had forgotten all about that…incident, Centurion. But," he pointedly looked back down at the scroll, "I confess I'm puzzled by something, and I'm sure you could help me understand." I did not bother answering, though he did not seem surprised. "How is it that you were born an Equestrian, as Gnaeus Claudius Volusenus, but decided to accept what is, in fact, a demotion down to the Head Count?" He paused again, and I could tell he was savoring the moment before he asked, "Was your father a...large man?"

I was faced with a choice; I was as certain as I could be that he had worked out that my natural father was Titus Pullus, while my mother was married to the Equestrian Quintus Volusenus. The choice was whether I indulged him as he toyed with me, and in the process shamed my mother Giulia, or whether I just acknowledged the truth. Frankly, it did not take me long to decide.

"I can see that you've already worked it out, Prefect," I said evenly. "Titus Porcinianus Pullus is my real father, a fact of which I was unaware until immediately after his death during our operation to rescue Segestes. An operation," I pointed out, "that also brought Arminius' wife and his unborn son to Rome."

"Yes, that was very impressive," Sejanus sniffed. "But that doesn't explain anything."

"Is it any of your business?"

"The personal life of any man serving me is my business, Centurion!" he snapped. "Now explain the circumstances of how you were born an Equestrian but are now the son of a lowborn Head Counter!" Then he gave me an unexpected opening when he asked, "Why would anyone deliberately leave the Equestrian Order?"

How, I wondered, do I explain that to someone like Lucius Sejanus, or even to myself, back when I was Gnaeus Volusenus, leaving Mediolanum to assume a post the man I thought of as my father had purchased for me?

"Because," I said honestly, "I've learned more from men of the Head Count about honor, courage, and commitment than I ever did when I was on the Campus Martius in Mediolanum with all the other Equestrian boys."

As I hoped, he did not like that, at all, and I braced myself for some sort of retaliation, but when it came, it was still hard to contain my rage.

"Yes, well," he sniffed, "clearly it was just that you were born of a mother who didn't know of such things." His tone told me that he was taunting me, but when I refused to reply, he decided to raise the wager, so to speak. "Did this Quintus Volusenus know he'd been betrayed by your mother?"

"My mother was not unfaithful to Quintus Volusenus, Prefect." It was difficult to get this out, my jaw clenched as tightly as it was. "She was already carrying me when she married him."

"Ah," his eyes widened, which I was beginning to understand was an affectation he seemed to be fond of, "so he took on damaged goods, as it were."

"I don't know anything about the circumstances back then," I lied. "Nor do I think it has any relevance on what my duties will be. Which," I pointed back down to the scroll given to me by Germanicus the day before, "the *Propraetor* has ordered me to report to you about."

"Yes, about that." Sejanus handled my abrupt switch with disgusting ease, but I took it as a warning to remain on my guard every moment around him. "I'm going to have to speak to the *Propraetor* about his direction to place you in the Second Cohort, and at the rank of Pilus Posterior."

"Oh? May I ask why?"

"Because that's not his decision to make," he snapped, and I made a mental note that I had my first piece of information that I thought Germanicus should know, because I could see he was truly angry about that.

It was only as I was walking to the Second Cohort barracks that I recalled something else; he had said the personal lives of anyone serving in the Praetorians was *his* business, and not the business of the Imperator, as if the Praetorians were for his use and not for Tiberius, and I reminded myself to have Alex pass this on to Lysander.

In the moment, and hoping to get him to say something even more damaging, I pressed, "Forgive me, Prefect, but he *is* a *Propraetor*, as well as being a Legate, and the Imperator trusted him to lead my Legion and the other seven against Arminius." I spread my hands as if I was trying to understand. "I just didn't realize that the rank of Praetorian Prefect was vested with more power than a man with the rank of *Propraetor*."

"There's quite a bit you don't know about how things work here in Rome," he shot back, but I was certain I saw a glimmer of hesitation in his expression. He gazed malevolently at Germanicus' order, his hands folded across his stomach, and I noticed that when he pressed his lips together, it accentuated his receding chin. I remained silent, and I was rewarded when he finally spoke after heaving a sigh. "But I suppose that for the time being, it's better to allow you to report to the Second Cohort...*temporarily*," he glared up at me, "while I sort this out with the *Propraetor*."

He did no more than snap his fingers, but one of the clerks, who must have been listening since he knew what to bring, came running over with a clean sheet of vellum. I watched as Sejanus dipped his quill, then wrote several lines, dipping into the inkwell several times, then handed it to the clerk, who took it a few feet to a desk that had a bucket of sand on it that is used to absorb the excess ink. With a speed that was impressive, the clerk threaded the ends onto two wooden spools, using the same wax to affix the ends to the spools that he used for the seal that, once I looked at it, bore the mark of Lucius Sejanus as Praetorian Prefect, which I would come to know very well, because he loved to send missives and edicts reminding everyone of his power.

"You will go from here immediately to the barracks where the Second Cohort is located." I was about to ask, but Sejanus beat me to it. "Philippus here will give you directions since you're new to Rome. You're to report to your Pilus Prior, Marcus Silanus Creticus, to begin the process of joining us. And," he pointed his quill at me, his thin lip lifted in what I would come to learn was his most common facial expression around his inferiors, as if he was smelling a foul odor, "you're never to be seen wearing a red tunic again, even when you're off duty, do you understand?" I assured him that I did, then he added, "And I don't know who varnished your leathers, but they deserve to be flogged for it." He laughed, a tittering sort of noise that was much higher pitched than his speaking voice. "But Pilus Prior Creticus will make sure that you're up to our standards very quickly. He knows how I like things."

The clerk had come to me to hand me the scroll, my record, and a tablet with the directions to the Second Cohort barracks, which are on the Esquiline Hill, which, as I would learn, is in the Third district, one of the fourteen created by Divus Augustus decades earlier, although it's more commonly called the District of Isis because of the temple there. I saluted, and at least this time Sejanus returned it, then I executed an about turn and headed for the door.

I do not know what possessed me to do so, but I stopped at the door to ask, "Will I be meeting the outgoing Pilus Posterior?"

It was actually the reaction of the clerks in the room, their expressions ranging from what I took to be surprise to acute discomfort, although it was the manner in which they uniformly looked towards Sejanus that gave me my first hint.

For his part, the Prefect gave that tittering laugh again before he answered, "Oh, I'm afraid that won't be possible. Secundus Pilus Posterior Crus is no longer with us either."

Now this is not uncommon; even when we are not on campaign, men die from illness or the occasional accident, and yet I somehow knew this was not the case with this Crus. Still, I could not help myself.

"How did he die?"

"He was executed," for the first time, Lucius Sejanus sounded not just cheerful, but almost jolly, "for plotting against the Imperator."

Following the directions, I walked due north, across the Palatine, trying not to ogle like a provincial at the massive villas, although there was one under construction that was along the northwestern edge of the hill that looked like it would at least rival the *Domus Augusti*, and I would learn later that this was Tiberius' future home. As I was descending the Palatine, I caught a glimpse of the roofs of what I knew were some of the temples and official buildings of the Forum, and I was sorely tempted to take a left at the first street heading northwest that appeared to aim directly at the heart of the Forum, but I resisted the urge. The flat area between the Palatine and Esquiline does not have a particular name, and it is equally mixed between businesses and *insulae,* but as I would learn, of a better quality than the Subura, and none were taller than three stories, while the pedestrians going about their day were a mixture of Head Counters, Equestrians, and I spotted a few men who were togate with slaves walking ahead and behind them while they were carried in a chair. There was a handful of covered litters, which I assumed meant that they were carrying wellborn Roman women going about their daily routines. Another thing I would learn is how common this separation is; while I had believed that there was a strict division between the upper and lower classes in Mediolanum, it is nothing compared to Rome, although I was not surprised that it is exclusively the upper classes reminding the lower classes of their respective places in our order. Reaching the base of the Esquiline, I stopped to consult the tablet, and I was so intent on trying to decipher the directions that when someone called my name, I almost jumped out of my skin.

I spun about to see Marcus Sempronius, our benefactor from the day before, and he called out, "*Salve*, Centurion Pullus! You look like you're lost!"

He said it in such a genial way that I had to laugh and admit, "I think I may be."

Sempronius reached my side as he asked, "Where are you going?"

"To report to my new post with the Second Praetorian Cohort," I told him.

"May I see that?" He pointed to the tablet, and I obliged, somewhat curious if he could read it. Opening it up, he frowned down at it, answering my silent query by muttering, "What *mentula* gave you these directions?" He suddenly seemed to realize I might find this offensive, so he hurriedly added, "I'm sorry, Centurion. I didn't mean any disrespect. It's just that this was clearly written by someone who never leaves the Palatine."

"No offense taken. And," I grinned down at him, "now that you mention it, he did look like a bit of a *mentula*."

Sempronius laughed, glanced up at the sun, then said, "I still have time before I have to be somewhere. I can show you where the barracks are, and a lot more quickly."

"I would appreciate that," I told him sincerely, and he immediately turned and began weaving through the people around us.

As he had done the day before, Sempronius called out for slower pedestrians to make way for a Centurion of Rome, but I cannot say that drew more attention than normal because of my size. There was one moment where I hesitated, when he suddenly darted in between a pair of *insulae*, where there was a gap not wide enough to be a street, and I felt a bit smothered within a couple of paces, the only sunlight coming from the gap above us. Nothing untoward or unpleasant happened, and as time passed, I would use this route whenever I was in a hurry to get to the barracks. Even a block away, I recognized the home of the Second Cohort for what it was; essentially a two-story brick building with a red tile roof that forms a hollow square occupying an entire block. Sempronius came to a stop, and I reached into my purse, happy that this time he did not argue.

Then, on an impulse, I asked him, "What do you do for a living, Marcus Sempronius?" The sudden change of expression on his face made me assure him, "I don't care what it is. The reason I'm asking is that, since you know your way around Rome, I wanted to hire you for the next few days to help me get my woman and my clerk's family settled."

He thought for a moment, then asked, "How much of the day?"

"Well, it depends on how much time I'm given to make my personal arrangements," I answered honestly, "but I can't imagine that it would be more than a half day."

"All right." He held his arm out, and I took it. "When do you want me?"

"Come to the inn tonight. I should have a better idea then what my immediate future looks like."

We parted with an agreement that he would come to the inn, and I walked up the street to the main entrance.

My reporting in to Pilus Prior Creticus was more aligned with my experience in the Legions, but I quickly learned that it was not because he had been under the standard. He was about ten years older than me, with thin, sandy hair, a square face, and a truly proud Roman nose, but what surprised me was when he stood up, and he was only a couple of inches shorter than me, although his build was slenderer. Fortunately, he did not play the game as Sejanus had, and in fact, he seemed a bit nervous, for which I would learn the reason in the near future.

"Welcome to the Second Praetorian Cohort, Pilus Posterior Pullus," he said as he returned my salute that accompanied my formal reporting, then indicated the chair in front of his desk.

I had handed the clerk Sejanus' order and my record, who in turn laid it in front of Creticus, and I watched his face carefully as he broke the seal and began reading, but his face gave nothing away. Then he set it down and folded his hands on his desk; I must confess it was slightly unsettling that our eyes were at very close to the same level.

"I reviewed your record already before I sent it to the Prefect," he began, "and it's very impressive, I must say."

"Thank you, Pilus Prior." It was all I could think to say, and he waved a hand.

"I'm not saying anything other than the truth, Pullus. In fact," his tone stiffened a bit, "it gives me some…concerns."

"Concerns?" I asked, confused.

"You're in the Praetorian Guard now, Pullus. And here, it doesn't matter how many barbarians you've slain. That's not what's important to the Prefect."

This was so outside of what I had expected that I could not really think of what to say, other than, "But if skill in killing the enemies of Rome isn't important, what is?"

"That," he nodded approvingly, "is the right question to ask. And…" Suddenly, he glanced over at the pair of clerks whose desks were side by side against one wall, ordering, "Leave us. Go help Diodorus make Pilus Posterior Pullus' office ready."

They did as ordered, of course, moving with a speed that gave me a hint about what Creticus expected from his clerks, both of whom were slaves. Once the door shut, he resumed.

"I won't lie to you, Pullus. Duty, and life in the Praetorians isn't going to be anything like what you're used to in the Legions. I," he answered my unasked question, "have never served, but my Optio has, as has about half of every Century in the Second Cohort, along with another Centurion, the Hastatus Posterior, Titus Plancus, who was in the 20th until three years ago." Mention of the 20th got my attention, sensing that the timing of his transfer to the Praetorians was not a coincidence, since the mutiny had occurred three years earlier, and I wondered how I might find out whether this Plancus' transfer was a reward for his actions during the mutiny. Oblivious to my internal musing, Creticus went on, "What we do as Praetorians is protect the Imperator in all ways, and to provide a…presence, if you will, for the representatives of foreign nations who are visiting Rome at any given time."

"So we're toy Legionaries." Will you never learn, Gnaeus?

Shockingly, Creticus was not offended; in fact, he burst out laughing, and it did not seem feigned in any way.

"That," he agreed as he wiped an eye, "is essentially it, Pullus." The smile faded a bit, but his tone was still friendly enough as he continued, "The Prefect has very…exacting standards about the appearance of the Praetorians, Pullus. If you were looking for training like you were used to in the Legions, I'm afraid you'll be disappointed."

"But what if we do need to fight?" I asked, trying not to hide my dismay.

"Who?" Creticus spread his hands in a gesture that I supposed was meant to encompass Rome. "Who would we be fighting? Oh," he allowed, "we get some sort of riot in the Subura every month or so, and we've had a couple of bread riots, but we're just there for backup because the Urban Cohorts are responsible for that, and we only get involved if it looks like they're going to take over the Forum or they get too close to the Palatine. Otherwise," he laughed again, "you Legions have done too good a job in keeping our enemies away from the city."

Now I cannot say that I expected to be manning the barricades around the Capitoline fighting off Brennus and a pack of Gauls, but I realized that I did not really know what I was supposed to be doing, and I tried not to show my disappointment.

"So what do we do?" I asked, trying not to sound plaintive.

"Honestly?" Creticus shook his head. "You're going to be

doing more inspections in a week than I suspect you do in a month in the Legions. And we have duty on the Palatine every fourth day, but only three Centuries at a time. Aside from that?" He shrugged, then seemingly out of nowhere, asked with what appeared to be some anxiety, "Please tell me you have a toga." I assured him that I did, and he was obviously relieved. "Good." He nodded, but then said nothing else.

When it was clear this was all he intended to say, I said, "May I ask why?"

"Because when we have the duty, that's what you'll be wearing." He said this as if it was an obvious answer, but I could only stare at him in disbelief, and again, Creticus dropped his eyes as he continued, "The Prefect requires Centurions to be togate when on duty out in public. He says it sends the wrong message to be seen wearing our armor as if we're expecting to be attacked at any moment."

Well, I thought, that explained why the Praetorian rankers I had run into at this point were only wearing their tunics and *baltea*, which prompted me to ask, "Does that mean I'll be unarmed?"

"No." He shook his head. "You can carry your *gladius,* but it has to be under the toga. And," he gave a shudder as if he was recalling something unpleasant, "by the gods, do *not* let the Prefect catch you where it shows, Pullus! He is," Creticus paused, giving me the sense that he was searching for the right word, settling on, "very particular about certain things, and that one is highest on his list."

I assured him I would be careful, while at the same time wondering how on Gaia's Earth I would draw my *gladius* in the event that I needed it, but shoved that to the back of my mind to mull over later.

"Who is my Optio, Pilus Prior?"

"His name is Publius Canidius Sabinus," Creticus informed me.

"Pluto's cock, does every man in my Century use three names? My hand will cramp writing them all the time!" I said this as a joke, but Creticus actually winced as he held out a hand to silence me.

"Pullus, first, no, only our officers are referred to in records by all three names. But," he warned, "this is another thing that the

Prefect is insistent on, and that's our language. The way you may have spoken in the Legions will *not* be tolerated in the Praetorians, and that is for the men of all ranks when they're on duty. However, the Prefect doesn't care how the rankers talk when they're off duty, but he *does* care about his officers, at least if they're out in the city. So consider this a warning. You must guard your tongue at all times while you're in the Praetorian Guard. Is that understood?"

My initial suspicion that Creticus was warning me about far more than just cursing was confirmed within days of our first meeting, and while we never spoke of it, once I got to know him better, I now believe that he was trying to help me in his own way.

Consequently, I assured him, "I do understand, Pilus Prior."

"Good." He seemed relieved, then stood up. "Now, let me take you to the *Quaestorium* so that you can draw your uniform tunics and other items you'll be needing."

Honestly, I was expecting to leave this building, but I was surprised when he led me into the interior square, which is large enough to fit a Cohort of men, albeit only if the spacing is a bit closer than I was accustomed to.

At that moment, there were no men in sight, which I found odd, but when I asked Creticus about it, he answered absently, "We don't have the duty today, so I suppose most of the men are at the races or napping in their quarters."

"The races?" I exclaimed. "You mean the chariot races?"

This did cause him to slow down, and he looked over his shoulder in surprise as he asked, "You mean, you don't know that we have free entrance to the races? Or any of the games?"

Could I look like more of a crude provincial if I tried? I wondered, but I simply shook my head.

"Now you know." Creticus resumed walking, and we reached a door in the far corner of the barracks, with a sign above it that declared it was the *Quaestorium* for the Second Praetorian Cohort, which he opened without knocking.

Inside, it was set up like what I was accustomed to, but the first thing I noticed was that there were no racks for javelins to be seen, while the racks for the *gladii* seemed to have enough for every man to have a spare. This was when it hit me.

"When we're not on duty," I asked Creticus, "what do the men do with their weapons?"

"They turn them in, of course," he answered, and this time, he seemed to be equal parts surprised and irritated at my obtuseness. "We can't have them out in the city armed, Pullus! It would frighten the citizens!" I did not accept that as the real reason for a moment, though I said nothing, and Creticus added, "Of course, that doesn't extend to officers. Besides," he shrugged, "yours will be hidden by your toga."

"But I thought you said that was only when I was on duty," I protested, and once again, Creticus refused to meet my eyes.

"Yes, well," he said uncomfortably, "it's true that there is no regulation that Centurions must be togate even when they're off duty, but that was because the Prefect's father overruled Prefect Sejanus when they were co-Prefects. But now that his father is the *Praefectus Augustalis* in Alexandria, Prefect Sejanus has stressed to us that it's…advisable that we wear them at all times we're in public." He glanced at me then, and I saw what I took to be some sympathy in his expression as he asked, "Not quite what you expected, eh, Pullus?"

"No, Pilus Prior." I had to laugh, though not without a bitter edge. "Not at all." I thought of something then, "I only have one toga. If I'm expected to wear them all the time…"

"I have six of them myself." Creticus understood my thinking. "I can take you to the man who makes them for me. And," he averred, "I'd go sooner rather than later. In fact, once we issue you your tunics that you'll wear under your toga and when you're in your quarters, then I show you your Century office, I'd suggest we go after that. He's not far from here."

The *Immunes* behind the counter had clearly been warned of my arrival, because he already had four blue tunics, and the white crest that replaced my red, while the Praetorian Pilus Prior's crest is black. Which, Creticus informed me, I would only be wearing twice a month when Prefect Sejanus conducted an inspection of the Guard attired in the kind of uniform I had assumed I would be wearing all the time I was on guard duty.

"What color does the Primus Pilus wear?" I asked, curious since in the Legions the white crest is worn by one Centurion.

"We don't have a Primus Pilus," Creticus answered, "because the Praetorians aren't a full Legion."

I confess I had forgotten this; when Divus Augustus, back before he was Augustus but after he was Octavius, in the aftermath of Actium and the final defeat of the Triumvir of the East Marcus Antonius and the woman who I still have trouble accepting was my half-great-aunt Cleopatra, he had reorganized what had begun as the Brundisium Cohorts, which was how they were known during my great-grandfather's time. In much the same way that he only appeared to relinquish power but retained Praetorships of every Senatorial province where Legions were located, by making it one Cohort less than a full Legion, he prevented the possibility of another Roman becoming powerful enough to challenge for full power. It was a lesson that Divus Augustus had taken to heart, although it was not until after I finished the Prefect's account once I completed my father's that I fully appreciated his genius. During the Pompeian civil war, and the Second Civil War, it was true that Legions became too powerful, and there were enough unscrupulous Primi Pili who were willing to sell their Legions to the highest bidder to a man like Marcus Aemilius Lepidus that Divus Augustus took steps to keep history from repeating itself. And, I thought as I followed Creticus out of the *Quaestorium*, it's also why not all nine Praetorian Cohorts are ever in Rome at one time.

Finally, we reached my quarters and the Century office, which was next door to the Cohort office, whereas in a Legion camp, they are separated by the rankers' section quarters, but those are all on the second floor in this configuration. Creticus opened the door, then stepped aside to allow me to enter first, which created something of an awkward moment, because the man I assumed was my Optio was standing there at *intente*, offering his salute, which of course I could not return because my arms were full.

"Optio Publius Canidius Sabinus, Pilus Posterior Pullus! Welcome to the Second Century, Second Cohort, and I am ready to receive your orders!"

I was saved by one of the three clerks, who I assumed was Diodorus since I did not recognize him from my time in Creticus' office, who relieved me of my burden so that I could return the salute. We stood facing each other, and again I was somewhat surprised, because while Sabinus was not as tall as Creticus, he was taller than average, but he was quite broad across the shoulders as well. As I would come to learn, in some ways, I fit into the Praetorian Guard better than I did the Legions, because it became apparent that men from the ranks are recruited as much for their physical appearance as for any other reason.

"Thank you, Sabinus." I tried to sound as if I had faced a situation like this before, but Optios are not traditionally there to greet a new Centurion. Not knowing what else to say, I offered, "I look forward to serving with you."

"As I am with you, Pilus Posterior." Sabinus nodded with a surprising enthusiasm. "I've heard of your exploits at the Battle of the Angravarian Wall! You were decorated by the *Propraetor* Germanicus Julius Caesar, no less!"

When I looked at Creticus with a surprise that bordered on shock, Creticus looked uncomfortable, but he said readily enough, "I let Optio Sabinus read your record."

There was no regulation forbidding a subordinate to view his superior's record, at least as far as I knew, but I still found it unsettling.

"Er, yes," I said, feeling awkward about it. "I was just blessed by Fortuna to be in the right place at the right time."

"I'm going to let you get settled in, Pullus," Creticus said as he headed for the door. "Once you're done, come see me and I'll take you to my tailor so you can get properly outfitted."

The clerks I had seen in the Cohort office followed him outside, leaving me alone with Sabinus and the clerk, who I had learned was indeed Diodorus, and I was already beginning to work out when I would be bringing Alex here to become one of my clerks, and wondering how much it would cost to bribe whoever needed to be bribed to make it happen. As I was thinking about this, I heard someone moving in the next room, which would be my private quarters, then the door opened and another man, very young and with the darker skin of a Greek, stepped into the outer office.

"Who's this?" I asked of nobody in particular.

"This is your second clerk, Pilus Posterior," Diodorus answered. "His name is Demetrios."

"That's…unfortunate," I muttered, and it was, both because I would not be needing him, but more because that was the name of our second clerk when I was the Quartus Pilus Posterior.

He and Alex detested each other, but not to the point that Alex was not haunted by Demetrios' fate when we were ambushed at the Long Bridges, and he was one of the hundreds of clerks and slaves slaughtered, while Alex managed to rescue Gaesorix Batavius, who had been badly wounded because of Albinovadus Pedo's incompetence and is now retired and living back in Batavia. I just hoped that Alex did not feel that this was some sort of omen from the gods or something.

"What was that, Pilus Prior?" Sabinus asked. "What's unfortunate?"

"Ah," I did not realize I had been overheard. "It's unfortunate because I won't be needing Demetrios because I'm bringing my own clerk in, Alexandros Pullus."

I saw the three of them exchange a glance, but I ignored it to walk to the door of my private quarters, which are far more spacious and better appointed than anything I had seen in Ubiorum or even Mogontiacum, even the Primus Pilus' quarters. Diodorus had lain the clothing and other soft items of my new issue on the bunk, while he had placed the other items on the desk, which was when I first noticed that, while they had given me a *vitus*, it had a distinct difference, because at one end, it was topped by a cap that was held in place by tiny nails, and atop the cap was a silver Roman eagle.

"That is how everyone knows that we're Praetorian officers when we're out in public."

I turned in surprise and asked Sabinus, who had spoken, "Optios carry a *vitus* in the Praetorians?"

"No using a turfcutter handle for beating Praetorians." Sabinus laughed. "It's beneath them to be whacked with one of those."

"So," I asked cautiously, keeping in mind all of the shocks of the day, "we're allowed to thrash rankers?"

"By the gods, yes!" Sabinus answered with a grin. "It's the only way you can get some of these dozy bastards to make an effort at keeping their kit in order." I was relieved to hear this, then Sabinus added, "Although the Prefect doesn't like us doing it in public. So sometimes Publius will get a smart mouth when we're out on duty and hope that we forget about it by the time we get back here."

"Does it ever work?"

"What do you think?" He laughed again, and I felt myself warming to Sabinus, although I still reminded myself to be on my guard. His smile faded, and he said, "Pilus Posterior..."

"When we're alone, Pullus is fine," I assured him, and he nodded his understanding, but went on, "I just wanted to...warn you about your idea of bringing your own clerk to the Century, Pullus."

"I got the impression there was some sort of problem," I said honestly. "Why?"

Before he answered, Sabinus turned to abruptly shut the door to my private quarters, and because of where I was standing, I caught a glimpse of the expression on Diodorus as the door shut in his face, instantly understanding why Sabinus had done so.

In a low tone, Sabinus explained, "What the Pilus Prior probably didn't tell you is that every decision we make, about anything, is reviewed by Prefect Sejanus, and that includes who we pick. Or," he added meaningfully, "we buy for our personal use."

It took a moment for me to comprehend what he meant, and while it did not impact me personally, I gasped, "You mean even a personal body slave?"

"Or a comfort slave," he confirmed. "The only exception is if you're using them as an investment, like leasing them out. But if they're going to be here at the barracks for any reason, it has to be approved by the Prefect."

That, I realized instantly, was going to be a problem, especially now, given my clash with Sejanus earlier in the day, but I made the decision to set that aside for the time being. With my newly issued items disposed of, I returned to the Cohort office, where Creticus was ready to escort me to the man who would be making my togas. As we walked, my new Pilus Prior got to experience something that I have long since forgotten; the looks, the widened eyes, and occasionally, the flash of fear that caused another person to suddenly steer a different course around me as they passed.

"Does this happen often?" Creticus asked.

"All the time," I confirmed, but then I pointed to my helmet, "although now that I know the Praetorians don't wear this, I think that's part of it."

"That's true." Creticus nodded. "We don't get many men from the Legions in Rome. And when we do," he said with a laugh, "they're a foot shorter and a hundred pounds lighter than you are."

"Pilus Prior," I spoke carefully, which he seemed to sense by the manner in which he turned to look at me, "what are the regulations for Praetorian officers as far as where they spend their off-duty time?"

Thankfully, he understood immediately.

"You have a woman with you?" I nodded, and he was right when he said, "Then you'll be relieved to know that Centurions are exempt and can spend their nights where they choose, provided they report for duty at the proper time and place and wearing the appropriate attire for the day." I thanked him, but he waved it away. "I've got a woman and three children. I spend the night before we have duty at the barracks, and before important inspections by the Prefect. Otherwise," he shrugged, "I'm with my family. Do you have any children, Pullus?"

"No," I answered, then added, "not yet. According to Bronwen and my clerk's wife, she's about four months away from it."

"Bronwen?" He regarded me with a raised eyebrow. "That's not a name I'm familiar with. Is she a Gaul?"

I spent the rest of our walk, and part of the time when the man who could have been thirty or sixty took my measurements as I stood on the floor instead of the stool that he said he normally used explaining to Creticus how Bronwen had come into my life, noticing something about the tailor as I did so.

"You're from Alexandria," I said, which surprised and clearly pleased him.

"Yes, Dominus, I am. But," he did not stop measuring, "how

did you know?"

"I was there not too long ago, and I heard enough of the accent to place it."

"Ah," he nodded, then an expression of what I took to be melancholy by his words, "I have not seen Alexandria for more than thirty years."

It was more to make conversation than from any real curiosity that I asked, "What brought you to Rome?"

Because he was using the marked stretch of knotted cord to measure my neck, I felt him stiffen.

"There was…some trouble," he said uneasily, refusing to look at me from the stool he was standing on, appearing to count the number of knots. "You have quite a large neck, Dominus. In fact, I cannot remember anyone other than Felix the Thracian who came here after he won his freedom who was your size."

It was a blatant attempt to change the subject, but I did not press him on it, nor did I tell Creticus after we left when he asked me about it that his tailor, while from Alexandria, was not Egyptian, but a Macedonian Greek, and by the manner in which he spoke, was an educated man, far more educated than necessary for a tailor. As I was learning, Rome was not Ubiorum, or Mediolanum, and was a far more complicated place, where seemingly nothing was as straightforward as it may have looked at first examination.

Chapter 3

Sempronius had been waiting for almost a third of a watch, but he did not appear to be irritated at my tardiness, and I found him playing a game of bounceball with Iras, who was still at the age that what her eyes saw and where her hands went because of what she saw was not always the same place, which Alex, Algaia, and Bronwen were watching in quiet amusement.

I apologized, then got immediately down to business. "I'd like to hire you for a few days to help us find a place in the city for us to live."

"What are your needs?" he asked, and I had to stifle a groan since, naturally, I had not given it any thought.

Thankfully, Alex, although I was certain that Algaia was behind it, was prepared for that question. "It obviously needs to be close to the Second Cohort barracks, and while having apartments side by side would be ideal, in the same building would do. And," he added, superfluously in my opinion, "it needs to be in a neighborhood that my wife and Bronwen can feel safe in."

"So that means the Subura is out." Sempronius chuckled, but he was nodding. "That's understandable. How much are you willing to pay per month?"

"Our quarters in Ubiorum cost a *denarius* a month," Alex told him. "I know that Rome will be more expensive, so..." he thought for a moment, then glanced over at me, and I provided no help whatsoever, just offering a shrug, "...two *denarii* a month?"

We got a warning in the manner in which Sempronius shifted uncomfortably, suddenly looking at the floor.

"That," he said awkwardly, "will make things...difficult, at least based on your needs. For two *denarii* a month, you wouldn't be in the Subura itself, but you'll definitely be down there near it in the Fourth District in that area between the Viminal and Esquiline."

"How much for what we described?"

97

"A minimum of six *denarii* a month," he answered, and to ensure we understood, "apiece."

"*Six?*" Algaia gasped, but while Alex made no overt response, I saw he was shaken as well.

"What can we get for ten *denarii* a month?"

My question surprised Sempronius, but it disturbed Algaia sufficiently to come to her feet off the couch.

"Gnaeus, we cannot afford that!"

"I know," I acknowledged, "but I can."

"I knew Praetorians got paid more," Alex said cautiously, "but how much more?"

"As a Praetorian Pilus Posterior of one of Cohorts permanently in Rome, while a Praetorian ranker gets two *denarii* a day, I get twenty," I told him calmly, although I had only learned this a short time earlier.

"You get paid six hundred *denarii* a *month*?"

I could not keep the grin from my face. "That's what my new Pilus Prior tells me."

"When you say ten *denarii* a month, I assume you mean apiece?" Sempronius asked.

When I nodded, Alex interjected, "But, Gnaeus, what am I going to be paid as a clerk?"

"I don't know," I answered honestly. "But it doesn't matter."

What I did not say aloud in front of Sempronius was that we still had four thousand *sesterces* of the five that my aunt Miriam had insisted I take when we left Arelate for Ubiorum, so I was not concerned with monetary matters. I also did not know how much of even a Praetorian's pay is deducted for items at the time, all of which are mandatory, particularly funds for the officer's mess, something that is unknown in the Legions, and as I would quickly learn, the Praetorians did not deign to eat regular soldier's fare, with the exception of bread, although the flour is milled twice and is much finer. Alex looked as if he was still inclined to argue, but I cut my eyes to Sempronius, and he gave a faint nod, whereupon I turned back to face the other man.

"For ten *denarii*, I can get you on the lower slope of the Esquiline, just a couple of blocks from the Temple of Juno Lucina." He thought for a moment, "Or, there might be something available down at the base of the Caelian Hill as well."

"How far are they from the barracks?" I asked.

He thought for a moment, then answered, "They're both about the same distance, just from different directions. There might be more traffic coming from the Caelian, but they're both less than a half-mile. But," he warned, "I need to make sure that I'm right, Centurion."

We agreed that he would return the next day, then he was gone, and I was now left with the others, all of them understandably intent on learning a bit more about what their lives would be like in the future.

"Well," I began, "I'm going to be wearing a toga more than I ever have in my life."

My introduction to the Second Century, Second Praetorian Cohort occurred the next day, when I got another shock.

"These men are bigger than any Century I've ever seen," I muttered to Creticus when I met him outside of our quarters as the Cohort assembled for the morning inspection. Glancing around, I saw that my Century was not unique, but Creticus seemed surprised.

"You don't know that there's a minimum height requirement for the Praetorians?"

"No, no, I did not," I admitted.

"Only big, strong farm boys from the home provinces," he assured me. "Etruria, Latium, Umbria, Picenum, Calabria, and Apulia, although not many of those."

Sabinus was standing in his spot in front of the Century, and as far as the ritual of reporting that the Century was gathered, and all were present, this is identical to how the Legions do it. The *Signifer* bearing the Century standard, which unlike the Legions, has the *imagii* of both Divus Augustus and Tiberius, while our standard only has the current Imperator, was also in his spot. The *vexilla* was blue instead of red, and whereas the Cohort number is engraved on a placard on top of the standard with the Legions, with the Praetorians, it is lettered in gold gilt that makes it stand out.

"I'll leave you to it, Pullus," Creticus said, turning and walking over to where his Century was standing, waiting for their daily inspection.

I had to take a breath, then I strode to stand in front of Sabinus, who saluted and gave his report. "All Praetorians of the Second Century, Second Cohort are present and ready for inspection!"

This was unusual, at least when compared to the Legions; at any given moment, there is almost always someone missing because they are on the sick list or have been given some punishment detail.

Sabinus saw my surprise and interpreted it correctly, using the fact that his back was turned to the Century to assure me, "This is normal for the Praetorians, Centurion. We don't get men on the sick list that often. And," he lowered his voice even more, "given the Prefect's...strict discipline, most of the officers look the other way on things because we don't like seeing men get striped with the scourge for a blemished buckle."

"That's good to know," I muttered, immediately scrapping my plan to be even harsher in my first inspection than was needed.

Sabinus stepped to my side as I stopped in front of the *Signifer*, who rapped out, "*Signifer* Vibius Herennius Flaccus, Pilus Posterior!"

Flaccus was a couple of inches shorter than I was, with an aquiline nose and regular features that, as is the norm, were partially obscured by the wolfskin headdress that was in better condition than anything I had seen in the Legions. The fact that he was wearing the headdress, yet like everyone else was dressed in only his tunic and not his full armor I put down to yet another quirk of the Praetorians.

"Flaccus," I made sure to look him in the eyes for this first inspection; in the future, I would be examining their uniforms, but on this day, I wanted to make the kind of personal connection that comes when one man looks another in the eye. "What's your experience?"

This confused him, and his eyes cut to Sabinus as he repeated uncertainly, "Experience, sir? I'm not sure what you mean."

"Have you ever served in the Legions?" I snapped. "Have you been on campaign? What's your experience and why are you qualified to be a *Signifer* in my Century?"

As I hoped, this shook him, but it also angered him, or so I assumed by the way his face flushed, yet he did not answer immediately.

Just as I began to lean over him, my normal tactic for intimidating a man, he said, "No, Pilus Posterior, I've never served in the Legions. I was recruited directly into the Praetorians."

"I see." I nodded. "Then you worked your way up to *Signifer*."

I got the answer I was suspecting by how he once more glanced over at Sabinus, but my new Optio gave him not a flicker of a sign he was going to help.

"N-no, Pilus Posterior. My father purchased the posting for me."

"And how long ago was this?"

"Three years, Pilus Posterior."

"And where are you from?"

He looked startled, but he answered readily enough, "I'm from Rome, Pilus Posterior. I grew up not far from here on the backside of the Esquiline."

Honestly, I cannot say why I had asked him that, but I am glad that I did, because it instantly put me on my guard with Flaccus. As far as his appearance, as much as I tried to find something, it was faultless, and I instantly saw what Sejanus had meant by the varnish job expected of the Praetorians, because every inch of his leathers shone to a degree I had never seen before. I also noticed that it was not confined to just the leathers, but this did not please me at all, and I pointed down to his *caligae*.

"What's this? You varnish your *caligae* too?"

Sabinus answered instead of Flaccus, his tone even enough, but I sensed something there that I needed to learn more about.

"Yes, Pilus Posterior. The Prefect expects us to set a standard that will make Rome and the Imperator proud."

"But that makes the leather stiffer," I countered. "Which means that you're going to have more foot problems than normal."

This was when Sabinus reminded me, "We don't do much marching, Pilus Posterior. Just to our duty posts and back."

I think this was when the enormity of how different my life was about to be hit me, but I did not say anything more to Flaccus, moving on to the next man instead. I knew that there was no way that I would remember the names of eighty men after just one inspection, but I did apply the trick my father taught me of learning the name of one man in each section, usually the Sergeant, and by the time I was finished, I did not know whether to laugh or cry. In appearance, the men of the Second Century would have put any Century I ever commanded to shame; their tunics were not just spotless, they were pressed, and I already mentioned their leathers, and there was a uniformity to their hair length that was something I certainly had never been able to achieve with the men under my previous command. Personally, I had adopted my father's practice of keeping my hair closely shorn, which in turn he had copied from my great-grandfather, not because of any vanity, but because our heads are so large and helmets are not made in anything other than one size that, if I wanted to wear the felt liner, I had to cut my hair. The Praetorians' hair was longer, though not by much, and it was all the same length, which, along with their larger size, made them look as if they were essentially made from the same mold. This was the positive takeaway from my first inspection, although it was outweighed by the fact that, of the eighty men, less than a dozen of them bore any kind of scars. This may seem...odd, and I suppose that it could have been because these men were so skilled that they had never suffered any wounds, but I was certain, and it was later confirmed, that this was not the case. It went deeper than that, however; they were also all sleek and well-fed, with a complacent air that was unlike anything I had ever experienced before. Even in garrison, during the winter months when the men of the Legions get fat and lazy, there is still an air of restlessness, as if men are just marking time before they are unleashed once again to do what they do best, killing the enemies of Rome. I did not get that sense from any of these men, and it served as a reminder of something that my father had said more times than I can count.

"Soft duty makes for soft men; hard duty makes for hard men."

And, I was unhappy to realize by the time my inspection was done, I was certain that I did not have a Century of hard men, and this was when I made the first decision that would put me in Sejanus' bad books.

"I'm sorry, Pilus Posterior. What?"

This came from the *Gregarius Immunes* in charge of the armory, because as I had noticed on my visit, there were not only javelins missing, and it was why I repeated, "Where are the *rudii*? For training?" Suddenly, I got a sinking sensation. "Please do not tell me that a Praetorian Cohort has no training weapons."

This made the *Immunes* flush, but he assured me, "Oh, we have them, Pilus Posterior Pullus. We just keep them in crates in the back."

"Then," I said pleasantly, "I want eighty of them."

He did not move, which ignited another, darker feeling in me, while he asked cautiously, "Have you spoken to Pilus Prior Creticus about this, sir?"

The fact was that I had not; as usual, my decision had been made impulsively, not long after I concluded my preliminary inspection.

Deciding that bluffing was my best chance, I said confidently, "Of course, I have. He thought it was an excellent idea. Now," I hardened my voice, "I need you to bring eighty *rudii* up here so that my Century can pick them up."

I did not wait for him to obey, although he did move in the right direction, towards the storeroom at the back of the armory, while I strode across the Cohort forum and went back to my office, where Sabinus was waiting.

"Assemble the men," I ordered. "We're going to the stakes."

In a manner eerily similar to the *Immunes*, Sabinus' first reaction was to stare at me, but it was for more practical reasons.

"The stakes, Centurion?" He frowned and shook his head. "There aren't any nearby."

I could not contain myself, uttering a half-groan, half-curse as I told myself, Of *course* there's not, Gnaeus. We're in the largest city in the world, so what did you expect?

To Sabinus, I queried, "Would I be correct in assuming that they're out on the Campus?" He nodded, but when I said, "I wonder if there will already be men out there?", it prompted a laugh from him.

"Pilus Posterior, I can practically guarantee that there won't be anyone out at the stakes. In fact," he mused, "I can't remember the last time I've been on that side of the Campus. They may not even be there anymore."

"There's only one way to find out," I said with a confidence I did not feel, but again, I was met with hesitation.

"Have you spoken to the Pilus Prior about this?"

"No," I snapped, getting irritated now. "Why? Do I need to clear everything I do with my Century with the Pilus Prior?"

Rather than answer me immediately, Sabinus turned to the clerks and ordered them to go outside, and only after we were alone did he begin to speak.

"Centurion, I understand what you're going through, I do," he said quietly. "I truly do. When I came from the 2nd, the first months were horrible, and we hadn't seen nearly as much campaigning as you lot on the Rhenus. But once you accept that difference, things get a lot easier."

It was good advice; I knew it when I heard it, and I knew it later.

Nevertheless, I said, "Thank you, Sabinus, I'll keep that in mind. Now," I picked up my *vitus*, "assemble the men. We're going to collect the *rudii* on the way to the Campus."

To his credit, he did not argue, although his salute and the ritual words we use were delivered curtly, and I was certain that he was not happy, but there was only so much I would bend.

Thankfully, Creticus had been summoned to meet with Sejanus, along with the other Pili Priores, so I did not have to explain myself until after the fact, and when we returned, just before the beginning of third watch, I did not know whether to laugh or to cry. I will not say that the Second Century was as bad as if they were all raw *Tirones*, but if I had marched with these men against Arminius, I would have immediately joined my father on the other side of the river. If there was a positive, it was that I could instantly see the veterans among them…all ten of them, although there was one pleasant surprise, in the form of the Sergeant of the Sixth Section, one of the older men in the Century. Only later did I realize I should have known from my inspection, because he was on the short side compared to the rest of the Century, of average height but tightly muscled. I had gone circulating among the group working; there were twenty stakes so that we had a line of four men per stake, two stakes per section, with Sabinus barking out the position, then a pause, then the barked command of execution, followed by the sharp cracking sound of the lead-filled wooden *rudii* slamming into the scarred wooden poles that, frankly, were not nearly as battered as I would have expected, although I supposed it was possible they had been replaced recently. I just happened to be at the right angle to see when the Sergeant was recovering from his thrust, standing one stake over as I was, and I immediately walked over to him.

"Sergeant…" I had to think for a moment, then ventured, "Valerius, yes?"

He had snapped to *intente*, although he was holding the *rudis* point down next to his leg, rapping out, "Yes, Pilus Posterior! Aulus Valerius, Sergeant, Sixth Section!"

I nodded my acknowledgement, but I was pointing to his *rudis*, and I said, "Show me how you're grasping your *gladius*, Valerius." He did so without hesitation, but I was certain that I read a sense of resignation in his expression, as if he was about to be reprimanded, but frankly, seeing it made me feel better than I had in some time. On the spur of the moment, I decided to pretend ignorance, and I asked him, "Where did you learn to hold your *gladius* like that, Sergeant?"

He swallowed, making the lump in his throat bob, then answered, "In Pannonia, Pilus Posterior. I was in the 8th Legion."

"Cohort and Century?"

"First of the Third Cohort, Pilus Posterior!"

I nodded, thinking that I should not be enjoying this, while

Sabinus, seeing I was talking to one of the men, had not issued another command, and I felt all eyes on us.

"Does this…grip have a name, by any chance?"

"Yes, Pilus Posterior." He did not hesitate this time. "It's called the…"

"…Vinician grip," I finished for him, relishing the look of surprise on his face. Suddenly, I had another idea, and I asked, "Are you a wagering man, Sergeant?"

"I've been known to make a wager or two, Pilus Posterior," he said cautiously, and I had to smother my grin at the sight of a ranker who knows that his Centurion has some sort of surprise in store and that it is highly improbable he will like it.

"I'll wager that I know who taught you how to hold your *gladius* in that manner," I said, then held up a hand, "but you don't have to risk anything. If I'm wrong, I'll give you an extra day off duty, but even if I'm right, it won't cost you anything."

I should not have been surprised this made him more suspicious, not less, but he also understood that he did not have much choice in the matter, so he nodded and said, "Very well, Pilus Posterior, I'll take those terms."

"The man who taught you that is named Titus Domitius," I said triumphantly, a sensation that only lasted long enough for him to shake his head.

"No, Pilus Posterior," Valerius answered soberly. "It was Gaius Petronius who taught me. He was our weapons instructor." I stood there like a lump, but then I saw his eyes turn down at the corners, although he remained straight-faced as he added, "Of course, Gaius Petronius was my Optio…and Titus Domitius was my Tertius Pilus Prior. So," he shrugged with a casualness that was completely feigned, "I suppose that it's possible that Centurion Domitius taught him."

"Oh," I growled, "so you're a clever man, eh, Valerius?"

I delivered this in such a way that he instantly understood, and he grinned as he answered, "That's what my Mama always told me, Centurion! That I was her cleverest child!"

"Yes, because you're the only one she had, Valerius."

I did not catch who said this, but it was from one of the men of his section, all of whom immediately roared with laughter, along with those within hearing. Signaling he had taken the honors, I clapped him, hard, on the shoulder, sending him staggering a step, but I decided to use this moment.

"Gather round me," I ordered, and the Century did so, whereupon I pointed to Valerius' hand, and with a gesture, indicated that he lift it up, then make a slow rotation. "See how Sergeant Valerius is holding this *gladius*?" Everyone nodded, and I was not surprised when I asked, "Does anyone else hold it in this manner?" that heads moved in the opposite direction. "Well, starting today," I said this using my command voice, "everyone in the Second of the Second Praetorians will learn how to use this. It's called the Vinician Grip, and it very well may save your lives one day." Turning back to Valerius, I gambled and asked, "What about you, Valerius? Did that ever save your bacon?"

"No, Pilus Posterior," he answered, but my disappointment did not last long because he added, "but it did save the life of my close comrade, Tiberius Fronto, back during the Batonian Revolt. He was able to hang on to his *gladius* even after some barbarian *cunnus* your size…" Immediately, he turned red. "Er, I didn't mean to imply that…"

"Yes, I don't think you're calling me a *cunnus*, Valerius." Then I grinned and said more loudly than necessary, "But I'll wager that you will at some point in the future, or I'm not doing my job."

I was pleased that this amused the men, and Valerius continued, "The barbarian had one of those giant double-bladed axes, and he swung it hard against Fronto's blade, but while it spun Fronto around a bit, he held on to the *gladius* while the barbarian was off balance and his shield was out of position. He told me later that if he hadn't been using that grip, he'd have crossed the river right then."

Although this sounded plausible, there was something about it that made me think that perhaps Valerius was being a bit…generous, but in that moment, I made the decision to accept it at face value and not just as an attempt for Valerius to ingratiate himself with me.

"It's saved me as well," I assured the other men. "In Germania. And it's saved the lives of men in the Centuries I've commanded.

But," I glanced up at the sun, "we'll begin that another day. Now we return to the Cohort. Sabinus, assemble for the march."

On our march back, my mind was filled with all sorts of things, some of them conflicting. Taking them out to the stakes had been both my chance to assess if what my eyes had told me during the inspection were deceiving me, and the fact that they had not was a mixed blessing. On one hand, it meant my judgment was good, on the other, now that I knew just how deficient these men were when it came to a bare level of competence as Legionaries, and given the resistance I was certain would be coming if I tried to correct that, it was a daunting prospect, to put it mildly. When we got back, Pilus Prior Creticus was there waiting, his eagle-capped *vitus* in his hand, but I did not need to know the man well to see by his expression that he was unhappy. But, I was certain, he was not angry; just...unhappy, as if he would rather be somewhere else.

Nevertheless, he waited for the ritual of dismissal before walking up to me, saying, "So you took your Century out to the stakes, eh, Pullus?"

"Yes, sir," I answered. "I wanted to get an idea of where the boys are when it comes to our business."

"Our business?" Creticus echoed, then shook his head. With a sigh, he said, "Pullus, let's go for a walk. I'll take you to a *taverna* down the street that the Centurions like. Let me buy you a cup of wine, eh?"

Even if I had wanted to decline, I knew this was not a request, although I did ask, "Shouldn't I put on my toga?"

"You didn't bother when you left the barracks and went to the Campus," he pointed out, which was true enough, but I protested, "That's because we were going to be working at the stakes, Pilus Prior."

This did not impress him in the slightest. "They were, but what about you? Or," suddenly, he looked a little uncomfortable, "did you perform the exercises too?"

"No," I admitted. "But only because I wanted to evaluate my Century."

"The Prefect isn't going to care about that," he shot back, then

I got a hint of what he was worried about, "but hopefully, he doesn't hear about this."

"About what?" I asked, not without some astonishment. "That a new Centurion wanted to assess the ability of his Century to perform their duties?"

We reached the *taverna* just then, and I followed him in as he went directly to a table in the far corner, holding up two fingers as he passed the bar, and we were barely in our seats before the man, I assumed the owner, was standing there with a pitcher and two cups.

"Do you want water today, Pilus Prior Creticus?" the man asked with a thick Greek accent, but Creticus shook his head.

"No, Philemon, it's close enough to the end of the day," Creticus replied, then waited for the man to return to the bar before he picked up the pitcher to pour into my cup. "It's not Falernian, or Chian, for that matter," he grunted, "but it's not the kind of swill that the men love." I waited until his cup was filled, and he lifted it as he said, "Welcome to the Second Cohort, Pullus, and it's time you learned some things."

It was close to dark by the time Creticus and I parted, with me heading back to the inn and him to his home not far away, but while my head was swimming, it was not because of the wine. Which, I confess, was actually very good, and he was being truthful when he said it was of a much higher quality than that favored by the men. What I did not tell him was that it was of a better quality than what the Centurions in Ubiorum favored.

"You need to stop thinking of the Praetorians as a military posting, Pullus," he said frankly. "Because it's not. It's a political job, nothing more." He took a swallow before he continued, leaning forward as he lowered his voice, but it was the intensity in it that struck me. "Which means you have to stop thinking like a Centurion. Oh," he gave a small wave before I could reply, "yes, we go through the motions, and yes, we use the same organization and the regulations are mostly the same. But our purpose here is much, much different."

I was almost afraid to ask, but I sensed that not only was Creticus being honest, he was trying to help me. "Then what *is* our purpose, Pilus Prior?"

This pleased him, and he gave me an approving nod. "*That* is the right question, Pullus! We're here to strike fear into the hearts of our enemies." Now, to me, this was exactly what the purpose of the Legions all around the Empire are for, but he cut me off. "I know what you're going to say, but there is one difference, and it is the crucial difference. The enemy of the Praetorian Guard isn't the barbarian tribes in Germania, or Pannonia, or the wild tribes beyond the Ister, or the Parthians, or the Pontics, for that matter. No," he tapped the table for emphasis, "our enemy is *here*, in Rome, and it's whoever our Imperator says it is." He paused to take a swallow, as if he needed the fortification. "Even if it's fellow Romans."

I did not reply, mainly because I did not know what to say, so I sat there trying to absorb what that meant, and I learned a great deal about Creticus that night, and it began when I asked bluntly, "And who is that determines what fellow Roman or Romans constitute the enemy of the Praetorians? Is it Tiberius? Or," I looked him in the eye, "is it Sejanus?"

His eyes suddenly shifted, looking over my shoulder, which was disconcerting in itself, then he reached out and grabbed my forearm resting on the table as he hissed, "Keep your voice down, Pullus! Pluto's cock, are you trying to make your stay in the Praetorians the shortest ever?" My initial thought was perhaps that this was not such a bad thing, but he immediately divined my thinking, because he added ominously, "And making sure that you never see the birth of your child?"

Even in that moment, with our acquaintance being less than two full days, I felt reasonably certain that Creticus was speaking out of at least partial concern for me, although I knew self-interest was involved, for which I did not blame him a bit.

However, this did not deter me from getting the answer, and I asked just above a whisper, "Well? Who is it that's making the decisions about who poses a threat to the Imperator?"

"Who do you think?" he snapped, and he seemed angry for the first time. I quickly learned it was not at me as he muttered, "I don't know how he's done it, and I don't know how someone as clever as Tiberius could allow it to happen, but right now..." He stopped to take another look around before he went on, "...Prefect Sejanus is the most dangerous and powerful man in Rome, and I mean that. Tiberius trusts him completely, and while I know that some of his oldest friends have tried to warn him about Sejanus, at least two of them have just…" He did not finish but used his hands to make a gesture that we use to indicate something going up in smoke or vanishing.

While this was informative, and chilling, I still did not fully understand, prompting me to ask, "So how does that have to do with me and whether I take my Century out to the stakes?"

Creticus did not seem surprised at my question, and he answered readily, "Because it's something that Sejanus didn't know about beforehand, Pullus. You must understand something about Sejanus. He trusts *no one* except for himself, and perhaps a couple of his lackeys. And of course he's got the Tribunes terrified of him because he has scrolls this thick," he held his thumb and pointing finger an inch apart, "on not just them but their fathers and families. Although," he allowed, "there is one Tribune that doesn't seem afraid of him. And, as I recall, he served in Germania under Germanicus as well. Worst of all," he grimaced, "he just happens to be the Tribune who commands our Cohort. You haven't met him because he's away on some personal business."

"What's his name?" I asked, thinking that I would at least be familiar with the name, because there were a lot of Tribunes during the two campaign seasons Germanicus had led the Army of the Rhenus.

I was, but it went much deeper than that, because Creticus answered, "Marcus Nonius Asprenas." It must have been my reaction that prompted him to say, warily, "It looks like you know him, or at least know about him."

"I do," I did not see the point in lying, but I had to decide how forthcoming to be, and I was aware of the possibility that Asprenas might not want his connection to the Pullus family known, so I said, "but only barely. We've spoken a couple of times, nothing more than that."

Creticus seemed to accept this, then leaned closer to warn me, "I'd be careful getting too…friendly with our Tribune. He's connected to a family that Sejanus has his eyes on."

"Eyes on for what?" I asked, initially puzzled, but I caught up quickly enough. "Ah," I said barely above a whisper. "The Asprenas family is one of those Sejanus is trying to isolate?"

Creticus nodded slightly. "Which is why you should be careful how…close you get to the Tribune."

Even if Creticus was sincerely trying to protect me, the instant I heard the name, I knew I would do no such thing. While we certainly were not close in any real sense, he had been with us the final year of our campaign against Arminius, and he had actually escorted me to meet with Germanicus after I ordered my Fourth Cohort to change our position, in a move that was at least partially the reason I found myself in Rome. But it went deeper than that, because it had been Asprenas who had accompanied my father on their mission to find Germanicus when he was conducting his census in Gaul to inform him of the Legions of the Rhenus revolting. Having read all of my father's account, it did not get off to an auspicious start, my father viewing the Tribune as just another spoiled young patrician who thought it was beneath him to be in the company of a lowly Centurion, even if that Centurion was Titus Porcinianus Pullus. However, both men came to respect each other, and of all the Tribunes about which my father spoke, Marcus Asprenas was one of a bare handful that, as he would have put it, were worth more than an amphora of his piss. Which, I realized, meant that if it was within my power to do so, I would help Asprenas, if only because I was certain that would have been what my father would have done, and what he would want me to do if he was still alive and back on the Rhenus. While my first thought was that it was unusual that Asprenas was still a Tribune—by rights, he should have been at least on the list for Quaestor—but I quickly learned that a Praetorian Tribune is in an entirely different category, all of them being older than the normal Tribune, which partially explained why Sejanus considered him a threat.

We remained in the inn for another week before Sempronius arrived one evening to announce that he had found something that he thought might be suitable.

"It's about halfway up the northern side of the Caelian Hill, so you can just go down the hill and cross over to the Esquiline to get to your barracks," he explained.

There was enough light left for us to go see it, although it would be dark by the time we came back, and I was about to suggest that just Alex and I go, not wanting Bronwen, Algaia, and young Iras out on the streets of Rome out after dark, but Alex gave me a warning shake of his head.

"They've been cooped up since we got here," he whispered. "If you want to sleep with one eye open tonight, that's your business, but Algaia and the baby are coming with us."

Naturally, that meant it was all of us, and we followed Sempronius through the throng of people, some of whom were heading home, while others were clearly heading out for a night of enjoyment, which seemed to be an every-night occurrence and not just the day before and the night of market days like Ubiorum. At least, the civilians of Ubiorum behaved in this manner; Legionaries would go into town to their *taverna* every day if they were allowed, so I suppose in that sense, Rome seemed to be full of Legionaries. We had become accustomed to the noise and the smells for the most part, and it was actually a pleasant late afternoon, and I was proud of the looks Bronwen received, even as she was now visibly pregnant. I was dressed in my Praetorian tunic and carrying my Praetorian *vitus*, so there was no need for Sempronius to shove people aside or warn others we were approaching, but there was now a different quality with the glances and looks I received that have been a part of my life for as long as I can remember, and it troubled me that I could not put my finger on what it might mean. Sempronius had been correct; the place was just two streets down from the top of the Caelian Hill, and it was in a neighborhood that was occupied by people in the Equestrian order, but best of all, it was essentially a two-story building with a small enclosed courtyard, and the floorplan was identical for both floors. It was also completely unoccupied, although Sempronius assured us that it would not remain so for long.

"It's a bit more expensive than you said, Centurion," Sempronius admitted.

"How much more?"

"Twelve a month," he answered, and I was opening my mouth to tell him to keep looking while I would keep this one in mind, when Bronwen, along with Algaia and Iras, returned from their tour of the place.

"This is where we will live," she announced. "It is perfect for all of us. We will live on the top floor, and Alex, Algaia, and Iras on the bottom floor."

I could say that I put up a fight, or that we had a spirited debate over the merits compared to the extra cost, but Bronwen had been pregnant for more than five months by this point, so I simply turned to Sempronius and asked, "Can you make the arrangements?"

It was easy for me to see that he was struggling to hide his amusement, not that I could blame him since I was acutely aware that the sight of someone like me meekly submitting to my woman's authority would have evoked merciless teasing from my fellow Centurions. Fortunately, Bronwen chose not to gloat about her easy conquest of her overgrown man, and as I quickly learned, she had been right, and it was worth every coin it cost me.

My first time with the duty where I had to wear my toga while carrying my *vitus* was when the Second Century was assigned to secure the Forum, a week after I took command. By "securing," I mean to say that we were required to stand there, arrayed by section, around the edge of the Forum, while one section essentially marched up and down the slope of the Capitoline and in between the temples and curiae and smaller forums, showing the people of Rome that the Praetorians were present and ready for anything.

Fortunately, Sabinus had warned me, "This isn't the worst posting we can pull, but it's close." He made a face. "I know how much you hate playing at toy soldiers, and this is probably the one that is the worst for that sort of thing. Although," he offered a leering grin, "the boys love it because it gives them the chance to flirt with the ladies of Rome."

Sabinus was correct in every detail, both in how much I hated it and how much the rankers loved it, and at his suggestion, I allowed every section to make at least one tour around the Forum. As far as what the officers did, I suppose it was essentially the same as the Legions, except that as the Optio made the rounds of every post with the *Tesserarius* and the Centurion stayed put, my station was at the base of the statue of Divus Augustus, enduring the heat in my toga. At least, I thought miserably, the boys on the walking post are getting exercise going up and down the Capitoline, which is not as steep a climb as the Palatine that was in front of me. From my vantage point, the *Domus Augusti* is barely visible, at least the edge of it closest to the Forum, although it is just the red tiles of the roof peeking up and over the other villas of the rich and powerful. Naturally, I got my share of stares, but it was during that first duty that I realized what was different in the expressions of the passersby who had some sort of business in the Forum, and that was fear. Now, I cannot say that it was completely foreign, and in thinking about it, I realized that it was a matter of degree, as well as the fact that that expression was always consigned to the men who eyed me as we crossed paths. I suppose I would characterize it in this manner: men, at least some men, view me with a sense of caution, as if by my very size and build I am liable to suddenly erupt in fury and begin smiting anyone around me. However, what I was seeing, and saw, was more than just caution but real fear, and it was not restricted to just the men. Usually, the glances I get from women are anything but unfriendly, and early on, it caused problems with Bronwen, including one memorable time where I had to grab her around the waist to keep her from launching herself at a woman whose appreciation of my appearance was a bit too forward for her taste. It clearly was not the toga that people were reacting to, because a good quarter of the men scurrying about the Forum on any given day are togate, and I saw several business transactions formally sealed, either in front of the statue of Divus Augustus or in Caesar's Forum. Before much time had passed, I considered concealing my *vitus* with its silver eagle head, since I was certain this was where the fear was coming from, but while most people steered a clear path around me, not everyone was intimidated.

"*Salve,* Centurion!"

I turned to see a balding, middle-aged man wearing a toga that, while it was draped well enough, could not conceal the pot belly, and it could only charitably be considered white, especially in contrast with one of my new ones. He was smiling broadly and was only missing a tooth on the bottom, while his skin had a slight sheen to it that might have been from the baths or might have been sweat.

"*Salve,* Citizen." I realized I had not been instructed by Creticus about the regulations concerning interaction with civilians, but I did not want to appear rude.

"I don't believe I've ever seen you before, Centurion." He sounded genial enough, reaching my side, and I took notice that he stood to the side and not in front of me, as if he did not want to obstruct my view. "And I'm in the Forum every day, and have been for many years, so I know all of our Praetorian officers by sight. And," he laughed, "some of them I know quite well."

There was nothing overtly objectionable in what he had said, and I answered honestly, "I'm new to the Praetorians, Citizen...?"

"Ah yes, my apologies." He did look slightly embarrassed as he pivoted to look up at me. "Where are my manners? My name is Marcus Livinius Appius. Not," he held up a hand, "any relation to the great Appius Claudius or any of the other esteemed men of Rome, alas. Or," he laughed, "if I am, I must be a poor relation."

The manner in which he said this told me that this was something he used quite often, which in turn indicated that he was in a business where he was meeting new people quite often; or, I thought, he uses this to put people at ease for some reason.

Courtesy dictated my own response. "I'm Gnaeus Volusenianus Pullus, Secundus Pilus Posterior. Of," I added, "the Praetorian Guard."

"Yes," Appius nodded, the smile still stuck to his face, "I assumed as much, given your attire. That," he pointed to the *vitus*, "and where you're standing, since this is where the duty Centurion always stands." He stopped then, and for the first time looked away from me to watch the people passing by. Then the smile vanished, and he frowned as he turned back to me. "Forgive me, Centurion Pullus, but it took a moment for me to make the connection. I'm getting old, as you can see." The smile came back. "But given your...size, would I be correct in assuming that you're connected to the great Camp Prefect Titus Pullus in some way?"

"He was my great-grandfather." I nodded, and despite a small voice warning me to be wary, I could not help feeling the stab of pride I feel every time he is mentioned.

I was completely unprepared for him to continue, "Then is it safe to assume that means that you're also related to the late Titus Porcinianus Pullus, formerly the Quartus Pilus Prior of the 1st Legion, who fell during the successful attempt to rescue Segestes and resulted in Rome now having Arminius' wife and their son as...guests?"

"How did you know that?" I gasped, but he behaved as if it was obvious.

"Why, what good and loyal Roman doesn't know of the exploits of the Pullus family?" He sounded surprised, but I was certain there was a false note there. "Was he an uncle, perhaps?"

"No," I answered coldly, "he was my father."

This earned a thoughtful nod, then he said, "So you're the Centurion who was stranded in Britannia then, but once you secured your freedom, you didn't return to Ubiorum as you should have. You went somewhere else instead."

I had glanced away because I spotted my Sixth Section marching past, and when I returned my attention back to Appius, there was not a trace of a smile or any good humor, although his eyes were on my men as well.

"How do you know that?" I demanded, and I was both angry, and while I was not frightened, I was also certainly alarmed, and now I turned slightly and moved closer to him.

As I intended, this made Appius take a nervous sidestep, nor did he look up at me, but his voice was steady enough as he replied, "It's my business to know such things, Centurion. I also know that you traveled all the way to Alexandria, again before you reported back to your Legion. And yet," he did look up at me then, and there was now a hard glint in his eye, with no sign of the affable Appius he had shown me a moment earlier, "when you returned to Ubiorum, instead of being punished, you were actually promoted into the Praetorians. The question is," he pursed his lips, "on whose authority...and why?"

He doesn't know that my orders came from Germanicus! This was my first, immediate thought, yet almost as quickly, a small voice warned me, *don't make that kind of assumption, Gnaeus. Remember what Germanicus told you about being on your guard.* However, I was also angry now, truly angry.

"First," I was lifting my *vitus* as I talked, "I don't know who you are or who you work for, and you're asking me questions that make me suspicious. And," that was when I tapped him on the shoulder with my *vitus*, "it makes me angry, Marcus Livinius Appius. And, do I seem like the kind of man you want to make angry?"

As I hoped, this made him visibly nervous, yet I also saw a hint of his own anger, although he answered, "No, Centurion, you do *not* seem to be a man it would be wise to anger. But," his voice hardened slightly, "while I have no illusions about how long it would take you to spill my guts here on the Forum stones, you should also know that I have *very* powerful…friends. And," he finished, "they have questions about how someone who not only violated Army regulations to pursue personal business but isn't even in the Equestrian order manages to land such a sweet and profitable posting here in Rome."

The voice I heard in my head then was, of all people, Alex.

"Don't assume that he knows, Gnaeus. Yes, he seems to know a great deal about you, but that doesn't mean he knows that it *is* Germanicus, and that could be why he's here now."

Aloud, I said, "If you don't know the answer, then that suggests that you're not supposed to know. And," I could not resist, "perhaps your friends aren't nearly as powerful as they think they are. Now," I pressed the eagle of my *vitus* against his shoulder again, applying pressure that shifted his weight, "move along, Citizen Appius. I don't have any more time to spend on someone like you."

I did not shove him all that hard, but it was enough to send him staggering, yet while he smiled, there was no mistaking the malice in it.

"We'll see each other again, Centurion Pullus," he promised. "As I said, I'm here every day."

Somehow, he managed to simply vanish into the crowd, even as I was watching, blending in immediately with all the other people. It was not long after this when Sabinus appeared to inform me that our watch was done and the Third Century was there to take the second part of the day's duty, whereupon we marched back to our barracks. By the time we arrived, my toga was sodden, and I understood then Creticus had been telling it truly that I needed more than one. As soon as we went through the ritual of ending our duty, I left for our apartment on the Caelian Hill, which we had moved into two days before. Alex was there, waiting; he had borne his inactivity with growing impatience, but I was not quite confident enough to make him a clerk for the Century yet. Neither of us knew that Appius had unwittingly offered us an opportunity.

I told him about what had transpired with Appius, and when I asked him if he thought this was worthy of getting a message to Germanicus, he said immediately, "Absolutely." When I asked why, he pointed out, "If this Appius was connected to Germanicus, he would have known the answer."

"Could he have been testing me?"

Alex considered for a moment, then shook his head.

"I doubt it, because once you passed, why wouldn't he tell you as much? Besides," he asked, "does that sound like something Germanicus would do?"

"No," I answered immediately. "That's not his style."

"Then I'll go talk to Lysander," Alex replied, but when he got up to leave, I stopped him.

"Sempronius should be here any moment," I reminded him. "I want him to go with you."

After Marcus Sempronius had proven so valuable to us, I had offered him what I suppose might be called a job, although it was not of a fulltime nature. Instead, I asked him simply to come to the apartment in the late afternoon, and if I had something to do for him, he was free to say no. I still was not clear what he did to make money, but I also assured him that I did not care, with the only provision being that it did not cause any trouble for me or for the others.

"Do you trust him, Gnaeus?" Alex asked, a perfectly reasonable question.

"Not completely," I answered honestly, "but so far, he's proven trustworthy. Besides," I laughed, "you're just as likely to get lost going to the Palatine."

"That only happened once," he protested. "When I was exploring the city."

Our conversation was interrupted by the knock on the door, which Bronwen opened, and as expected, Sempronius entered. I explained what I needed, and he did not hesitate, but when I began writing in the tablet I intended to give Alex containing my message, Sempronius cleared his throat in a manner that I interpreted as a warning.

"Centurion, if I were you, I wouldn't write anything down that's going up to the Palatine," he said soberly. "The Praetorians have been known to just randomly stop men and demand to see what they're carrying."

While I appreciated the warning, I saw Alex's expression, so I was expecting it when he asked Sempronius, "How do you know that, Sempronius?"

"It's common knowledge," Sempronius answered with a shrug, either missing or ignoring Alex's obvious suspicion. "Besides," he addressed me, "it's as dangerous for whoever is sending the message as it is for whoever's carrying it."

That, I realized, was certainly true, and a glance at Alex saw that he agreed.

"You remember the name?" I asked, not wanting to repeat it in front of Sempronius because, while I did trust him to a degree, Alex also had a point.

"Yes," he assured me, then the pair left, while Bronwen brought me a bowl of porridge, and in a surprise, a roast chicken.

"I didn't smell any chicken roasting," I said, and she smiled.

"That's because I did not have to roast it myself," she replied, her face alight. "Did you know that there is a shop right around the corner where you can buy all manner of roast meats?" She sighed with contentment as she dropped onto the bench next to me, and as had become her habit, reached over and tore a leg off of the bird on my plate, which Alex had informed me was a woman's way of claiming ownership of a man, which was perfectly fine with me...provided she did not take more than a leg. "Isn't Rome *wonderful*?"

Who was I to disagree?

"Marcus Livinius Appius works for Sejanus," Alex informed me on his return to the apartment, but only after we had seen Sempronius off. "I talked to Lysander, and he knew immediately who I was speaking of, and he knew that he works for the Prefect."

While this was what I had suspected, there was a part of it that did not make sense, which I expressed to Alex.

"But when I reported to Sejanus, he made it clear that he was aware that my orders came from Germanicus!"

"I know," Alex agreed, "and I told that to Lysander. Now," he allowed, "Lysander made sure I knew that this was a surmise on his part, but Lysander thinks that Sejanus doesn't *really* know with any certainty, and that was his guess."

"Then who else would it be?" As soon as the words left me mouth, I knew. "He's worried that it was Tiberius, not Germanicus."

Alex nodded. "That's my belief as well, and it's Lysander's too." He hesitated then, but I knew him too well to know that his reason for doing so was important.

"What is it?"

"I want to make sure you understand that this is *not* based on anything Lysander told me, or any other kind of information. But," he paused, "it has to do with Dolabella."

"Dolabella?" I frowned, not seeing any connection.

However, I also knew I needed to listen, so I motioned at Alex to continue.

"Remember you told me how Sejanus basically gloated about either killing Dolabella or being behind his death?" Since it had happened barely a month earlier, I did, although I simply nodded. "Well," Alex continued, "what information did Tiberius Dolabella have that concerned your father?"

I instantly understood then, at least to an extent.

"About the…things my father did for Tiberius," I said slowly. Still, I was unconvinced there was a connection. "But that was my father, not me! So why would…" This was when it hit me, much like a punch to the gut. "Who better to continue working for Tiberius than me? At least," I added, my conviction strengthening, "as far as Sejanus is concerned."

"Exactly," Alex replied quietly. "A man like Sejanus, who sees webs and connections and plots everywhere he looks? Who better than the son of Titus Pullus to continue to do Tiberius' bidding in those things that Tiberius doesn't want known?"

"Fuck me."

It was really all I could think to say. I think back to that moment, when I thought my life had become hopelessly complicated and how wrong I was. Indeed, within a month, I would look back at that night with longing.

Despite the differences, and despite what I still view as the inanity of duty in the Praetorians, as with all things, once one learns the routine, it becomes easier to bear. And I was getting to know the men better; more importantly, I was developing my own opinions about who I could trust and who bore watching, and in my Century, at the top of the list was my *Signifer* Flaccus when it came to the latter. It was not his behavior as much as it was learning from Sabinus that, while Flaccus had said truthfully that his post was by virtue of his father's friendship with someone highly placed, the fact that it was Sejanus himself kept me on my guard. He also asked a great deal of questions, and some of them sounded suspiciously like the kind of questions Appius had asked. I also continued my practice of taking the men out to the stakes at least once a week, mainly because, while Creticus was clearly unhappy, he never forbade it, and when the Secundus Princeps Posterior Vibius Antistius Rufus came to my quarters to ask if I minded if he brought his Century along, I naturally agreed. The next week, we were joined by the Sixth Century, commanded by Titus Fufius Plancus, which was when Creticus called a meeting.

"This doesn't reflect well on the Second Cohort! Not well at all!"

I suspected that Creticus wanted to sound thunderous, but to my ears, it sounded more like the shout of a petulant child, and one glance at the other Centurions, at least one of whom, Titus Fufius Plancus, the Hastatus Posterior who was one of only two other Centurions who had served in the Legions with the 20th, told me he at least felt the same way as he caught my glance and rolled his eyes.

Before I could say anything, it was Rufus who raised his hand and said, "Pilus Prior, we need to do something more with these men than what we're doing. We spend more of our time polishing things than anything else. And," he held up a hand, "that's certainly important for what Praetorians are here for, but what harm can come from at least reminding these men they're supposed to be able to know which end of the *gladius* to hold?"

As soon as Rufus finished, I could see that Creticus, if not swayed, at least saw the sense in this, but he still shook his head.

"I won't forbid you from working at the stakes, but neither do I condone it," he said, not looking at us but down at his desk, with a set to his jaw that reminded me of Iras when she was being stubborn about something. "And," he continued, although he did look at us, "only one Century at a time will be allowed at the stakes. No more of two or three Centuries going on the same day. Is that understood?"

I was not happy, and I could see Rufus and Phillipus were similarly dissatisfied, but I also decided to follow their lead, so when they muttered their understanding and did not push the issue, I went along.

Once we were dismissed and outside, I approached Phillipus, the other Centurion from the Legions who had only served for five years with the 3rd in Syria and was a paid man like I was. His only campaign experience had been against a band of bandits who were waylaying travelers to Damascus, but he did not pretend that he was a grizzled veteran, and in fact, he is only three or four years older than I am.

"What's Creticus worried about?" I asked him, making sure to keep my voice down as we walked across the square. Before he could say anything, I hurried to add, "I know it's related to the Prefect for some reason, but any idea why?"

Phillipus continued walking, heading towards his quarters, but he glanced over his shoulder before he answered, his tone suggesting he was choosing his words carefully. "About a year ago, the Quartus Pilus Prior was arrested and accused of plotting against the Imperator. And," he glanced up at me, "he had been spending time with his entire Cohort on the Campus for about two months before he was arrested. That," he shrugged, "is why Creticus is so upset."

"He could have stopped us," I pointed out, but Phillipus laughed at this.

"Pullus, you haven't been here that long, but surely you've noticed that our Pilus Prior isn't the most…decisive man."

That was certainly true, but while this could be a deadly weakness under the standard, as time passed, I became more sympathetic to the plight of Creticus.

The day that I had been dreading inevitably came, with the Second Cohort assigned to the Palatine on the daylight watch. My hope that my Century would be assigned to another part of the hill and not the *Domus Augusti* lasted all of the time it took for Creticus to read off the assignments. The fact that he would not meet my eyes as he did so also gave me a strong indication that the selection of the Second was not random. However, while I was, and am certain that Sejanus was behind this, I am equally sure that he could not have foreseen what happened. We marched down the Esquiline, skirting the Subura, and ascended the northern side of the Palatine. By doing so, we passed a stretch of two blocks where the residences had been razed for a new construction project, which I had been told was going to be Tiberius' personal residence, whereupon he would vacate the *Domus Augusti*. The speculation was that either the *Domus* would be permanently converted into a building for all the various government offices that were scattered about the area and brought under one roof, or that the half of the *Domus* that was designated as private quarters would house whoever Tiberius selected as his heir. On that subject, there was an unwritten but strictly enforced rule with the Praetorians that we never spoke about this, for reasons that should be obvious. Naturally, trying to tell any Roman, no matter whether they're a member of the Head Count or a Praetorian, not to discuss political matters is like telling us not to breathe, so what it did mean was that whatever talk there was occurred in dark corners and in hushed tones. And it should not be surprising that, once my fellow officers learned that I had served under Germanicus, rarely a day went by during my first month where one of them did not just happen to stop by to try and pump me for information about the man. Which, I will say, I was happy to offer in very general terms, but they quickly learned that I would never venture my opinion about any of the things in which they were most interested. That day, we arrived outside the *Domus*, whereupon we began the ritual of relieving the guard, the three Centuries of the First Cohort who had stood the night watch, which meant I met the First's Pilus Prior for the first time. He was in his forties, his name Sextus Sulpicius Cinna, and he wore enough perfume that I smelled him from two paces away, while his hair was slicked back with what I am certain was an expensive pomade. He was handsome, in a pretty way, with pouty lips, the corner of the upper one curled slightly upward, and I wondered if it always looked like that, or it was the sight of me that did it. I detested him immediately, and as I would quickly learn, the feeling was mutual.

I began by saluting as we are expected to do, and at least began, "Secundus Pilus Prior Pullus, reporting to…"

I got no further, as Cinna cut me off with a wave of his *vitus*, the kind of mortal insult that no Centurion would offer another in the Legions.

"Yes, yes, yes," he said impatiently. "I know who you are, and I know why you're here, there's no need to waste any more time. I," he drew himself up to his full height, I supposed so that he was only four inches shorter than me than five, "am already late for my meeting with the Prefect. I don't have time for this…" he used his free hand to wave it around at his men and mine, standing facing each other, "…sort of thing. So," he sniffed, "I consider myself relieved." Then, in another insult, he turned his back to me to call his Optio. "Carry out the relief, then march the men back to the barracks, Optio." Then, without even a glance over his shoulder at me, he strode into the *Domus Augusti*, presumably to meet with Sejanus.

The Optio looked desperately uncomfortable, but I assured him, "Don't concern yourself, Optio."

Then, turning to my *Tesserarius,* Spurius Dido, I indicated that he come forward to begin the process of the relief, while I walked over to Sabinus.

As we stood and watched Cinna's Optio and their *Tesserarius* exchange the four men at this post outside the main entrance, then begin marching off to the next post, neither of us spoke for a moment, then Sabinus, after glancing over his shoulder, said softly, "I should have warned you, Pilus Prior. I heard that Cinna had some sort of…show in mind when you and he met the first time."

"Any idea why?" I asked, although I suspected I knew the answer.

"Because he and Sejanus are…close," Sabinus said, which at first I took as confirmation of my guess.

Then something in the way he had said it registered, and I looked down at him, but Sabinus was staring down the street, watching as Dido and Rufio reached the next post, and exchanged four more men so that Rufio's group grew, while my Century shrank.

There are more than a dozen four men posts spread at roughly even intervals over the Palatine, while the other two sections are, as with the Forum, divided into two walking posts of a section apiece. The other difference is that, while we are not wearing armor, the men are armed, the signal that this area represents the heart and soul of Rome.

"Do you mean what I think you mean?" I broke the silence, but Sabinus just shrugged.

"It depends on what you think it means, Centurion," he answered reasonably. Then, he added, "But if you think it means that they're lovers? Then, yes. At least," he hurried to add, "that's the rumor."

This was interesting, and it was certainly titillating, but it is also the sort of thing that was just as likely to be baseless gossip as the truth, yet there was certainly something effeminate in Cinna's manner. And, I will say, nothing I saw after my first meeting has led me to believe that it is gossip.

One improvement of this duty over being assigned to the Forum was that I was not required to stand under a statue looking like a statue, and I took full advantage of it, making the rounds of every post, then pausing for perhaps a hundred heartbeats outside the main entrance to the *Domus* before doing it again. By this time, I had learned the names of all of my men, although on occasion, I still mixed them up, and I made a point to speak to a different man at each post, although I limited myself to spending a brief moment doing so. Certainly, I wanted to minimize the amount of time I had to spend standing in a spot where it was possible that the Prefect might appear, yet I did not want to be obvious about it. Nevertheless, never in my worst imaginings could I envision what happened when, as I was returning back to the *Domus* by the street where Germanicus was living, I saw several lictors emerging from his residence. It at least gave me an instant's warning for when Germanicus himself emerged, but my hope that I could simply slow down and allow him to go down the street once I saw he was heading in the same direction I was lasted long enough for him to give the kind of casual glance one does in the opposite direction. I was too far away to make out what he said, but when the eleven lictors he was entitled to because of his status as *Propraetor* came to a halt, I used the distance between us to groan aloud, although I did not break stride and I did try to appear pleased.

"*Salve*, Pullus!" Germanicus called to me, a smile on his face.

He was togate, as was I, but I still came to *intente* and saluted, which as I had learned, is hard to do in a toga and takes some practice.

I was not surprised that he returned it flawlessly, but then he beckoned to me in a gesture that told me he wanted me to walk with him, and as I fell in beside him he said, "I have some good news."

I was unsure what to say, so I asked, "Oh? What's that?"

"You're going to be reunited with the 1st," he answered, and I felt my jaw drop as my heart started pounding so hard that I heard it in my ears. And, I saw, he immediately understood, because he added quickly, "Not permanently, Pullus. I mean, not yet. It's just that my father has granted me a triumph for our campaign against Arminius, and the 1st is one of the Legions who are going to be marching in it." It is impossible to describe the mixture of emotions running through me; certainly I was happy that I would be seeing my Cohort and the other officers of the 1st, especially Marcus Macer, but my hopes had soared for the briefest period of time at the thought I would be leaving Rome, so it was hard to hide my disappointment. I suppose Germanicus interpreted my expression correctly, because he said, "I apologize for that, Pullus. I can see now how that might have sounded."

While I appreciated the apology, it did not lessen the sting, but I decided to move on, and I asked him, "When will they be here?"

"Not until late April or early May," he told me. He paused then, so there was only the sound of hobnailed soles slapping against the paving stones. Then, he continued, "And as soon as the triumph and festivities are over, I'm leaving Rome." He lowered his voice. "It's not exactly a secret, but I'd prefer that you not spread around what I'm about to tell you." I assured him I would not, and he continued, "My father is sending me to the East on something of a...diplomatic tour of our provinces there. And, I'll be meeting with the kings of some of the countries who are of Friend and Ally status."

"For how long?" I asked, but he could only shrug and say vaguely, "As long as it takes, I suppose."

He was about to say something else when, to my utter horror, yet another group of lictors emerged from the *Domus*, but along with them came three other men, two of whom I instantly recognized by sight, while the other, a man in his fifties, I only knew by his likeness on the coins that I am paid with for my service to Rome.

"Pluto's..." Germanicus muttered, then he gave me an apologetic glance. "My father and I are addressing the Senate shortly, but I didn't know he'd be bringing Sejanus and his pet with us. I apologize again, Pullus. I know he's going to have something to say about it."

And, of course, Sejanus was already staring at me as he stood there, while Cinna stood just behind him, that fucking lip lifted again, although the expression on Sejanus' face was the one that concerned me more.

Once we were close enough, Sejanus inclined his head, "*Salve, Propraetor.*" Then, more coldly, "Pilus Prior Pullus, I confess I was...surprised to see that you weren't at your post here when you knew your Imperator was going to be leaving on his way to the Senate."

I was more startled than alarmed, but I was also massively confused, because Tiberius was standing no more than a dozen feet away, saying nothing and seemingly content to watch whatever was happening, while I wondered if I was supposed to salute the Imperator before I opened my mouth.

Before I could make a decision, my mouth made it for me as I blurted out, "That's because I wasn't told that the Imperator would be going to the Senate, Prefect."

"Oh?" Sejanus seemed surprised, except that instead of addressing me, he turned to Cinna, demanding, "Didn't you tell him when he relieved you, Cinna?"

And, without a flicker of hesitation or any other indication, Cinna lied, "Of course I did, Prefect. It was the first thing I told him when he reported to me. But," he held up a hand, "I also know that this is the Pilus Posterior's first time standing the most important posting in the Praetorians." He gave a laugh that was as artificial as his words. "I remember my first time. It's quite...overwhelming, so it's easy to see why it might have slipped his mind."

128

"It didn't slip my mind because you didn't tell me."

Gnaeus, you *fool*! You're doing exactly what they want! I saw the truth in Sejanus' sudden smile, and he opened his mouth.

"Your father served in the 1st, did he not?"

I turned to face Tiberius, but when I began to render a salute, he held up a hand.

"I'm no longer a Legate, Centurion. I'm simply the Princeps," he said. "And I don't need men bowing to me and behaving as if I was a King, because I'm not. Nor," I was certain his voice both raised a bit and hardened, "will there ever be a King in Rome."

He fell silent, so I took advantage by answering before Sejanus could say anything, "Yes, Princeps. My father did serve in the 1st, and under your direct command."

"I know that!" he snapped. "There's nothing wrong with my memory, Centurion!"

"Yes, Imperator. I apologize." The words tumbled out, for which I blame my addressing him as Imperator instead of Princeps. "I meant no disrespect nor to imply you wouldn't remember." If I hesitated, it was only for an eyeblink. "My father considered serving under you one of the greatest honors of his career, sir. He spoke of it often."

If I am being honest, Tiberius reminds me of a snapping turtle, with a great beak of a nose and something of an underbite, although I also know that this might be colored because I have read my father's account and he described him the same way.

I do not know if this mollified him or whether he was ready to move on, because he said, "Your father served Rome well, Centurion. And," he added, "on occasion, he served me personally just as faithfully as he did Rome." My stomach dropped all the way to my feet even before he asked, "Can his son be counted on to follow in his father's footsteps?"

It was one of the few times I was thankful for my toga because the sudden rush of sweat that covered my entire body did not show through, and while I kept my eyes on Tiberius, I saw Sejanus out of the corner of my vision as I answered immediately, "Of course, sir. I'm ready to serve Rome and you to the death."

Tiberius did not reply, though he did give an almost imperceptible nod, but then he turned to Germanicus and asked abruptly, "Do you have your words prepared, Germanicus?"

"Yes, Princeps," Germanicus assured him.

"Then we're wasting time," Tiberius said as he turned to begin walking, sending his dozen lictors scrambling, and to my surprise, Germanicus did not order his lictors to begin moving immediately.

Instead, he turned to Sejanus, and there was no mistaking the coldness in his tone as he extended a hand, "Go ahead, Prefect. You and...Cinna are part of the Princeps' party, not mine."

I was certain that his pause before using Cinna's name was meant as an insult, as if he either wanted to use another word or he could not remember his name, but even if he did not, just by Sejanus' reaction, it was easy to see he took it that way.

Nor could he do anything about it; as arrogant as I had already seen Sejanus is, he is no fool, so he knew better than to argue, although he did say, "As you wish, *Propraetor*," as if he was granting a request, then spun about and stalked away with Cinna in tow. When I glanced at Germanicus, I expected to see that he was angered by this, but he was clearly amused, although it did not last long. Once Sejanus and Cinna had hurried to catch up to Tiberius, where they were allowed to join the Imperator in the cordon of lictors, Germanicus then ordered his own eight lictors to begin moving.

"Walk with me a short way, Pullus," he commanded again. He lowered his voice so that I could barely hear him. "I apologize for that, Pullus. I had no intention of putting you in that position. Although," he sighed, "I suppose it was bound to happen sooner or later. Now that you're in the Praetorians, you're going to be around my father, and Sejanus is never far away. Even," he did not move his head, but I saw his eyes move to the right, then left, where a lictor was on either side of us, "when he's somewhere else."

"It's not necessary, sir," I lied.

"So have you settled in yet?" he asked, his voice back to a normal tone, and I told him about the place on the Caelian Hill. When I was finished, he frowned. "I'm familiar with the area, but I can't really place where you're living."

It seemed to be an idle question at the time, which I answered in more detail, explaining where it was in relation to the landmarks Romans use with their city, which are usually temples, fountains, and small parks.

"I won't delay you from your duty any longer, Pullus," he said when I finished. "Go back and keep the Palatine safe."

I knew he meant this humorously, so I offered a polite laugh, then moved outside the moving formation as, without looking back, Germanicus strode down the hill, heading for the Curia Julia where the Senate meets, while I returned to my Century, wondering glumly what consequences I could expect from essentially promising to kill for Tiberius, right in front of Sejanus.

I learned that Germanicus had not been asking out of curiosity that night, when there was a knock on the door, after dark, and after I had informed Sempronius he was not needed.

"Are you expecting anyone?" Alex asked, but I assured him that I was not.

We had quickly fallen into a routine where Alex, Algaia, and Iras spent their evenings in our apartment, where Alex and I played tables, while Algaia helped Bronwen sew pieces of clothing for Bronwen as she grew larger, for Iras as she grew larger, and for the coming baby, which I was growing increasingly nervous about with every passing day. And, in what had become something of a running joke, Bronwen issued her regular threat that that quantity of undyed, unfinished silk I had insisted on buying in Alexandria would be used only for the babe's diapers, which she found quite amusing. When the knock came that night, I did not draw my *gladius* because I had gotten in the habit of hanging the blade Scrofa made for me from a hook pounded into the wall next to the door that was normally used for wet cloaks, so I always opened the door with my left hand. Certainly, I was not sure what to expect, but seeing Lysander standing there was nowhere near the top of my imaginary list.

"Centurion," he looked up at me calmly enough, although he seemed amused at my openmouthed surprise. "May I come in?"

Stepping aside, Lysander entered the room, and while Alex was surprised as well, he had also heard the freedman scribe's voice, so he was able to offer the first verbal greeting, except that he immediately got down to business, saying, "I'd ask what brings you here, but Titus already told me about earlier today, so I suspect I know."

I introduced Lysander to Bronwen, while he greeted Algaia, having met her before, and Alex and I exchanged a surreptitious grin at the sight of his combination of surprise, and I am certain, envy.

"I had heard the stories," he bent and kissed Bronwen's hand as if she was a fine patrician lady, "but I didn't think it was possible that Pullus here could attract such a jewel."

"Yes," she answered, but she was looking at me with the expression I had learned meant she was feeling mischievous, "he is blessed by Fortuna to have me. Perhaps you could remind him, Lysander?"

By this time, I had witnessed Bronwen's talent for putting men both at ease, and being blunt, under her spell, and Lysander was no different, blushing deeply, although he also understood the game, turning on me.

"Really, Pullus," he said severely, "how could that be true, eh? If she were mine, I would remind her every day how precious she is to me!"

"I do!" I protested, then glared at Bronwen who, now that Lysander had turned back to me, stuck her tongue out at me.

The scribe's good humor faded away, and I asked him to sit at the table while, without being asked, Algaia and Bronwen left the room as Alex brought cups and the pitcher.

"I'm assuming that you know why I'm here," he began bluntly, even before he took a sip, which he partially explained by saying, "and I don't have much time. I lost the man following me, but he's going to be walking the streets, and I don't want to be seen leaving here."

While unsurprising, it was still alarming, and I was thankful that the women were out of the room. He did take a sip then as he formed his thoughts. "Clearly," he began, "what happened today was *not* something Germanicus wanted to happen, but now that it has, he's more concerned about you than ever."

"Why?" Alex asked, but he was looking at me, and I got the sense he thought I had left something out, but I assured him, "I told you everything that happened!"

"It was Tiberius who complicated matters," Lysander explained. "He told Germanicus later that he thought he had seen a *numen* when you walked up."

"He certainly didn't *seem* surprised," I commented.

"That's because he's Tiberius," Lysander replied. "He's had a lifetime of practice of keeping his thoughts and feelings hidden." This certainly made sense once I thought about it, and I gestured to him to continue. Now Lysander looked uncomfortable. "What Master Germanicus wants me to tell you is that, while Tiberius didn't say as much, Germanicus feels certain that someone will approach you on his behalf to bring you into his service for the same type of...things your father did for him."

"Sejanus," I groaned, but Lysander shook his head, and said adamantly, "It won't be Sejanus. Nor," he hurried on, "anyone associated with Sejanus."

"I thought Tiberius trusts Sejanus," Alex interjected. "The Prefect or someone attached to the Prefect would be the perfect choice, wouldn't it?"

Lysander did not answer directly, instead saying to Alex, "Remember when we talked a few weeks ago and I said there were things I knew and things I *thought* were happening?" Alex nodded. "Well, I've learned more since then, so there are some things that I thought were happening that have been confirmed." He stopped to take another sip, which reminded me to follow suit since my throat was threatening to close up. "While Sejanus was able to...extract a great deal of information from Tiberius Dolabella before he died, I've learned that there was one subject that Dolabella refused to give up." Lysander lifted his gaze from his cup to look me directly in the eye, "And while there were some other things, the one that matters to our discussion is that he never divulged to Sejanus what kind of things your father did for Tiberius. And," he gave a grim smile, "our Prefect is someone who does *not* handle not knowing everything well."

I confess that I was touched at this display by a man who, for most of their association, my father loathed, although during their last time together during the revolt, things had changed between them, which I learned from reading my father's account, but neither did I see the connection to me, and I said as much.

"Another thing that I have learned about Prefect Sejanus is that he has a *very* active imagination when it comes to things like plots and schemes," Lysander explained. "Couple that now with his frustration that he never learned exactly in what capacity your father worked for Tiberius, and the Princeps' words with you today, it means that there's something going on, and he doesn't know what it is, so he's going to be watching you even more closely."

By this point, I was expecting Lysander to say as much, but I suppose I was trying to look at the bright side by commenting, "Well, he can watch, but that doesn't mean that Tiberius has any kind of plans for me."

It was the manner in which Lysander suddenly looked down at his cup that wrenched a groan, but I looked at Alex, hoping for some sort of assurance that perhaps I was reading the scribe incorrectly.

Lysander took a deep breath then said carefully, "While Germanicus told me that the Princeps didn't say as much, the questions he asked Germanicus on their walk back from the Senate about you convinced the *Propraetor* that you can expect a visitor from Tiberius."

I was too stunned to say anything, but Alex spoke for me when he said, "What does Germanicus want Titus to do if and when that happens? What is he supposed to tell whoever shows up?"

Whereas Lysander had seemed unsettled before, he suddenly looked acutely uncomfortable.

I learned why, when, breaking his gaze on me, he looked back into his cup as he said, very slowly, "Germanicus says that ultimately the decision is up to you, and that you should follow your conscience." He stopped then, but I sensed there was more coming, and I was right when he resumed, "Having said that, he also told me to remind you that, while Tiberius is a fair man, he is *not* a forgiving man."

"So," I could not keep the bitterness out of my voice, "I actually have no fucking choice if I want to live to an old age."

I got my answer in Lysander's silence, and I gulped down the cup of wine I had been sipping.

"How do you think this will affect things with Sejanus?" Alex asked.

This seemed to lighten Lysander's demeanor slightly, but he addressed his answer to Alex's question to me. "Actually, I think that in regard to Sejanus and whatever designs he might have to engineer anything to damage your career, you're going to be safer rather than in more danger." He held up a hand. "As long as you don't say no," he cautioned.

"Like I said, no fucking choice."

Lysander left shortly after that, after which Alex and I quietly debated about how much to tell the women. Of course, as we quickly learned, there was no need for discussion, because we were still in the middle of the discussion when the door opened and both of them walked in, Bronwen leading the way.

"You know what you must do, Titus," she said simply as she dropped onto the bench next to me and grabbed my cup.

"Were you listening at the door?" I demanded, only partially feigning being irritated about it.

"Of course." She laughed. "Did you *really* think I would not?"

"No, I suppose not. But next time, can't you at least give me time so that I can pretend to be thinking about telling you?"

"I will consider it." Her lips were curved up as she lifted the cup to her mouth. Any sign of levity was gone when she set it down, and in fact, she looked anxious. "But you know that I am right, do you not, my love? You know that you must agree to whatever Tiberius wants from you."

I realized then that she was truly concerned that I might reject this offer for some reason, so I squeezed her arm as I assured her, "Yes, I know, *meum mel*. I'm not going to pretend that I'm happy about it, or that I wouldn't like to say no, if only because now that I've read my father's account, it was something he was ashamed of doing. But," I could not help sighing, "he didn't have a choice then, and I don't have a choice now."

The knock on the door never came, but that does not mean a message from Tiberius was not sent. It was the identity of the messenger and how it was delivered that it took me some time to come to terms with, and I suppose in some ways I still am struggling with it. It was the day after our duty on the Palatine, and I had scheduled my Century's time at the stakes, which only Sabinus knew would be the last time because I was about to change things again. In general, I was pleased with the progress that my Century had made, but I had not been expecting the level of enthusiasm they displayed once they got over their soldiers' grumbling about being made to do something new. More than once, the thought crossed my mind that it was as if these pampered pets had always yearned to be more than that, to actually do the kind of job for which the Legions are made. Naturally, there were exceptions, men like Flaccus who were perfectly content with shining their helmets and varnishing their leathers as being the most strenuous activity in their daily routine. Thanks to men like Valerius, the veteran of the 8th, who worked on and with their comrades during their copious off-duty time, these laggards and complainers were in the minority, and it was thanks to my veterans, few in number as they were, that the moaning and complaining of men like Flaccus was muted and did not reach my ears. Or, so they believed, anyway, since I had long before learned the value in a Centurion either ignoring or pretending not to know as much about their men as the men thought. All in all, I was actually in a good mood when we secured from duty that day, and as had become my habit, I headed for the bathhouse that was directly across the street from our barracks that was for our exclusive use. Feeling clean and refreshed, I begged off a game of tables that Phillipus was trying to goad me into, mainly because he is a better player than I am, and I left the bathhouse, whereupon I ran into none other than Marcus Sempronius, which I considered a happy accident.

"I'm glad that I ran into you, Sempronius," I said after we greeted each other. "I actually was hoping I could hire you for something."

At that moment, I did not notice the subtle but unmistakable change in Marcus Sempronius, nor was I forewarned when he said, "Would you mind if we kept walking to your apartment, Centurion?" Not suspecting anything, I agreed, but before I could bring up what I had thought of for him to do, he said, "And before you tell me what you have in mind, Centurion, I have a confession to make."

Oh, I was certainly somewhat disturbed at his words, but it was a shade compared to how I was feeling not much later.

"And what's that?" I did not falter in my stride, while my tone was not completely cordial.

"When you saw me outside the gates of Rome, it wasn't by accident," he began, and this caused me to look down at him, but his eyes were on a pair of men ahead of us carrying a wooden crate between them. "I had been waiting there for you."

"Why?" It was all that came to mind to ask, honestly.

"I was sent there on orders," he replied, and he seemed remarkably calm for someone who was essentially admitting he had gained my acquaintance through false pretenses.

Truthfully, when I thought about it later, this was where I got the first idea that there might be a connection to the events of the day before.

Still, I was confused, repeating, "On orders? Whose orders?"

He did not answer me, choosing to continue staring straight ahead, but now I did slow as my mind finished putting the pieces together. I was about to say it for him, but I had what I suppose was a divine inspiration, because the name I supplied was, "Sejanus. You're working for Sejanus, aren't you?"

I got my reward, and confirmation, by the manner in which he turned his gaze away from ahead of us to look up at me directly, and if he was not truly surprised, he deserves a place on the stage.

"No, Centurion!" He shook his head adamantly. "I do *not* work for Prefect Sejanus! You must believe me!"

The fact was that I did believe him, yet I was also angry about his deception, which was why I refused to indicate that as I demanded in a cold voice, "Why the fuck should I trust anything that comes out of your mouth, Sempronius? Or," it occurred to me, "is that even your real name?"

To his credit, Sempronius did not flinch, and he was looking up into my eyes as he acknowledged, "There's no real reason that you should, Centurion." He spread his arms out. "And whether you believe me is your decision, and I know that there's nothing I could say that would help you in that."

I decided to resume walking because we were beginning to get curious glances from the people passing by; it is one of my least favorite things about Rome, how you are never alone whenever you are outside, and are always surrounded by people, although I actually felt more comfortable around the Head Counters than I did with people of the order I was once a part of, which I ascribe to my time under the standard.

Once we were moving again, I said, "Let's say that I believe that you're working for…" I caught myself before I said his name, which I saw Sempronius recognized, acknowledging as much with a nod. "That still doesn't answer the question of why you were waiting for us. Although," I said this to myself, albeit aloud, "now it makes sense why you always seemed to show up."

"Centurion, I wasn't told why," Sempronius answered, then he countered, not in a contentious manner, "How often are you told why you've been given orders by a superior?"

"Not often," I had to admit, though I did not like it all that much.

He surprised me then by continuing, "If I had to guess, it was because he was concerned about your wellbeing once you were in Rome."

For the second time, I came to an abrupt stop, completely forgetting myself.

"*Gerrae*! That's ridiculous! I didn't even know he was aware of my existence until yesterday!"

"Centurion." Sempronius had to stop as well, and he glanced about before he asked, "Do you remember what they said about Divus Augustus? I mean, as far as how much he knew?"

I did, and I repeated something I have heard more times than I can count. "He knew about a sparrow falling in the Forum even before it hit the ground."

"My master learned a great deal from Divus Augustus." He resumed walking, which irritated me further, but we were at the base of the Caelian Hill, and it is a bit more open down in the bottom, so I made a couple of long strides to catch up in order to be surrounded by buildings. He resumed by allowing, "And my master is a...complicated man, Centurion. In fact," he gave a humorless chuckle, "the truth is I very rarely ever know his mind when he uses me and for what purpose. Which," his tone audibly changed to the point I looked at him, "is probably better for me. And for anyone who works for him, for that matter."

"Which," I was growing tired of this dance, "is why you just 'happened' to be waiting for me outside the baths, eh? You're speaking on his behalf?"

"Yes," Sempronius answered simply.

"What would I have to do?"

Now Sempronius' voice hardened, just a fraction, but noticeably. "Whatever he orders you to do, Centurion. Just like you would have to follow his orders if you were on the Rhenus."

This was nothing but the truth, as unpalatable as it may have been, yet I still only grudgingly acknowledged it, then I asked, "When?"

"When what?" Sempronius frowned, then his face cleared. "Ah, I understand." He shrugged. "I have no idea, Centurion. In fact, he may never call on you at all."

This made me laugh, although it was just as humorless as his had been a moment earlier.

"Would you care to wager on that, Sempronius?"

"No, Centurion." He did not laugh, but he did smile. "That wouldn't be a wise wager."

"And I suppose that you'll be the one to relay them to me?"

"Yes," he said immediately, but then he went on, "and in fact, I was going to warn you of something." We had just reached the end of the first block on the lowest part of the hill, and Sempronius suddenly sidestepped into a narrow alley. Naturally, I followed, but I was on my guard, which I made clear by putting my hand on the hilt of my *gladius* through the sewn-in slit in my toga that Creticus had suggested. He pretended not to notice, but despite being out of the traffic, he still lowered his voice. "It's possible that the Prefect might try and determine your real purpose here by sending you someone you don't know who claims to be sent by my master. Do *not* believe them, because I will be the only one who will ever come to you with some sort of orders."

Even as he said this, I recalled that the same was true with my father; he only dealt with Tiberius Dolabella and nobody else.

Consequently, I answered, "I understand, and I'll remember that." I was struck by a thought, and I asked, "Do you know a man named Marcus Livinius Appius?"

His reaction was immediate, and I was certain unfeigned, his mouth twisting into a sneer, then he spat on the ground as he made the sign.

"I know that *cunnus*," he snarled. "And I owe him a fucking debt that I swear on the black stone that I'll repay in a way he'll never forget!" He took a breath, then in a calmer voice, he said, "He works for Prefect Sejanus." Glancing up at me, he asked, "I take it that you've met him?" I described our meeting at the Forum, and when I was finished, he nodded and said contemptuously, "Yes, that's our Marcus all right. He smiles a lot and is always friendly, at first. Did he make that joke about being a poor relation of the Appius family?" This made me chuckle, and I told him that I had indeed been subjected to that joke. "But he's still dangerous, Centurion. And," he hesitated, which I understood why when he said, "from now on, I need to be informed whenever you're approached, either by Appius or someone else. Although," he mused, "knowing the Prefect, he's unlikely to send Appius again."

"I'll let you know whoever it is," I assured him.

Thinking that he was through, I turned to get out of the alley, but he caught me by the toga.

"Centurion, I know that you have no reason to trust me, but there's something I want you to know," he began. When I said nothing, he continued, and I was completely unprepared to hear him say, "Tiberius Dolabella was a friend, but he was also something of a...mentor to me when I first began in our master's service. And," he continued, "I've been wanting to tell you for some time that he considered your father one of the greatest men he ever met, and he was happy at the end of his life that they had become friends. Although," he said bitterly, "he didn't know he was near the end of his days, thanks to Sejanus."

Suddenly, I recalled the circumstances of our meeting outside the gates, and how he had known about my family. While I cannot say that it convinced me he was being sincere, neither could I deny that it made sense now that I knew at least part of the truth.

Not really knowing what to say, I finally managed awkwardly, "Well, I'm sure they're together across the river now, arguing about something or other. And I do know that my father considered him a friend after they came back from Pannonia."

"I just wanted you to know that," he said.

Then he led the way out of the alley, but when we reached the door of the apartment, I told him, "I'm not inviting you in, Sempronius."

I could see that while he did not like it, he also understood, and he hurried down the street as I watched, knowing that I was stalling for time before I had to face the others. Finally, I entered through the outer door and ascended the stairs, finding, as expected, the other three occupying themselves.

Alex glanced up from his scroll and saw enough in my expression to understand something had happened.

"Someone approached you," he said instantly, which naturally caught the attention of Bronwen and Algaia.

"Yes." I nodded, then took my time unwrapping my toga, which I draped across the back of a chair, which as I knew it would, got Bronwen on her feet to go pick it up and take it into our bedroom while saying things in her tongue that I have never asked her to translate. I dropped onto the bench, waiting until she returned before I began, "Yes, I have been approached." I stopped, briefly wondering whether or not I should tell them, then I realized it was inevitable they would find out anyway. "And it was by Marcus Sempronius."

That was the last relatively quiet moment for the next span of time, and naturally, it engendered a very lively debate, since Bronwen's initial reaction, with Algaia's fervent agreement, was that I should cut Sempronius' tongue out. As I had been informed by Bronwen, this is the traditional punishment for a man who lies after taking an oath in the Parisii tribe, but from the way it sounded, either Algaia's Bructeri do this as well or she just thought it was a good idea all around. Only Alex remained quiet, and while I was engaged with my woman and his wife, I kept my eye on him as he sat there with that frown that tells me he is thinking things through. The women gradually subsided in their invective for Sempronius, who I freely confess I did not go to any length to defend, and they became focused on Alex along with me as he sat there with his head bowed as if he was praying.

Finally, he lifted it, and I was surprised to see a slight smile on his face, which he explained, "This actually gives us an opportunity, Titus."

I heard Algaia's gasp, but while I did not, I was no less surprised; it had been almost a year since the last time Alex had mistakenly called me by my father's name, and he turned a deep red, but when he opened his mouth, I asked quietly, "What's the opportunity?"

By the time he was finished, I had forgotten all about his mistake, because I knew he was right.

"I've decided to replace one of my clerks," I informed Creticus the next day. "Effective immediately."

I was not surprised in the least at the unhappy expression that came over the man's face, but he did not immediately begin protesting, instead choosing to ask, "Why is that?"

"Because I don't trust him," I answered immediately, which was the truth. "And I've found several mistakes in his accounts with the Century that lead me to believe he's skimming from the men."

That *may* have been true, at least the last part, but I did not really have any evidence to believe this was going on, and I suppose the use of the word "several" is a relative term; I had caught four arithmetic errors, which Alex had confirmed when I brought the ledgers home.

"Which clerk is this?" Creticus asked cautiously.

"Diodorus," I answered, and his reaction both warned me and confirmed my suspicions.

"You can't replace Diodorus!" He gasped, shaking his head as he said it.

"Why not?" I asked pleasantly. Then I threw the dice because I had actually not done so beforehand, "Perhaps you could show me in the regulations where it says that a Centurion can't select his own clerks? Is it different in the Praetorians?"

"Well, no," Creticus answered unhappily. "It's more of a...practice that the Prefect provides the Pilus Prior of each Cohort with a list of names, and then we allow our Centurions to choose."

"So it's *not* a regulation," I pressed.

"I said it wasn't," he snapped. Then he raised his voice to command, "Leave the Pilus Posterior and me alone!" I heard the scrape of chairs, and he added, "Be where I can call you when I need you back!" He waited until we heard the door close before he sat back in his chair and tossed the stylus he had been fiddling with down as he asked, "What are you up to, Pullus? What's your game?"

"My game?" I echoed, pretending to be confused. "I'm not sure what you mean, Pilus Prior."

"Why," he at least tried to sound patient, "do you seem determined to antagonize the Prefect?"

"That's certainly not my intention, Pilus Prior," I assured him. Then I took another roll of the dice, trusting my instinct that, while Creticus was not a strong leader, neither was he in Sejanus' purse. "In fact, I want to do the opposite. I want my Century to be the best Century in the best Cohort of the Praetorian Guard. Surely the Prefect doesn't object to that."

"While I appreciate your enthusiasm, Pullus, as I recall, I did warn you that the Praetorians aren't the Legions."

"Maybe they should be," I said without thinking, but he surprised me then.

"Believe me, Pullus, you're not the first man to say that. And," he allowed, "I don't necessarily disagree. But that's not the reality." He heaved a sigh, then said, "I'm not going to stop you, Pullus. But," he warned, "if the Prefect asks me, I *will* tell him that I warned you that this is highly unusual."

I thanked him, saluted, then left. Walking into my Century office, I wasted no time with Diodorus.

"Pack your things," I told him. "You're being replaced."

For a moment, he looked disposed to argue, but he quickly realized this would be a bad idea, although he did ask, "Where am I supposed to go, Centurion?"

It was, I instantly realized, a fair question, because Diodorus was a slave, not a freedman, which I should have thought about, because Demetrios was a freedman. However, Sabinus had never warned me about Demetrios, but he had about Diodorus, and not for making errors in his accounts.

I chose to take the coward's way out, telling him, "Report to Pilus Prior Creticus. Maybe he has some use for you."

I watched as he gathered his belongings, and I allowed him to use a box that we store tablets in. Once he left, I waited a few moments, then I left the office, exited the barracks, and walked down the street to the fountain, where Alex was standing, with a slightly larger box.

"It's done," I said, and he followed me back to my office. It was just before I opened the door when I remembered something, and I winced at the idea of telling him, but I turned and said, "I forgot to tell you the other clerk's name. It's," I swallowed, "Demetrios."

For a moment, I thought he was going to turn around and leave, but instead, he gave me a glare and muttered something about the gods, then I opened the door.

I expected some sort of confrontation the next day, anticipating that I would be summoned to the *Domus* to stand in front of Sejanus, but nothing happened, nor did it the next day. Initially, I ascribed it to the fact that, rather than send Diodorus back to Sejanus for reassignment, Creticus had simply added him as part of his staff, so the First Century had three clerks instead of two. Nevertheless, I was certain that there would be some sort of reckoning, but the fact is that I am still waiting for it to happen; although, I should amend, I am still waiting for a reckoning about Alex in particular. Who, as I expected, immediately discovered several areas of improvement in the running of the Century, to the point where a month after his arrival, Creticus summoned me to his office.

"Whatever your freedman is doing," he told me, "I want him to teach it to the other clerks, including mine. Your Century is the only one where I never have to wait on reports, and there are never any errors caught by the Prefect's staff."

Naturally, I was happy to comply, and as I knew would happen, by the time he was finished, two weeks later, he knew almost as much about each Century, and most importantly, their Centurions and Optios. Best of all, however, was that he did it so skillfully that none of them suspected anything.

"Atticus is the most crooked," he informed me once he had consulted his notes back at the apartment. "He's skimming, but he's very clever about it, and in fact, when compared to some of the Centurions back in the Legions, he's not very greedy." When I speculated why this was, Alex had an answer, "Because he thinks he's cleverer than the rest of you, and this is his way of demonstrating that."

"But not if nobody knows about it," I protested, not seeing the point, but Alex was adamant.

"That's what it's about with him, Gnaeus. He's proving it to himself and nobody else. Which," I remember hearing a note of respect, "*is* clever."

Moving on, he continued, "With Rufus, it's the opposite. It's not that he's slow-witted, but his chief clerk Menander is one of the slyest clerks I've come across, maybe even better than Patricius." I did not recall the name immediately, but he reminded me, "He was the chief clerk for Maluginensus, remember? And after Maluginensus died, he vanished?"

I did recall Patricius then; he had been the clerk to the Tertius Pilus Prior Maluginensus, whose cowardice had been a contributing factor in the death of my father. I also remembered that, in the aftermath of the events after our rescue of Segestes, this clerk had vanished in the night, taking what we had heard was ten thousand *sesterces* that he had been skimming over the dozen years he had been the clerk.

"Did you tell Creticus' clerk?" I asked, and he shook his head.

"I wanted to talk to you about it first, but it can wait." He moved on, "But as far as his Centurion, I think Rufus is one of the men you can trust. He's been unhappy his entire time in the Praetorians, for the same reasons as you, that we're not soldiers." This aligned with my sense about him, and I nodded for him to continue. "Phillipus is another man I think you can trust, but I also think that he's not quite as...solid," was the word he used, "as he should be."

"How so?" I asked, not understanding.

He did not reply immediately, thinking about how to answer, then he finally said, "His intentions are good, I think. I just don't know if Sejanus puts pressure on him in some way that he'd be able to withstand it. I learned from one of his clerks that his transfer from the 3rd was due to some...irregularities that were occurring in his Cohort." This alarmed me, but he hurried on, "Not because of what he was doing, but because of what his Pilus Prior was doing. And," his tone turned ominous, "the Pilus Prior was found guilty based on the evidence that Phillipus provided."

I considered this for a moment, but I was not really accepting Alex's premise.

"That sounds to me like he saw his Pilus Prior committing some sort of wrongdoing, and he came forward about it."

"That," Alex granted, "is one way to look at it. And," he added, "another way to look at it is that he provided the Legate in command with information based on the promise of a promotion to the Praetorians."

This earned him a glare from me, only because the instant he said it, I considered this as just as likely an explanation.

"You know," I told him, "sometimes, I really don't like you very much."

As I hoped, this made him laugh.

"Don't blame me for thinking like a member of the upper orders," he shot back. By silent consent, he moved on, "Plancus is one I worry about."

"How so?"

"Because his clerks say all the right things about him, as far as how he performs his duties, and how he approaches being a Praetorian. But," he shook his head, "I can't put my finger on it. I just think that there's something else going on with him that bears watching."

"If I'm hearing you correctly, you're telling me to guard my tongue around Plancus. At least until I have a better idea of what he's about."

"Exactly." Alex nodded, and his obvious relief that I had understood him irritated me a bit.

"I'm not thick, you know," I growled. "You don't need to explain everything to me like you would Iras."

He was completely unimpressed, and he retorted, "Oh, I know that you're clever enough. It's not your mind that's the problem, it's your temper."

I did not try to argue, if only because there was nothing I could say to refute it.

As May approached, the tension within not just the Second Cohort but the entirety of the Praetorian Guard noticeably increased, to the point that I broached the subject at our weekly meeting of all Centurions of the Second. I will confess that I did not mention my excitement and anticipation at the thought of reuniting with my friends, and seeing the men of the Fourth Cohort again, although as I look back, I realize there was no need, since I have never been very good at hiding my emotions.

Creticus bore his usual expression at everything I asked, as if it pained him to have to talk about it, but he answered readily enough, albeit with a question. "Pullus, what do the Legions of the Army of the Rhenus think about the Praetorians?"

I was surprised, if only because the two Cohorts of Praetorians Germanicus had brought with him for the last part of our campaign against Arminius had acquitted themselves well.

"We, I mean, they," I corrected myself, "thought that the Praetorians performed well with Germanicus. And," I allowed somewhat hesitantly as I thought about it more, "there was some surprise at that."

"Do you know which Cohorts they were?" Creticus asked,

which was when I got a glimmer of where he might be heading.

"As I recall, it was the Seventh and Eighth Cohorts," I answered cautiously.

"You are correct in your recollection," Creticus confirmed, but he was not done. "Those are two of the Cohorts who aren't permanently stationed in Rome." He hesitated, and I noticed that he actually glanced over at Atticus before he continued, "And let's just say that you would probably have enjoyed being under the command of either of the Pili Priori a bit more than with me, because they're both veterans of the Legions."

I still was not understanding the connection, but Creticus waved a hand at Atticus, who explained, "One reason Germanicus requested those two Cohorts in particular was because he knew that being away from Rome meant that they weren't under the...influence," I instantly noticed how carefully he used the word, "of the Prefect as the Cohorts here in Rome are."

"So they're trained to fight and not just look pretty."

For perhaps the thousandth time, my tongue got ahead of my mind, but the damage was done, at least as far as Creticus was concerned, who interjected, "Frankly, Pullus, the attitude you're displaying right now is what concerns us. When the Legions arrive, they'll be kept outside the walls certainly, because they can't cross the *pomerium* until the day of the triumph as Legions." I barely contained myself from laughing at this nod to the ancient laws of Rome that the men in power have ignored since before I was born, but somehow I managed. "However," he continued, either ignoring or missing my incredulous expression, "it's very unlikely that the Imperator will forbid these men from entering Rome during their free time individually and in small groups. And," he actually pointed at me, "you *know* that no Primus Pilus worth his salt would ban men who will be marching in a triumph to celebrate their victory from coming into the city in the days before the actual triumph." This was true, so I did not bother even trying to deny it, and Creticus continued, "What your fellow Centurions," he corrected himself, "what *I* and your fellow Centurions are concerned about is what's going to happen when your former comrades show up in the *tavernae*, and the brothels, and the races while our rankers are there."

Frankly, I was embarrassed, for the simple reason that it was so obviously a cause for concern, and I had missed it.

This was what prompted me to admit, "I should have thought of that. And," I hesitated, wondering if it was politic to do so, "you're all right to be concerned." Rather than be happy to have their judgment confirmed, what I saw instead were unhappy glances at each other, which served as a reminder that I still was not really a part of this group. And, I acknowledged to myself, I may never be. Nevertheless, I felt as if I owed it to them to try and explain, although I chose my words carefully. "The Army of the Rhenus has been involved in the hardest fighting of our lifetimes."

Before I could continue, Creticus interjected, asking skeptically, "Compared to the Batonian Revolt?"

This put me in a potentially delicate position, since I had a unique insight into that rebellion thanks to my father's service in the *Legio Germanicus* and his account of it, but I thought I could explain without divulging too much.

"What you may not know is that my father was with Germanicus during the Batonian Revolt," I began, and I saw by Creticus' and the others' reactions they had been unaware of this, and I decided to take advantage of that by lying. "And I actually asked him which was the tougher campaign, against Bato and the Pannonian tribes, or Arminius. What he told me was that, while there was one battle that was the toughest fight he had ever been in, when they took a town that the Pannonians set fire to themselves, campaigning against Arminius was different, because he had served Rome and knew our way of fighting." I paused then, and seeing their heads nodding in acceptance, I returned to the original subject. "It's because of that that the Rhenus Legions are a bit..." I tried to think of a word other than the one that had popped into my head, "...unruly," I said, instead of "wild." "Between the revolt..."

"Which you were a part of," Creticus interjected, and while this was technically true in the sense that I was serving in the 1st at the time of the rebellion by the bulk of the Armies of the Rhenus and Pannonia, his tone ignited that flame deep inside my belly.

"I was *present* during the rebellion," I countered, trying to keep my tone just respectful enough, yet also sending him the message that I did not appreciate his words, "but that doesn't mean I was part of it."

Surprisingly, Creticus' reaction was one of embarrassment.

"I apologize, Pullus," he said quickly. "I realized how that sounded, but that wasn't my intent."

Nodding my thanks, I had continued thinking, and my heart began sinking downward as I realized that their concerns were completely justified.

This was what prompted me to allow, "But I think that it's going to be inevitable that there will be some trouble between us and the…" I almost said "Praetorians" but caught myself in time, "…and the Rhenus boys."

"Unless," Creticus countered, "you use your influence with your former Primus Pilus. What's his name?"

"Sacrovir," I answered, realizing this had been Creticus' purpose all along. "Primus Pilus Sacrovir. But that's just one Legion, Pilus Prior. As I understand it, half of the Army of the Rhenus is coming, which means four Legions will be here in and around Rome."

"I understand that," Creticus answered irritably, "but we need to do whatever we can to make sure that we show the Prefect that we're not the ones who are the instigators, and in fact we tried to keep the peace."

"I'll do my best, Pilus Prior," I promised.

The meeting ended immediately after that, and as I filed out with the others, I thought, so *that* was what this was about. Once again, it was about appeasing Sejanus, not Tiberius. This led me to a recognition that, when it came down to it, at least the Second Praetorian Cohort was more afraid of Sejanus than they were of Tiberius.

Chapter 4

Certainly I had heard about what marching in a triumph was like, although the only firsthand account I had encountered was from my great-grandfather, when the Equestrians had marched in four in succession. With the passing of time, it has become accepted as fact that the roots of what befell Divus Julius were sown with his penultimate triumph, celebrating the defeat at Thapsus, because that victory was over other Romans and not an enemy of Rome. Frankly, after reading about how Caesar had ordered the construction of a diorama that depicted Cato's botched disembowelment, where he was depicted pulling his own guts out of his body, I tend towards accepting this view. There had been two triumphs for Tiberius, one for his actions in Germania the year after his brother Drusus died, my father's first campaign when he was decorated by Drusus for his slaying of Vergorix, and the second for his role in crushing the Pannonian tribes during the Batonian Revolt while Divus Augustus was still alive, but I did not know anyone aside from Titus Domitius who had participated in the second one. For the Centurions of the marching Legions, it would be a period of time where they got little sleep, since every Primus Pilus would insist that the men of his Legion outshine the others, but this was where I got a pleasant surprise, because as far as the Praetorians were concerned, this was simply another day in the life of a Praetorian. I suppose I should acknowledge that, in that sense, Sejanus' apparent obsession with our appearance paid dividends in the form of not putting much more effort into our preparations. This turned out to be a good thing, because on a night a month before the triumph and a week before the scheduled arrival of my comrades and the other Legions, five days after the Ides of April, Bronwen wakened me with a sharp elbow to the ribs.

"My waters have broken," she just managed to get out before she let out a sharp cry of pain, but I was already up and moving.

I ran downstairs, but I was met by Algaia, who had heard Bronwen's scream, emerging from their apartment before I had finished descending the stairs. Alex's wife charged up the stairway, shoving me aside as if I was an obstacle to be overcome, which I suppose I was.

"Go get Terentia," she said over her shoulder. "She knows to be ready."

Terentia was, after several interviews with other candidates, all of whom had been rejected by Algaia and Bronwen for one reason or another, the midwife who would help bringing my babe into the world.

Algaia had moved so quickly that when I called out, "How do I get to her *insula*? I don't know the way!" I was speaking to nobody.

"I do. I had Algaia write out the directions." I spun about to see Alex, standing outside his apartment at the base of the stairs with an oil lamp in one hand and a tablet in the other. Most importantly, he had taken the time to put on his boots. "Go back upstairs, Gnaeus. I'll get Terentia."

Since he is sitting here across from me as I dictate this, I know that even if I did not recount my actions that night, he would find a way to insert it. Consequently, when Alex told me to go upstairs, I would liken my reaction to it being the same as if I had been ordered to assault a band of Cherusci all by myself, unarmed.

"What am I supposed to do?" I called out.

"Nothing but stay out of the way!"

Alex had to shout this because he was already leaving the building, and I will admit that I stood there on the steps, debating whether or not I should do the prudent thing and go hide somewhere. But then, Bronwen cried out again, this time with an edge to it that simultaneously got me moving and stabbed me with fear as I dashed up the stairs and into the apartment. The door to the bedroom was open, and Algaia had taken the time to ignite one of the lamps, the light spilling into the main room.

"Gnaeus," she called out. "Come here. Bronwen needs you."

With the light, I saw the sheen of sweat on my woman's face, but it was the expression in her eyes that look like emeralds that is seared into my mind, because they were wide with fear, and when she extended her hand towards me, I rushed to take it.

"You stay with her while I get things ready," Algaia instructed, and I knelt by the bed so that I was not towering over her.

As soon as Algaia was out of the room, Bronwen whispered, "Gnaeus, I am scared."

So was I, all of the stories about the Pullus women who did not survive bringing us into the world rushing into my mind, but I tried to keep that from my voice as I assured her, "You're in good hands, *meum mel*. And you're strong and healthy."

"Because I am a barbarian." She actually gave me a smile as she said it, reminding me of the times I had slipped up early in our relationship when referring to native tribes.

"Why do you think I chose you?" I smiled back. "You barbarians are tough."

"*You* chose *me*?" she began, but then her body tensed, and she let out another cry of pain, cutting off what I am certain would be a correction about who did the choosing of the other.

Despite my joking tone, I was serious about Bronwen's strength, which I felt as she gripped my hand so tightly that I had to bite my lip to keep from yelping like a pup, knowing I would never hear the end of it. This spasm seemed to last longer, and was intense enough to make her start panting, which I supposed was an effort to dissipate the pain.

"That was two hundred," Algaia called out from the kitchen, and now there was light in the other room, but from the way it danced against the wall, I knew she had lit the fire in the stove.

"Two hundred what?" I asked of Algaia, raising my voice to be heard because of the distance.

"Heartbeats," Bronwen answered for her. "This is how we know when the babe will come."

Her grip had relaxed a bit, and I desperately wanted to let go of her hand so I could flex my fingers a bit, which felt as if they had been caught between two heavy stones, but instead, I tried to distract the both of us.

"So have you decided on what to name her if it's a girl?"

Once more, she smiled weakly, this time at my concession in what had been a long-running debate about how, as *paterfamilias*, I was the one who decided on the names for all of my children, which Bronwen had countered by saying that she was not Roman, and the Parisii had a different custom, the woman having the responsibility for selecting the name for female infants. I had refused to give in, but only because it had become more a source of amusement for both of us than a real bone of contention; besides, I had resigned myself months before that I would lose this debate. And honestly, I have my suspicions whether this is actually the case with the Parisii, but since she is the only one I know, I have to take her word for it.

She surprised me greatly, when she said shyly, "I was thinking that Giulia would be a good name."

Before I could reply, we were interrupted with the arrival of Terentia and the coming of another spasm. I had never laid eyes on the midwife before, but I suppose I had formed some image in my mind of a crone, bent with age, probably toothless, which meant that when the woman was brought into the room by Algaia, I was completely unprepared to see a woman who was perhaps in her mid-thirties, with pleasant features and a slight smile on her face.

"The midwife is here," I announced.

In between her panting, Bronwen managed, "I am pregnant, not blind, Gnaeus!"

There was anger in her voice then, but Algaia did not seem surprised, and she told me briskly, "All right, your part is done, Gnaeus. Now go into the other room. Or," she added, "perhaps you and Alex go downstairs to our apartment."

My retreat was as hasty as it was welcomed by me, but I did lean over to give Bronwen a kiss on the forehead, and I was disturbed by the clammy feel of her brow but decided that since neither Algaia nor Terentia seemed alarmed, it was normal. Alex was standing there in the main room, but when he turned and headed for the door, I stopped him.

"I'm staying up here," I told him. "I want to be close by if she needs me."

While Alex came back to drop onto the bench on the other side of the table, he assured me, "I can't count the number of times my mother and Algaia have reminded me of just how useless men are when it comes to childbirth. But," he lowered his voice, "I didn't want to be anywhere else when Iras was born."

I noticed that, along with heating a basin of water, Algaia had refilled the pitcher of wine that we kept on the table as well as putting two cups out, so I filled one, handed it to Alex, then as I filled the other, for the first time, I voiced my fear in a whisper. "You know why I'm worried, don't you? I mean, more than a man would normally worry?"

"I do," he replied gravely. Lifting his cup, he said, "Which is why Algaia has been making offerings to Juno Lucina and Magna Mater every day for the last two weeks, and today, she went out and found a small temple to Egeria in the Subura, and she made an offering there as well."

I cannot say I was happy with the thought of Algaia being alone in the Subura, although she had obviously returned unharmed, but I was more concerned with the timing.

"You mean she knew that Bronwen's waters would break tonight?"

"If not tonight, then tomorrow." He shrugged. "Or maybe the next day."

"How do they know that kind of thing?" I wondered, and this did make Alex laugh.

"Gnaeus, once we cross the river and we learn just how much more women know than men, I think we're going to feel like utter fools."

Despite my best attempts, I dozed off, which I had thought impossible because of Bronwen's cries, but I came awake when Bronwen issued her shrillest, sharpest cry, jerking upright from where I had been dozing with my head on the table. I looked at Alex in alarm, but before he could say anything, there was another sound, a squalling cry of what sounded like angry protest that was also the sweetest music I had ever heard. Naturally, I jumped to my feet and headed for our bedroom, where I was met by Algaia, who for the second time shoved me, this time out of the bedroom instead of the main room.

"Not yet," she said firmly. "We'll call you when Bronwen is ready."

"Is she all right?" I asked, and to my intense relief, Algaia obviously understood there was more to my question.

"She did well, Gnaeus," she assured me. "It was a...difficult birth, but she was never in danger. And the baby is healthy."

If it had been in front of Terentia, who was out of sight somewhere in the bedroom, I would have behaved differently and not collapsed to my knees as my eyes filled with tears, but I consider Algaia as much of a family member as those who were born with the Pullus name, so I felt no shame at doing so. I suspect I was babbling, thanking every god I could think of, and I felt her hand on my head for a moment as I did so, but when she removed her hand, that was when the other important thing occurred to me.

"And? What is it? A boy or a girl?"

"You don't think I'd tell you and not let Bronwen do it, do you?"

To my ears, she sounded obscenely cheerful, but she shut the door so quickly that I could not have offered a rejoinder even if I had thought of one. Climbing to my feet, I turned back and returned to the table as I wiped my eyes, where Alex was waiting with a cup, which he offered me.

"Congratulations, Gnaeus," he said in a manner that got my attention, and when I looked at him, I saw the tears there as well, reminding me again of the loyalty of the children of Diocles to my family. "But," he joked, "you're never going to be sleeping the same again."

I quickly learned how right he was, and still is, albeit the sleepless watches are for different reasons now. We sat there as I tried to determine what was happening in the other room, as my babe seemed to be suffering some sort of indignities, at least going by the quality of its lusty cries.

Alex proved to be a great help, explaining, "They're cleaning the babe's mouth and nose so it can breathe. Then they're going to wipe it down before they give it to Bronwen to suckle for the first time."

There is no way I can determine how long we sat there, but I heard the scraping sounds of footsteps before the door was opened, again by Algaia.

"Gnaeus, come meet your child."

The manner in which she said it, with a teasing tone because she had not said "son" or "daughter," earned her a glare from me as she moved aside so that I could enter our bedroom. My memory of that moment is that the first thing I noticed was the smell, unlike anything I had ever experienced before. It was not unpleasant; it was just...different, I suppose, a smell of life at its most basic and elemental, yet my entire attention was on Bronwen, propped up against the bolsters we use for our heads, her beautiful hair down and arrayed on her shoulders, my favorite way that she wears it, but it was the smile on her face that elicited from me a feeling of such happiness that, even now a few years later, I feel my heart quicken at the memory. As eager as I had been before, suddenly, it was as if my feet were stuck to the floor, and a glance over at Algaia, who was now standing next to Terentia, seemed to indicate that I was behaving in a manner they had both seen before, which seemed to be an indulgent amusement, I think. Somehow, I do not even remember doing it, I crossed the room, my eyes now fixed on what looked like nothing more than a small cloth bundle. I started to sit down on the bed, then stopped myself, worried that my weight would cause Bronwen pain.

"Gnaeus," she said, her voice understandably hoarse, but with obvious amusement, "you need to sit next to me so that you can meet..." She stopped then, and I realized that she was teasing me as well, so I did sit, albeit carefully, which was when she finished, "...your son, Titus."

She leaned forward, offering me that bundle of cloth that was so much, much more than that, while I was able to see my son's face for the first time. I had been warned, most recently by Alex, that newborn babes are not much to look at, that they're quite red, wrinkled, and bear little resemblance to what they will become, and while he, and the others who had told me this were right, they were also wrong; he was, and still is, the most wonderful thing I have ever seen. His eyes were open, and I had also been warned that a babe's eyes are almost black in the first few days after they were born, but as I stared down at him, I was certain that he was doing the same as we examined each other, and I remember wondering what was going through his tiny mind. I have no idea how long this moment lasted, as I made sure to burn this image into my mind, but it ended, when suddenly, his tiny, toothless mouth opened, yet instead of crying, he yawned, then shut his eyes. It is amusing now to think about it, but my initial thought was that I had somehow crushed the life out of him, and Bronwen must have seen my face and correctly interpreted the look of alarm.

"Titus has had a very big day, my love," she said as she gently, but firmly, took the babe from my arms. "And," the smile she gave me was tired as she said with unusual understatement for her, "so have I."

She and my son were almost instantly asleep, Titus cradled in her arms, but when Algaia tugged on my sleeve in a signal that it was time for me to leave, I shook my head.

"I just want to watch for a moment," I whispered, and promised, "I won't make any noise. I just want to…look at them."

And I did, sitting there for what I was told later was a full third of a watch, just watching the mother of my child and my son enjoying a well-earned slumber, and the thought that kept running through my mind was a deep sadness that my father would never see his grandson.

Not surprisingly, the Praetorian Guard does not particularly care when one of their Centurions has a child, so I had to endure an upbraiding from Creticus because I had been tardy for duty, not arriving until almost midday, although Alex had gone ahead to the barracks to inform the Pilus Prior. However, Creticus' heart was clearly not in it, making it clear that this was a formality that he had to go through with, so I stood there and solemnly swore that I would not be late for duty for the foreseeable future, and hopefully, the next time my woman went into labor, she would make sure that it was at a convenient time. He clearly did not appreciate my levity, but he did not make an issue of it either, and I was dismissed to my quarters. There was one benefit that the Second Cohort did not have the duty that day, and since Sabinus had held the morning inspection in my absence, I had nothing more to do than retire to my private quarters and get some sleep. Alex roused me at the end of the duty day to hold the dismissal formation, and the men raced off to go to either one of the *tavernae* frequented by the Second Cohort, or catch the last few races at the Circus, while I headed to my apartment and my new son. Just before I ascended the stairs, Alex stopped me.

"Gnaeus, if you're like I was, you're going to want to run away before you get to the count of five hundred," he warned. "But trust me, do *not* do it. You need to stay there."

Honestly, I had not intended to flee, but I said, "But Terentia is going to be with her for the next week. And I assume Algaia will stop by."

"She will," Alex assured me. "But remember what I said."

Alex was wrong about one thing; I doubt I made it past the count of two hundred before I was thinking of what excuse I could offer, but this was a time when I followed his advice, and I look back on that first night with my new family fondly. I learned how to hold him properly, which was a good thing, since I had no idea there was a wrong way, and how a rocking motion soothes an infant. I also learned from Terentia that my son was larger than normal.

"He's the biggest baby I've ever delivered," she told me when I took her out into the main room to speak to her. When I asked how Bronwen did, she smiled. "She bore it well, Master Gnaeus, especially for her first time. She said that you were worried because of your size that she was in danger." I briefly explained why, and I could see that she was not surprised, and neither was I when she said, "She also told me that she's going to sacrifice to not just her gods but yours that next time, she has a girl."

And I could not blame her for that.

I had been looking forward to the arrival of the 1st, my anticipation at being reunited with the men I still think of as my true comrades growing every day. Then, on the day that the four Legions that had been marching for more than a month arrived on the Campus Martius, it was perhaps at that same moment that the knock on my door came, and when I opened it, Marcus Sempronius was standing there. I was not happy about it, but I let him come in, while Bronwen was reclining on the couch nursing young Titus, who was sucking noisily, and from what I could tell, quite happily.

"*Salve*, Centurion," Sempronius began, clearly uncomfortable, which put us in the same frame of mind, "and I offer my salutation on the birth of your child to you and," he turned and gave Bronwen an awkward bow, "to your lady."

Bronwen had always treated Sempronius very warmly, but once she learned his role and after I allowed her to express her feelings about Tiberius' spy, for one of the first times since we were together, I ordered her to hide her true feelings around him, and I regret to say that it became quite heated until I essentially bellowed at her in the same manner I would to a ranker who was being disobedient. Consequently, I was holding my breath, but Bronwen offered him a smile that only I knew was false.

"I thank you, Sempronius," she said, and while I was turned towards her, I watched him out of the corner of my eye, and I was certain he did not detect any falsity.

"Have you chosen a name?" Sempronius asked, and I immediately understood that asking for his name was Sempronius' way of determining whether we had a son or daughter.

Nevertheless, I saw no reason to withhold the truth, telling him, "We named him Titus, in honor of my father and great-grandfather."

He was clearly not surprised at this, but his eyes had never left Bronwen and the babe, and there was something in his expression that forewarned me when he commented, "Truly, I'm not an expert in these matters, but it appears that young Titus will be his father's size."

"That's how it looks," I agreed. Then, tiring of this little game, I said, "What brings you to my door, Sempronius?"

For a bare instant, he allowed his irritation to show at my bluntness, but he recovered quickly, which in the moment I ascribed as a necessary skill for a spy.

"It concerns a...sensitive matter, Centurion," he spoke carefully. "One that, while I have no wish to cause offense, is best heard by your ears only." Suddenly, he added, "It's just that I need some advice about a matter that's...embarrassing."

It was neatly done, and if I did not know who Sempronius really was, I would have been completely fooled, but in order to keep up the pretense that Bronwen did not know about his real role, I cast her an apologetic glance.

"I'm going to step outside for a moment, *meum mel*, if that's all right."

"I believe I will be able to manage, my love," she answered dryly, and since my back was turned to Sempronius, I threw her a wink.

We went out into the atrium, but Sempronius still kept his voice just above a whisper, pulling out a small scroll as he said, "I bring instructions from our master, Centurion." He handed me the scroll so that I could see the seal, and I recognized it immediately, that of a sphinx that I assume is now the official seal of whoever is Imperator. When I began to tuck the scroll in my belt, Sempronius shook his head, saying flatly, "You're to read your orders in my presence, and acknowledge them." His tone softened slightly as he added, "It's one of his...quirks, Centurion."

Naturally, I did not like it, at all, but neither did I argue. I cracked the seal, unrolled it, and in the span of a couple heartbeats, felt my heart drop and my stomach tighten.

"When am I supposed to do this?" I gasped; frankly, it was all I could think to say.

"Immediately," he confirmed my fears. "Preferably tonight, but by no later than midday tomorrow."

"But I have duty tomorrow," I protested, but this did not sway Sempronius, and I began getting angry. "What do you think will happen if I'm not with my Century tomorrow? Maybe you're not aware, but it's our turn for the Palatine again, and there's no way that Sejanus won't find out that I'm missing."

"Then," he shrugged, "you need to do everything in your power to talk to those men tonight."

"How the fuck am I supposed to manage meeting with the Primus Pilus of every Legion?" I asked, feeling anger and despair in equal measure.

"Actually," Sempronius answered calmly, "I have a suggestion."

He explained briefly, and while I was still not completely mollified, I did allow, "That might work. But," I set this aside for the moment, "what am I supposed to say to them?"

"To begin with, that it's in their best interest that their men don't create any trouble in the city," Sempronius answered, but I gave a snort.

"I doubt they have to be told that."

"There's more," Sempronius said quietly. "The Imperator also wants them to understand that the consequences for their failure won't be confined to whichever of the Primi Pili and their Centurions whose men break the peace inside the city."

"What does *that* mean?" I demanded, but he did not answer verbally, just regarded me steadily for a long moment as the import of his words hit me, and I gasped as if I had been hit in the stomach.

"You mean he'd do something to their *families*?"

"What families, Centurion?" Sempronius countered, but I did not take his meaning immediately, prompting him to ask, "Isn't it true that men of the Legions are forbidden from being married?"

This wrenched a groan from my lips, because I suddenly understood, or thought I did.

"So Tiberius can pretend that he didn't order the execution of the Primi Pili's and other Centurion's families, since those families don't legally exist."

"Centurion, remember when I reminded you that our master is a fair man, but he's not a forgiving one? And," he added, "while he didn't say as much, I believe that he would take this failure on their part personally."

"So your suggestion is that I threaten their families," I said sourly.

"No." He shook his head. "Not *you*, Centurion. And you need to make it clear that you're only the messenger. And," he shrugged, "if it helps your cause, tell them the only reason that you're doing this is because the same threat was made to your woman and son."

It had not even occurred to me that this might be the case, and the realization struck me like a thunderbolt from Jupiter, and before I knew it, I had grabbed a handful of Sempronius' tunic; my anger was sufficient that I snatched him up off the ground so that his toes were barely touching it.

"You just threatened my family, you *cunnus*." Somehow, I managed to keep my voice down, though I dearly wanted to bellow in his face. "Do you have any idea what I'd do to you if any harm came to them?"

He was scared, certainly, but he was not terrified out of his mind, although his voice was choked because my grip had tightened his tunic around his throat.

"Do you think you're the only one with a family, Centurion? That you're the only one with more to lose than your own life?"

Honestly, I had never considered the possibility that Sempronius might have a family of his own, so while I did not really want to, I let go and dropped him back onto the ground, taking some satisfaction in the manner in which he had to pause to regain his breath.

I was not about to apologize, so instead, I said tonelessly, "You can tell him that I understand...and will obey."

"Centurion," Sempronius' tone was apologetic, "please believe me that I don't enjoy this any more than you do." I did not say anything to indicate I cared, but neither did I tell him to fuck himself, and I suppose he took this as a sign to continue, "We're both working towards a larger goal, Centurion."

"And what goal is that?" I asked sourly, not really caring; or believing I did not.

"That we expose Sejanus' true nature to Tiberius," he replied immediately. "We need to convince the Imperator that Sejanus can't be trusted." Before I could say anything, he reminded me, "Remember, I owe Sejanus for what he did to Dolabella, and he always said that your father was one of the few true Romans he knew, a man who could be counted on to do what needed to be done for Rome, not just one man. And," he finished, "from everything I've seen, you are your father's son in every regard. Was I wrong?"

Oh, I wanted to punch him right in his face, but I confess that, even in the moment, I realized it was because he was right.

Instead, all I said was, "All right. I suppose I better get going immediately. I need to go tell Bronwen that I'm going to the Campus and that I won't be back soon."

I made him stay outside when I informed Bronwen, and I did not tell her the truth, but I was certain that she was not fooled. However, for some reason I never asked her about, she simply nodded and returned her attention to Titus, whose belly was now full and was sleeping soundly in her arms. And, as it always happened, when I looked at my woman and my son, I was assailed by a sensation that I was still becoming accustomed to, and the truth is that I doubt I will ever fully absorb, and that is the fear that comes from the recognition that it was no longer just myself I had to worry about. I put on my *baltea* with my *gladius* on over my blue Praetorian tunic, then went and donned my toga, certain that I would be spotted out on the Campus and did not want to have Creticus chewing on me after Sejanus chewed on him for not being properly attired. Leaving the apartment, I went downstairs to Alex's apartment, but when Sempronius began to object, I silenced him with a look. As I had with Sempronius, I bade Alex to come outside, except that I did tell him the entire truth, but when he insisted on coming with me, I flatly forbade it.

"I want you here," I told him, and I used the tone that told him it was his Centurion speaking and not his friend and *de facto* family member.

He did not like it, but I did not expect him to, but I also knew he would obey. There was one surprise when I rejoined Sempronius, but he made no move to come with me.

"I'm going to wait a bit after you leave, Centurion, just to make sure that we're not seen together."

The irritation I felt was aimed at myself because I should have thought about it, but I still snarled something at him as I left the apartment and stepped out onto the street, holding my *vitus,* and prepared to perform my first task for the Imperator, and in the process, probably declaring myself as an enemy to the Prefect.

It is difficult to describe my feelings on my walk down the Caelian Hill, and I could say that I took the long way by going around the Circus on the western side so that I would not be skirting the Palatine, but that would only be partially true. This route took me through the Forum Boarium, where all of the animals that feed a million people are slaughtered and butchered, which means that you can smell the Boarium long before you get there. I was slightly concerned that, given how crowded the Boarium is, I ran the risk of colliding with a freedman or slave hauling parts of a carcass to some shop in the city, but I quickly learned the extra benefit that came from not just my size, but the Praetorian *vitus* that I carried, so my toga was still white when I exited on the opposite side. Marcellus' Theater is a short distance north of the Boarium, and it reminded me that Bronwen had wanted me to take her to some sort of entertainment before the baby came, but I had put it off. It is just one of the many benefits of being a Praetorian; free admission to not just the Circus and to any games, but to the theater, although from what I had been told, not many Centurions attended, and certainly no rankers were eager to watch plays written by some dead Greeks, although if the Theater had been used for the mimes and farces that are far more popular, it would have been full of Praetorians.

I reached the southern edge of the Campus just as the sun was going down, and the Legions were camped on the far side next to the river, so once past the *Praetorium* that is second only to Pompey's Theater in dominating the area, in the last bit of light, I saw the sea of tents, and I felt a tightness in my throat, while my heart began pounding more heavily. It was not just dread of what I had to do; the sight of a Legion camp, where the men I led and those I called friends were brought back a flood of memories, and while the thought of my father dominated them, along with the memory of Structus who had fallen at the Angrivarian Wall, it was not just sadness and loss I was feeling. If it had not been for the visit of Sempronius, I would have been beside myself with eagerness to see Macer, Saloninus, Gillo, Fabricius and my old *Signifer* Gemellus, who had been with me since my time as Hastatus Posterior. While there was no ditch and wall, the picket stakes had been set out to delineate the boundaries of the camp, so I headed to the Porta Praetoria, which was manned by a full section of men and was a bit unusual. It was just dark enough that I had to get closer before I saw by the symbol on their shields that these were men of the 5th Alaudae, which told me the identity of one of the Primi Pili I had to see this night. The torches were just being lit, and the extra light enabled me to see the white stripe of the Optio who stepped forward, his features slightly shadowed by his helmet.

"*Salve*, Centurion," he called out, but held a hand up. "Please stop there." This was not unusual, so I did as he asked. "I see you're a Praetorian, so forgive me, but do you know the watchword?"

Of course, I did not, but I stopped myself from snapping at him, simply saying, "No, Optio, I don't know the watchword."

"May I ask your business, then?" he asked, and I felt a stab of sympathy for him, knowing that he was in an awkward spot. "Who are you here to see?"

"I'm here to speak to my former Primus Pilus, Tiberius Sacrovir," I answered, but I was completely unprepared for what came next.

Since I was focused on the Optio, I did not notice that just beyond him within the picket stakes, a Centurion was walking by, but he noticed me.

"Pullus? Is that you?"

It took me a moment to recognize the voice, but I was helped when he stepped into the steadily growing pool of light from the torch.

"Gallus?" I was relieved to see a familiar face, although I did not know the Octus Pilus Prior of the 1st that well. "Can you explain to the Optio here who I am?"

Gallus addressed the Optio, but he decided to have a bit of fun at the same time.

"Optio, do you not recognize *the* Hero of the Army of the Rhenus? He's been decorated by Germanicus himself!"

This was embarrassing enough, but I saw the dawning expression on the Optio's face, and he gasped, "He's *that* Pullus?" He snapped to *intente*, offering a salute as he said, "My apologies, Centurion Pullus! I should have recognized you immediately, just by your…"

"By my size," I finished for him, torn between being amused and irritated at Gallus, saying this as I returned his salute.

What mattered was that he stepped aside and allowed me to pass, and I walked over to Gallus, clasping arms with him.

"Nice to see that you got all dressed up to come see your old comrades," he commented, then laughed at the face I made.

"This," I grumbled, "is my uniform."

"*Gerrae!*" he exclaimed. "We heard that, but we all thought it was just camp gossip."

"No," I sighed. "It's true. So," I asked, "is the 1st in its normal spot in a four Legion camp?"

I am glad I asked, because I was already heading in the wrong direction.

"No, I'm actually heading over to see a friend in the 20th," he replied, giving me the identity of the third Legion. He turned and pointed back in the opposite direction. "We're on the opposite side this time, northern right quarter."

"Next to the river." I said this aloud, but more to myself, wondering how the men felt about this.

I got my answer when Gallus spat on the ground, then said bitterly, "Yes, the Legate fucked us pretty good. The bugs are terrible, and the smell isn't great."

"Who's the Legate?"

"Who do you think?" Gallus gave me a sour smile. "Caecina."

When I heard the name, I realized that I should have guessed it; Caecina was in his sixties, and while he was not incompetent by any measure, he was still angry about the revolt almost three years earlier, thinking that the men were ungrateful, lazy, and had been spoiled, at least when compared to the Legions of his youth. The fact that the Princeps had arbitrarily extended the term of enlistment to twenty years was, as far as he was concerned, completely immaterial, nor did he think they deserved the raise in pay that Tiberius was forced to agree to in the aftermath of the death of Divus Augustus. None of which mattered in the moment, and Gallus and I parted as I headed for the largest tent in the northern Porta Dextra side of the camp. Because of the direction I was coming from, it meant that I had to decide whether to walk through my former Cohort's streets, meaning it was inevitable that I would run into someone I knew, and I admit that I felt guilty when I chose to take the longer route, not because I did not look forward to seeing old friends and comrades, but I had four visits to make before the sun came up the next day and I had no idea how long it would take to convince the Primi Pili. Instead of simply entering through the flap of the Primus Pilus' tent, I rapped on the piece of wood outside, but it was a matter of a couple of heartbeats before the flap was thrust aside, and Menander was staring at me, except this time, he did not seem as surprised as he had been when I appeared in Ubiorum a few months earlier with a Parisii woman and quite a story to tell.

"*Salve*, Centurion Pullus," he stepped aside, giving me a bow. "The Primus Pilus told me to keep an eye out for you. Although," he added, "he expected you tomorrow."

"*Salve*, Menander," I answered cordially, having been taught by Alex the value of being on good terms with the chief clerk of the Legion; when that chief clerk is also the personal attendant of the Primus Pilus, it is even more important. "You haven't changed a bit. Is he in his quarters?"

"Yes, Centurion," he answered my question, then smiled as he fingered the toga, "but I have to say, I didn't expect to see you like you were going to the Senate."

"Trust me," I said frankly, "I didn't expect that either when I got here. It's," I tried to keep my tone neutral, "by orders of Praetorian Prefect Sejanus."

I do not think I fooled him, but he wisely said nothing and excused himself to leave the outer partition that bisects the tent to inform Sacrovir of my presence, while I pretended the sweat I felt soaking my tunic was because of the stuffiness of the tent now that the lamps were lit. I heard the exchange, but I could not make out the words, although what mattered was that Menander returned immediately.

"The Primus Pilus will see you now, Centurion."

As I stepped past Menander, out of the corner of my eye, I saw that his eyes were on my forehead, seeing the beads of sweat there, the frown on his face telling me that he was sure it was not because of the heat, serving as another reminder of how those in a subordinate position are always watching for any signs that might impact their own fate. Sacrovir was seated behind his desk, but quite unusually, he stood as I centered on his desk and rendered my salute, which he returned immediately.

"If I didn't recognize you, I'd think a Senator had come to visit," he joked, which was unusual in itself. When I started to drop onto the stool, he said, "Let's sit at the table."

Walking over to the wall of the tent, I saw that there was a full pitcher and two cups, and it reminded me of the last meeting we had had between us, when he handed me Germanicus' orders.

We took our seats, and he poured a cup for me, saying, "Now, tell me about life in the Praetorians, Pullus."

How do I do this? This was the thought pressing against my mind, so I naturally plunged into the cold pool without checking it first.

"I would love to, Primus Pilus," I began, "but unfortunately, I'm here on official business tonight."

He stopped in mid-pour of his cup, all hint of friendliness gone from his face, although he did not seem angry…yet.

Setting the pitcher down, he said tonelessly, "Go on, Pullus. What business do you have with me?"

"Actually," I answered, changing my strategy on the fly; I had intended to give Sacrovir Tiberius' warning first, then inform him that it was not just him, but I realized this was better, "I have to see all four of you Primi Pili tonight, Primus Pilus."

"About?" He showed the first glimmer of worry, but it was a shade compared to what his expression would be when I finished.

We sat there for a long moment after I delivered the warning, and as Sempronius had instructed, was explicit in what the consequences would be, neither of us speaking, the silence dragging out as he regarded me with an expression I could not identify.

Finally, he broke the silence. "Why you, Pullus? Why," he leaned forward to fix me with an intense stare, "would Tiberius choose you to be his…messenger?"

"I…I don't know," was all I could think to say.

He shocked me then. "I don't believe you, but on the off chance you're telling the truth, I'll tell you why." He paused, giving me the sense that he was gauging my reaction when he continued, "Because of the work your father did for Tiberius before he became Imperator."

He was clever to do so, because I was shocked to the point that I gasped, "How do you know about that?"

"Because I'm not a fool," he snapped irritably, but then he held up a hand. "I apologize for my tone, Pullus. This is none of your doing." He took the time to sip from his cup before he went on, "I had my suspicions, and I confronted your father about it. And," he looked from his cup to my face, "he told me the truth. He didn't try to lie about it. That," his voice softened, "was the kind of man your father was, Pullus. I know it bothered him, but while he didn't go into much detail, I learned that he didn't have much choice. Which," he concluded, "is my assumption with you, that you were put in a position where it would be suicide to refuse."

There were a couple emotions running through my body, but the predominant one was relief, and I assured him, "Your assumption is correct, Primus Pilus. I was informed, in detail, what awaited me if I refused."

Then, Sacrovir said something, an offhand comment that instantly changed things.

"That explains why you were assigned to the Praetorians." His voice contained a measure of satisfaction, as if he had figured out part of a puzzle. "And," he went on, "it makes sense that Tiberius would work through Germanicus, given his connection to your father. And," he looked embarrassed, "you, of course. You both served the *Propraetor* well, so it was natural of me to assume that Germanicus was behind your transfer and not Tiberius."

I was faced with a choice at that moment, and I am still not certain whether I chose wisely or not, because I did not correct his mistaken assumption that Tiberius was behind my assignment.

Frankly, I had more pressing matters, but Fortuna decided to offer me a smile when, slapping the table, Sacrovir stood up and announced, "All right, come on, then. We need to go see the others."

"You're going with me?"

Sacrovir seemed surprised by my reaction and gave a bark that was his version of a laugh. "Of course! Not only will you need me to make sure they know how serious this is, I want to see their faces when we're all dropped in the *cac*."

As we left his quarters, I was struck by the amusing thought that some things about the army never change; no matter what your rank, if you're going to be dropped in the *cac*, as Sacrovir aptly put it, there is nothing more enjoyable than seeing your comrades suffer the same fate.

Of the other three Primi Pili, we spent the most time with the Primus Pilus of the 5th, and while I was grateful for Sacrovir's assistance with all of them, it was with Quintus Nerva that he was most needed, because I am certain that if he had not been there, I would have struck Nerva…or worse. When Gallus had informed me that the 5th was one of the Legions marching in the triumph, I suppose it was in the back of my mind that Nerva might have something to say about the incident almost two years earlier when I pummeled his Quintus Pilus Prior, Lucius Petronius, when I was in Mogontiacum. Nevertheless, I was not prepared for him to immediately begin snarling and hurling curses at me, although that was not what angered me, but I suppose when he saw he was not getting under my skin, he switched to the subject of my parents.

"Petronius was just speaking the truth!" He had started out loud, but now he was bellowing at the top of his lungs, face red and the cords of his neck standing out. "Your father and mother were never married, and that makes you a…"

"Nerva."

I do not know how or why, but my guess is that it was Sacrovir speaking in a quiet tone that caught the other man's attention. Nerva was a bit taller than average, and with a stocky build, but he was also in his late forties, and speaking truly, the biggest impediment to me beating him to death would have been that I was wearing a toga. Nerva swiveled his head to glare at Sacrovir, who kept his tone at the same level, but his words were delivered in the flat, matter-of-fact manner that we use when offering a report, a simple statement of fact.

"You're about to utter a slur against the Centurion here that honor will force him to respond in a manner you won't like. And," he said coldly, "I won't lift a finger to stop him. You *do* remember what he did to Petronius, *neh*? What do you think he'd do to you? How long do you think you'd last against the son of Titus Pullus?"

If I had slapped Nerva, I do not think his reaction would have been much different because of Sacrovir's words.

"You'd allow a subordinate to strike a fellow Primus Pilus?" he gasped, and actually staggered back a step.

"For calling him a bastard?" Sacrovir asked dryly. He gave a shrug. "Even if I didn't approve of what he did, I'm no fool. Remember, I've seen him fight, and I wouldn't be able to stop him. Besides," he pointed out, "he's not only a Praetorian now, he's been sent here specifically by Tiberius to send us a warning."

For a long moment, Nerva seemed to seriously consider finishing his slur; whether it was the manner in which I laid my *vitus* carefully on his desk while bunching up the sleeves of my toga dissuaded him, what mattered was that he let out an explosive breath.

"So," he asked sourly, "what's this warning?"

I expected him to balk, or bluster, but he went pale as he fell back against his desk, looking over at Sacrovir.

"Is he telling it true?" he asked Sacrovir, which was insulting, but I ignored it. "Do you believe him?"

"Even if it wasn't Pullus standing here, yes, Nerva, I'd believe that Tiberius is willing to do anything to keep our boys from tangling with the Praetorians. But," he indicated me with his head, "the fact that it's Pullus means that I'm as certain as I have been about anything that this is a warning we need to take seriously. And," he finished, "to heed."

Nerva's shoulders sagged, and he looked down at the hardpacked ground, saying dully, "And my son just had a child in Januarius." He looked at Sacrovir, and I realized I had forgotten that my former Primus Pilus had a son in the Eighth Cohort as Nerva said, "He's like your boy, followed in his Tata's footsteps." Only then did he return his attention to me, but while he was still angry, he took Sacrovir's warning to heart. "Very well, Centurion Pullus. I'll get together with my officers, and if there *is* any trouble, it won't be from the men of the Alaudae."

It was not until we were out of the tent and heading to the 20th, the third Legion in camp, that Sacrovir informed me, "I don't suppose you had a chance to hear about Petronius."

Without thinking, I replied flippantly, "Other than the fact that I beat him like a slave who'd stolen something? No, I suppose I haven't."

This brought Sacrovir to a stop so that he could glare up at me. Poking me in the chest, he hissed, "Yes, well, that beating you gave him shamed him to the point that he opened his veins!"

I was certainly not expecting this, and I could only stammer, "I...I...I didn't know that, Primus Pilus."

"Well, now you do," he snapped. "And now maybe you know why Nerva was so angry."

This was true, and we lapsed into silence as we resumed heading across the camp. I found that I was profoundly disturbed by this news; certainly, I had wanted to beat the man to the point his toes were dipping in the river, as we say, but it had never occurred to me that he might be unable to live with the shame of such a beating.

"Why didn't Nerva make some sort of trouble for me?" I asked Sacrovir.

"Why do you think?" he answered flatly. "I convinced him that it would make things worse, not better." I suppose he sensed I needed more, so he explained, "You know that Petronius had a...reputation, yes?"

In fact, I did; it was why Alex had selected him as the man to make an example of, because he was the most notorious brawler in his Legion, and while he was usually victorious, this was not always the case. And, as Alex knew, I was not the first Pullus to give Petronius a bad beating.

What came out of my mouth was a simple "Yes."

"That's why nobody in the *Praetorium* at Mogontiacum was willing to lift a finger when Nerva went to them and tried to have you arrested and executed."

It should not be surprising that this stopped me in my tracks, since this was the first that I had heard about it.

"When was this?" I gasped.

Sacrovir did not stop, but he did slow down as he said over his shoulder, "It was during your...festival days, when you were traveling the world."

I hurried to catch up to him to ask, "Why didn't you tell me when I reported in?"

"Because," he shrugged, "the matter had already been settled. I didn't see much point in bringing it up."

We were just a few paces away from the quarters of the Primus Pilus of the 20th when a thought struck me.

"You said nobody in the *Praetorium* would intervene?" When he nodded, I asked, "Did you ever learn who it was? That doesn't sound like something Caecina would ignore."

"Caecina never learned about it," he answered, then shrugged as he added, "but I never found out who kept it from the Legate."

Our conversation ended when the chief clerk answered the knock at Neratius' quarters, pushing aside the flap to allow us to step inside to continue my mission.

The conversation with Lucius Neratius was certainly not as hostile as with Nerva, but he took quite a bit more persuasion, although his objection was more practical in nature.

"I can make sure that they don't start anything, but what happens when one of those arrogant Praetorian pretty boy bastards starts something with one of our boys?" His expression changed suddenly, and he looked from Sacrovir to me. "I apologize, Centurion Pullus. I meant no disrespect to you personally."

"None taken," I assured him, then grinned, "and yes, a good number of the men in my Century and Cohort fit your description," thinking of Flaccus. "But," I warned, "not all of them are that way. About a third of the rankers came from one of the Legions. Although," I allowed, "there are only a handful from the Army of the Rhenus, and not many more from the Army of Pannonia, so they're not particularly experienced."

"You mean those boys from the Gallic, Spanish, and Syrian Legions?" Neratius scoffed. "They're as soft as pudding."

I was not inclined to argue the point, for the simple fact that he was speaking the truth; there has not been any action with any of those Armies in the last decade, but I also felt the need to press the larger point.

"While I agree with you, Primus Pilus, they're still men of the Legions and," I was forced to admit, "if there is trouble from the Praetorians, it will likely be with those men and not the ones recruited directly into the Guard. But," I assured him confidently, "you're not going to get any trouble from the Praetorians."

"Oh?" Neratius looked skeptical. "And how can you guarantee this, Pullus?"

"I can't," I acknowledged. "But Prefect Sejanus can, because every man in the Praetorians know that he speaks for the Imperator. So," I felt even more assurance about this, "you don't have to worry about the Praetorians."

This convinced him, at least to the point that he offered the same declaration as Nerva that it would not be the 20th who caused trouble, leaving us just the 14th, the last Legion. After Sacrovir and I left Neratius, and we were walking down the Via Praetoria to the 14th's area, there was a sudden roar of laughter coming from one of the tents one street over, but the tents blocked our view. In the moment, I assumed it was just some men laughing at a joke told by one of their comrades; now, I think it might have been the gods laughing at me and mocking me for my hubris.

Looking back, I believe that the fact that my task, with the exception of Nerva, turned out to be not as difficult as I thought was what led to my upcoming lapse. The 14th's Primus Pilus, Lucius Frugi, immediately assured me that he had already warned his Centurions that if any of their men were the cause of trouble in the city, that not only would the rankers be scourged, but their Centurion would be demoted, not down to Optio, but all the way down to the ranks. Indeed, he agreed so quickly that I did not even have to mention Tiberius' name, and while I was slightly troubled at how easy it was, neither was I so disturbed that I gave it more than a passing thought. Sacrovir and I walked back in the direction of the camp forum, and he asked me if I intended to visit my former Cohort that night.

"I thought about it," I admitted, "but I decided that I need to get home. What are your orders for tomorrow?"

"Polishing and varnishing," Sacrovir answered, his tone making me chuckle. "That's really all we're going to be doing until the triumph. At least," he added sourly, "that's what our Legate has told us."

"Then I'll be back tomorrow, if you approve," I said, and I saw that it pleased him to be asked, while it reminded me that he was viewing me more as a Praetorian than as one of his Centurions.

"Of course," he replied. Then, in a complete surprise, he offered his arm, and he actually smiled as he said, "And I don't blame you for wanting to get home, Pullus. I remember your woman very well."

"We have a son now," I told him, a bit embarrassed that I had forgotten to mention this, and he offered his felicitations, then I left the camp with his invitation to stop for a longer chat the next day.

That, I remember thinking, went much better than I expected, and I suppose it was natural that my mind began wandering, thinking of the warm bed waiting for me and feeling good about having accomplished my task. As it should have been, the Campus was deserted, but I had learned that, while the traffic is not nearly as heavy at this time of night, Rome never really sleeps. I certainly had been warned that anyone I was likely to run into at midnight or later was not up to anything good, but this was where my confidence in myself and ability to handle any civilian with mischief on his mind came into play, because quite frankly, I was not paying attention. And, I will maintain to my dying day, even with being caught completely by surprise, and as I quickly learned, hampered by my toga, if there had been three and not five men, I would have prevailed without difficulty.

Since it was empty, I decided to cut through the Forum Boarium, intending to use the Via Caelias, the street at the base of the Palatine so that the Circus was on my right. My attackers used the empty stalls on both sides of the street as cover, but one of them either got anxious, or perhaps it was by design since his sudden lunge from the deeper shadows from my right made me instinctively pivot to face him, thereby exposing my back to what turned out to be a pair of men on the other side of the street, and if they had used either a *pugio* or *gladius*, I would not be here dictating this to Alex; who, I confess, is giving me an angry glare about my refusal to let him go with me that night, despite this being some time after the fact. All I saw was a dark shape charging at me with something about the length of a *gladius* in his hand, but just by the manner in which he was holding it above his head, I was certain that it was a cudgel.

What mattered was that my left hand, holding my *vitus*, was sweeping upward with the *vitus* parallel to the ground, the standard maneuver to block an overhead blow, while my right hand was thrusting through the slit in my toga for my *gladius*. I have no idea whether the blow across my lower back landed an eyeblink before my *vitus* blocked the cudgel aimed at my head, or if it was simultaneous, but what mattered was that I somehow managed to block the overhand blow even as my legs collapsed from under me, while the aim of my second attacker from behind was thrown off so that instead of hitting me in the back of the head, I felt the disturbance in the air as he missed his swing by a couple of feet. I now was on my knees, but while I do not have any memory of doing so, I somehow managed to draw my *gladius*, which happened to be the Scrofa blade, just as two other men materialized in front of me. One of them came rushing towards me, also armed with a cudgel; I only knew this because I heard the sound of wood dropping to the paving stones after I launched a completely wild backhand horizontal swing just as he was stepping into his own attack. For yet another time, the grip taught to me by my father served me well because of how deeply the edge cut into the man's side about halfway down the blade's length, and while Scrofa's *gladius* is not the match of the Prefect's Gallic blade, it is still incredibly sharp, so that I almost cut the man in half at the waist, the only thing stopping me his spinal column, and I have no doubt that, even as strong as my grip is, I would have had the *gladius* wrenched from my hand when iron struck bone with that much force without the Vinician grip. Under other circumstances, I would have at least noticed the shower of blood and offal that drenched my arm and the sleeve of my toga, but I only became aware of it later. While I still had control of my *gladius*, before I could wrench it out of the man's body, who did not scream as much as seem to just exhale in a great moaning sigh as he fell away in the opposite direction, I took another blow, this time to the side of my head, an explosion of light blinding me so that I could not even tell from where it came. Oddly, I did not hear anyone saying anything to this moment, just the harsh panting and the grunting of men trying to kill me, one of those grunts coinciding with another blow from behind, this time striking me on my left shoulder, sending a shock of pain that ironically did more to clear my head than anything else, but I heard the clatter of my *vitus* as it dropped from my hand, which told me that they were trying to disarm me.

My mind was screaming at me to get back to my feet, except my legs did not respond at all, and it was about this moment when I realized that my knees did not hurt from kneeling on the paving stones. This did not anger me as much as it terrified me, and I began flailing wildly with my *gladius* now that I understood that they were trying to disarm me, which was confirmed by yet another blow, again from behind, this time striking me on my upper right arm, my large muscles and the thick folds of cloth cushioning the blow, which in turn gave me an opportunity to twist at the waist and make another wild backhand swing, whereupon I was rewarded by the sudden tug as my blade bit flesh, although the shout of pain told me that it was not mortal. This was destined to be my last successful blow since, by twisting my torso and without my *vitus*, I had no defense for the final blow, this time to the opposite side of my head but at the same spot above my ear, yet I was still aware that I was falling, toppling over to my right so quickly that my arm was trapped between my body and the filthy stones of the street. My toga is ruined; I have no idea why this was the thought in my head, but for the first time, someone spoke, breaking the relative silence.

"That's enough. We don't want to scramble his brains. At least, not yet."

Where had I heard that voice before? I was seeing double, or I believed I was, although it was possible that there were two pairs of shoes just a few inches from my face, but when I tried to peer up into the darkness, one of the feet lifted from the street to kick me in the stomach.

"Don't look up here!" the same man snarled. "If you want to live, you're going to answer some questions! Understand me?"

I tried to answer, but I had no air in my lungs from the kick, so I nodded my head.

"Good," he grunted. "Now, who sent you to the camp tonight?"

"I...I went to visit my old Cohort." It took me a heartbeat to get enough of my breath back to speak, and I barely recognized my voice, it being more of a gasping moan than anything else.

The words were barely out when I was kicked again, this time in my left thigh, and while it was painful, I was also certain that it had been aimed for my groin, but my assailant had missed, though it still wrenched another groan from me, and I hated myself for showing that kind of weakness.

"Don't lie to me, you *cunnus*," my interrogator snarled. "Do you think I'm stupid? Eh? Is that it?" This time, I saw the kick coming because it was my interrogator who launched it, but while he did not aim for my groin, it was not much less painful being kicked in the chest. "We have eyes everywhere, you stupid bastard! We know exactly where you went and who sent you!"

"Then if you know, why are you asking?"

This earned me another kick, except this came from behind, striking me in my right kidney, and once more, I could not stop the groan.

"You think you're clever, eh?"

It was the way he said it that made the pieces come together, and while I was in tremendous pain, the one blessing from Fortuna was that since I had not taken another blow to the head, my mind was clearing, although there was a sharp pain above both of my ears, which were now wet and sticky. Once I had time to think about it, I realized that it was that sensation that also sent the message to that beast deep inside my belly, curled up and sleeping, because it was also one that I had experienced before. It was the day my father sacrificed himself to save my life, after I had rushed headlong and rashly to the aid of Tertius Princeps Posterior Trigeminus who, along with most of his Century, were already doomed, the only difference being that the blow to my head sent me to the ground immediately.

This growing rage is the only reason I can offer for saying, "I'm clever enough to recognize your voice, Appius."

I was rewarded by a ragged chorus of shock and, judging by the quality, of dismay from more than just Appius himself, but this time, I anticipated the kick, actually seeing it coming this time, enabling me to roll in the opposite direction so that the blow only glanced off my left arm, the heavy cloth of the toga once more helping absorb some of the force. More importantly, it freed my right arm, although I instantly saw that my *gladius* had been kicked out of my reach.

"You're going to die for that, Centurion!"

I will never know if Appius was going to say something else, but the only warning I got that the situation had changed was when, now that I could turn my head enough to see Appius in the darkness, I saw his head jerk up from me to look behind me, his mouth dropping open in shock, at the same instant one of the men behind me let out a sharp cry; or that was how it started, but it instantly transformed into the kind of gurgling sound I have heard more times than I can count, and an eyeblink later, I felt the vibration of a body hitting the ground immediately behind me.

"On your feet, Centurion! I need you!"

While I recognized the voice as belonging to Sempronius, it was a Sempronius I had never heard before, the words barked out as a command that would have not discredited any Centurion I ever served with; most importantly, it made me take something of an inventory of my condition, and I was surprised, happily, to see that when my mind told my legs to move, they obeyed, although I still could not feel them. Consequently, it took me a bit longer to scramble to my feet, and I was just in time to see that Sempronius was swinging away with a *gladius*, although he was only just keeping two of the three surviving men at bay. I do not know how he managed, but immediately after Sempronius shouted this, he kicked my *gladius* in my direction, sending it skittering across the paving stones, creating little sparks as I somehow managed to bend down, scoop it up, and in two quick strides, reach Sempronius' side, instantly earning me the attention of one of his attackers. The man wasted what little chance he had with a poorly aimed and clumsy thrust with what I assumed was a cudgel since he had been one of the men behind me, but when I knocked it aside, there was the sharp clanging sound of metal on metal as my blade slid off of his, then I immediately recovered and made a second position thrust right into his throat, although I was careful not to punch all the way through his neck so that my blade did not get stuck in his spinal column. My attention was still on the dying man when, suddenly, Appius moved, not to attack me or help his two remaining men, but in an obvious attempt to escape.

"Centurion! He can't get away or we're both dead!"

I reacted immediately, but I was still hampered by the lack of feeling in my legs. It was the oddest sensation, being able to move yet not feeling anything other than the jolting impact shooting up my legs into my lower back. And, being honest, if Appius had not been so clumsy and unfit, he would have gotten away, but he chose to try and squeeze himself in between the stalls, and I heard him colliding with something, which served both to slow him down and to locate him since, I confess, I had almost immediately lost sight of him. It was actually his curse that pointed me in the right direction as I lengthened my stride, but I was almost as clumsy as Appius, my hip hitting the edge of one of the stalls because my legs were only obeying my commands to move in a general sense. Fortunately, this only lengthened my pursuit of Appius a couple of heartbeats, and just before he reached the next street between the stalls, I was close enough to reach out and grab hold of the back of his tunic while sliding to a stop. Thankfully, my hobnails got a grip on the stones, so I was treated to the sight of Appius' upper body coming to a sudden stop while his legs kept going, while I took advantage by jerking my left arm holding his tunic down so that he slammed, hard, onto the stones. This time, it was his turn for all the air in his lungs to be expelled in an explosive gasp by the impact, strongly enough that even as I was standing above him I could smell the wine, garlic, and rotting teeth. For the span of a heartbeat or two, I was concerned that by doing as I did, I had caused the back of his head to slam into the stones and knock him senseless, but even with the darkness, I could see the whites of his eyes as he stared up at me as I returned his gaze, panting in an attempt to catch my own breath. I suddenly realized something in that moment, and all I can say is that it bothered me only later, but the truth was that I was happy, actually relishing the sight of this man lying at my feet, terrified and quivering and knowing that I had the power of life or death over him.

I suppose he probably read this savage joy in my face, because he regained enough of his wind to gasp, "You know you can't kill me, Pullus! You know who I work for!"

I knew that Appius was right, that it would be both foolish and dangerous to kill him, and for a long moment, we stared at each other, his head between my feet, his face upside down and almost glowing in the darkness because it was so pale. Oh, I suppose I could blame what was about to happen on the sudden sound of someone approaching at a run, and that it might have meant that Sempronius had been killed two streets behind me, but that would be a lie, and in keeping with my oath to tell the truth, no matter how painful, or how it might make me seem to my son when he is a man and reads this account, the truth was that Appius was doomed from the first moment he and his men attacked me. The fact that I was outnumbered meant, and means, nothing to me; I am a Pullus, and men like Appius and those who work for men like him are fodder for my *gladius*, but they had caught me by surprise, and while I was beginning to actually feel the pain more acutely at every spot of my body where they had struck me, it was actually my pride that had been savaged worst of all; they had humiliated me and driven me to my knees, meaning that it did not matter who it was closing in on us.

"You're right," I agreed, at least seemingly. "I do know who you work for, and I do know that Sejanus is a bad man to have as an enemy." My pause then was for the simple purpose of prolonging the moment, enjoying the sudden look of hope in Appius' eyes, but the onrushing footsteps were immediately behind me, so I was forced to cut the moment short, and my blade was moving as I finished, "But you're still a dead man, Appius."

This time, I did not take care not to thrust into his neck bones, my downward thrust only stopped when the point struck the stone underneath his body, and while I experienced a pang of regret, it was because I was afraid I damaged my blade, but any thought of that was driven from my mind by a shout from behind me, almost in my ear.

"Centurion! NO!"

Fortunately for both of us, even as I yanked the blade out of Appius' body and spun about in one motion, I recognized the voice as belonging to Sempronius, but he still came sliding to a sudden stop, just out of the reach of my *gladius*, instantly cautious. He barely glanced at me from what I saw, his eyes immediately going to Appius, and the growing pool of blood that could have been mistaken for black ink.

"By the gods, Centurion!" he gasped. "What have you done?" It was then he tore his eyes away from Appius to look directly at me, and I could tell that between his panting from his run and what he had just witnessed, he was struggling to sound composed. "Do you know that you've probably gotten both of us killed?"

How do I answer that? I thought. How do I assure him that I actually was aware of the danger I had just brought down on not just my head, but Bronwen's and my infant son's, not to mention Sempronius...but in that moment, I did not care? Because this was another lesson that I had to learn firsthand, despite my father's warning to me shortly before he died, that this beast that resides within the Pullus men is not under our control, that we are as much at its mercy when it is roused as men like Appius.

Aloud, I said, "Not necessarily."

"How's that?" Sempronius asked skeptically, and I could not blame him for that.

I explained my idea, such as it was, and he was actually beginning to nod when the budding plan was destroyed by the sound of a horn.

"It's the Urban Cohort! Someone must have heard the fight!"

"We don't know they're coming this way," I countered Sempronius, though it was more of a hope, then the horn blasted again and it was louder, telling us both that I was wrong.

"Give me your toga," he ordered me. "Then you need to leave, Centurion. You're going to have to take the long way around back to your apartment so you don't run into whoever's coming."

"Why do you need my toga?" I asked, mystified.

It was when he pointed to it that I looked at myself for the first time, and I immediately saw that he was right.

"You look like you work here in the Boarium," he replied, but I was already shrugging it off.

He also had a practical purpose, because essentially, a toga is nothing more than a large cloth that, as I quickly saw, could serve as a shroud.

I stood there watching him wrap up Appius' corpse, but when he glanced up, he asked in surprise, "Why are you still here, Centurion?"

"Because I can't leave you here by yourself," I answered without thinking, which this time surprised us both, and even in the gloom, I could see he was also moved.

"This isn't the Legion, Centurion," he said quietly. "While I appreciate it, the most important thing is to make sure that you're not implicated in this."

"But I'm the one who did it," I protested. "I should..."

"Pullus!" He cut me off sharply, and it was also the first time he had called be my name and not rank. "We don't have time for this. You need to leave."

"Not until you at least tell me what you intend to do." I refused to budge, knowing I was being mulishly stubborn.

"I plan to take Appius with me and making sure that he's never seen again," Sempronius assured me.

"What about the others? Won't someone connected with Sejanus know that they worked for Appius?"

"Probably," he agreed. "But Appius is the only one who matters, and as long as he's never seen again, Sejanus will be suspicious, but that's all he'll have. Besides," he said this as he heaved Appius' body up over his shoulder, "I've got an idea of my own to help throw them off the trail. Now," he reached out with his free hand and gently but firmly pushed me, although he did say, "please, Centurion. Get away from here. I'll come to your apartment tomorrow if it's safe. But," he warned, "if I don't show up, then you need to take that as a sign that something has gone wrong."

I did not have a chance to say anything, because he immediately walked away, and after a heartbeat, I turned and went in the opposite direction, able to hear the echo of hobnailed feet trotting in our direction.

By the time I made it back to the apartment, I was hobbling and bent almost double from the pain from what, to this point, is the worst beating I have suffered. My head was pounding, but the bleeding had stopped at least, although I could feel the stickiness all the way down my neck, while the feeling had returned in my legs, reminding me that I had been kicked in my left thigh and my self-inflicted blow to my hip was throbbing. Breathing was difficult, and I suspected I had at least cracked ribs, but perhaps the most potent proof of my distress was when I passed a fountain and thought, I need to stop and get cleaned up so that I don't scare Bronwen, but I quickly realized that if I did so, there was a chance I could not complete my journey home. The idea of her seeing me in this state hurt my pride more than anything, although I was thankful that Titus was far too young to be disturbed at the sight of his battered father, and since this is the first time I have spoken of that night, if the gods are kind, he will not learn of this for years to come. I knew I had been seen on my return, but there was an unexpected benefit of being only in my tunic, because the handful of other people who were out in the streets unanimously avoided me, and I realized that it was because of the *gladius* in my scabbard. A *gladius,* I realized, that still had the blood of three men on it, yet another thing I had to remember to do. Using the key hanging around my neck, I opened the door to the building, my intention to go upstairs to rouse Alex, since I was certain that he would be guarding Bronwen, but I immediately realized that I would be unable to ascend the stairs without a great deal of effort. Thankfully, this was one thing I did not have to worry about.

"Gnaeus!"

If Alex had been an attacker, I doubt I would have turned in time to face him as he emerged from the shadows on the far side of the atrium, and he informed me that he had been standing there since I left. His gasp after he lit one of the hanging lamps told me my concerns about Bronwen's reaction were not unfounded.

"I'd ask what hurts most, but I think I know the answer." He did not speak in a whisper, although he kept his voice low, and I was about to admonish him, but realized it was pointless.

"I was going to go up to get cleaned up, but I don't think I can make it up the stairs without help," I confessed.

Whatever he intended to say was interrupted by the rattling sound that signaled the opening of the door to my apartment, and I had to move carefully to face Bronwen, who was thankfully without the baby, but holding a lamp of her own as she stood at the top of the stairs.

"Come inside," she said, but then in what I took as a deliberate signal, she turned away from me to go inside before I could respond; all I got from Alex was a sympathetic glance that told me I was on my own, at least in one sense.

Nevertheless, I obeyed what I knew was a command, and Alex did help me up the stairs, where I saw that she had already started the fire to heat up a basin of water as Alex helped me to take a seat at the table. I heard footsteps coming up the stairs, and when Algaia entered, she was already carrying several pieces of cloth.

"I knew you would need some sort of cleaning up," she said, in a tone that told me Bronwen had a likely ally for what I was certain was a reprimand coming.

She handed the cloths to Bronwen, who had refused to look at me, which I took as a sign of her anger, and she took a couple of the cloths and dipped them into the water before she finally turned back towards me. I learned I was in error by her sudden gasp and how her eyes went wide, the lamplight making them shimmer as they filled with tears.

"Oh, my love! What happened? Who did this to you?"

It was the manner in which she thrust the basin into Algaia's hands so that she could come to stand in front of me, the tears now plainly visible, and I saw her hand shaking as she reached out to gently touch the bloody gash above my left ear while I hid my wince at the flash of pain, despite how her fingers barely brushed me.

"It looks worse than it is," I lied. I took her hand, and said as gently as I could, "Bronwen, why don't you let Alex do this? He's had more experience at patching men up."

I saw the look of relief on her face, making us of the same mind, and she turned and handed the dripping cloth to Alex as she stepped aside.

"You might as well talk while I work," he said. "What happened?" He was dabbing away the dried blood from my ear when he stopped suddenly, saying with a gasp, "Did this happen in the camp? Were you attacked by someone in the Legions?"

"No," I answered immediately and decisively. "It was on my way home. In fact," I decided to start with the good news, "I got the message to all four Primi Pili, thanks to Sacrovir."

"So he *did* help you."

"Yes." I actually nodded in answer to Alex's statement, which was a mistake that got a yelp of pain and I reminded myself not to move my head again. "And I didn't even have to ask him to; he just did it on his own."

"Sacrovir is many things, and one of them is clever," Alex commented, while I had to stop speaking because I was gritting my teeth too tightly as he began working on the wound itself. I was not surprised when he said, "This one will need stitches, although not many. The one on the other side isn't as bad."

This was good news as far as it went, but I immediately thought of something.

"I have duty tomorrow, and there's no way that Creticus will miss this."

"So we need to come up with a story." Alex understood immediately. "But we'll do that after you finish telling us what happened."

I did so, but I left out one detail, although as soon as I was alone with Alex, I told him the whole story, including who I had slain, but in that moment, I did not want Bronwen to worry more than she already was. I also realized that I had not had time to learn from Sempronius what his idea about Appius was, which was a distinctly uncomfortable sensation, knowing that I had to trust Dolabella's successor, but I also forced myself to be fair. He had followed me from the camp and had come to my aid when I was attacked, putting himself at risk; more importantly, he had insisted that I leave him to deal with the mess that I had made with Appius, in both the literal and figurative sense, and I made the decision that night to trust him in the same manner my father had come to trust Dolabella. And, so far, it has been a good decision. Once Alex was finished with my head, I stripped out of my tunic, leaving me in only my *subligaculum*, the sight of the bruises and welts on my body unleashing a fresh set of tears from Bronwen, while Algaia went pale, but it was Alex's reaction I was most worried about.

"Judging from where that bruise is," he pointed to my stomach, where the skin had colored to such a degree that you could clearly see the outline of the front part of a shoe sole, although thankfully, Appius had not had the military style hobnailed soles, "you might be bleeding inside."

"Wouldn't I know by now?" I asked, more for Bronwen's benefit than my own.

"If the bleeding was very bad, yes," Alex granted, but he still sounded grim. Then he reminded me, "But we've both seen someone who we thought was fine who wasn't."

He did not mention a name, but he did not need to; he was referring to one of the rankers in the First Century who had gotten kicked in a brawl in Ubiorum between us and men of the Seventh Cohort, his name Lucius Severus. His visible bruises were almost healed when, a week after the brawl, he suddenly collapsed during the morning formation, and while he lived another day, he never regained consciousness. The camp physician was puzzled enough to cut him open and found that his belly was filled with blood from a damaged liver.

"But Severus wasn't as muscled as you are," he pointed out. "Even in your stomach muscles, so I think it's a low chance."

Obviously, he was right, but in the moment, he had me stand up and turn towards the light, and when he probed my lower back, I gave another yelp.

"You're going to be pissing blood for a day or two," he guessed, and again he was right.

When he got to my ribs, he was more optimistic, assuring me that my ribs were not broken, although he did use a pair of bandages from his *medicus* bag to bind my lower chest just underneath my sternum, but when I complained it made it hard to breathe, he told me to stop whining like a little girl, which told me he was not overly worried.

"It's only a watch before dawn, and I think if I lie down, it will be hard to get back up because I'm too sore," I decided, but while Bronwen argued about it, I did not change my mind.

Fortuna smiled on me in the form of a tiny but powerful set of lungs as Titus decided that he was hungry, or so I was assured by Bronwen as she immediately forgot all about me and my condition to leave the three of us in the outer room.

"How does she know that he's hungry?" I asked Algaia, because it was truly a mystery to me. "He might have pissed or *cac*'ed himself, because he cries about that too."

The look Algaia gave me immediately reminded me of my mother Giulia, one of equal parts amusement and scorn at our thickness.

"Because a mother knows the difference," she said as if it was obvious, and I suppose it is for mothers. "You men aren't around long enough to learn the difference!"

I opened my mouth to argue that I had a job, but Alex stopped me with a touch of my arm, and when I glanced over, he just shook his head in that kind of silent signal that we men have learned to use when it comes to dealing with our women, informing me that this was a battle I would not win.

Algaia left, and as was the routine, Titus and Bronwen fell back asleep, with him lying on her chest, and I had learned that this was when she slept most soundly, when she was physically connected to her babe, which in turn enabled Alex and me to talk freely. I quickly informed him of the rest of the story, bracing myself for what I viewed as the inevitable remonstrance I had gotten from Sempronius, although much more pointed and detailed.

He shocked me then by saying, "I would have been surprised if you let Appius live after hearing this."

Certain that he was toying with me somehow, I asked suspiciously, "What makes you say that?"

"Because you're your father's son," Alex did not hesitate. "And no Pullus man has ever let a beating like you sustained go unavenged, no matter what the cost."

I cannot say I liked the tone that he used when he said this, but I could not argue the truth of his words.

I tried not to sound defensive when I said, "Well, Sempronius says he has an idea to cover up what I did to Appius. Now we have to decide what story to tell about why I look like this."

"You said you were attacked," Creticus was clearly choosing his words carefully, "on your way back from seeing your former comrades in the Fourth Cohort." I was standing in front of his desk, where he was seated, but I nodded in answer. "By four men," he continued, and I nodded again. "Who were trying to rob you? *You?*" Now he did not bother to hide his skepticism. "Not only are you...you," he apparently thought I would know what he was referring to, "but you said you were togate and carrying your *vitus*. There's not a man in Rome, no matter what class they are, who doesn't know that means you're a Praetorian."

"It *was* quite dark, Pilus Prior," I reminded him, while inwardly I was thanking Alex for thinking about Creticus' likely reaction. "And," I tried to sound contrite, "I might have imbibed a bit more wine than was wise with my friends. I think that what they saw was a drunken man of the upper class and thought he'd be easy pickings."

Creticus said nothing for a span of time, but he was not looking at me; he was looking at a wax tablet that, somewhat unusually, I could not read from where I was standing, and I realized that he had moved it closer to his edge of the deck while tilting it slightly, telling me this was not an accident.

I learned what it was when he said abruptly, "As it happens, all of the Praetorian Pili Priores are sent the nightly report from the Pilus Prior of the Urban Cohort on duty for the night. And," he indicated the tablet, "this arrived shortly before I summoned you, and it *does* say that there was some sort of...incident last night. Where did you say this attack happened?"

"The Forum Boarium," I replied, although I actually had not said anything about where it happened to that point.

"And how many attackers were there?"

"Four," I lied again; this was where things would get interesting, Alex had warned me.

"Are you certain?" Creticus pressed. "Could it have been more than four?"

Heeding Alex's advice, instead of repeating the lie, I tried to sound genuinely doubtful as I said, "It's certainly possible, Pilus Prior. As I said, it was dark, and there aren't any night torches in the Boarium."

For a span of perhaps a dozen heartbeats, Creticus just sat there, regarding me steadily as I stood there, doing my best not to appear uneasy at the silence, certain that it was a tactic on his part.

Finally, he gave a curt nod, then said, "Well, you put paid to all four of them according to this report." I felt my body relax, but he was not through, because he suddenly frowned as he continued reading from the tablet. "Although, there is one strange thing."

When this was all he said, I was forced to ask unconcernedly, "Oh, what's that, Pilus Prior?"

"It says that the Centurion ordered a search of the entire Boarium, and while they didn't find any other bodies, they did find a large pool of blood two blocks from where the four men were."

Before I could say anything, his eyes widened, and for the first time, he looked up at me. "Is this true? That one of the men you killed you almost cut in half at the waist?"

"I...suppose I did, Pilus Prior. Although I don't remember all that much."

"I knew you were strong," he gave a low whistle, "but this proves it."

I was actually tempted to say I had suddenly remembered that when I had done so, I was on my knees and robbed of the power from my legs, but I knew that was my pride talking and not my mind, so I refrained.

Instead, I pretended to consider the matter of the blood, and while I cannot say it was divinely inspired, I did think it was clever of me to point out, "The Boarium *is* where all the animals are slaughtered. I know they're supposed to wash the blood away every day, but I haven't been in Rome long enough to know if they're thorough or not."

"Actually," Creticus grunted, "they're terrible about doing a good job, which is why it stinks all the time." This seemed to answer the question in his mind, and he set the tablet down in a signal that this matter had been closed, which was confirmed when he asked, "Will you be able to conduct your duties, Pullus?"

"Absolutely, Pilus Prior," I assured him. Inwardly, I was thinking, thanks to being in the Praetorians, but I kept that inside.

"Very well, you're dismissed." He returned my salute, and I left his office, returning to mine, where I just gave Alex a nod that this part had gone well.

Now that the Legions had arrived, Sejanus had ordered that three of the four Cohorts inside the city stand duty every day, but only required three Centuries per Cohort. In another change, he had authorized that, instead of our normal practice of tunics and *balteae*, we turn out fully armed and armored, along with our plumes, which are dyed the same shade of blue as our tunics, with the exception of the Centurions. And, probably as a way for the gods to remind me that they still controlled things, it was the turn of the First, Second, and Third Centuries to stand duty, which meant that I had to struggle into my *hamata* with Alex's help, while Sabinus was outside bellowing at our men to assemble for inspection.

"What about your decorations?" Alex asked.

I blame the pain for distracting me enough that I did not think it through, and I nodded, whereupon he attached the *phalarae* to my harness, then the torq I had been awarded by Germanicus, which was not nearly as ornate as the one given to my father by Germanicus' father for slaying the Chatti chieftain Vergorix, and I was tempted to swap them but decided against it. Finally, the arm rings that, speaking for myself, I like wearing the best because of the way it accentuates the size of my arms, for which neither Alex nor Bronwen never tire of teasing me about.

Once I felt properly attired, I stepped out of the Century office to find the Second standing at *intente* already, returned Sabinus' salute, then began the inspection, starting with Flaccus. I confess I was disappointed that I could not find any fault with the *Signifer*, and while I did briefly consider inventing something, I dismissed it because it was likely to cause me more trouble than it was worth. Frankly, the time it took to conduct an inspection of the Praetorians compared to the Legions do not really compare because I had learned that it was rare to find a smudge on a buckle or a scratch on the varnish. I had also become resigned to the practice of varnishing the *caligae*, only because we did not actually march enough for it to be that much of a problem. Satisfied, I returned to my post, waiting for the other Centurions to finish, and as usual, Rufus was the last one to raise his *vitus* in his signal to Pilus Prior Creticus that the Cohort was ready to depart the barracks.

Normally, Creticus' next words would have been a command to execute a right facing turn before stepping off, so I was not watching him when, instead, he called out, "Pilus Posterior Pullus, attend to me!"

This startled me to the point where I instinctively pivoted and began to trot over to him, but I did not make it more than a couple paces before I had to stop or I would have groaned aloud. It was bad enough that I caught Flaccus smirking at my obvious discomfort, and I regretted my earlier decision not to find something to put him on *cac* detail for, but I quickly had something else to worry about.

Creticus returned my salute, but immediately pointed to my harness. "What are those?"

My first thought was, Does he really not know what *phalarae* are, so I said without thinking, "Those are *phalarae*, Pilus Prior. They're used by the Legions for..."

"I know what they are, idiot!" he snapped, then he took a breath as if to calm himself, and in a quieter tone, "What I want to know is why you're wearing them?"

"Because I earned them?" I heard how I made it sound like a question, but I was honestly baffled.

"Did you earn them as a Praetorian?" he countered, then answered for me, "No, you didn't. Those are Legion decorations, Pullus." His anger seemed to fade, and he indicated I follow him with a jerk of his head, and we moved a few paces away from his Century, while he made sure to turn his back to them. I will say that his tone was not unkind as he explained, "Pullus, look at the other Centurions. Look," he indicated himself, "at me. Do you see any decorations?"

"No, Pilus Prior," I answered, understanding now what this was really about, so before he could say anything more, I assured him, "I'll be back in a moment, Pilus Prior."

He nodded his dismissal, and I reentered the office, where Alex was finishing the morning report.

"He told you to take them off, didn't he?"

"Yes," I answered tersely, somewhat irritated at Alex because he had suggested it in the first place. "Help me get these off."

He came and did so, commenting as he worked, "You know that Creticus is actually doing you a favor, don't you?"

"How so?" I asked, surprised. "I thought it was just because he was embarrassed that I'm the only Centurion in the Cohort who has earned any decorations."

"Oh, that's certainly part of it," he allowed as he unfastened the torq. "But what do you think Sejanus' reaction would be if he saw you? And," Alex said positively, "he *will* be around today. This is too important for him to stay up on the Palatine."

This was certainly true, I realized, but I was still irritated, so I just gave him a nod as I left the office, my harness now bare so that the symbols of my actions would not cause my Pilus Prior and my fellow Centurions embarrassment for their lack of such things. Creticus just gave me a nod of approval, while I ignored Flaccus again, although I had begun to think of ways to make his life miserable, then Creticus gave the command and we marched out of the barracks.

Chapter 5

I knew within a third of a watch that it would be a very tough day for me, mainly because we spent as much time motionless as we did marching about the city, making the battered parts of my body stiffen up once we had stopped for a time. The Second Cohort was given the Sixth District north of the Forum, using the Via Longus that runs between the Viminal and Quirinal Hills, where Creticus' orders were essentially to march in a large rectangle around the Gardens of Sallustius, which had been opened to the public for the week, although we were stopped at intervals, presumably for the citizens to admire us, and I wondered if this was by Sejanus' order. Since we would not be marching in the triumph—the Seventh and Eighth Praetorian Cohorts who had distinguished themselves at the Angrivarian Wall had arrived the day before and were now on the Campus as well and would represent the Praetorians—I supposed this was as close to it as we would get to marching in one. It was supposed to be festive, and while there was some cheering as we marched past, I also was certain I felt an undercurrent as well, one of resentment and sullen anger, and during one of the times we were stopped, although Creticus never gave the reason for them, I called Sabinus to me.

"Is it my imagination, or are there people who aren't all that happy to see us?"

"It's not your imagination, Centurion," Sabinus assured me. When I did not say anything, he shrugged and explained, "It's just that the Praetorians here in Rome have a... reputation for treating the citizens of the lower class poorly."

"How so?"

Now he looked uncomfortable, but he did not hesitate, "Sometimes the rankers don't pay their bill at a *taverna*, or at a brothel," he said. "And if the owner is a member of the Head Count, he's likely to get a beating if he tries to make them pay."

"Can't the owner just go to the Urban Cohort?"

This evoked a snort from Sabinus, and I sensed he thought I was jesting by the look of dawning surprise on his face.

"Pullus, the Praetorians own the Urban Cohorts," Sabinus said seriously, but he quickly amended, "or I should say, Prefect Sejanus owns the Urban Cohorts because their Prefect was suggested to Tiberius by Sejanus. And," he lowered his voice, and while he did not move his head, I saw his eyes dart over to where the men were standing with their shields grounded, although Creticus had forbidden the Cohort from leaning on them, "Sejanus handpicked the Tribunes of each Urban Cohort as well. So," he finished with a shrug, "to answer your question, no, the Urban Cohort won't lift a finger to stop what's going on."

"How many men in our Century behave in this manner?" I asked coldly. When he did not seem disposed to answer, I decided it was time to employ a favorite tactic, although some might call it a trick, leaning closer to Sabinus so that I was essentially towering over him as I fixed him with a hard stare, ignoring the pain it caused me to do so. "Sabinus, you seem to be a good Optio, and up to this moment, I've been pleased with your performance, and you've been a big help as I learn my way with the Guard. But," I tapped his chest with my *vitus*, "you need to decide where your loyalties lie: with your Centurion, or with some of your men who may be behaving in a manner that reflects poorly, not just on me, but you and the Praetorians."

He was clearly nervous, which I liked to see, but he argued, "Centurion, we're just one Century in one of the four Cohorts. And believe me, this is something that every Praetorian officer has to deal with."

I was about to snap that I did not give a fart in a *testudo* about the other Centuries or Cohorts, but I managed to refrain and instead suggested, "Sabinus, take another look at those people watching us. Are they looking at us the way they'll be watching the Legions in a couple of days? Are they cheering us the way they will the Legions?" He shook his head, and I pressed, "No, they aren't, and the Legions are returning to the Rhenus, while we're going to stay here...along with all those people staring at us. At the very least, we can put a stop to what *our* men are doing."

I deliberately chose to refer to the Century as being under both of our commands, which meant that we were equally responsible for each of them, and I was pleased when I saw his head move slowly up and down.

"You're right, Centurion, and I apologize for forgetting that."

"No need to apologize." I smiled, but there was an edge to it that he did not miss. "Just give me the names of men who are robbing these people."

By the time he was finished, I had been given my opportunity with Flaccus, and I was not surprised at the names of the others, since they were all close friends.

I was exhausted by the time we marched back to the barracks, while my head was throbbing from my helmet rubbing against the gashes on my head, for which I accept the blame since I refused to allow Alex to wrap a bandage around my head, not wanting to draw more attention to my injuries. However, I was equally disturbed at the sight of my men, almost all of whom looked how I felt, and none of them had the excuse of having sustained a beating the night before, telling me just how soft these men were. That, however, I decided was for later, because I needed to hurry to my apartment the moment we were secured from duty to wait for Sempronius. Such a rush was I in that I risked flaunting the regulations and did not take off my armor, but we managed to slip out of the barracks without Creticus noticing me. Alex was with me, naturally, but we did not talk on our walk to the Caelian, mainly because I was huffing and puffing from the bandage restricting my breathing and the pain deep inhalation caused. I had not told Bronwen that, if the gods favored me, Sempronius would be showing up, and I knew that if he appeared it would raise questions with her, but this was also a problem for later. The people in the streets who already steered clear of me when I was togate or carrying my *vitus* now leapt out of my path since I was fully armored, and I was still wearing my helmet despite a deep desire to pull it off. When we got to the apartment, the stairs once more proved to be a daunting task, but I told myself that I did feel better, if marginally, than I had in the night hour. Bronwen was surprised to see me attired as if I was back with the Legions, but she helped me shed my armor while Alex spent time with Algaia.

"Sempronius might be stopping by." I tried to sound casual about it.

At first, I thought I had succeeded when she only commented, "It has been some time since he's stopped by." She disappeared, lugging my armor into our bedroom, refusing my offer to carry it with a tart reminder that I had undergone a beating a handful of watches earlier. It was when she returned and dropped down onto the bench next to me to give me a level look that told me she was at least suspicious of something as she asked, "And why did Marcus Sempronius suddenly stop showing up here? I thought you had things for him to do. Are they all done now?"

I glanced over at her, and I saw that she was not fooled; oh, she may not have known the details, but she knew that Sempronius' absence had nothing to do with the fact that I had run out of errands for him.

Regardless, I lied, "Yes, but something has come up that I need to talk to him about."

Instantly, I knew I had blundered, and I barely managed to avoid compounding it by groaning aloud.

"And what is that?" she asked directly, but it was the crossing of her arms that told me she would not be deterred. "What has come up that you need his help for, Gnaeus?"

The sharp rapping on the door startled both of us, but I offered a silent thanks, both for the temporary rescue, and because if it had been Alex, he would have entered after knocking and this visitor did not, making me certain I knew who it was. I got up with some difficulty and hobbled to the door, but there was no way I could have been prepared for what I saw when I opened the door.

Which was why I inhaled so deeply that it caused me to give a bark of pain before I gasped, *"Lysander?"*

It took some doing, and it was not accomplished without some acrimonious words between my woman and myself, but Lysander had absolutely refused to divulge the purpose of his visit to the apartment with her, or Algaia, in the same room. Finally, the two women and the children were banished downstairs, though not without a dire warning from Bronwen that our conjugal bed would be so cold that night, I would be better off finding somewhere else to sleep.

"She," Lysander observed mildly, "has a temper."

I had to chuckle at the understatement, which unleashed a fit of half-cough, half-groan, but the moment of levity did not last.

"I doubt you're going to feel like laughing after this," he began ominously, and I glanced over at Alex, trying to get a sense of what might be coming, but he was as mystified as I was. Naturally, he had been offered refreshment by Bronwen, even as she was castigating him, and me, for being excluded. He was eyeing the cup as if he was trying to decide how to begin, or maybe he was worried that Bronwen had put something in his wine, then continued, "Someone has disappeared from Rome, Centurion. And," he looked up at me, "his absence could prove to be dangerous to a number of people. Depending," his voice changed slightly, "on why he vanished...and whether he's coming back."

Alex told me later that he was buying me time when he asked suddenly, "Did Germanicus send you?"

"Not directly," Lysander replied carefully, "but suffice to say that he's aware of this situation."

"And I suppose he's one of those concerned that it could be dangerous?"

"Not for him." Lysander shook his head. "Not personally, but there are people around him who may fall under suspicion, through no fault of their own. And you," Lysander turned to address me, "you are one of them, Pullus. Germanicus...suggested that someone should warn you to expect some sort of trouble."

He doesn't know! It took all of my self-discipline to keep my expression the same, or at least I hoped it was, but I could not stop myself from glancing over at Alex. He is better than I am at masking his true thoughts, but I saw in his eyes the same confusion I was feeling, since I had resigned myself to being told that I was at least suspected in Appius' disappearance.

"Do you want us to guess who we're supposed to worry about?"

I saw immediately that Alex's pointed question made Lysander both irritated and uneasy, but he answered readily enough, "I think you know who."

He wants one of us to say his name, I thought, so more to keep

Alex from uttering it, I said, "Sejanus. He's the threat."

Lysander nodded slowly.

"Yes. The missing man was one of his...agents, I suppose is the best way to put it."

"Wait," I pretended to guess. "Are you talking about Appius?"

"Yes." He was clearly surprised, but when I reminded him that I had reported our encounter in the Forum, he looked chagrined. "Yes, that's right. I forgot. So yes, it's Appius who's missing."

This was when he pointed to my head, which Alex had insisted on bandaging on our return. "Does that have anything to do with Appius being missing?"

"No," I lied immediately and without hesitation. "I visited the camp last night to see some comrades, and on the way back, I cut through the Boarium, and some bully boys from one of the *collegia* either had been following me or were just waiting for some drunk they could rob."

"How many were there?"

"Four," I lied again, sticking to the story that we had concocted to tell Creticus.

Lysander regarded me for a long moment, saying nothing, then gave a shrug in seeming acceptance.

"Fortuna smiled on you, then," he responded, then returned to the subject of discussion, "but you're going to have to be more careful than you were last night until this Appius situation is resolved."

"We'll stay alert," I promised Lysander, but before I could say anything else, there was another knock on the door.

The sound made me jerk in surprise, although I was not alone, as the other two did as well, but it was Lysander who, clearly worried, asked, "Are you expecting someone?"

"Actually, yes," I said offhandedly. "A man I've used on occasion to run some errands."

Instead of doing it myself, I gave Alex a beseeching look, and he heaved a great sigh as he stood up, muttering something about not being a servant, which I answered with a broad grin and a shooing motion towards the door. While it was Sempronius standing there when Alex opened the door, it was Lysander's sudden gasp of shock, accompanied by him leaping to his feet that gave Alex and me a presentiment that our plight was about to become more complicated.

"*This* is who you were waiting for?" Lysander's tone sounded accusing to my ears, but I managed to not react in the way that his words inspired in me, saying only, "Yes. This is Marcus Sempronius."

"I know who he is!" Lysander snapped.

When I turned to look at Sempronius, who was still just inside the door although Alex had closed it, while he did not appear angry, I could see that he was at the very least deeply unsettled to see one of Germanicus' most trusted scribes in my apartment, but he was the one who actually broke the brief silence.

"*Salve*, Lysander. It's been a while."

"And you know why!" Lysander shouted, but there was something in his voice besides anger that made me turn back to him and examine his face more carefully.

He's not just angry, he looks...hurt, I thought, though I decided for once to keep my mouth shut, as did Alex, leaving us as mute witnesses to this tense reunion. Once more, the silence dragged out, then Lysander expelled the breath he must have been holding before dropping back down on the bench.

"That doesn't matter now," he said almost to himself. "What does is why you're here." Either ignoring or forgetting where we were, he extended a hand to indicate the seat on the opposite side of the table, but Sempronius looked at me, and I nodded, though I was not particularly happy about it. My hope that Sempronius' visit would be brief was clearly not going to happen, and he sat down on my side of the table, but at the opposite end of the bench. "This is obviously about Appius," Lysander said the instant Sempronius' ass hit the wood of the bench.

"Yes." Sempronius wasted no time answering Lysander, but then he turned to me and asked bluntly, "Does he know?"

I do not know why I was surprised that he asked me this; I blame still being distracted by the beating, which made me slow to respond.

Lysander, however, immediately understood the implication of the question, and he looked at me accusingly. "So that story about you being robbed was just that, a story."

"Yes, but that's my responsibility," Alex interjected, having returned to sit next to Lysander. "I convinced Gnaeus that it would be in his best interests to lie to Pilus Prior Creticus."

"No it's not," I snapped in irritation. "I'm not a simpleminded fool that has to be told what needs to be done. I made the decision on my own."

"It doesn't matter," Lysander said, sounding tired, and I wondered how much weight he carried on his shoulders for his master. Keeping his gaze on me, he said, "Tell me what happened. And," he held up a hand, "I mean *everything*, Pullus. No more secrets. We're past that now, and it's too dangerous."

"I didn't lie," I protested, very weakly, "not exactly. I was ambushed in the Boarium like I said, but there were five, not four of them."

"And the fifth man was Appius," Lysander muttered. He thought for a moment, then asked, "So how many of them got away?"

This prompted Alex and me to exchange a started glance, but he beat me to it by asking, "Didn't you see the report from the Urban Cohort about what happened last night?"

"What report?" Lysander shook his head. "I don't know what you're talking about."

Alex went on to explain how the Praetorian Guard received daily reports for both the day and night watches from the Urban Cohort; judging from Lysander's reaction, this was news to him, which he immediately confirmed.

"Those reports aren't sent to Germanicus, because I would have seen them." He was clearly angry, slamming one hand on the table. "Yet another thing that viper Sejanus is keeping from us!" He glared down at the table for a couple heartbeats, then returned his attention to me. "Judging from your surprise, that clearly means those men didn't escape?"

"No," I assured him, bracing myself for what was coming next.

"What about Appius?" Lysander asked. "Are you saying that he's dead as well?"

I opened my mouth, and on the black stone I was going to tell the truth, that I essentially executed the man, but Sempronius spoke up. "Yes, he is, but it's not the Centurion's fault. It's mine."

Lysander let out what sounded like a curse under his breath as his attention snapped from me to the man sitting across from him, but he sounded calm enough when he asked, "How is that?"

"I was following the Centurion to the camp and back here," Sempronius answered. "But I let him get a bit too far ahead of me, and Appius and his bunch were waiting for him when he was about halfway through the Boarium. By the time I got there, the Centurion was on his knees, then I..."

"Stop." I will not deny that part of the reason I refused to allow Sempronius to take the blame for Appius' death was that his mention of me being on my knees was a blow to my pride that I could not endure, but it was also that, while I appreciated the gesture, Sempronius should not suffer the consequences for something I had done. Turning to Lysander, I said, "I killed Appius, but it was only after Sempronius came to my aid. He ran off, but I caught him. And," I said flatly, "I didn't have to kill him, but I did." Only then did I look over to Sempronius. "Thank you, Sempronius. I appreciate that you tried to take the blame for killing that *cunnus*, but it's not right that you might suffer Sejanus' wrath because of a lie."

I cannot say what I expected Sempronius to say, but it certainly was not his lips pressing into a thin line as he retorted, "It's better for all of us that it's me and not you that Sejanus comes after."

"Oh, *now* you're willing to sacrifice for the greater good?"

The sarcasm in Lysander's voice was scathing and impossible to miss, but while I saw Sempronius' face flush, he replied mildly, "That was a long time ago, Lysander. Men change." This evoked a snort but nothing else from Lysander, then Sempronius moved on by saying, "But I don't think Sejanus will have more than just a whisper of suspicion that the Centurion is responsible, and there's a far more likely suspect."

Not surprisingly, this riveted the attention of the three of us, but I suppose it makes sense that of the three of us, Lysander was clearly the most skeptical.

"And who could that possibly be?" he demanded. "You know that Sejanus ordered Appius to go after Pullus to find out what he was up to. Which," he turned back to me, "you should know that I don't buy your story about why you were in camp last night, not after knowing you lied about Appius."

I was rescued by Sempronius again, when he offered a single word; more accurately, a name.

"Fidenus."

I had never heard of him, and a glance at Alex earned me a shrug, but Lysander clearly had, although he seemed unconvinced, replying, "I've heard about Fidenus and Appius, but I don't think Sejanus will believe that the man would be bold enough to do anything to him."

"Would either of you care to explain who this Fidenus is?" I demanded, not liking the feeling of not knowing anything about what was being discussed, especially given that it involved me.

"He runs one of the Aventine *collegia*," Sempronius explained. "And he and Appius used to be partners for a protection scheme until Sejanus recruited Appius." He paused, which appeared to be a silent signal to Lysander, because he was the one who continued, "The story is that Appius had promised to put in a good word for Fidenus with the Prefect. This was back when Sejanus was still a Tribune," he explained. "But while nobody knows with any certainty, what is known is that Fidenus has never been on Sejanus' payroll. But," Lysander shook his head as he addressed Sempronius, "that's not enough for Fidenus to kill Appius, not all these years later."

"No, it's not," Sempronius seemingly agreed, but he paused, and while I never asked, I am certain I heard a note of satisfaction as he continued, "but the fact that Appius borrowed money from Fidenus to buy a small estate outside Rome, and when Fidenus came to Appius demanding repayment, Appius used his relationship with Sejanus to threaten Fidenus? That," he finished, "is more than enough for Fidenus to risk it."

"How do you know this?" Lysander demanded, but Sempronius shook his head.

"You have your sources, I have mine," he countered. "But if you don't believe it, send one of your little birds over to the Aventine to Diana's Lair, which is right across the street from the Temple. If they sit there long enough, they'll hear about it."

Lysander considered this for a long time, although frankly, I did not see why he was still doubtful, because I saw absolutely no reason for Sempronius to fabricate this story, because it could not be corroborated. As I would be learning, however, I was also still a raw provincial who had been thrown into the labyrinth that is Rome and its politics, from the heights of the Palatine with all the plots and counterplots by men like Sejanus, to the depths of the Subura, where men like Marcus Sempronius were engaged in as deadly and, to them at least, as important a contest as any patrician. Despite what I was to learn, I will also say that Sempronius was not lying about the falling out between Fidenus and Appius, which would be confirmed not long after this meeting, in a grisly fashion, when we heard that Fidenus' body had been found. More accurately, part of him was discovered, namely his head, which had been deposited on the doorstep of the building that had been the headquarters of his collegia. Which, as one might imagine, engendered all manner of jests about how this was now the appropriate name for it.

Finally, Lysander shrugged and said, "No, I believe you. But," he warned, "what's most important is that Sejanus believes it."

"He will," Sempronius assured him, "and I've taken steps to make sure he hears the story from a reliable source."

Not surprisingly, Lysander pressed him for more about this source, and I was as interested as the scribe, but on this, Sempronius refused to budge, saying only, "I'm the only one who knows who it is, and it's going to stay that way."

Whether Lysander was satisfied, or he was resigned to the idea this was as much as he would learn, and that his warning had been delivered, he stood up and announced that he was taking his leave. Before he got to the door, however, Sempronius spoke up again.

"Lysander, wait, please." It was easy to see he was reluctant, but he did so, and again I was certain I saw something besides anger or dislike in the scribe's expression. "I have something to tell the Centurion that I think will interest you. And," he added with a tentative smile, "hopefully please you as much as it will your master." He turned to me and informed me, "You didn't know this, but the *Propraetor* made a formal request of the Princeps that you be allowed to march with the 1st in the triumph. And," the smile he offered seemed genuine, "my master told me to tell you that he approved the request. You'll be marching with your old Legion in the triumph."

Alex leapt to his feet, and even Lysander gave a cry that sounded like happiness, but I just sat there, unable to move, while the lump in my throat prevented me from saying anything for several heartbeats.

When I was able to speak, my voice was husky to my ears, but all I could think to say was, "Please tell both of them I offered my deepest thanks and appreciation for this honor." It was more to keep my composure that I looked over at Alex, who was smiling broadly, and said, "At least I'll be able to wear my *phalarae* this time."

"Even better," Lysander said, and now he was smiling as well, his feelings about Sempronius at least temporarily in abeyance, "this will drive Sejanus mad. And," he chuckled, "there's nothing he can do about it."

Sempronius got up then, bidding Alex and me goodbye, but he turned to Lysander and asked quietly, "May I walk with you, Lysander? I'd like to talk to you."

I was certain Lysander would rebuff him, but to my surprise, he only hesitated a moment before giving a nod, although he did not say anything, and the pair opened the door and disappeared into the night.

"I wonder what that's all about," I mused.

"So do I," Alex agreed, then shrugged as he added, "but I doubt we'll ever know."

He was right, at least to this point in time. My happiness was tempered by one thing, and since it was just Alex and me, I did not try and stifle my groan as I got to my feet.

"Now I have to go face Bronwen," I said, feeling a bit grumpy and apprehensive about it.

"Tell her about the triumph first," he advised me.

It was good advice.

"I've received orders about you, Pullus," Creticus informed me the next morning. He eyed me for a moment before continuing, and I guessed that he was waiting for me to confirm that I knew what it was about, but I stood there looking at him blandly. Finally, he sniffed and said, "Yes, well, orders have come from the Prefect that you're being allowed to march with your Legion in the triumph tomorrow."

I did try to appear surprised, but I do not think he was fooled, nor was it all good news.

"Since it's tomorrow, Pilus Prior, I request your permission to turn over command to Optio Sabinus today so that I can prepare my uniform."

Creticus looked uncomfortable, but he did not hesitate to say, "Request denied." When I opened my mouth to protest, he cut me off with a hand. "It's not me, Pullus. This came from the Prefect. He's...not pleased about this, for some reason."

I seem to have a streak of perversity in me that tempts me to say intemperate things, and I certainly was tempted to tell him the reason for Sejanus' displeasure, but I refrained. And while I cannot say I was surprised, I still was unhappy, and I took it out on my Century, who found themselves performing exercises in the barracks square. Admittedly, part of the reason was because of my anger, but I also remembered how they behaved as if they had been on a thirty-mile forced march with full equipment instead of what was by Legion standards a leisurely stroll through the Sixth District. I did not participate in the exercises, something that I normally did, but I was still exceedingly sore from the beating, so I had to content myself by strolling through the ranks, tapping my *vitus* in my hand, and on occasion, using it to encourage one of the men I deemed was not putting the right amount of effort into their exertions.

"The more you sweat now, the less you'll bleed later."

I had adopted one of my father's favorite sayings for my own, and while it was not in my plan, either the gods decided to do me a favor or it was just a happy accident, because I happened to be walking past Flaccus, his face red and glistening with sweat as I uttered this again.

"We're Praetorians, not some fucking arrow sponge Legionaries."

He had muttered this, and I suppose he felt emboldened because I had just passed him and was behind him, but I heard him say it, and I heard some of the men snickering, which made it even worse for him. My initial instinct was to use my *vitus* from behind and bring it down across his back, but I managed to refrain, and instead, I walked slowly back to where he was lying, face down, since at this moment, I had the men performing press-ups, and I made sure to move so that he could see my *caligae* right under his nose after he pressed himself up. As I intended, this got his attention, his head snapping up, his eyes wide at the sight of me staring down at him.

"On your feet, Flaccus," I ordered calmly.

He obeyed, although he seemed to take his time, but I refused to believe that he would be that openly defiant just judging by his expression as he drew himself to *intente*.

When I did raise my voice, it was to bellow at the others, "Nobody told you to fucking stop, you *cunni*!"

Sabinus was on the opposite side at the rear of the formation, and over the prone bodies of the men, I pointed to one in the Fifth Section who had used this diversion as an opportunity to rest. Sabinus nodded, then stepped over the other men to begin thrashing the ranker; the fact that I knew that this man, Arvina was his name, was a close friend of Flaccus meant that this was not a random decision. And, just as I expected, when Arvina yelped in surprise and pain when Sabinus smacked the back of his legs, Flaccus immediately looked over his shoulder.

"And nobody gave you permission to look, Flaccus." I did not yell this, but I was pleased to see that when he snapped his head back to face front, he looked acutely nervous, which I took to mean that he correctly heard the menace in my voice. "Now," I continued to keep my voice low, and now that Sabinus had made an example of Arvina, I could see bodies moving up and down as they panted and groaned from their exertions, "I'm curious about something, and I hope that you might be able to enlighten me about it."

As I hoped, a look of wary confusion replaced his expression of an eyeblink earlier, but he tried to sound earnest as he answered, "If I can be of any help, Centurion Pullus, I'm happy to help."

"Good, good." I nodded, wondering if it was wrong that I was enjoying myself. "I appreciate that, Flaccus. Now, I heard you use a term that I haven't heard used before." I was rewarded by Flaccus suddenly closing his eyes for a moment as he realized that I had heard him. "Arrow sponge?" I pursed my lips as I shook my head. "I don't believe I've ever heard that term before. What does it mean?"

Flaccus' mouth seemed to have gone dry, because I saw him swallow twice before he finally got out, "It...it's a term some men use at times." He stopped, but while I did not speak, I raised an eyebrow, and he let out a breath as he said resignedly, "Some men call the men of the Legions arrow sponges."

"Some men?" I echoed. "What kind of men would use that term? You know I'm new to Rome, and I haven't had much time to meet anyone here. So who calls the Legions arrow sponges? Is that what the people in the Subura call them? Because," I pointed out helpfully, "as you may know, there are a lot of men from the Urban tribes under the standard. So," I shook my head, "I don't think they would say that."

I suppose Flaccus decided there was no point in prolonging the suspense, because he said tonelessly, "It's a term that some Praetorians use, Centurion."

"Ah." I nodded, as if this was some sort of news. "I see. And," I pointed out, "you *are* a Praetorian, *neh*?"

"Yes, Centurion," Flaccus answered, and I heard the resignation in his voice, and I thought, You just think you know what's coming.

"Have you ever been hit by an arrow, Flaccus?" I asked.

This startled him, just as I intended, and he not only shook his head, but he actually gave a small laugh. "No, Centurion. You know that I've only been in the Praetorians. And we don't have to worry about anyone shooting arrows at us."

"Have you ever wondered what it feels like?" His mouth was just opening when I struck him, not hard enough to kill him, but enough that the eagle of my *vitus* would leave a bruise right below his sternum, and I was blasted in the face with his breath as he collapsed at my feet, curled up into a ball and gasping for breath. I leaned over so I did not have to raise my voice as I informed him, "That's what it feels like, Flaccus. Except," I allowed, "it hurts a lot worse when that arrow is buried deep in your guts, and your *cac* fills your belly. You know," I said conversationally, "you can always tell if a man is doomed by getting close and sniffing the wound. If you smell *cac*, he's already in the boat." Straightening up, I said, "You need to keep that in mind for the next time you want to call the men who keep Rome's borders safe an arrow sponge."

Suddenly, I was in a better frame of mind.

I would have liked to actually visit my friends that night, but I was too busy making myself presentable for what is the ultimate reward for men who march under the standard. And for once, I didn't rely on Alex as I had in the past; this time, I did everything myself. As I worked, I was surprised at the wave of emotion I was feeling, but it wasn't all excitement and anticipation at seeing my former Cohort. Instead, without warning, I felt a wave of sadness as I realized something: my great-grandfather had marched in four triumphs, my grandfather had marched in one as part of the Army of Pannonia when Augustus awarded the grandson of Marcus Crassus a triumph for his campaign against the Bastarnae, and now I was about to march in a triumph, meaning the only Pullus man who was left out was my father. It was this thought that got me up to go to the chest that contains all of my uniform items, including the decorations, and from it, I took the torq that my father had been awarded by the Imperator's brother for slaying Vergorix of the Chatti in his first battle, and replaced the one that I had been awarded for the rescue of Segestes, which I had always found to be bittersweet when I wore it because it also was the day my father was killed.

"This way, you'll be marching in the triumph for Germanicus like you deserve," I whispered as I attached it to my armor, and so absorbed was I in this that I did not hear Bronwen enter our bedroom, holding young Titus.

The baby coughed, which made me jump out of my skin, and I

turned to see her standing there, with Titus in her arms, but it was the way her eyes were shining that told me she had heard me.

"I wish," she said as she came to me, "I had gotten to meet your father."

"So do I." It was all I could manage, but Bronwen handed me my son without a word, understanding that this was the best thing she could have done.

He was at the age where he was learning how to explore things, although he had not begun to crawl, but when he leaned down to grasp the torq, I did not stop him, choosing instead to watch his face as his eyes fastened on the intricately worked golden torq, enjoying the change of expression on his face as he did so.

"You just polished that," Bronwen protested, but I shook my head.

"I know, but I can do it again," I barely recognized my own voice as I watched young Titus touching something that had belonged to his grandfather, for whom he was named, and I wondered if there was some form of magic where some of my father's *animus* was still contained within that golden device, and if so, was it being transferred into my son. It is a silly notion, I know, yet in the moment, it seemed possible. But then, his tiny hand curled into a fist around the torq, and if it had not been attached, he would have picked it up, and as I had observed he did with everything, put it in his mouth. This made me laugh, and I pried his fingers loose as I told him, "No, this isn't to eat, son."

I should not have been surprised that young Titus took this as a mortal insult, because he began bellowing in indignation, waving his little arms around and turning red in the face. And this battle-hardened Centurion immediately turned around and thrust the baby out to his mother, who gave me a mock glare as she took him while I detached the torq and beat a hasty retreat to the other room to re-polish it.

After a sleepless night, I rose with Bronwen and Titus, and as she nursed him, I broke my fast. Alex and Algaia came in, and we discussed the plan for the day, which included me taking full advantage of one of the benefits of being a Praetorian.

"You'll have seats at the Circus," I reminded them. "Which is probably the best spot to be with Iras and the baby. I don't want you in the crush of the crowd along the route." Turning to Alex, I asked for what he later assured me was at least the fifth time, "You've already got the tokens from Creticus?"

"Yes, Gnaeus," he sighed, pulling them out of his purse to wave under my nose.

"The earlier you get there, the closer you'll get," I grumbled, knowing I sounded defensive.

While I had done everything myself, Alex came into the bedroom to help me don my uniform, ignoring my fussing when, once again, I wore the red tunic of the Legions, along with the red transverse crest that marked me as a Pilus Prior and not the black, which I had been informed I would be allowed to wear because this was the rank I held at the end of the campaign. One reason I had wanted to visit my comrades before the triumph was to speak with Licinius, who was the acting Pilus Prior...or perhaps he was now the permanent Pilus Prior, I reminded myself, to ensure there would be no confusion about my place in the formation, and if there was some tension, try to at least reduce it. Now I would be finding out when I went to the Campus, where the Legions were at that moment beginning their day as well. The marching part of a Triumph actually takes place relatively late in the day, at least for Legion men, starting at the beginning of the noon watch, but I was leaving my apartment shortly after dawn. The streets were busier than normal, I noticed immediately, but I quickly saw why when I entered the Boarium and there were already people lining the Via Boarium, which is part of the route. At first, I got the kind of looks from the citizens that I had become, if not accustomed to, at least familiar with as a Praetorian, but when the sun peeked over the tops of the buildings on the eastern side of the city and I was easier to see, they apparently realized I was not a Praetorian. Indeed, it was somewhat embarrassing to hear people cheering me, and I also felt slightly guilty, as if I was stealing the thunder of Germanicus and the Legions who were out on the Campus.

"Gods, he's huge!"

"I can see why they beat those German savages if they all look like him!"

This was the sort of thing people were saying as I strode by, but while I tried to maintain an impassive demeanor, I confess that before I exited the Boarium, I was smiling from ear to ear, and actually replying to some of the people who called out to me.

The most memorable comment, however, was when a man turned to a companion and remarked, "How would you like to be walking in the Aventine after dark and run into *him*, eh, Vibius?"

You, I thought with grim amusement, have no idea how truly you speak. Having learned my lesson the hard way about not having some sort of bandage on my stitched cut, Bronwen had fashioned something of a pad that was held in place by the felt cap and extended down just above the top of my ear, and one had to get close to notice it, but it was beginning to itch. Leaving the Boarium and entering the Campus, the crowd was actually thicker, despite the fact that they still had almost two watches to midday, but there was a festival atmosphere, where people brought folding stools, and more than one of them brought liquid refreshment with them. How drunk are they going to be by the time we march by? I wondered. The gates to the camp were wide open, but while I expected to be stopped, none of the men standing watch gave me more than a quick glance, and I realized that there was probably a stream of Centurions and Optios returning from whatever debauching from the night before. There certainly had been no word of any trouble, but frankly, all I was concerned about was that, if there was, it was not with men from the Fourth Cohort of the 1st, or the Second Century of the Second Praetorian Cohort. I suppose it sounds odd that my immediate concern was for my former Cohort, but that was where my loyalty still lay, which should not really be a surprise. I had shed blood with, and for those men, as they had for me, whereas all I had done with the Second Century was make sure they looked good and marched them about as toy soldiers. Since it was so early, the men had yet to don their full uniforms for the final inspection, and while I would not call the atmosphere leisurely, there was a lack of tension, which surprised me a bit. I decided to head to the Primus Pilus' quarters, but I did not even have to go inside because he was standing with a group of Centurions, still in their tunics. As I got closer, I recognized one of the Centurions from behind since his back was to me, and my grin was so broad and sudden that it caused a tweak of pain from the stitches pulling, but while he is not the shortest Centurion in the 1st, he is the shortest Pilus Prior. I suppose Primus Pilus Sacrovir caught movement out of the corner of his eye, and he turned away from the others as I approached.

"You're late..." Sacrovir said, his face expressionless, yet only for a moment, when he added with a smile, "Pilus Prior Pullus."

The next few moments were consumed with greetings from the other eight Pili Priores, some cordial, one or two cool, but there was only one man whose smile matched mine, and that was Marcus Macer, my father's closest friend and my first Pilus Prior.

I should have known what was coming, because after we clasped arms—we would have embraced if I had not already been in uniform—Macer's smile vanished and he pointed up to the pad above my ear, demanding, "What's that?" I opened my mouth, but he beat me it to add, "Who did you make angry this time?"

"You sound like Bronwen and Alex," I protested. "Why do you immediately assume it's because of something I did?"

"Because it usually is," Macer shot back, then the smile returned.

Even Sacrovir was in a jovial mood, commenting, "Whoever did that didn't know that hitting Pullus in the head doesn't do anything because there's nothing in there to hurt."

This brought a roar of laughter, and while I joined in, it was more because it was so rare to see Sacrovir in such a lighthearted mood.

Once the laughter subsided, but everyone was still looking at me, I explained, using the lie we had used with Creticus, which seemed to satisfy everyone...except for Macer, and I felt him studying my face.

Resigning myself to more questioning about this later, I addressed Sacrovir. "Primus Pilus, if Germanicus authorizing me to march as Pilus Prior is a problem for Licinius, I'd like to talk to him about it."

Sacrovir looked surprised, and I learned why when he said, "That didn't come from Germanicus, Pullus. I mean," he lifted a hand, "yes, the order was his, but it was because I specifically requested that you march as the Pilus Prior." I was surprised at this, which obviously showed in my expression, because Sacrovir looked somewhat embarrassed as he offered a shrug. "You deserve it,

Pullus. That's the only reason. And," he assured me, "I've told Licinius and he actually agreed."

While this was a relief, I did not completely believe Sacrovir that this was just a case of justice applied; now that I was favored by Germanicus, it was a politic thing to do, but as soon as the thought crossed my mind, I dismissed it as unworthy. Yes, the Primus Pilus and I had had our problems, but I had become aware that he did not bear me anywhere near the enmity I had assumed he did. However, I tucked this away in the back of my mind to talk to Macer about when I had the chance.

"We're going to be holding full inspection a third of a watch before the end of second watch," Sacrovir informed me. "That should give you some time to go see the boys of the Fourth."

With that, we were dismissed, and while the others, like Clepsina and Gallus, seemed disposed to walk with us, I think they saw that I wanted to have a word with Macer alone, and they hurried away towards their areas.

"So how are the Praetorians?" Macer asked me, which made me laugh.

"Where do I even begin?" It was all I could think to say. "And," I took a glance around then lowered my voice, "I don't want to talk about it out here."

Macer nodded, then in a tacit signal, he asked, "And how is Bronwen? Has she had the baby?"

"She's fine and yes, she has," I confirmed, but then said nothing else, enjoying his look of anticipation that transformed into a glare.

"Well?" he demanded. "Is that all you're going to say?"

"That's all you asked me," I answered innocently, which earned me a shove, and I laughed, telling him, "Yes, mother and babe are fine, and he's a son."

Macer's smile was as broad as it was genuine, and he teased me, "Do I even need to ask what his name is?"

"I can tell you what it's not." I grinned down at him. "It's not Marcus."

"Marcus is a fine name!" He tried to sound indignant.

"There've been many famous Romans named Marcus!"

"Yes," I seemingly agreed, then extended a finger. "There was Marcus Crassus. He ended up having his head cut off. Then," another finger, "there was Marcus Antonius." I made an exaggerated show of looking around with my eyes wide then whispered, "And we're not even supposed to say his name!"

"Oh, go piss on your boots," he grumbled, but we had reached his quarters by then, and before he entered his tent, we agreed to get together privately before the 1st returned to Ubiorum.

I spotted Saloninus before he spied me, and it enabled me to sneak up behind my former Optio and the current Pilus Posterior by approaching from his blind side.

"If I didn't know better, I'd think you lost your other eye if you can't see a big bastard like me coming," I commented.

He had been in the process of berating Tiberius Vitruvius, the Sergeant of the First Section of his Second Century, which I had commanded as well, but Vitruvius had seen me coming and heeded my silent warning, which meant Saloninus yelped in surprise in a manner completely unbecoming for a Centurion of Rome. Which, of course, Vitruvius and the other men who witnessed it thought it was the funniest thing they had ever seen, and it reminded me of how the simple things tend to amuse rankers the most, reinforcing my father's and my own observation that, in many ways, Legionaries are like little children.

"That wasn't funny," Saloninus protested, but his visible eye was alight with pleasure as he thrust out his arm.

"The men seemed to think so," I pointed out, grinning back at him.

"That's because they're idiots," he growled. Then, echoing Macer, he asked, "So how's life in the Praetorians?"

"About like you'd expect." I decided on a partial truth. "A lot of standing around looking pretty."

"And how are the men?" he asked, and I thought about it for a moment, then shrugged, and I was a bit evasive when I answered, "Not that much different than the Legions, I suppose. We have some men from the Legions, but the Second doesn't have any Rhenus veterans, and I think there's only a handful in the other Cohorts, and it's the same with men from the Pannonian Legions."

That was as specific as I was willing to be, but Saloninus understood instantly, another example of why I had been willing to go against tradition and risk the wrath, because he replied, "So you mean even the veterans in the Praetorians haven't seen much action."

"No, they haven't," I was secretly relieved that he had understood what I was trying to say. "But," I pointed out, "there's not much danger of Gauls invading Rome anymore. Actually," I admitted, "I think that it's about how they look as much as whether they can fight."

"Oh?"

"I'm still the tallest, at least in the Second Cohort, but not by that much, and the average height is at least four inches taller."

Saloninus was unimpressed, but I did not expect him to be, and he scoffed, "If they can't fucking fight, I don't care how big they are."

He excused himself then, and I wandered down the Cohort street, heading towards what would have been my tent, and despite Sacrovir's assurances, I was still apprehensive about my meeting with Licinius. Part of it stemmed from the situation I have already mentioned, but it was also because I did not know Licinius as well as the other officers of the Fourth Cohort, because he had come from the Third Cohort after the death of my father. He was certainly competent, and his men responded to his commands with the kind of promptness that one would expect, but there had been an awkwardness between us that, I confess, was mostly because of me and my feelings about what had happened with the Third Cohort when we escorted Segestes and his daughter pregnant with Arminius' child. It was true that one reason Licinius came to our Cohort was because he was one of the three Centurions of the Third who had kept their head, while the Pilus Prior, Maluginensus, had panicked, almost literally losing his in the process. As I approached the tent, I was determined to set this aside, and I knocked on the wood. When the flap was thrust aside, I enjoyed seeing the surprise on Balio's face, and I like to think that the smile was genuine.

He did hesitate for an instant, but I understood that he was trying to decide how to address me, and I did not fault him for settling on, "Centurion Pullus! This is a surprise!" The clerk stepped aside to let me in, and I remembered to take my helmet off because of the soot that coats the roof of the tent that would mar my red crest, and feeling quite smug about it at that.

"Is he in his quarters?" I asked, my own attempt to avoid the subject.

Balio opened his mouth, but it was Licinius who answered, "I'd know that voice anywhere."

He emerged from the rear portion of the tent, but he was still just in his parade tunic, and he smiled as I did, yet I was certain I saw the hesitation there, which prompted me to do what I normally do in such situations, open my mouth without thinking.

"We've got to be the only Cohort in the Roman army with two Pili Priores," is what came out of my mouth, but his response was to roar with laughter, then he crossed the room to thrust out his arm.

"That," he agreed, "is certainly true, and that's a good way to put it."

For a brief moment, I thought about asking to go into his quarters so that I could say what I wanted to say, but then I realized that it was essentially pointless; canvas walls do not do much to dampen sound. Besides, the odds were that Licinius would tell Balio about the conversation later.

"I just wanted to come here and tell you that I didn't know anything about this, Licinius," I began.

"I know, Pullus." He held up a hand to stop me. "The Primus Pilus told me that it was actually his idea. And," he hesitated, but I suppose since I was being honest with him, he felt inclined to be the same, "I can't lie and say I was happy about it right after he told me. But then I thought about it, and it's the right thing to do."

I was pleased, but I was also embarrassed, and I did feel a bit guilty, to the point I proposed we split the time marching as the Pilus Prior, which I could see in turn pleased him, although I was surprised when he shook his head.

"That won't work," he said, but when I asked why, he offered a rueful grin. "Because I asked the Primus Pilus about that as a possibility and he said no."

"Oh." It was all I could think to say.

"What matters," he said, and the smile had returned, "is we get to drink all we can drink, eat all we can eat. And," the smile turned to a leer, "if everything I've heard about the women of Rome when soldiers are around is true, they'll be wet as October and ready for plowing, and we won't even have to pay for it!"

This made me laugh, reminding me that, even for those who wear the transverse crest of Centurion, they're still rankers at heart, at least those who worked their way up through the ranks. And, prior to my meeting Bronwen, it was certainly an attitude that I not only approved of but had adopted as my own.

The mention of women must have reminded Licinius, and he asked me, "So are you still with your Briton? What tribe was she from?"

"Parisii." I nodded. "And yes, we're together. And," I was still at the stage where I felt a surge of pride whenever I said, "she bore me a son a couple months ago."

"That didn't take long!" Licinius joked. "But while I never saw her, I've heard enough about her to know why. She was all Saloninus talked about when he got back to Ubiorum, and he didn't even know that you two ended up together! He just talked about the most beautiful woman he'd ever seen, and how it made him think about staying."

While I laughed, I do not deny that I felt a stab of what I suppose was jealousy, for which I immediately chastised myself, thinking, Why should you be upset with Saloninus for thinking the same thing that you do?

Aloud, I said, "Well, even if I *was* inclined to take advantage of the...rain," Licinius grinned, "there's no way I'd do it now."

"Oh?" He raised an eyebrow. "Why's that?"

"Do you have children, Licinius?" I asked pleasantly, and this made him laugh.

"By the gods, no." I knew it was coming, because he waited just a heartbeat then gave me a wink as he finished, predictably, "At least, none that I know of!"

This is probably the most common answer to that question, and it is funny the first two or three times you hear it, but I laughed politely and explained, "I've learned something. When women are pregnant, they go a bit mad."

"I've heard that," he agreed.

"Well, that's true, and I've also learned that the madness doesn't go away after the baby. So, if I were to...stray, she'd cut my balls off when I was sleeping," I said simply; and, I was being honest. This made him roar with laughter, and thinking this was a good note to part on, I took my leave so he could finish getting ready.

The rest of my time before the *Bucina* sounded the assembly in the camp forum for inspection was spent going from one tent to another, not just with the First Century, but the others as well, stopping to greet the men with whom I had served. I suppose it was natural that the First and Second got most of my attention since we had shared so much in our adventure in Britannia, and I was extremely flattered to see that their pleasure that I was marching with them was genuine. I listened to some stories, all of them about the debauching they had done and were intending to repeat in Rome. Seeing men like Acisculus again, who had proven to be so valuable in repairing the ship *Brizo* that ended up carrying the First and Second back to safety from Britannia, and Laevinas of the Eighth Section who broke his ankle during the storm that crippled the ship was extremely enjoyable. I jokingly asked Acisculus if he was going to retire to become a shipbuilder, while I teased Laevinas for his slight limp, then endured their revenge as they retold embarrassing stories about their Centurion that I do not feel the need to repeat here. All in all, it felt good to be back where I belonged, even if it was temporary. Finally, the camp *Bucina* sounded the call to assemble in the forum, and the men responded immediately, streaming out of their tents, and there was an air of excitement that was unlike anything I had experienced. If I were to describe it, I would liken it to the air of anticipation when the men know they were about to march out of camp and into battle, just without the stench of fear sweat.

"All right, you *cunni*," I barked. "Stop your chattering. The Fourth isn't going to be seen babbling like women at the fountain."

I was stepping into my old spot next to Gemellus when, from behind me, I recognized the voice of Vitruvius, who muttered, "It's like he never left."

Fortunately, my back was turned and he did not see my broad grin as I gave the order to march the Fourth to the forum.

Four Roman Legions, with every man spotlessly clean and everything that could gleam highly polished, with every bit of leather shining from varnish that would have done credit to my Praetorians, is a stirring sight, and this most potent symbol of Roman power never fails to move me. Since we were marching in numerical order, the 1st had the honor of being the first of the Legions, following the two Praetorian Cohorts who had been with Germanicus and the army at the Angrivarian Wall. It should come as no surprise that there was a lot of grumbling about this, and the sentiment could be summed up by what Gemellus said to me.

"They were there for one fucking battle," he complained, "not for the whole two years we were! It's not right, Pilus Prior."

While I agreed in spirit, I could not really bring myself to feel the outrage; I suppose my exposure to the realities of Rome and the politics that are part of it colored my view to the point I was more resigned to it than anything.

"Pullus! Pilus Prior Pullus!"

The call came from behind me somewhere, and my initial thought was, That sounds like Germanicus, but I dismissed it as impossible. When I turned, I saw him just as he stepped into the *quadriga*, the triumphal chariot, but it was a very different Germanicus. He was wearing the purple toga called the *toga purpurea,* while underneath it and barely visible was a white tunic that had green palms stitched around the collar, and on his head was the laurel wreath of the victorious general. I also noticed that he was driving the chariot himself, and he slapped the reins lightly and the four matched white horses moved at a walk as he made his way to his spot. He drew up for just a moment next to us, but the only way I could tell he was in an understandably jovial mood was by his voice, because his face was a mask, and I mean that literally.

"I can't smile." He pointed to his face, which was a deep, dark red. "If I do, it will flake off."

"Paint?" I asked, surprised. "I thought they used blood."

He shook his head, but I saw how carefully he did it as he explained, "They haven't done that for centuries, because the blood flakes off even worse. I remember my grandfather telling a story about how it also washes away because of sweat, and how it looked like some Legate had been weeping the entire triumph." Changing the subject, his tone also changed, and he raised his voice a bit louder than was necessary. "I'm glad to see you at the head of the Fourth Cohort, Pullus. And," he shocked me then, because he pointed directly at my torq, "I was hoping that you'd wear your father's torq that my father gave to him." He gave a slight shrug. "Maybe that means that your father is marching with us just like my father is by wearing this." He lifted his hand to show a large gold signet ring that I presumed belonged to his father Drusus. I did not know what to say, and even if I had known the right words, I doubt I could have gotten them out, but he saved me by giving a nod, then in a cheerful voice he called out, "Men of the Fourth! Enjoy this day! You and your comrades around you deserve the glory, not me!" Then, dropping his voice to a more conversational and lighter tone, he added, "My children are at the camp gates waiting for a ride, and I can't keep them waiting or I'll have to listen to them complain for most of the triumph."

He slapped the reins and made his way up the column as we all bellowed our acknowledgement of his words to his back. It was only then that I noticed that it was Lysander who was playing the part of the slave who, I assumed, would be the one holding the laurel wreath for the official part of the triumph. He glanced over his shoulder and gave me a smile, which I returned, although I wondered if this was some technical breach of the rules since it was supposed to be a slave and not a freedman. Because of the two Praetorian Cohorts, our view was even more obscured, so we could not see the war trophies and the displays that commemorated important moments until we reached the Circus, when they would pass by us in the opposite direction as we circled the track. We could definitely hear where the crowds began by the sudden roar as Germanicus left the camp boundary. Then we were marching at what can only be described as a leisurely pace, and once it was our turn to march out of the camp, we were assailed by a riot of sounds and sights as the people of Rome cheered us. Women were throwing flowers, while youngsters dashed out and tossed flower petals in our path, although the street was already littered with what they had already offered to Germanicus and the Praetorians. A crowd that seemed to be equally divided between men and women stood four and five deep on either side, and this was just the beginning; once we entered the city itself, our guess was that the people were ten deep. We passed by Pompey's Theater, and more daring souls had shinnied up the columns for a better view, making me wonder how much wine they had consumed beforehand.

Gemellus had to shout, "Do you think there will be any flowers left for those bastards in the 20th?"

This made me laugh, and I raised my voice more than necessary so the rest of the Century could hear. "I hope not! If the gods are just, by the time those *cunni* reach this spot, the people will be bored and have gone home already!"

As I expected, this was accepted as a perfectly wonderful idea, and my boys shouted out prayers to their favorite god to make it so. The Portico of Octavia was absolutely packed, and I saw that people, almost all younger men and boys, climbing up to get a better view was not restricted to Pompey's Theater. From up ahead, Paterculus, the Legion's senior *Cornicen,* began playing one of the marching tunes that was popular, and he was immediately joined by the other *Corniceni,* including Poplicola, the Fourth's *Cornicen.* Naturally, the men began singing, making it even louder, and the crowd loved it. As we wound around the Portico then in between it and the Temple of Bellona on one side, with the Theater of Marcellus on the other, things became rowdy, raucous, and quite graphic, as women began darting out from the crowd to bare their breasts, while the more daring drew up their gowns.

"Be sure to come to the Den of Aphrodite, boys, and ask for Cleopatra! I'll be sure and show you how grateful we are!"

"Cleopatra has the pox! What you need is a *real* woman like me, Niobe! You can find me at Isis' Grotto!"

The reason I'm relating this exchange, just one of many of this type, is that I knew about Isis' Grotto because it was one of the spots where the Praetorians of the Second Cohort frequented, and I made a mental note to remind the men that they were to stay away from the place, something that I forgot until it was too late. In the moment, however, it was all good fun, and flattering, despite knowing that these invitations were of a commercial nature. Entering through the Porta Carmentalis, if anything, the noise intensified, bouncing off the city walls and the buildings that line the Vicus Iugaris, which we followed, heading in the direction of the Forum, although we would be doubling back onto the Vicus Tuscus, which took us through the Velabrum, where among the stalls and small structures, there is a lone fig tree that is supposed to have been the one that the basket carrying Romulus and Remus was snagged on during a flood of the Tiber. I had been told by other Praetorians that, while this was drained centuries ago, the area is still prone to flooding, which was why it is not heavily populated and is used more as a market area and an informal gathering spot. We smelled the Forum Boarium before we entered it, and while the crowd was still thick, a large number of the spectators were wearing bloody aprons, the sign of the immense slaughter that was going on for the banquet that would be held out on the Campus for us, where at that moment, hundreds of slaves were setting up tables and making ready.

By this point, I, and every other Centurion, had given up trying to keep the men from interacting with the crowd, the only requirement that, while the citizens could come rushing out into the street, any man who broke ranks, no matter what the temptation, would get a striping. And, I will admit, some of the offers being made were very tempting, including one maiden who, from what I could tell, was not a whore, but was so stricken with passion that she lay in the street and pulled her gown up, begging one of the boys to relieve her of her burden of lust. Licinius was actually at the back of the First Century, but on my side, across from Mus, who had been confirmed as Optio, and I glanced over my shoulder as we passed the young woman, offering him a glare that was only partially in jest. He actually took a step away from the formation, as if he was going to stop and render his assistance, but it was only to tease me, immediately returning with a broad grin on his face. As we left the Boarium, my attention turned to the Circus, wondering if I would be able to spot Bronwen, Alex, and Algaia. For the first time, because of the long expanse of open track, once we stepped out onto it through the open end through the wooden gates where the chariots lined up, we could see the entirety of the procession ahead of us, but the most striking thing about this moment was how the sound intensified even more, something I would have sworn was impossible until I heard it for myself. In all honesty, it was a daunting sight, even if the crowd had been silent, every tier packed with people, most of them members of the upper orders, at least in the choicer seats near the track. The top tiers were filled with people more like the ones who had been lining the route to this point, while the lowest rows were a sea of white togas, punctuated by the many colors of the *stolae* worn by the upper-class women. How, I thought with dismay, am I going to be able to find them in all of this? It was so noisy that it was hard to concentrate, but it also gave all of us an opportunity to actually see Germanicus and his children, including young Gaius, who, as expected, was wearing his tiny Legionary uniform and was solemnly recognizing our calls to him and his father as they drove by, the paint covering Germanicus' face still in place as he offered what I suppose was a regal gesture of acknowledgment to the crowd who was in full throat, the single flowers and baskets of petals now replaced by full bouquets that rained down in front of his *quadriga*. Following this were the Tribunes who had participated in the campaign, all of them on horseback and wearing their uniforms, and I barely glanced at the lot of them. Behind them came the wagons hauling the displays that were in the procession, among which were mockups of several battles, including the final two of the campaign, the Battle of Idistaviso, and the Angrivarian Wall.

I confess that I only glanced at it as it approached on our left on the opposite side of the barrier that runs down the center of the course because I was searching the stands for a woman with red hair, but then Gemellus reached out and grabbed my arm.

I was irritated, but when I turned to him to rebuke him for distracting me, he was looking across the barrier and pointing at one of the wagons, shouting, "Look, Pilus Prior! That's the Battle of Idistaviso! Look what they did!"

And when I did, any irritation evaporated. Later, when we had an opportunity to examine it, there were two sides to the diorama made of two large boards that were angled against each other. The opposite side had tiny figures made of what we were told was clay, each of them painted, with the men of Arminius' army painted in the same variety of colors as their real counterparts were wearing that day and with different colored shields, while the Legions were arranged in neat rows that accurately depicted our disposition...with one exception. On what was the left side of the wagon, which was what we could see, there was a group of figures positioned perpendicular to the otherwise straight and ordered lines of the four Legions of the front line.

"That's us!" Gemellus had to shout this, because the other men of the First of the Fourth, seeing the same thing, began shouting like Gemellus. "They're showing what you did, Pilus Prior! That's the

Fourth!"

It is impossible for me to describe the emotions that ran through me when I realized he was right, that for whatever reason, whoever was responsible for creating this had depicted the moment when I decided to move without orders because I saw an opportunity to be the man to strike Arminius down. But, whatever my reason, it had become accepted as an article of faith, and confirmed by Germanicus himself, that we had turned what looked to be a bloody draw into a victory that sent Arminius fleeing for his life and shattered the German host. At least to this moment, seeing this so clearly depicted is one of the proudest moments of my life. The next wagon was the tableau depicting the Angrivarian Wall, but on our side, the Praetorians were identified by blue, which made them stand out from the red of the Legions, and the moment depicted on this panel was when Germanicus had led them in their assault on the German left flank.

"They aren't showing how we plugged the gap," Gemellus said disappointedly, a point that Poplicola fervently agreed with, but frankly, I was still overwhelmed by the first diorama.

However, before I could really pay attention to the Angrivarian display, another sight captured our attention, one that would be the talk of Rome for days to come.

Following the dioramas, there were three wagons piled high with the spoils, mostly captured weapons, helmets, and shields, while the last wagon was loaded down with all manner of glittering gold and silver in the form of torqs, arm rings, chains, and cups. It was what came next, however, with the prisoners, that instantly riveted our attention, and explained why, if not the volume but the quality of the sound of what we were told was created by almost two hundred thousand people present changed. This wagon had no sides, just a flat platform, upon which there was what I counted to be a dozen people, but there was one in particular that held every eye, and I confess I felt a stab of what I suppose might have been shame that I think was prompted by the flaming red hair that, while brighter than Bronwen's, was a close enough match that it was unsettling. I realized that I had forgotten what Thusnelda, the wife of Arminius and daughter of Segestes, had looked like, and the truth is that I had only caught a glimpse of her a couple of times during our frantic retreat back to the Rhenus. Despite the fact that she was not alone—her brother Segimuntus, chief of the Cherusci, a priest named Libes of the Chatti, and a variety of other high-ranking German nobles were all standing behind her on the same wagon—I doubt I was alone in barely noticing any of them. The only other figure who caught my attention was a small boy who was standing just in front of her, her hands resting on his shoulders in a manner that suggested that she was holding him upright, which was understandable given his age, which I would guess was around two, if that.

"That's got to be Arminius' brat," I heard Gemellus comment, but I just nodded, not taking my eyes off of his mother.

It was not just her appearance that was striking, although she was, while not beautiful in the way we Romans prefer, a handsome woman, it was the manner in which she stood there, head erect and not once responding to the taunts and jeers of the crowd. In fact, by the time they had made the turn and were returning on the opposite side of the Circus, to my ears, most of the reception was one of admiration, a reminder that we also value courage, even when it is displayed by our enemies. Who else but a Roman could appreciate the kind of arrogance she was displaying, a complete disdain for the reality that she was in fact another trophy of a conquered enemy? I am certain that she was completely aware that she was the object of everyone's attention, but one would have never known it by looking at her, and despite the fact that I hated her husband and his warriors with a passion, and bore her a fair amount of hostility because of what had happened during our rescue attempt, I also felt some admiration and respect for her, knowing this must have been hard for her to endure. Then came the rest of the prisoners, and these men earned our complete attention, and it was fortunate that we were marching near the stands on the right hand side while the head of this part of the procession was now moving next to the stands on the left hand side, because I think that one of our men who had lost a friend might have leapt across that barrier to attack the prisoners. They were all chained, and as one might expect, they were plodding along and, much like Thusnelda, were pretending they did not see the crowd who, once Arminius' wife passed by, had resumed their full-throated expression of their contempt and disdain for our conquered foes. We quickly saw that the assault was not just verbal, as pieces of refuse came arcing out of the stands, some of them striking one of the prisoners. For the most part, it was things like rotten vegetables and fruit, but I just happened to be watching when one of the

Germans was struck in the head by something that was solid enough to drive him to his knees and cause blood to begin flowing down his forehead. Although they were chained, their hands were in front of them, and one of his comrades moved to him, helping him to his feet, but they immediately resumed moving, and most importantly, their gaze returned to the dirt of the track.

"Gnaeus! Gnaeus! *Gnaeus!*"

So absorbed was I in watching the prisoners be abused that it took Alex calling my name several times for me to return my attention back to the stands on our right, but I had absolutely no trouble finding them, because Bronwen was standing next to him, her auburn hair standing out among a sea of black, brown, and a few blonde heads, the sun catching her tresses. They were four rows up, and I was sorely tempted to move from my spot and trot over to the wooden wall that separates the spectators from the track, which only comes up to my waist. As I had hoped, she was attired in a gown made of the green silk that we had bought in Alexandria, but cut in the Roman style; I had been afraid that she would wear her everyday clothing because of young Titus' propensity to spit up on her, but there he was, on her hip as she smiled down at me.

"Pilus Prior," Gemellus had to shout, but he was still hard to hear, "I believe that Fortuna loves you more than anyone else I know!"

"And," I replied with as much conviction as I could offer, "I know it."

As we drew even, I raised my *vitus*, and on an impulse, I bellowed, "Century, eyes to the right!"

She was clearly delighted, while the people around her clearly understood there was a connection between this beauty and the big Centurion, and they began shouting even more loudly, waving their arms in my direction, while the women around her called out to her. My face, which had already begun to ache a bit from the smiling, hurt even more, yet it was worth it just to see her cheeks flushed with happiness, her green eyes that her *stola* matched shining as she lifted baby Titus' little hand to wave it at me, which I happily returned without a modicum of self-consciousness. Then, the moment was over, and we reached the end of the track, rounding the barrier to reverse our course on our way out of the Circus. The sun was out, the weather could not have been better, and I had never, ever been happier in my life than at that moment.

Once out of the riot of the Circus, while the crowds outside were still cheering, it seemed as if it had suddenly gone quiet in comparison. We marched down the street paralleling the Circus as the procession headed for the Forum by way of circling between the Palatine and the Caelian Hills so that we would be approaching the Forum from the southeast. The men resumed singing their songs to the accompaniment of the horns, while the invitations resumed, but if I am being honest, I was getting a bit weary of all this, if not downright bored. It is certainly a wonderful thing to be the object of an adoring crowd, even if we were the secondary attraction to Germanicus, but there came a point where I had had enough. However, one glance over my shoulder at my men informed me that I was in the vast minority, so I did my best to appear as excited and happy as they still were.

As we had been warned, the procession came to a stop when Germanicus reached the Capitoline and the Temple of Jupiter Optimus Maximus, whereupon he ascended the stairs to the temple, where Tiberius was waiting as Imperator, along with the various priests like the *Flamen Dialis*, and the most senior members of the Senate, who had left the Circus and come directly to the Capitoline. This was the moment where the prisoners were taken off to meet their fates, and it served as a reminder of something that at one point in time I would have scoffed at, the idea that the upper classes of Rome treat the nobility of other nations, even if they are enemy, differently than the lower classes of our foes. None of the dozen people on the wagon were executed, although I had been certain that Thusnelda would have been spared, along with her son, because they not only provided a strategic bargaining chip since, despite this triumph, Arminius was still uncaptured and beyond our reach, but because of Segestes, who as we were about to learn, was with the official party waiting at the Capitoline as an honored guest and ally. Once Germanicus had ascended the steps of the Capitoline, the march resumed, minus the wagons and the prisoners, who were hurried off by one of the Urban Cohorts, while the Praetorians led the way up the slope, where they would halt and allow the rest of the Legions to join them, surrounding the Temple. This was the moment I had been dreading, because I was certain that, among the party of dignitaries, I would see Sejanus among them, although I did hold out a faint hope that perhaps he would be shoved to the back of the crowd by all the Senators who wanted to fawn over the Imperator. It never occurred to me that the moment would be because of Tiberius, who proved that, as my father and Sempronius had warned me, never forgot or missed anything.

Chapter 6

By virtue of being the first of the Legions atop the Capitoline, it meant that we had the equivalent of the front row seats at the Circus, perhaps not the most prime viewing spot, that went to the Seventh and Eight Praetorians, but a clear view nonetheless, even if it was a bit cramped. Instead of the normal spacing between the first row of Cohorts and the second, the Sixth through Tenth were essentially aligned behind us so that it appeared as if it was just a series of very long files. We stood at *intente* as the other Legions marched past, but I had given the men a warning beforehand about keeping their mouths shut and not engaging in the usual barbed banter that takes place. Since we had relaxed our discipline along the route, allowing the men not only to sing but to have exchanges with the crowd, I was concerned, but only with the Fourth. Because of the Temple to Jupiter, which is massive, and the Temple of Juno Moneta behind us, which is smaller but still large, the sound created by the hobnailed soles of the thousands of Legionaries marching by was so overwhelming that even if the men had yelled at their counterparts, I doubt they would have been heard. The 5th Alaudae, with Nerva leading them, marched past, and like us, they were looking straight ahead, sensing that the time for frivolity was over now that they were under the eyes of our Imperator, until they drew abreast of the Imperial party, and as we had done, snapped their eyes to the right. Tiberius, as might be expected, was standing on the top step of the Temple, but to my surprise, he was only wearing a toga of a dazzling white and, while it took me a moment to spot it, was carrying in one hand an ivory baton that declared his *imperium* and status as supreme leader of every soul on the Capitoline, the city, and the entire Empire. Germanicus was now beside him, the paint still in place, and the pair were surrounded by the senior members of the Senate. I did see Sejanus, but as I had hoped, he was relegated to the last row, and I wondered how he felt about that. Following the 5th came the 14th, and by this time, the 5th had marched around the Temple to take up their spot on one side, while the 14th marched past them and arranged themselves on the opposite side of the Temple, which meant they would be unable to see anything at all, something that made our boys very happy. Finally, Neratius led his 20th past, where they made an entire circle of the Temple to end up on the fourth and only unoccupied side, signaling that the series of sacrifices could begin, whereupon each animal, ending with the sacred white bull last, was led out from inside the Temple where their handlers had been keeping them waiting docilely for their slaughter, albeit with the help of the drugs that the animals are fed. One by one, the *Haruspex* offered up the ritual prayer, then with the bronze knife honed to razor sharpness, sliced the throats of the animals, all of which obediently collapsed without causing a disturbance, whereupon they were dragged off. Meanwhile, it was up to the *Haruspex* to examine the entrails, and none of us were surprised that all of the omens were favorable; it would have been a very brave, or stupid, man to declare bad omens when standing that close to Tiberius, or to Germanicus, for that matter, since it was his day. Frankly, I found the entire thing boring, and I know I am far from alone, but when the sacred white bull was brought forward, for the span of a few heartbeats, it looked as if things might get interesting, as the animal began tossing its head, jerking the arms of the two slaves leading it to the point where the feet of one of the slaves left the ground.

"It probably smells all that blood and knows that's not a good sign," Gemellus murmured, and while I managed to quell my snicker, the others who heard him were not so circumspect.

I cannot say this was the moment when I came to Tiberius' attention, but because of where we were standing, the tittering got his attention to the point that I saw his head turn slightly to his left, putting us directly in his gaze.

"I swear by Dis," I hissed through clenched teeth, "if you *mentulae* don't shut your mouths, you're going to get in the square with me and my *rudis!*"

As I suspected, this was all it took, and Tiberius had already looked away, nothing in his expression indicating that he had noticed anything. And, thankfully, this was the only commotion the bull caused, dropping to its knees when the bronze hammer hit it squarely in the forehead, then the *Haruspex* secured the hammer while pulling the bronze knife from his belt and drawing it across the bull's throat, all in one motion. Naturally, the basin for the bull was larger, and it quickly filled up, but it was a testament to the skill of the *Haruspex* that not so much as a drop of blood spattered onto all the sparkling white togas around it. The examination was made, the announcement given, then it was our turn to acclaim Germanicus *Imperator* three times, our last official act of the triumph before we marched back to the camp. Only, we did *not* shout Germanicus' name but Tiberius', and once again, as I learned later, it was by Germanicus' express orders. Then our part was done, and we were waiting for the Praetorian Cohorts to turn to face in the proper direction so they could march off of the Capitoline, though on the opposite side from where we had ascended, and I watched idly as Germanicus and his adoptive father addressed each other, while the Senators waited for their turn to flatter and ingratiate themselves with both the Imperator and the man who was at worst the third most powerful man in Rome. This was why I was distracted and did not see the man approaching us until he was just a few paces away, but while I did not recognize him, he wore the symbol that he was part of Tiberius' household around his neck. Even then he was only a matter of idle curiosity, at least until I realized he was heading directly for me, just as Paterculus blew the warning note that the 1st was about to march.

"Pilus Prior Pullus, you are to remain here for a moment. The Imperator would like to speak with you."

I barely managed to avoid groaning aloud, although I did have the presence of mind to remember Licinius, and I waved to him.

Once he got to me, I said, "You're going to march the boys back to camp. I'm staying here for a bit."

I could see Licinius was dying from curiosity, but he also understood that it would be impolitic on his part to ask why; besides, I thought with sour amusement, Gemellus heard and he'll tell Licinius before they're off the Capitoline. He did not have to do so, but he saluted anyway, then the movement note sounded, and he immediately bellowed the order to begin marching. Not wanting to endure the scrutiny of these men with whom I had just reunited a few watches before, I turned my back as they marched past.

"Where does he want me to go?"

"Follow me," the scribe, if that was what he was, said.

He did not take me up the main steps of the Temple, but instead led me around to the side where, behind a row of laurel bushes, there was a well-hidden door that offered another entrance into the Temple. Following him in, I literally found myself at the feet of Jupiter, sitting on his throne with his huge arm pulled back as he held the thunderbolt that was an article of faith was made of solid gold and not just gold leaf, poised to strike. I had brought Bronwen to the Temple shortly after we arrived in Rome, and she had been suitably awed by how lifelike the statue was, but it was on this occasion that I noticed for the first time that Jupiter's eyes were blue. Supposedly, Caesar had blue eyes, and given that it was Divus Augustus who was responsible for rebuilding the Temple and having this new statue created, I wondered if this was a tribute to the man whose name he bore. I am not certain how long I waited, but I was acutely aware that I was sweating now, despite it being cooler in the Temple than outside. I heard someone approaching, and when I turned, it was the man who had summoned me.

"This way," he said curtly, and I followed him back in the direction of the main entrance, then out the doors and onto the front porch.

Tiberius was not alone, exactly, but only later did I realize that his separating himself from the cluster of men, including several Senators, as well as turning so that his back was to them, was no accident. I saluted, not knowing how else to behave, and my mouth was so dry that I was afraid that, if he required me to speak first, I would be unable to do so. For several heartbeats, he regarded me silently, then with a frown, he pointed, in my direction but not directly at my face.

"I recognize that torq," he said abruptly. "My brother gave it to your father during your father's first campaign, then your father's Primus Pilus took it and gave it to me." Suddenly, he looked up into my face, asking sharply, "Are you aware of any of this?"

"Yes, Imperator," I answered, surprising myself that I was able to do so, but this was the wrong thing to say.

"You address me as Princeps," he snapped. Then, almost as if it was to himself, he muttered, "I do not care for that...other title." Returning to the original topic, he continued, "I gave it back to your father, both because it was the right thing to do and in honor of my brother's memory." He paused for just a heartbeat, then asked quietly, "This was your father's to wear, not yours. So why did you choose to wear an award that is not yours to wear?"

"I...I..." I heard my voice stammering like an idiot, but I could not seem to control it, then in that instant, I decided to tell the truth. "I wanted my father to be part of this triumph in some way,

Princeps." The sound of my words gave me the strength to risk Tiberius' wrath. "He deserved to be here for this, and this was my way of making that happen."

I cannot say that his expression noticeably altered, yet I was certain that my words had hit home for him in some way, although he just regarded me for a few more heartbeats.

Finally, he said, "That is an acceptable reason, Centurion Pullus. But," his voice hardened, "this will be the only time that you wear an award that you didn't earn. Is that clear?"

"Yes, Princeps," I assured him, relieved beyond measure, but Tiberius was not through with me.

Seemingly out of nowhere, he asked, "How are you finding life in the Praetorians, Centurion?"

It was probably his intention to catch me off balance, yet somehow I managed to think before I answered, "It's certainly...different than the Legions, sir."

This elicited something that sounded like a snort as he replied derisively, "I'm aware of that, Centurion. The Praetorians *are* different. But," he asked bluntly, "what do you think of them as a fighting force? Based on what you've seen?"

Since I was completely unsure of where this was going, I answered carefully, "The Seventh and Eighth certainly acquitted themselves well."

He cut me off with a dismissive wave.

"That's because they aren't stationed here in Rome, so they spend more time on proper training than the Cohorts that are here permanently." My hope of escape evaporated when he asked bluntly, "I'm asking what you think of the Praetorian Cohorts permanently stationed here in the city."

"They're soft." It came out before I could stop it, but then I hurried to add, "That doesn't mean they can't be an effective fighting force, sir. They just don't spend much time on that kind of training."

"You mean," he shocked me by saying, "like taking them out to the stakes?"

"You knew about that?" I gasped.

For the first time, Tiberius' face, which seems to be carved out of stone with a perpetual scowl, altered in a way that indicated to me that he was amused, and he answered, "Oh yes. I heard about it from the Prefect the same day. He was...unhappy about it." While I was not surprised, given that Creticus had said essentially the same thing, the thought that I was talking to Tiberius about it made my stomach clench, but there was no way I was prepared for what came out of his mouth next. "I'm ordering you to continue training your Century in the manner in which you see fit, provided that you fulfill your other duties, and that you're never more than a half-day's march from Rome. I," now he did smile, but it was not pleasant, "am about to inform Prefect Sejanus of my decision." Which means, I thought miserably, Sejanus will instantly suspect me of convincing Tiberius to do so during this conversation. Following hard on the heels of that thought was the question, why would Tiberius do something like that to me?

"Very well, Centurion," Tiberius intruded into my thoughts. "You may return to the Campus Martius and enjoy the feast that my son has prepared for all of you. But," he said as he turned away, "I expect to see you back in Praetorian colors tomorrow, training your men."

Despite the fact that he was walking away, I saluted his retreating back, but as I did so, I saw the gaggle of Senators standing there looking in our direction and, I assumed, dying of curiosity. There was only one man I was concerned about, however, and as I turned to head towards the small door, I tried to surreptitiously scan the faces; just as they were moving out of my vision, I spotted Sejanus, and even out of the corner of my eye, I could see the poisonous glare he was giving me.

My walk to the Campus was hampered by the crowds, which were breaking up as citizens began rushing for one of the spots where free food was being served, similar to what awaited me at the camp, although it would not be as plentiful or with as much variety for the citizens as for us. Tiberius had announced that he was paying every citizen the sum of three hundred *sesterces*, supposedly out of his own purse, although from what I could tell, where Tiberius' private finances and those of the Empire diverged seemed to be something of a mystery. The people were in a merry mood, and understandably so, yet I barely noticed any of it, aside from being forced to shove my way through knots of people, some of whom wanted to personally congratulate me, blasting me with their breath that told me the wine had been flowing for some time already. Instead, I was trying to understand why Tiberius had put me in this spot, and I was sorely tempted to detour and return to the apartment to talk to Alex about it, but I had been waiting for this opportunity to be reunited with my comrades for so long. By the time I arrived, the men had been dismissed, and they were in their tents, stripping off their armor and chattering with their closest comrades about the sights they had seen on the route, arguing with each other about what women had been the prettiest, and who these young maidens had tossed a flower to, which to my ears seemed to be the biggest point of contention. The idea that whatever woman had tossed a flower in their direction was doing so indiscriminately was the only thing there was mutual agreement on, as every man involved in the dispute was certain she had spotted him personally.

It was strange for me to go to the tent that had been mine, but instead of entering the private quarters, taking off my armor, helmet, and greaves, and laying them on Lucco's desk, reminding myself to come back after the banquet to retrieve them. Once everyone was suitably attired, we marched to the huge area just beyond the northern edge of the Campus where the tables had been set up, in long rows so that the men of each Cohort were in the same row, designated by the standard of each Cohort and Century being driven into the ground next to their spot. There was a gap between the Legions, but the only way to avoid the inevitable would have been to set up barriers between each Legion, and even then, once men had had enough to drink, they would crawl over the barrier to get at someone in another Legion because of some past dispute out in Ubiorum or Mogontiacum.

Because of my late arrival, I had missed the previous week where the officers stressed on an almost watch by watch basis the penalty for instigating a fight with men from another Legion, but as I was told by Macer, "Sacrovir will be happy if the men just beat on each other instead of the other Legions."

And I can attest to the fact that the hard feelings that can arise between Cohorts, or even Centuries of the same Cohort are at least as strong as the hatred between Legions. That said, I would be remiss in not saying that, even if that was the case, if a Fourth Cohort man of the 1st saw a Third Cohort man of the 1st being assaulted by men of another Legion, despite the fact that there had been hard feelings between the two since the Segestes raid, a Fourth man would not hesitate to jump in on the side of the man or men of the Third. From what I have been told by Alex and other men with brothers, this is common behavior; brothers may try to kill each other, but if anyone from outside the family tries to hurt one of them, they will find double the trouble, or more. Regardless of this reality, we reached our assigned seats with the entirety of the Legion in a festive mood, eager to gorge themselves, aided by the knowledge that for the next week, they would be pulling no duties and would be free to essentially do as they pleased, with the warning about starting trouble with the Praetorians hanging over their head, of course. My place was at the end of the table reserved for the Fourth, with Licinius sitting on the opposite side and Mus next to him, Gemellus next to me, then more or less in Section order, although this was more from habit than any requirement. Once men have sat around the same fire for years, those are the men they gravitate towards, and it quickly became apparent that half a section was sitting on one side and the other half sitting opposite. Of course, we were not allowed to take our seats until every Cohort had reached their spot, meaning that the grumbling of the first line Cohorts began almost immediately as we stood there waiting.

Finally, we were in place, and our eyes went to Sacrovir, who had climbed up onto his table to be seen, and after a moment, he bellowed, "Men of the 1ˢᵗ Legion....*seats!*"

The sound of more than four thousand men dropping onto their benches at one time created a noise that I had never heard before, and I was not alone in being impressed, not by the noise itself, but that so many men could act in complete unity, as one, which summoned a thought I have had more than once; who else but Romans could behave in this manner...or appreciate it as I just had? The moment was not quite over, because one of the four priests that traveled with the Legion as part of the *praetorium* staff, an older man who, we would learn, would be retiring from his post after this, was helped up onto the table. Thankfully, because of his age, it meant that he was experienced enough to know there were times to make the prayers brief, and this was one of them. By the time he vanished from sight, the real noise began as men began talking to each other as we waited for the first course.

"I wonder if they're going to serve us dormouse?" Mus

considered aloud, reminding me that this was his favorite dish.

"How many dormice do you think there are in the world?" Gemellus laughed. "Because that's what it would take to feed this lot."

"A man can dream," Mus shot back.

It was about that time a line of slaves appeared from somewhere, although I did not bother to look to see from where, each of them bearing a large board stacked with loaves of bread, and each man got a loaf, still warm from the ovens.

"Boy," Gemellus called out to the youth who was serving us, and he pointed to me, "if you know what's good for you, you'll give the Centurion here two loaves instead of one."

I had been expecting something like this; before I became a spectacle for the Parisii to watch as I ate, the men of the Fourth had long been fascinated by my appetite.

"M-master, we were told only one loaf per man," the slave, dark-skinned but clean and wearing a tunic that announced that he was owned by the state, looked between me and Gemellus, his eyes wide. "I was told we'd be beaten if we did."

This was enough for me, and I was about to dismiss him, but my *Signifer* pointed at me and asked pleasantly, "Does your master look like this?" The youth shook his head vigorously. "Then who would you rather be beaten by? Your master or the Centurion?"

The second loaf was dropped onto my plate, but while I felt a bit guilty, I did not return it. Pitchers of olive oil were already out on the tables, along with small pots of garum that we would be putting on the meat dishes that were coming, which was what I was looking forward to the most. This proved to be a forlorn hope; just as I was about to shove a hunk of oil-soaked bread into my mouth, Licinius looked up sharply over my shoulder in a way that got my attention, and I turned my head just in time to see Creticus' chief clerk standing there, holding a tablet. And, I noticed with a sinking feeling, an expression on his face that warned me that he was bringing bad news.

"Pilus Posterior Pullus," he thrust the tablet more or less in my face, "I bring orders from Pilus Prior Creticus. You've been summoned to return to the Second Cohort barracks immediately."

I was opening the tablet as he spoke, and I instantly recognized that it was Creticus' handwriting, but what I was reading did not seem to make any sense, and I asked him sharply, "Emergency? What kind of emergency?"

"That I don't know, Pilus Posterior," the clerk answered immediately. "I was just sent to summon you immediately."

I did not answer him, but I did turn to Licinius and say, "I suppose you're back in command of the Fourth."

While I cannot say he looked all that unhappy, neither was he beaming at the idea of my disappearance.

Standing up, I said, "I'm going back to your tent to get my things. Tell Macer that I'll try and see him sometime in the week."

Patting Gemellus, who did look upset, on the shoulder, I turned in the direction of the camp, but the clerk, who now *did* look unhappy, said, "I was instructed to tell you that you're to come immediately with me, Centurion."

This was too much, and I snarled, "Then it's up to you to stop me."

Then I stomped off, and while he came scampering after me, he did not try and stop me. And as I expected, nor did he mention a word to Creticus about my deviation from heading straight to the barracks.

I learned the ostensible reason for my summons when I reported to Creticus, only after a quick stop at my quarters to switch tunics, not wanting to risk some sort of censure for appearing in my Legion red.

"There's been an emergency called," Creticus said, but unlike me, he was actually wearing his armor. "There's been a report of trouble at the banquet in the Velabrum."

This did nothing to lessen my confusion, which prompted me to ask, or perhaps demand is more accurate, "What does that have to do with us? That's a job for the Urban Cohorts."

I got the first hint when, suddenly, Creticus looked away from me and down at his desk, "The First Urban Cohort has specifically requested the assistance of the Praetorians."

"So we're marching all four Cohorts to help one Urban Cohort?" I laughed, although it was a bitter one. "That seems to be a bit of overkill, don't you think, Pilus Prior?"

The second tile fell onto the imaginary board when Creticus, still looking everywhere but at me, said, "Only the Second Cohort is being mobilized, Pullus."

Despite part of my mind recognizing what was happening, there was another part that refused to believe that a man could be so petty, and it took an effort for me to ask, "By whose order is this, Pilus Prior?"

Creticus closed his eyes, sighed, and said wearily, "Who do you think, Pullus?"

So, I thought, he *would* be petty enough to concoct an "emergency" just to keep me from enjoying my time with my comrades. In hindsight, I should have known there was far more to this than just mean-spirited vindictiveness.

Realizing that there was no point in arguing, I pointed at his *hamata*. "Am I to assume that we're to be in armor?"

"Yes," he confirmed. "Sabinus has already alerted your Century, and I'm about to sound the call to assembly." Thinking he was done, I saluted, but he did not return it, and instead asked me bluntly, "What did the Imperator want with you today, Pullus?"

I realized immediately afterward he had said this to throw me off balance, and it worked, because I gasped, "How did you know about that? Who told you?"

The instant the last question was out of my mouth, I knew the answer, and Creticus did not bother to answer, instead asking again, "And what did he want?"

I considered refusing to answer, then I realized that he would be finding out, probably before the end of this day from Sejanus, so I told him, "We're going to start training like we're part of the Roman army, Pilus Prior."

Watching the color vanish from his face as his mouth dropped open was a bit of a consolation, and without waiting, I turned and exited the office; somewhat surprisingly, he did not call me back. I had just walked into my office when the Cohort *Bucinator* sounded the call for assembly, which was my excuse for what I did. Alex was not there, still being with Bronwen and Algaia, so I gave Demetrios the task of swapping my crest on my helmet while I put the *hamata* back on, and in a small act of rebellion, I left the awards attached. By the time I had strapped on my greaves and snatched up the Praetorian *vitus*, my helmet was ready so that, when I strode out of the office, the men of the Second Century were just shuffling into place themselves, and to my delight, both the Fourth and Sixth Centuries were slow in getting ready. The weapons had already been issued, but I noticed that, unusually, the men had been issued a single spear instead of the two javelins, although once I thought about it, it made a certain amount of sense.

"Pilus Posterior Pullus!"

I knew what to expect when I turned to face Creticus, but this time when he pointed at my harness, shouting a reminder that we had had this discussion before, I shrugged but did not move.

"You informed me this was an emergency, Pilus Prior," I answered in a matter-of-fact tone. "If you think that it's worth delaying the entire Cohort so that I can take off these decorations, decorations that I was authorized to wear today because of the triumph," I reminded him, "then of course I'll return to my quarters and take them off."

As I expected, he did no such thing, just giving me a glare before giving a curt nod to sound the call to march out of the barracks.

"I hope your disobeying orders doesn't cause you any problems, Pilus Posterior," Flaccus commented; if he intended to sound sincere, he failed miserably at it.

"Flaccus," I glanced over at him and smiled, "you've got much bigger problems than worrying about me."

That made me feel much better.

As I expected, the only trouble waiting for us on the Velabrum came from the utter boredom of standing there watching as several thousand other Romans gorged themselves and guzzled as much wine as they could manage. The First Urban Cohort was standing there on the Forum side of the Velabrum, with three Centuries blocking the Vicus Iugarius, and the other three on the Vicus Tusculus. On our arrival, we took up the position on the Vicus Iugarius.

"The Senate and the various city and Imperial officials are having their banquet in the Forum," Creticus explained to us after a brief conversation with the Pilus Prior of the Urban Cohort who, to my eyes, looked as if he might have been a Sergeant of a tent section at some point twenty years earlier. "The Prefect doesn't want them disturbed by this rabble once they get a skin full of wine and decide they deserve to mingle with their betters."

"Why do they need us?"

I was not the one who asked this, but I am glad someone else did, although it earned Rufus a glare from the Pilus Prior, who snapped, "Because we were ordered to assist by the Prefect. Is that good enough for you, Rufus? Or do you want me to let Prefect Sejanus know that one of his Centurions is unhappy with his orders?"

"No, Pilus Prior," Rufus assured him quickly.

Once we arrayed ourselves, we spent the rest of the time watching the people of Rome gorge themselves, the only bright spot that, on our arrival, the noise level dropped dramatically while those closest to us kept glancing anxiously over their shoulders at us. They're probably expecting us to come and take their food from them, I thought sourly, and that's not a bad idea. I was famished, even more than my normal state of perpetual hunger, and I did take some consolation looking at the faces of my men, who were clearly as unhappy about being forced to watch all of this food consumed right in front of them as I was. It would not be right to say that things did not become rowdier as the wine continued to flow, and a number of brawls broke out in the space between tables, but we did not move, relying on the Urban Cohort to deal with it. Unlike us, they were armed with cudgels instead of spears, although they were also armed with *gladius* and *pugio*, but for the most part, they were content to use their shields to shove combatants apart and issue a warning to stop the brawling. From what I could see, every single time a quarrel became physical, there was a woman or women who leapt up onto their bench, and while some of them certainly did so from alarm and a desire to get out of the way of potential harm, I believe that fully half of them were avid spectators, and had their own favorite who they urged on, usually by baring their breasts or lifting their gowns, which I took to be the equivalent of the auditor announcing the prize for a given gladiatorial contest. I suppose it did break up the monotony a bit, but I was beginning to tire, having temporarily forgotten that I had just marched in a triumph, and I must have been fidgeting a bit because I sensed how Flaccus' headdress kept turning as he glanced up at me. More to stretch my legs than anything, I walked over to Creticus.

"Pilus Prior, may I have permission to allow the men to stand at *otiose*?"

I was expecting him to say no, but to my surprise, he actually looked a bit embarrassed and agreed, "Yes, Pullus, that's a good idea." He called to his Century and issued the order, then told me to pass the word down, but then before I saluted and left, he added, "Just make sure they're ready to come back to *intente*." Lowering his voice so that only I could hear, he explained, "I have a feeling that the Prefect will be coming around soon."

Stifling the groan, I saluted Creticus, then trotted back to my Century, stopping only long enough to give the command, then went to tell Atticus, hearing but not acknowledging the thanks from the men who understood that had been my purpose in speaking with the Pilus Prior. When I came back, some of the men were facing the man next to them, while others were actually faced in the opposite direction, since the position only requires that their left foot remain in place and their shields are leaning against them. What I did not expect is that just listening to the men talking with each other, arguing about the chariot races, or what they planned on doing with their off duty time helped me forget how hungry I was.

There was one unfortunate effect, which I learned when I heard Flaccus clear his throat, then ask, "Pilus Prior, may I ask you a question?"

"It depends on what it is," I answered him, but I kept my eyes on the revelers, mainly to throw him off balance.

I heard him take in a breath, making me think that he had not expected that as an answer, and I thought, Now you have a decision to make, you little worm.

Apparently deciding to be bold, he asked, "Have I done something to offend you, sir?"

How do I count the ways? I kept this inside my head, and aloud, I countered, "Why? Have you done something that you know would offend me?"

This was when I did turn my head to gaze down at him, and I was rewarded by the sight of his mouth hanging open as he tried to determine what the right answer would be; perhaps he suspected that there was no right answer he could give me.

"I...I...don't believe so," he stammered, then insisted, "certainly not intentionally."

"What do you think might offend me, Flaccus?" I asked conversationally, returning my attention to the feasting. "Can you think of any behavior or actions that your Centurion might find offensive?"

I could see his mouth working out of the corner of my eye, and it took a couple of times before he managed, "I...I suppose that I haven't been as...respectful as I could be."

"That's a start," I agreed. "But that's not what I find the most offensive." I thought about prolonging his agony, but I was getting bored, so I turned to face him and lean towards him, a favorite Centurion trick, even for men shorter than I am. "What I find the most offensive is hearing about how you refuse to honor your obligations out in the city."

"I'm not sure I understand, sir." Flaccus shook his head, but the color leaving his face told me he was lying.

"Yes you do," I snapped, then I used my *vitus* to poke him in the chest for emphasis. "You and some of your comrades think that because you're Praetorians, you don't need to pay your debts when you go out whoring and drinking, especially at Isis' Grotto."

"But that's how it's always been, Pilus Posterior!" Flaccus insisted, and I began wondering if he was as stupid as he seemed for arguing with me. "That was how it was when I showed up, I swear it! I didn't do anything anyone else isn't doing!"

"Are you saying that every man in the Century stiffs the owner?" I scoffed. "He'd be out of business in a week!"

"Well, no," he admitted, but then his mouth snapped shut, but I was not through.

"How many men?" I demanded, but before he said anything, I held up a hand, "I don't want their names. I'll find that out on my own. Although," I pretended to consider this, "I can't imagine that they'd be very happy with you if they thought that you had given them up."

I thought he was pale, but this made him go deathly white, and by the way his eyes fluttered, I thought he might actually faint to the point I started to reach for the standard, but he managed to stay on his feet.

"You...you're not going to do that?" he asked with an understandable anxiety.

"No," I told him, but I could not resist adding, "at least, not yet." One thing at a time, Gnaeus, I told myself. Suddenly, I experienced what I suppose was an inspiration, because I said, "You know that you're an officer of this Century, don't you, Flaccus?"

"Yes, sir," he answered readily enough, but he frowned as he tried to figure out where I was going.

"But you came into this Century at your current rank, yes?" He clearly did not like this, but he did not bother denying it, although he only nodded. "So you have absolutely no leadership experience," I continued. "And that means that I don't really know if you have what it takes to be an officer in my Century." I paused for several heartbeats, returning my attention to the crowd before I said, "For example, if I was to learn that the owners of Isis' Grotto and the other establishments our boys frequent are being paid what they're owed, that would get you in my good books, and it would prove to me that you're the man for the job. Because," I warned him, "the regulations for the Praetorians is the same as in the Legions. I know because I checked," I lied, "and the Centurion in command of a Century has the authority to promote or to *demote* any man in his Century that he deems deserving."

I thought he was disposed to argue for a span of heartbeats, but he finally said, "I understand, Pilus Posterior." He swallowed hard enough that I could see how it choked him to finish, "And I will obey."

We'll see about that, a thought that again stayed in my head. With this settled, I began thinking about what was coming tomorrow, and whether Flaccus would still be of the same mind.

As I expected once I learned the real cause for this "emergency," we were not called on to stop a stampede of drunken Head Counters rushing for the Forum, and at least I can say that it was fairly entertaining to watch. In many ways, despite being civilians, they exhibited the kind of behavior I observed with rankers out in Ubiorum on a random night, making me wonder whether it was the work they did or the class from which they came that dictated their behavior. This is not to say that our time on duty passed completely uneventfully, because as Creticus had warned, the Prefect arrived, along with a bodyguard of a dozen Praetorians, which I thought odd. Fortunately, I had a moment's warning when Numerius Blaesus, Creticus' Optio, who was standing on my side of his Century, called my name, and when I turned to look at him, he pointed over his shoulder. Thanks to my height, I saw Sejanus coming, which gave me the time to call the Century to *intente*, so that by the time he reached Creticus, at least the First and Second were no longer at *otiose*. Unfortunately, Atticus was engaged in a spirited discussion with his *Signifer* and had his back turned to me, which in turn meant that the other Centuries on the other side of the Third were not warned either. It required Creticus ordering his *Cornicen* to sound the call for the Cohort to come to *intente*, earning me a glare from Atticus, and I reminded myself to explain later. However, there was another consequence of this horn call, because the mood of the crowd instantly changed, the laughter cutting short, but it was the change in their demeanor that worried me, and I was not alone. Thousands of people suddenly snapping their heads around in our direction was unsettling enough, although it was more the expressions on the faces of those nearest us that made my stomach flutter as I remembered all the stories of what angry Head Counters in Rome could do to those who incurred their wrath. I do not believe there is a Roman citizen alive who has not heard the stories about the Gracchi and of the aftermath after the death of Divus Julius. My hope was that not doing anything other than changing our posture back to *intente* would be enough to settle what was one action away from being an angry mob back to the more important business of drinking themselves insensible, since the food had already been served and devoured. Perhaps it was a blessing that very quickly I had other matters to worry about, though it certainly did not feel that way in the moment as, out of the corner of my eye now that I was staring straight ahead, I sensed movement that, on getting closer, I saw that it was Creticus and Sejanus, but it took another moment for me to recognize the third figure, although he was in uniform, wearing the helmet that identified him as a Tribune. When I did recognize him, I was unable to greet him properly because I suddenly found myself looking over Prefect Sejanus' head as he glared up at me, just inches apart.

Pointing at my torq and without any preface, he snapped, "What. Is. That?"

"It's the torq awarded to my father by the Princeps' brother, Prefect," I answered.

"And why are you wearing it now?" Sejanus pressed. "Especially after you were expressly forbidden from wearing Legion decorations?" He was close enough to smell the wine on his breath, and I am certain that he was at least slightly drunk, because that is the only reason I have for him deciding that poking me in my chest in the exact same manner I had with Flaccus not long before was a good idea, and he poked me in rhythm with his words. "Who authorized you to wear these things?"

Honestly, I would have loved to draw the moment out longer, but as angry as I was, and as little fear I had, or have for a man like Sejanus if we are facing each other with a *gladius* in hand, I reminded myself that made him no less dangerous, which made me answer fairly promptly, "The *Propraetor* did, Prefect." I could have stopped there, but then I added, "And as you saw, the Princeps and I had a conversation, and he voiced his approval of the *Propraetor*'s decision."

"That's a lie!" Sejanus snarled. "The Princeps would never have said such a thing! When I became the only Prefect, I explained my reasoning about allowing you..." I think he wanted to call me scum or some such, "...men from the Legions wearing your decorations that you didn't earn as a Praetorian!"

I fully expected that I was on my own, but to my utter shock,

Creticus spoke up, after a fashion, clearing his throat in a manner that did manage to jerk Sejanus' glare from me to him.

"Actually, Prefect, I saw the order. It had Germanicus' seal, and as you know, as the triumphing general, he has the right..."

"I don't need to be told about our traditions, Pilus Prior Creticus."

The fact that Sejanus said this in a quieter tone than he had been addressing me must have made him sound even more menacing, judging from the manner in which Creticus' face took on a deathly pallor. Apparently deciding that was enough to yank Creticus' leash, Sejanus returned his gaze and his attention to me.

"I will discuss this with the Princeps later, Pilus Posterior Pullus. And," he was using the same soft tone, "if he tells me a different story, I am afraid that the consequences for putting lies in the mouth of the Imperator are...severe."

You think I don't know that, you *cunnus*? It was becoming clear to me that Sejanus was underestimating me, but it seemed as if he also bore me a personal enmity that went over and above just viewing me as an annoyance or a minor obstacle in whatever it was that he was trying to achieve.

Aloud, I only said, "I'm aware of that, Prefect."

"So," Sejanus' tone changed, becoming friendlier, or perhaps oilier would more accurate, "how was your moment with the Imperator?"

"It was an honor, Prefect," I answered honestly. "The fact that he remembered my father and all that he did for Rome is a moment I'll treasure forever."

While he nodded as he said, "Indeed. Your father did serve Rome well," it was obvious that he did not like the taste of the words. "Granted," he added, "he had a streak of...arrogance in him. Just like you do."

Is he baiting me? I wondered.

Deciding to be honest, I replied, "You aren't the first man to say that about him, or me, for that matter, Prefect, and I suspect that you won't be the last."

His look of disappointment confirmed my hunch, but he returned to the real reason for this confrontation, demanding, "What else did you talk about with the Imperator?"

Even in the moment I took notice of how Sejanus kept referring to Tiberius as Imperator, despite the fact that Tiberius himself insisted on being addressed as Princeps, just as his adoptive father had up until his death, but it was only a random thought.

"I'm not sure that I should divulge the details of our conversation, Prefect," I replied coldly, while my stomach began twisting and turning.

As I expected, this infuriated him, and while he did not shout in my face, it was close.

"I am your superior, Pilus Posterior Pullus, something you'd do well to remember!"

"Who serves at the pleasure of the Princeps, Prefect. Or have you forgotten?"

If I had kicked Sejanus in the balls, I do not believe he could have gone paler, although he did not double up and fall to the ground, and in that instant, I wondered if he would feel any better knowing that I was the one who felt like moaning because of what I had just said. If someone had asked me before this moment if I was confident that, while Sejanus could make my life miserable, and he could do something behind the scenes like send scum like Appius after me, he would never have the nerve to try and have me executed for some official reason, if only because it would come to the attention of Germanicus, and as powerful as Sejanus was, and as powerful as he has become at the moment, he would have been foolish to risk Germanicus' wrath, especially for some trumped-up charge, I would have agreed. In this moment, standing on the Vicus Iugarius, if I had been forced to wager on that prospect, I doubt I would have put a brass *obol* on me surviving my time in Rome.

To his credit, Sejanus recovered quickly enough, but his countenance turned poisonous, his mouth twisting into a sneer as he assured me, "I don't forget *anything*, Pullus. You would do very well to remember that."

Without another word, and without inspecting the other Centuries, Sejanus turned and stalked away, snapping at Creticus and the Tribune I now recognized to follow him, but the Tribune hesitated for a moment.

"It seems that you have your father's talent for picking powerful enemies, Pilus Prior Pullus."

This was said with some amusement, and despite my fluttering stomach, I did laugh as I answered Asprenas, "It must be in the blood." As he turned to go, I asked, "Are you back on duty, Tribune?"

"Yes," he answered, then turned to hurry after the other two so it was over his shoulder as he called, "I'll tell you about it later."

If I live that long, I thought dismally, and this prompted me to glance down at Flaccus, who suddenly looked happy again, and I was so tempted to tell him what was in store for him the next day, but I refrained. Let it be a surprise, I told myself, and I savored the image of what his face would look like.

Sejanus dismissed us immediately after this, and the mood of not just my Century but the entire Cohort was quite surly, certainly the angriest I had seen them in my months with the Praetorians. When we returned to the barracks, Alex was there, but when I entered the office wearing the blue tunic and Praetorian crest, he was understandably surprised.

"What are you doing wearing that? Why aren't you at the banquet on the Campus?"

"Don't ask," I said sourly, but I did not stop walking, entering my quarters as he followed me in.

Naturally, I could not keep my mouth shut, so as he helped me out of my *hamata* and unfastened the decorations, I told him what had happened. Initially, I was not going to mention my clash with Sejanus, but then I thought about it, and with a sinking feeling in my stomach, I realized he needed to be informed, mainly because of what I had planned. He listened, his expression going from sober to grave, but to my surprise, he did not chastise me for my rashness.

"Do you think he's going to do anything? Like he tried with Appius?" he asked me, but when I shook my head, it was not just to make him feel better, because I had thought it through.

"The only way he can call me a liar is if he asks Tiberius, and if he does, it will be up to the Princeps to decide what to tell him. And," I took a deep breath, "I think Tiberius will tell him the truth. Maybe not everything," I allowed, thinking of the more important part of our conversation, which I had described to Alex along with the personal aspect about the training, "but enough that it would be very rash of him to come after me. Displeasing Germanicus is one thing, but Tiberius?" I shook my head, feeling more confident as I talked. "He's no fool. Still," I went on, "I'd feel better if you went back to the apartment."

"What?" This startled Alex. "Aren't you coming with me?"

"No, I have too much to do to be ready for tomorrow. Tell Bronwen that I'm sorry, but I'm staying here tonight."

I had to suppress a grin at the expression of alarm that flashed across his face, and he asked plaintively, "Can't you come with me and tell her yourself, then come back?"

"What, are you scared of my woman?" I laughed.

"I'm not the one who's afraid to tell her and wants me to do it for him," he shot back. With a shake of his head, he said, "She's better than when she was pregnant, but..."

"Not by much," I agreed, then gave him a playful clap on the shoulder as I intoned, "May Mars and Bellona favor you when you face the savage Parisii."

"Coward," he grumbled, but he was walking out as he did it, nor did I argue the point since it was essentially true.

After he left, I told Demetrios to go get Sabinus first, then to find me something to eat, and I passed the time outlining what would be facing my Second Century in the morning on a tablet. When Sabinus arrived, the way he entered my office, displaying a caution as if he expected me to be in a rage actually made me laugh.

"You're not entering an arena full of lions, Sabinus," I assured him, and I did not miss the look of relief that flashed across his face as he dropped into his seat. Turning the tablet around, I handed it to him as I explained, "I do need you to go to the armory to make sure that we have the wicker face shields, and enough padded sleeves."

Before he began reading, he asked with a frown, "What for?"

"If you read that, you'll see why," I answered, then sat back and watched as his eyes roved across the incised lines.

Since he had read enough of my handwriting, he only needed to go over it once, but he let out a gasp, sitting back in his chair to stare at me with an expression that might have been of a type that one uses on someone who has lost their wits.

"Have you talked to Creticus about this?"

It was his first question, and it was a good one, but while I made what I thought was a valid assumption, I would be learning shortly that it was erroneous.

"No," I said airily, waving a hand as I dismissed this as the trivial matter that I thought it was, "but I don't have to. It comes from a higher authority than the Pilus Prior, and I'm sure he knows by now."

I awoke even earlier than normal, and I roused Demetrios with orders to begin my meal immediately. While he was occupied and after my trip to the latrine, I went and knocked on Sabinus' door, pleased to see that he was already fully dressed.

"Did you get everything?" I asked.

Before he answered, he yawned, sending the signal that his slumber had been cut short, but he must have seen I was not sympathetic in the slightest, so he assured me that he had everything ready.

"Once you've eaten, get everything ready," I instructed as I returned to my quarters to do the same, then make myself ready.

When the *bucina* sounded the call for assembly, the men of the Second Century, Second Praetorian Cohort rose with the expectation that it would be a normal day, a fiction I was happy to allow until we were issued the orders of the day by Creticus, although I did hold my dismissal so that they were still in formation as their comrades in the other Centuries fell out of their formation, but it was really to wait for Creticus to enter his office.

"I suppose you're wondering why I'm not dismissing you right away." I used a conversational tone, wanting them to be lulled into a sense that this was just slightly out of the routine. "That's because the Second Century is going to be doing something a bit different today." This caused some mutters and glances, but they were completely unprepared for me to inform them, "When I dismiss you, you're going to go to your quarters...and put on your armor and helmets, but that's all you'll need." Now there was real concern, to the point that when I dismissed them, they did not move; I was about to bellow at the top of my lungs, but I was not ready to alert Creticus, so instead I just raised my *vitus*, which had the desired effect, and they scrambled to their quarters. Putting on my armor, I was met by Sabinus, who was standing next to two boxes, and a few *rudii* and training shields, which he had arranged leaning against the wall of our quarters, so we were ready and waiting when the men exited from their quarters, some of them noticing the equipment.

"Starting today," I began, "we're going to start behaving more like the Legions. I've seen your work at the stakes, and while it's far from where I'd like it," I started pacing back and forth so that I could catch the eye of every man in the Century, "it's good enough for us to begin sparring, which begins today." My purpose in moving around was twofold; I wanted their attention completely on me, and to see who looked eager at the idea of bashing each other and who did not. For the most part, the men like Valerius and the other veterans who were suddenly grinning, I was expecting, while men like Flaccus looked nervous, but none of them were ready for what was coming, because I stopped suddenly back in my normal spot, and while I was smiling, it was not a friendly one as I continued, "However, before you start facing each other, you're going to be facing me first, one at a time."

It was ambitious; in fact, it was not very well thought out on my part, but I wanted to make a demonstration that would leave a lasting impression, and while this was certainly partly due to my frustration and overall discontent, I also wanted to send another message, knowing that somehow Sejanus would hear about it and perhaps this would make him hesitant to try something again. What I did *not* think through well was the fact that, unlike the Legions, the Praetorians are rarely if ever understrength, while the opposite is true in the Legions, with the exception of right before we begin on campaign and have been plumped up, and as I would learn, eighty men is a lot.

"What order do you want to start in, Pilus Posterior?" Sabinus asked me, another thing I had not thought of, and frankly, I was distracted because I was expecting Creticus to reappear, although the rest of the Cohort was now re-polishing their helmets and oiling their armor from the day before because of all the wear that came from standing in one place. After thinking about it, I shrugged and said, "Let's start with the veterans first so I can see how rusty they are."

Instead of acknowledging my order, he stood there, an uncertain expression on his face, and when I raised an eyebrow, he grinned and asked, "Why not start with me?"

While it was a challenge, I could see that it was meant in a friendly, if competitive, manner, so I matched his tone and his grin, asking, "You sure you want to start with me when I'm fresh? You might have better luck once I'm tired."

"There's only one way to find out," he replied cheerfully, and my regard for Sabinus went up even more.

Certainly, I had had my reservations about him, and I was not sure I could trust him, but those doubts had been quelled by this moment, so I picked up a *rudis* and pointed to one of the boxes with it and said, "Get on your padding and faceguard and meet me in the square with a shield."

As I walked away, Sabinus called out, and I heard a note of concern. "What about you, Pilus Posterior? About your padding and faceguard, I mean?"

"Don't worry, I won't need it," I assured him.

Pacing out twenty paces to a side, the men formed a square, and while there was a lot of apprehension in the air, there was excitement as well.

As part of my plan, I pulled out my purse and addressed the Century, "I'm offering up fifty *sesterces* to any man who beats me!"

"Who's going to judge?" I was facing the opposite direction of the man who asked this, and I recognized that it belonged to Flaccus, but I was a bit dismayed to realize I had not thought about this.

Turning to face him, I said, "You are," I indicated all of them. "You're going to be the judges. If you think that I've been bested, then I'll trust on your honor as Praetorians and accept your decision. Is that fair?"

There was general agreement, although I cannot say it was all enthusiastic, but I hid my grin when I heard someone muttering about "knocking this cocky bastard on his ass." By this time, Sabinus had attached the padded sleeves and tied the wicker faceguard to his helmet, and he was carrying the *rudis* and training shield, but when he pushed through the men to enter the square with me, he stopped.

"Where's your shield?" he asked.

I raised my *vitus* in answer; I had picked up my Legion *vitus* and not the Praetorian for the simple reason I had never trained with a *vitus* that was weighted on one end, and neither did I intend to explain that, as a paid man, I had never gotten comfortable with a shield. Not surprisingly, the atmosphere was now charged with excitement, and I was certain I did not have much time before Creticus heard the commotion and came outside.

"Are you sure you know what you're doing?" Sabinus called, but because of the faceguard, the only way I could tell he was grinning was by his voice.

"There's only one way to find out," I echoed, then dropped into a first position, which Sabinus copied, though not before cracking his *rudis* against his shield a couple times.

"Come on, Optio! Show the Centurion what we're about!"

This was not Flaccus, but while I thought it was Glabrio of the Third Section, his voice was quickly joined by the others, their cries bouncing off the four walls of the barracks as Sabinus shuffled forward. I was content to let him come for the moment, because to my chagrin, I realized that I had not really paid as much attention to him as I should have when we were working at the stakes, so I needed a moment to learn about him. His position was good; tightly held, with his left elbow locked in as it should have been, and while he slid more than stepped across the paving stones, he never opened his stance too much. And I was impressed by his speed; when he launched a first position thrust, I barely managed to knock it downward towards the ground with my *vitus*. He was also ready for my first counterthrust, catching it on his shield, but even with the shouting, I heard the same gasp of surprise that every man who faces me for the first time offers as the shield rocked back towards his body, the sharp cracking sound also unique. Macer was the first, but he was far from the last who had told me that the only man they had ever seen who could create that kind of sharp cracking noise when striking something with the *rudis* was my father, but I have yet to achieve what he did, snapping a *rudis* in half edgewise. The men were all shouting now, and while it was not in my nature to be so passive, I still wanted to get a better idea of Sabinus' style and proficiency, although what I had seen to this point was impressive. He did not hesitate, this time coming after me with his shield, punching it at me, but he only grazed my right arm with the edge, and he let out a curse.

"Pluto's *cock,* you're fast," he called out, but I was not fooled, expecting another lunge even as he spoke, this time from over the top of his shield, which I used my *rudis* to deflect, then brought my *vitus* around the inside edge of his shield to strike him, hard in the stomach.

Even above the yelling, I heard him gasp with pain, but when I tried to press my advantage, he did an excellent job of using his shield defensively while shuffling backward to recover.

"That hurt!" he complained. "I haven't been hit with a *vitus* since I was a ranker in the 2nd!"

"Come on, Optio! Get after him!"

"Let's see what you're saying in a bit, Valerius!" Sabinus snapped, which elicited laughter.

I was standing there, waiting for his next move, and as I did, pivoting as he sidestepped to try to get a better angle of attack, I realized that I was happy, probably the happiest I had been since the day Titus was born, even more than the day before when I saw the diorama. Naturally, this was when he lunged; whether he sensed my mind was wandering or not, I did not know, but now I found myself doing the same thing he had just done, sliding backward as I parried three thrusts, a punch with the shield that struck me on my right shoulder, momentarily turning my arm numb, then a slashing blow down around my knees. This is frowned on, and I barely managed to block it with my *vitus*, causing a cracking sound that told me one of the twisted vines that make it up had been damaged. Deciding I had seen enough, I slid towards his shield side as he pivoted to remain squared up on me, and I feinted, not with my *rudis* but with my *vitus*, out wide enough that he could not bring his shield across his body, so he used his *rudis* to meet this threat. It was what I had been waiting for, and I twisted my wrist as I swung my *rudis* down, having learned that even with padded sleeves, with the strength I applied, if I had used the edge, it would have snapped at least one bone. Despite using the flat of my wooden blade, I caused his *rudis* to fly out of his hand, spinning wildly before it clattered to the ground as he shouted in pain and surprise. Nevertheless, he kept his composure so that he was ready for my following thrust, except this time, I had my hips underneath me so that, despite blocking the thrust with his shield, it sent him staggering backward, and I pressed my advantage.

It took two more thrusts before Sabinus began shouting, "I yield! I yield!"

To my embarrassment, I did not stop immediately as I should have, landing one more thrust before I stopped, and I was pleased that, while I was breathing hard, I was not panting as hard as Sabinus.

"The Pilus Posterior wins!"

That this came from Sabinus was the signal to the other men that he bore no grudge, and I made sure to quietly thank him.

"You hit like a fucking mule," he said ruefully as he shook his arm, but while I was concerned, he assured me that it was just bruised.

"Have you ever been kicked by a mule?" I asked, though in a bantering tone.

"Well, no," he admitted.

"I've been told that I hit harder than a mule," I assured him, and he chuckled a bit as he rubbed his arm some more. Turning serious, I said, "You're very skilled, Sabinus. And," I was not lying when I told him, "if I had faced you last instead of first, you would have gotten me."

As I hoped, he clearly saw that I was being sincere, but before he could say anything, we were interrupted by our Pilus Prior.

"What in Hades are you doing??"

My first thought was that, if Creticus shrieked like this in front of a Legion Century, he would never have heard the end of it, but he clearly did not care as he shoved a couple of my men out of the way to enter the square, coming right up to me and, for the first time during our brief association, his anger outweighed his caution as he glowered up at me.

"What's the explanation of this, Pilus Posterior Pullus?"

Determined to be calm in direct proportion to his ire, I did come to *intente* and explained, "I'm training my men, Pilus Prior."

"Like they're fucking *gladiators*?" he snapped, his face redder than I had ever seen it, but it was poking his finger in my chest that got my attention, and he demanded, "Who authorized this?"

Now it was my turn to be surprised; as it would turn out, I had made a bad assumption, which I displayed by asking in surprise, "The Prefect didn't tell you yesterday?"

Now Creticus' expression changed, a cross between confusion and, if I was any judge, apprehension, although he was speaking more loudly than necessary.

"Tell me what?"

Without mentioning Tiberius in the hope that Creticus would be satisfied, I explained to my Pilus Prior how the Princeps had changed the training regimen of the Praetorians to make them combat ready against more than just unarmed citizens of Rome.

I realized my error when, after rubbing his chin in thought, he asked, "And how do you know this since the Prefect didn't utter a word about it to me yesterday?"

Gnaeus, you're truly a prideful idiot; I almost groaned this aloud but managed to keep it inside my skull, and I realized I had no choice.

"The Princeps informed me of his decision when we were talking about my father, Pilus Prior. He said that I should continue to train my men as if they were in the Legions, and that he was directing the Prefect to issue orders to that effect for the entire Praetorian Guard. Although," I thought to add, "it might only be for the Rome Cohorts."

"I distinctly recall you being asked by the Prefect about your conversation." His voice was cold. "Why didn't you divulge this then?"

On an impulse, I decided to roll the dice, turning it around on him by asking quietly, "What would you do, Pilus Prior? And," I added, "who would it be more dangerous to offend? The Princeps or Prefect Sejanus?"

I cannot say what I was expecting from him, but it was not Creticus sighing and, almost at a whisper, telling me, "For men of the upper classes, it would be the Imperator. But," he looked up at me, and I believe the sympathy I saw there was real as he finished, "for men of the Praetorian Guard, there is no more dangerous man in Rome than the Prefect, Pullus." Before I could say anything, he shook his head. "But I believe you, Pullus. I'd heard rumors that the Imperator has been...unhappy with us. So," just as abruptly as he shoved his way into the square, he spun on his heel, his parting words being, "you might as well continue what you're doing while I seek confirmation from the Prefect."

The main challenge for me was not because my skills were tested, my endurance was, although I take full responsibility for this. I did realize early on that my pride, by way of my mouth, had gotten me into a situation that was of my own making, so by the time I was finished facing the First Section, I decided not to prolong any bout for the purpose of showing off. Alex had arrived when Sabinus and I were facing each other, but I was unaware that he did not stay long, instead dashing back to the apartment to retrieve something. I only learned of his absence by his presence when, just when I was halfway through the Century, he pushed his way into the square with a small stoppered bottle in his hand.

"If I'd known you were going to act like an idiot, I would have brought this with me," he muttered as he shoved it into my hands.

Immediately knowing what it was, I only briefly hesitated, mainly because of the memories associated with what we jokingly called the "magic elixir" that Alex's father had either concocted himself out of necessity during my great-grandfather's participation in the brutal campaign conducted by Marcus Antonius in Parthia, or paid for, none of us in either family really knowing. What I do know is that it works, although one is also left with a frightful headache after the effects wear off, but I also had a plan for ameliorating that as well, which I revealed afterward. Regardless, thanks to two doses of the thick, granular, and bitter-tasting liquid, my toughest opponent was my own fatigue. Otherwise, I wish I could have said I was pleasantly surprised, but the Second Century was about what I thought they were, a group of men for whom their training had been almost exclusively devoted to appearance, and not to the actual duties that I believe are required by anyone who marches under the standard for Rome, whether it be Legion, auxiliary, or Praetorian. The one change in plan was that I did not punish Flaccus to the degree I had originally intended, mainly because he was so comically inept that I was certain the effects of the mocking laughter of his comrades would last longer than any bruises I could inflict. As far as damage to myself, I had one bruise on my left arm when I admittedly got sloppy and extended it out too far, giving the First Section Sergeant, fittingly named Titus Plautius, the opportunity to stab me in my forearm with the blunt end of the *rudis*, fortunately hitting the meaty part and not the bone. And I would be remiss if I did not add that I made Plautius pay for it; he was moving gingerly for the next few days. However, while the men performed about like I expected, I was heartened to see that it was not from a lack of effort, and their enthusiasm helped me through the last section. That they were cheering against me and urging one of their comrades to best me I did not mind at all, because they showed a unity that I had thought was missing, only realizing later that they just needed the opportunity.

Before I dismissed them, I lifted my purse, hiding the grimace from the effort to seemingly taunt them. "Since none of you bastards were good enough to take my money, it looks like I have fifty *sesterces* on my hands." I paused, then heaved a theatrical sigh as I said, "I suppose I might as well waste it on you at Isis' Grotto tonight."

I was not the least bit surprised they all thought this was a splendid idea, and when I dismissed them, they could have been just another Century in a Legion in an army town and not in Rome, taunting each other about their performance against me and arguing who was going to drink more of my money. Sabinus caught me by surprise; I did not see him approach as I watched them streaming to their quarters, so when he gave a small cough, it made me jump in surprise.

"You shouldn't sneak up on a man like that," I grumbled, albeit facetiously.

I was disappointed that he did not seem to take it in the spirit I meant it, but I quickly learned he had something else on his mind, and I could not really identify his expression as he said, "I've never seen anything like that before, Centurion Pullus." Shaking his head, he turned his gaze on the backs of our men. "I know I came from the Legions like you did, but I don't ever recall seeing anyone, Centurion, Optio, or any rank, for that matter, do what you did." I was uncertain where this was going, but I got my answer in the manner he turned to look into my eyes with an intensity that was almost unsettling. "How can I become that good, Pullus? How long did it take you to be able to face seventy-nine men, and take care of most of them in a dozen or two heartbeats?"

How *did* I do these things? I wondered, and the truth is that I am still searching for an answer, but I decided to be honest.

"When I came to the 1st Legion," I explained, "in most ways, I was like you see me now. I," I shrugged, "am bigger, I'm stronger than most men, and for my size, I move quickly, and that's just the way it had been my entire life. It wasn't until I stopped being a stubborn, prideful ass that I learned how much more there is to this life, and it was my father who taught me all that I know now."

Since I saw the flicker of hesitation flash across his face, I was somewhat prepared for him to say awkwardly, "After you came here, I asked around, and I heard some...stories about you and your father."

When I see the written words, I can see how one might think this would anger me, but in the moment, I was sure that he was not trying to cast aspersions.

However, I was not willing to say more than, "That's for another time." Returning to the topic, "What I learned from him is that for any man who aspires to not just survive, but to excel under the standard, it takes a *lot* of hard work, and while I've been remiss since I came to the Praetorians, I spent a third of a watch a day at the stakes, working on my forms."

"Every day?" he asked in surprise, but I decided I owed him the truth.

"I'm not going to say I don't miss a day here or there," I

admitted. "But what I learned from my father is that, once you make something a habit, it's when you don't do whatever it is that makes you feel bad, like you're missing something you should be doing."

"That," he nodded slowly as his eyes followed the backs of the men, "makes sense. Still," he looked up at me, "I just wanted to tell you that what I saw you do today is something I'll never forget." I did not know how to respond to that, but the most important part came when he waved a hand in the direction of the section quarters. "And neither will they, Centurion. I think," he finished with a sober expression, "today, the Second became your Century."

I will not deny that this had been my hope, knowing that the only real way to form a bond between a Centurion and his men is through combat, but hearing Sabinus confirm it was gratifying to hear.

To cover up my emotion, I said gruffly, "Well, we better get to the baths. I want the Second smelling sweet when we're out on the streets of Rome."

When I entered my quarters, I suppose I have to take responsibility for not paying attention to Alex when I told him what I had planned for the night, but I was in a hurry to get cleaned up, because I wanted to go to the apartment to inform Bronwen that I would be out late after spending a night away from her.

"You're going to do *what*?"

Bronwen did not shout this, nor did she seem all that upset, which should have been my warning. I did hurry home after the baths, the sun just going down as I entered the building, and I found her rocking young Titus, talking quietly to Algaia. My second warning was how, the moment I entered, Algaia said something I could not hear, then got up and walked past me to the door while keeping her eyes averted.

"I told you." I wanted to sound patient, although I was certain I had explained myself well enough the first time. "Today I sparred with my Century, and tonight I'm going to go to Isis' Grotto to stand them for drinks. It's something that Centurions are expected to do from time to time," I explained helpfully.

"I see," she responded, then said nothing else, her attention seemingly on Titus, who was sleeping peacefully as she continued to rock him.

I made the mistake of thinking, This is going better than I thought, which was why I opened my mouth to say, "And I'm going to be spending a fair amount of money tonight, *meum mel*," giving myself a pat on the back for being so responsible.

Perhaps I can be excused for forgetting, albeit temporarily, that I was not only speaking to my woman, but to the daughter of the Parisii merchant Prausetaugas who, with every telling by Bronwen, became shrewder and more astute when it came to matters of commerce and money.

"How much money?" she asked suspiciously, and while I was prepared to answer this, she then complicated matters by demanding, "And on what?"

"Wine," I assured her, and perhaps if I had broken eye contact and not continued to stare into those green eyes that were regarding me steadily, I could have gotten away with it. Somehow, however, without any conscious decision to do so, I heard my voice say lamely, "Isis' Grotto is a...multi-purpose establishment."

I do not know why I thought throwing an unfamiliar phrase at her would work, but I was still surprised when she immediately snapped, "You mean whores! You are going to buy your men whores!" This was true, yet I was completely unprepared for her eyes to start glittering, and she stopped rocking my son to put her face in her hands and begin weeping. Because of that, I barely heard her muffled voice say, "And you are going to buy one for yourself! I know it!" If the window had not been shuttered already, I would have thrown myself out of it, but this was just the beginning, and she wailed, "Now that we are in Rome, you see all these women who are more beautiful than I am, and now you cannot wait to get away from me!"

It was my turn to be the one reeling from the surprise, and I actually staggered over to the bench, dropping down next to her with no idea what to say. How, I wondered miserably, could she think that? How could she possibly believe that there was a woman, here in Rome or anywhere, who matched her beauty? Before I knew it, I found myself on my knees, holding both of her hands in mine, trying to send through that contact the depth of my feelings for her, even as in the back of my mind, I thought, If your men saw you now, they would be snickering behind your back. Immediately on the heels of that was the memory of what this woman had endured with me, leaving her family, people, and everything she knew, then sailing across Our Sea with a man she barely knew.

"Bronwen," I assured her, squeezing her hands just hard enough to get her to look at me, "there is no other woman for me, I swear it on Jupiter's black stone, and on your gods as well. This is..." I tried to think of the proper term, latching on to, "...business."

"Business?" she scoffed, but I could see the dawning of hope in her expression. "What kind of business is that?"

Inspired, I asked her, "Are you saying that your father never took men out, bought them drinks, and...other things, in order to conclude some business?" She did not like it, I could tell, but after a heartbeat, she nodded, though she kept her eyes on our entwined hands. "That's essentially what this is," I went on, hurrying to continue when she lifted her head, her mouth open to say something. "I don't have the same bond with these Praetorians that I had with the Fourth. We haven't gone into battle, and we're not going to. So," I shrugged, "today I sparred with them, and tonight I'm going to get them drunk."

She did not reply immediately, just looking me directly in the eye, and I knew she was searching for some sign of duplicity, but while it is not something a Roman man likes to admit, the truth is that Bronwen of the Parisii is all I want in a woman.

"So," she asked hesitantly, "it is just business? You are doing this for your men?"

"I'm doing it for the men," I answered firmly, "and nobody else."

"Very well." She nodded, then wiped her tears with the back of her hand, something that I find endearing because it is something that I have seen little girls like Iras do. "Go to this Isis' Grotto and do what you must."

I kissed her, then I leaned over to kiss the baby and picked up my *vitus* leaning next to the door, but when I opened it, Algaia had just mounted the stairs.

"Alex is going with you," she said, and while she was not angry, she seemed more resigned to it than anything. As I walked past her, she grabbed my arm, looking up at me, and I remembered the first time I met her, when she came to my father's funeral rites. "This isn't unusual, Gnaeus," she said quietly. "New mothers often feel that they're no longer desirable to their man, and when they're left alone, they have nothing but time to think about what their man is doing when they're not around."

I do not know if she meant this in an accusing manner, or perhaps I did not choose to take it that way, and I assured her, "Bronwen has nothing to worry about, Algaia."

"I know that," she replied immediately, and actually smiled up at me. "Anyone with eyes can see that. But she," she nodded in the direction of the apartment, "she does not know that, Gnaeus. Not right now."

While I did not, nor do I, really understand this, I believed Algaia was speaking the truth, and I thanked her, then descended the stairs, where Alex was waiting. I was wise enough to wait until we left the building and was a bit down the street before I nudged him.

"Are you ready for some debauching?"

I had only been in Isis' Grotto once before, when I sat with Sabinus and had a cup of wine as he gave me the rundown of the Second Century, and I did not stay long. It is actually a large place, with a basement storage area that enabled the owner to use the entire first floor for benches and tables, while the second and third floor was divided into what were little more than cubicles with a swatch of fabric hanging down across the opening where the whores plied their trade. Before we walked in the place, I had resolved to myself that I would not even go above the ground floor, and I told Alex to remind me of my vow if I drank too much, because I know myself well enough that the clearheaded Gnaeus and the drunken Gnaeus are two different men. Because of my trip to the apartment, I was the last of the Second to arrive, and I was greeted by a cacophony of shouts and banging on the table, so I had to speak up to Alex to be heard.

"At least they're happy to see me," I said with a laugh.

"They're happy to see your purse," he commented, and had his own laugh at my sudden scowl.

It was packed, the patrons almost equally split between men and women, although all of the men were wearing the blue Praetorian tunic, and it seemed darker than I remembered the last time, then remembered we had visited the place during the day, when the windows were not shuttered. It took Sabinus standing up and waving to me to see that he was seated at a smaller table than the long ones that comprised the majority of the furnishings, another sign that this place catered to soldiers. The table was near the rear, so my progress was slowed as I was stopped by one or some of the men, all of whom seemed to have gotten an early start on the night's festivities. While each man said something slightly different, the overall tenor was that, despite their defeat at my hands, they had thoroughly enjoyed themselves and were asking when it was going to happen again, and the most common question was when they could start beating on each other, all of which I took as a good sign. By the time I made it to the table, Alex skirting around the middle of the room to get there first, I was ready for a cup, but before I ordered, I asked the serving slave to summon her master for me.

"Do you know the man?" I asked Sabinus, who shrugged, and I noticed for some reason he did not want to look at me as he said casually, "I know his name and I'm sure I've spoken to him a time or two, but that's all."

Before I could probe further, a squat, extremely hairy man wearing a dirty apron over a tunic that was not that much cleaner approached, following behind the girl, and while I did not need to do so, I stood and offered my arm to him.

"*Salve*, I'm Pilus Posterior Pullus of the..."

"There's no need, Centurion!" He wore what I believe my father called a proprietor's smile that never really reached his eyes, but his tone was certainly cordial. "I've already heard quite a bit about you from the boys here!" Why, I wondered, is he so happy to see the Centurion of the Century whose men did not pay their bills? I knew that it was not all of them, and Flaccus had been vague on the number of men who were involved. As he clasped my arm, he introduced himself. "Aulus Pomponius Gallus, Centurion." With his free arm, he made a sweeping gesture, "And my establishment, as humble as it may be, is proud to be frequented by the men of the

Second Century of the Second Praetorian Cohort."

This was not going at all as I thought it would, and suddenly, I decided that this needed to be held in a more private setting, realizing that all eyes were on us, which I realized might intimidate Gallus and keep him from being honest.

I was also struck by the thought that I could accomplish two things at once, so in front of everyone, I extracted my purse, and while I did not yell, I did raise my voice as I said, "Since I'm a man of my word, I'm handing this over to you to pay for these thirsty bastards to drink their fill." Naturally, this earned me raucous cheers, but I was not through. "And depending on how they behave, I *might* be persuaded to let them take a trip upstairs." I was expecting an even louder response, but the only surprise is that it did not make the dust sift down from the rafters. Taking advantage of the noise, I leaned over to Gallus, "I'd also like to talk to you more privately. Something has come to my attention and I want to discuss it with you."

The smile vanished as if it was never there, and while he was not scowling, it was close, and I heard the caution in his voice.

"What about?"

"Nothing that won't be to your benefit," I assured him, and the smile came back as quickly as it had vanished.

Signaling the slave, Gallus said something, the slave nodding, going back behind the bar, but she quickly returned with a stylus and tablet, which I assumed, correctly, was to record just how much the damage was going to be to my purse. Leaving the table, I did notice that Sabinus looked uncomfortable, though I did not think anything of it, and I followed Gallus down to the basement, which was only marginally quieter than upstairs and was dimly lit.

"What is it that you want to discuss, Centurion?" Gallus asked, and I explained how I had been made aware that there were men who were not paying, and while I would not commit to them paying what they owed, I assured him that the practice would cease. I was completely unprepared for his reaction; even with a single lamp, I saw what I took to be a look of alarm. "That's not necessary, Centurion, I assure you! It's only a handful of men, and I don't want to cause any trouble!" This made absolutely no sense to me, so I asked him to explain why he was willing to lose money, even if he considered it a trivial amount. Breaking eye contact, he began tugging at a thread on a sack of what smelled like chickpeas, then finally said bitterly, "I did complain once, to your predecessor, and all it got me was a beating. And," he looked at me, a trace of anger surfacing, "I lost two of my best girls!"

"Lost them?" I did not understand. "Lost them how?"

"Well," Gallus laughed, but without any humor, "I didn't misplace them, Centurion. They were valuable." Talking about it seemed to bring it back to him, at least emotionally. "One of them was a Thracian girl, only fourteen! Still fresh and fetching top price! And Layla." His eyes actually started to glint, and for an instant, I thought he might have had feelings for her; he did, but not in the way I thought. "I paid more than two thousand *sesterces* for her because she came from Damascus." Shaking his head, he expressed the reason for his sadness. "I hadn't recouped my investment in her yet."

I am no wide-eyed provincial rube, or at least I am not one any longer, and I knew that, while there are a handful of women who manage to control their own destiny selling their bodies, most of them are like this Thracian girl and Layla, being viewed as nothing more than investments from which a good businessman extracted profit down to the last *as* before the woman's body wore out, she succumbed to one of the diseases common to her profession or, as I have witnessed now that I have been under the standard for a few years, drank herself to death. Nevertheless, I felt disgusted by Gallus' callous attitude, but I hid it as best I could.

"How long ago was this?" I asked.

He thought a moment and said, "A bit more than three years ago now."

"And you've been letting men not pay all this time?"

"It's not all of them," Gallus insisted. "It's only a dozen, and they're the ones who have been in the Second the longest and back when another Centurion was running the Century."

I do not have a good reason why, but I realized that I had never bothered to ask who I had replaced, so I asked, "What was his name?"

"Cethegus," Gallus spat the word like a curse. "Numerius

Salvius Cethegus."

Why, I wondered, is that name familiar? Since I did not place it immediately, I set this aside for the moment; my concern about this Cethegus was not why his name registered, and I asked, "Where is Cethegus now? Does he still come around?"

"Oh yes," Gallus nodded unhappily. "He's now in the First Praetorian Cohort, and he's a Pilus Posterior like you. And," he spat, "he drops by every few months to make sure that I'm still taking care of 'his boys'."

"They're my boys now," I told him quietly. "And they're going to start paying what they owe...tomorrow." I grinned. "Tonight is on me."

"They drink a lot, Centurion." Gallus beamed up at me, his good humor restored.

"Which is why I'm only doing this once. Now," I offered my arm again, "I better get back up there."

Ascending the stairs, I was hailed like a returning hero, just in time to see that the slaves had brought the last of the first round of cups to the men. Picking up mine, I thought about standing up on the chair, but not only did I not really need to, I had had one collapse under me before.

When I lifted the cup, it quieted down enough for me to be heard, and I waited for the men to lift their own before I said, "Men of the Second Century of the Second Praetorian Cohort, today I tested each of you. And," I paused, actually struggling with the idea of telling a small lie, "while I bested each of you, many of you tested me, and all of you gave me your best effort." Pausing again, I turned to where Flaccus was sitting, having spotted him earlier. "Even if some of you looked like you'd never held a *gladius* and shield in your life. Flaccus, were you trying to beat me by giving me a cold waving those around like you did?"

As I hoped, the room erupted with roars of laughter, while Flaccus turned a red that might have been a close match to a veteran Legionary's tunic, while more than one man jumped up and mimicked Flaccus' performance, flailing wildly about with both arms. Finally, I raised a hand, feeling confident that I had humiliated Flaccus enough, and once they got quiet again, I said, "But, while you may not be where I want you to be right now when it comes to your *gladius* work....you will be, because I know now that you will give me your best. To the Second!"

"*The Second!*"

There was a momentary silence as every man tried to outdo each other in draining their cup before slamming it down on the table, and inevitably, several men were a bit too enthusiastic, shattering their cup in the process; which, of course, would be added to my bill. My part done, I dropped back down into my chair, but Sabinus was looking down at his cup, so I looked at Alex, who gave me a shrug to indicate he had no idea why my Optio seemed so morose.

I got my answer when, as the men were being served their next round, he looked up at me and said, "Centurion Pullus, I need to tell you something." I did not reply, though I nodded, and he said, "I'm one of the men who hasn't been paying Gallus."

It took a moment for the words to impact me, but once they did, I stared at him coldly, although I did allow, "I think you'd better explain yourself, and why you didn't tell me, Sabinus."

"When I joined the Century three years ago, I was like you," he began. "I didn't know anything about the Praetorians, so I followed Pilus Posterior Cethegus' lead..."

"Cethegus?"

We both looked at Alex in surprise since he was the one who said this, but he was staring at Sabinus as he asked, "Do you know his full name?"

"Numerius Salvius Cethegus," Sabinus supplied and it was hearing the name the second time that lodged something loose in my head, but Alex was ahead of me. "Is he a bit taller than me, with a large wart on the side of his face?"

Not surprisingly, at first, this startled Sabinus, then his face cleared. "Ah, you must have heard his name and seen him when we paraded with the First Cohort."

"I didn't see him then," Alex replied, then glanced over at me, raising an eyebrow as I tried to think.

"Wait," it came to me, "he was one of the Praetorian Centurions that was part of the *Legio Germanicus*?"

"Yes," Alex nodded. "It was when I began serving your father, during the Batonian Revolt, and Cethegus came from Rome." He stopped abruptly, still watching me as I began recalling the details from my father's scrolls where he described that period...and most importantly, why Cethegus was there.

"As you can see," I pointed to Alex, "he knows Cethegus. And," I decided not to go into detail, "now that I'm reminded of his name, I recall my father talking about him." While knowing his identity now was interesting, and might have been relevant, it was not at this moment, so I pressed, "So he told you this was how it was done?" Sabinus nodded, and when he said nothing else, I hid my irritation. "And you simply went along with it."

"He said that it was the least Gallus could do because of all the business he brought them, that some of us didn't have to pay."

"I told Flaccus I didn't want names," I replied, "but you're my Optio, and that doesn't apply to you. Now," I hardened my voice, "I want you to provide me a list. Not," I held up my hand because he looked as if he was going to stand up and go get a tablet, "now. Tomorrow is fine. But, Sabinus," I warned him, "you understand..."

"...That this stops immediately." He nodded and sighed, then looked me in the eye as he said, "I should have told you before this, Pilus Posterior."

"Yes, you should have," I agreed, "but this is the last we speak of it. And," I felt I owed him this much, "I understand why you did what you did. You were new, and your Centurion was telling you this is how things work. I can't change the past, but I can stop it moving forward. Now," I slapped the table, "enough of this talk. Let's drink!"

With Alex's help, I returned to the apartment, and while it was not the drunkest I had ever been, it was the drunkest Bronwen had ever seen me, yet for reasons that were not clear to me, she was not in a receptive frame of mind to my advances, which were prompted in me by thinking of what Algaia had said earlier. Yes, I was in a drunken state, but after I sobered up, and even to this day, I am not quite clear on why she viewed my gesture with such disdain. She had complained that I did not think her beautiful, and here I was crawling into our bed, professing my love.

"You stink."

Thinking that she was in a playful mood, I lifted an arm, took a deep sniff, then grinned, "It's not me! I went to the baths today!"

"If you did, you must have fallen into a wine vat." She was now sitting up, which I took to be a sign of progress, and I did laugh at what I thought was her jest. "I could smell you before you entered our room."

I tried tickling her, this having been successful in the past, but what I got for my attempts were two tiny feet placed against my middle, then with a force that reminded me that she was quite strong, she kicked me out of the bed, and I was drunk enough that when I landed on the floor, I thought it was not such a bad spot. My last memory of that night was her peering over the edge of the bed.

"I do not sleep with drunken men," she pronounced, then her face vanished, leaving me to try and untangle what she had just said.

"I thought I was the only one!" I said indignantly as I tried to sit up, but she was in no mood.

"You know what I mean, Gnaeus," she said firmly. "Now, you can join me in bed if you behave yourself, or you can sleep on the floor for all I care."

I believe it was as I was pondering my choices that I fell asleep, or passed out, depending on whose version one chooses to believe.

Chapter 7

I knew I would wake up sore, but for some reason, I never connected the fact that waking up sore and with a ferocious headache and sour stomach at the same time would make everything worse. Thankfully, today, Germanicus was sponsoring another round of games, including some *venatores* who would be in the arena with only a single spear and shield against several lions, although it was always difficult to determine if there were truly going to be twenty lions at one time as the posters plastered everywhere claimed. The gods smiled on us by having the Second and Third off duty, and as I had been informed on my arrival, there was a section of whatever venue reserved for Praetorians. Bronwen was still cool towards me, although it was not as frosty as it had been the night before, and I thought that I would appease her by taking her to the games. At first, she seemed interested, but when I explained what the main event was, her reaction was close to contemptuous.

"So you have these poor beasts caged up, then you put them in this place where there is no escape and they are slaughtered for your amusement?" Shaking her head, she said, "And you call us barbarians."

"The *venatores* only have a spear and shield," I pointed out, "so the lions aren't exactly helpless."

"And if the lions are victorious, are they freed?" she countered, completely unimpressed, but her naivety, which was how I viewed it, made me laugh.

"Gods, no! It takes a lot of money and effort to capture that many lions. No *auditor* would ever let them go, especially if they killed a *venator*. If people know that a lion has killed a man trying to kill him, they'll pay even more to come and watch."

Her reply was to say nothing immediately, just giving me a long, level look before she asked quietly, "And you think this a good thing? That it is normal?" She pointed down to Titus, who was in her lap trying to grab at a necklace I had given his mother. "Is this how you want our son raised? To be cruel? To enjoy watching suffering?"

Even as I said it, I knew how lame I sounded when I protested, "But that's the Roman way! That's why we control most of the known world."

"That does not make it right," she countered quietly. "And I do not want my son raised to be this way." Before I could object, Bronwen continued, "Brave? Yes, certainly. I want him to be as brave as his father." I cannot say whether she did this in a deliberate attempt to soothe my feelings, but it helped. "But I also want him to be kind to those who are weaker than he is. And," she pointed down to him, "you can already see that he is your son and will probably be close to your size, Gnaeus. I do not want my son to be someone who abuses the gifts your gods, and mine," she emphasized, "have given him by tormenting someone simply because he can." Shaking her head, she said, "No, I will not go to these games, Gnaeus." As somber as she had been, she smiled suddenly and said, "Now, if you want to take me to the chariot races, that is different. I *love* the races!"

Setting aside my consternation for the moment, I rolled my eyes as I asked, "Do I even know what team you support?"

As I expected, she cried out, "The Greens, of course!"

Deciding that this was a good point to end this conversation, I kissed her and said, "Well, this is one Roman who wants to see a lion eat a man."

I almost managed to dodge her swing, reminding me once again that, despite her size, she was very strong; I told myself that the only reason it hurt was because my arm was already sore. When I went downstairs, Alex was waiting, without Algaia, since only a Praetorian can bring a guest and not clerks or scribes. Still bemused, and unsettled, by my conversation with Bronwen, I broached the subject with him, but he had his mind on other things.

"I think this Cethegus situation is deeper than we think," he said.

"How so?"

Glancing up at me, he seemed surprised, which he explained. "Don't you remember why Cethegus was sent to serve with Germanicus? And," he added, "who your father thought he was sent by?"

I blame the fog in my mind for not making the connection beforehand, but once he said it, I did recall from my father's account that it had been the current Princeps, back when he was the unofficial heir to the title of Imperator, who supposedly sent Cethegus to spy on Germanicus.

"That's right. Tiberius," I answered, but I was surprised when Alex shook his head.

"That was never proven, and your father accepted that this was the case because Germanicus believed it to be the case. But I've been thinking about it since last night."

"You were able to think?" I joked.

"I didn't drink as much as you," he countered immediately. "I'm surprised you're sober now."

This made me laugh, which in turn sent a stab of pain through my head, and I shoved him then groaned, "Don't make me laugh, you bastard."

Turning serious again, which is one of Alex's greatest talents, he explained his reasoning.

"What I realized last night was that Tiberius didn't need to have Cethegus watching Germanicus because he already had someone there."

As fuzzy as my head was, I still understood immediately.

"My father," I said, and he nodded.

"At Dolabella's direction," Alex reminded me. "Back before..."

He did not need to finish; the Batonian Revolt had occurred several years before the revolt of the Legions, back when my father and Dolabella had what could charitably called an adversarial relationship.

Tacitly acknowledging this, I asked, "So who else?"

"I thought about Drusus," Alex said, but then added quickly, "but he and Germanicus have always been close."

"That may have been true back then," I granted. "I'm not so sure now."

"Since it's back then we're talking about, I think that rules Drusus out," Alex said somewhat tartly, and I was reminded that, just as I take immense pride in certain aspects pertaining to myself, the son of Diocles is no different. I nodded, which he took as a signal to explain his reasoning. "So if it wasn't Tiberius, and it wasn't Drusus, that leaves Augustus."

I only deduced later that he had offered this up to allow me to work it out, and I will say it only took a heartbeat before I shook my head.

"But Augustus wouldn't have any reason to spy on Germanicus, because they had a very close relationship, and even back then, most men thought that Augustus would be naming Germanicus at least second in line as his successor."

It was Alex's turn to nod, then he asked the important question, "So who does that leave?" When I did not answer immediately, he added, "What's the one connection that Cethegus has with someone we know takes a very active interest in everything Germanicus does?"

"Sejanus," I groaned, but it surprised me when Alex shook his head.

"Not necessarily," Alex said. "Remember when this was; Sejanus was only a Tribune who was reporting to the current Prefect of the Praetorians."

"His father." I understood now, and this earned me a nod.

"And we also know that father and son were almost identical when it comes to their ambition, and their methods..."

"...He learned at the feet of his father," I finished for Alex, which was something I had never heard about Sejanus and his father before arriving in Rome but had heard many times since, and always from men who would know. We were silent for a moment as I thought this through, then concluded, "So we need to assume that Cethegus is Sejanus' man."

Alex nodded, but he kept looking at me as if he expected more, while all I could offer was a shrug.

"I think it's safe to assume that if Cethegus is Sejanus' man, Cethegus has men of his own," he advised.

This brought me to a stop, and I slapped my forehead, which did not help.

"Of course," I groaned. "So that means I've got a dozen men in my Century who are reporting to Cethegus."

"I don't think it's a dozen," Alex said. "It might only be one or two."

If he had said one, I already had my suspect, but the way he said it made me ask cautiously, "If it's two, who are you thinking? Sabinus?"

"No," Alex said firmly. "I thought about him, but after last night, I think that he was being honest. He was told by his Centurion that that was how things ran, and he trusted him. Now," he held his hands out, palms up, "should he have asked more questions?"

"Probably," I sighed. "But I think you're right. I just think he didn't want to be the turd in the pot of honey by poking his nose into something, especially when he benefited from it."

We had reached the arena, which was a temporary structure out on the Campus, and the opening bout had just started, two pairs of slaves chained together, and while the section set aside for the Praetorians was not further subdivided, just as with the Legions, men from the same Century tended to sit together, meaning it was easy to spot my men. Since we had the day off, it was clear that most of the men, who I had left behind at Isis' Grotto after arranging with Gallus to send someone to my quarters with the balance of the amount the men had spent with the whores, had essentially not stopped their celebrating and were still drunk. As I sat down next to Sabinus, who had saved us seats, I pointed down at the action, which to my eye looked as if there were basically four men like Flaccus flailing at each other.

"What's this?"

"You know how it is." He shrugged, trying to make himself heard above the noise. "They found some slaves who were willing to risk their lives for freedom. But," he became enthusiastic, "the next bout is going to be between a *Retiarii* and a *Murmillo*. That doesn't happen often."

"Because the *Retiarii* usually wins," I commented.

While it had not been since I was known as Gnaeus Volusenus and lived in Mediolanum, I had once been an avid follower of the local gladiators, and the *Murmillo* was still relatively new back then, having been introduced by Divus Augustus because the former heavily armed type, the Gallus, had become offensive to all those Gauls who were no longer our enemy, but Roman citizens.

"Not against this one," Sabinus scoffed. "I've seen him, and he's at least your size, maybe bigger!"

I eyed my Optio, and that was when I saw how flushed his face was, while he was grinning at me like an idiot, telling me that he had been celebrating heavily as well.

"Being big isn't everything," I pointed out. "Let's see how he moves."

The bout with the slaves ended quickly, but while there was one man of the four left standing, before the *auditor* gave him the scroll of manumission that was the prize for this bout, he collapsed, and judging by the limp quality of his body as they dragged him out with the others, he was dead, which the crowd, particularly the Praetorians, thought was a fine joke by the gods. Alex and I exchanged a glance, and I saw that he was of a similar mind, neither of us finding it that funny. It was something I began noticing not long after our arrival in Rome, that there was a level of callousness, especially towards non-Romans, freedmen, and slaves that was not nearly as noticeable on the Rhenus. If I had to describe it in a word, I would say that Rome is a crueler place than where I had grown up, and where I have spent the bulk of my adult life in Ubiorum. While I cannot say this definitively, I believe that it has to do with the fact that, as relatively settled as Ubiorum is now compared to when my father reported to the 1st, it is still a frontier town, as is Mogontiacum, and we Romans are a minority who are surrounded by native tribes. Even as Romanized as some of these tribes may be, like the Batavians, there is still a difference between us, and all of us on the west side of the Rhenus are united in their hatred and distrust of the tribes on the opposite side of the river. Not that any of that mattered in the moment, and I settled down to watch the bouts as we waited for the *venatores*, but when the vendor selling cups of wine passed by, I demurred, getting a cup of water instead, earning me some commentary from the men around me, which I bore as gracefully as I could. Gradually, I got into the spirit, as did Alex, although in the back of my mind, my argument with Bronwen was lingering there, and I realized that I was unsettled by her words because I had never thought about it in the way she expressed them. I barely had any warning when Alex elbowed me, hard, but when I turned to glare at him, he was gesturing with his head lower down in the seats, just behind the box reserved for Senators and their guests.

Leaning closer so he did not have to raise his voice, he warned me, "I just saw Cethegus. He was talking to Pilus Prior Creticus, and I saw Creticus point up here." I began turning my head, and he hissed, "*Don't look*. But I think he's heading this way."

Alex was right, because while I kept my gaze seemingly on the sand that had been hauled from somewhere for this arena, I could see Cethegus approaching. However, while it was not that he stopped next to our row that surprised me, who he addressed first did, although he did actually give Sabinus, who was sitting on the opposite side of Alex, a perfunctory nod before he spoke.

"By the gods, I know you, don't I?" Naturally, since he was speaking, I turned my head, but he was not addressing me, he was looking down at Alex, and he was smiling as he went on, "You served Titus Pullus during the Batonian Revolt, didn't you?"

"Y-yes," Alex stood up and accepted Cethegus' hand, while I tried not to stare at the mole on the side of his face as I thought, Alex, you didn't tell me it was *that* big. "*Salve,* Centurion Cethegus."

"I apologize, I don't remember your name." Cethegus did look embarrassed, but I did not believe him, especially when, after Alex supplied his name, he only gave a perfunctory nod because he was already looking at me.

"I'd ask who this is, but not only is it obvious, his reputation precedes him," Cethegus' smile got even broader, and I realized that I would have to stand up. "Aulus Cethegus," he introduced himself, then pointed at Alex, "and I'm assuming that you heard how I know Alexandros here."

"I did," I answered cordially, then feeling mischievous, I cocked my head and said, "but I must apologize, because I don't remember hearing my father ever mention your name in connection with the Legio Germanicus."

Just as I hoped, this angered him, although he managed to shrug and say, "There's no reason why he should have, really. We weren't together that long."

Then he seemed content to just stand there, and I had the feeling he was expecting something more from me, but all I said was, "It was a pleasure meeting you." Then, as if I did not know, I asked, "So you're obviously a Praetorian. Which Cohort?"

"Second of the First," he replied, but I got the sense that he did not really believe that I did not know that. Then, from a few rows up, men from the Third Century of the Second began complaining about their view being blocked, but when I began to sit down, he asked, "Pullus, may I speak with you a moment?"

"Can it wait?" I asked, and I was only partially lying when I said, "I've been looking forward to this match." I offered him a grin. "My Optio says this *Murmillo* is my size, and I'd like to see how he acquits himself."

Cethegus clearly did not like this, but neither could he argue the point without showing the dice in his cup, so he agreed, grudgingly, then turned and walked back down to his spot.

"Why don't you want to talk to him?" Alex asked. "The sooner you find out what he wants, the better."

"Because I want to watch the *Murmillo*," I answered, which was true enough, but not the real reason; I wanted Cethegus to stew in his own juice, and I explained this to Alex.

"That's not like you," he remarked. "Usually, you like to get something potentially unpleasant out of the way."

"Maybe I'm maturing." I shrugged.

I was not surprised that this made Alex laugh.

"I should live that long," he replied.

The *Murmillo* was large, that was true, and he did move well for his size, but this *Retiarii* was very skilled, making for an exciting bout. Eventually, the *Retiarii* simply wore down his opponent, but the crowd made it clear that they wanted the *Murmillo* to live, albeit with a gash just below his shoulder pad and three neat wounds in his upper thigh from the trident that had crippled him and enabled the *Retiarii* to move in for the kill, and the *Murmillo* yielded.

"That's happening less frequently," Sabinus commented as the two combatants left the arena, the victor having taken off his helmet to show his face to the crowd, and I noticed that he was very young, with a mop of curly black hair, looking as if he came from one of the African provinces, while the *Murmillo* kept his helmet on as he limped out of the arena, probably to avoid the shame of being recognized.

I also saw how the smattering of women among the Head Counters, who were confined to the uppermost tier, showed their appreciation for the victor in much the same way they had with us in the triumph.

Distracted by the sight, I was not much interested, but I asked him, "What's happening less frequently?"

"That the loser is allowed to live," Sabinus replied. "When I first reported to the Praetorians, almost half of these bouts weren't to the death, but now it's about one in three."

I cannot say why, but I had mixed feelings about this. I was not altogether surprised that the people were becoming more bloodthirsty; I just could not determine why this bothered me, but it did. Not that I had any time to think about it, because the instant the bout was over, Cethegus rose from his seat and climbed up towards us.

"I don't think you're going to put this off any longer," Alex murmured.

I knew he was right, so I stood up, thinking that Cethegus would want to go somewhere private, and from what I could see, it would have been beneath the wooden scaffolding that served as the frame for the seating area, which meant we would descend to the nearest exit. Instead, he climbed the steps past me, but I saw why, because the upper couple of tiers were not full, and he dropped onto a bench that only had two other people but at the opposite end.

My ass had barely touched wood when he said, in quite a different tone, "I understand that you had a discussion with Gallus last night."

"I did," I agreed, then said no more, determined to force him into divulging the reason for this conversation.

This obviously displeased Cethegus, but he maintained an even tone as he continued, "And I've been told that you've made some...changes that concern Isis' Grotto and some of the men from my old Century."

"Who told you this?" I looked directly at him. "Flaccus?"

I am certain I guessed correctly by the way he flushed, but he shook his head.

"That doesn't matter."

"It does to me," I shot back. "Flaccus is already in my bad books, and if I can't trust him to not go running off and tattling to his former Centurion, then I need to know that."

"Why?" Cethegus crossed his arms, and I give him credit that he looked me in the eye. "What are you intending for Flaccus?"

"Frankly, Centurion, it's none of your business how I run my Century." I barely managed to disguise my anger, and I did think it wise to add, "I can't imagine you'd take it very well if I came and started meddling with your Century. How a Centurion runs his Century is between him and his Pilus Prior, and the men of that Century."

"This isn't the Legions," Cethegus retorted, which was one of the worst things he could have done.

"So I've been told, over and over," I snapped. More to catch him off balance than change the subject, I asked suddenly, "Haven't you gotten the new orders about training yet? Don't you know who they came from?"

He did look surprised, asking, "How did you know about that?" I was opening my mouth to answer, but he beat me to it. "You're the one behind it," and he said this as if it just occurred to him.

"And what makes you say that?" I countered.

"Because everyone knows that you were seen talking with the Imperator." Cethegus shrugged, but I was not content with that.

"And who told you?" I challenged, which earned me another direct look, although this time, I could not decipher his expression, barely knowing the man.

"Who do you think?"

"I didn't realize that you and the Prefect were so close," I tried to make it sound as if this was just an idle comment.

Matching my tone, he shrugged. "I've served in the Praetorians for more than ten years, and I've gotten to know the man." Then, dropping the pretense, he returned to the original topic. "Which is why we need to discuss this Gallus matter."

"Why would Prefect Sejanus care about one Centurion requiring a dozen of his men to start paying the bills they run up when they're out in the city?"

"You don't need to know why," Cethegus said coldly. "Just that it displeases him."

I was becoming confused, and this was the moment it first occurred to me that there might *not* be a deeper meaning behind this, that Sejanus might very well be that petty. I also realized that there actually was a simple solution to this by telling Cethegus I would rescind my order, because no matter the reason, I had no business antagonizing the man who was the commander of the Praetorian Guard, no matter how Germanicus might act as a shield against reprisal.

"I'm not doing this to displease the Prefect," I began, "and I certainly don't want to." I believe it was the way Cethegus started looking smug that made that beast in my belly to stir, and his expression quickly changed when I finished. "But unless you or the Prefect can point me to a specific regulation that states that men of the Praetorian Guard aren't required to pay for goods and services they incur in the city, or anywhere, for that matter," I added, "then the men of the Second Century are going to honor their debts."

Whatever satisfaction I got from wiping the smirk from Cethegus' face was quickly washed away because, while he kept his voice at the same pitch, the words were chilling.

"That would be a fatal error, Pullus," he said coldly. As he stood up, he looked down at me with what might have been pity. "I'm guessing that you think that Germanicus will protect you, but this isn't the Rhenus; this is Rome."

This brought me to my feet as well, and it was a real struggle to contain the beast, but I suppose it could be said I gave him a peek at it, because before I opened my mouth, four men on a row above us began shouting at us to sit down; all it took to silence them was a look from both of us and Cethegus lifted his *vitus*, which settled them down.

"Since you and the Prefect are close," I took advantage of the momentary distraction to move so that there was barely a hand's width between us, and since he was already in the aisle, he could not back up any more without running into the bench behind him, "you might want to ask him if he ever found Marcus Livinius Appius and those other men he sent after me."

It did feel good, I confess, but Cethegus was openly skeptical, which he expressed by scoffing, "The Prefect knows who was behind that already, and it wasn't you, Pullus."

"If you say so." I shrugged, then deciding on a slightly different approach, I asked, "You said you served with my father, and Alex says it's true, but did you ever see him fight?"

"Not directly," he admitted uncomfortably, "but I heard the stories from men who were there and who I trust."

"And?"

"And," he broke eye contact, vaguely looking down at the arena, where the lions were being hauled out in their cages, "they said they had never seen anything like it. But," he did turn back to look at me, "what does that have to do with this?"

"Do you know what my father told me the day before he died?" I asked, but did not wait for him to reply, lying, "He told me that I was better than he was. That I was faster, and stronger, and the only thing missing was experience. And," I leaned forward to look down on him, "I've had a lot more experience since then."

I could see he wanted to say something clever, or more likely threatening, but I suppose I intimidated him enough, because he simply turned and descended the stairs, quickly. I followed behind at a more leisurely pace, so that by the time I sat down next to Alex, I was no longer in the mood to watch lions kill and eat men, or men kill lions, or even lions eating each other.

"I think," I responded to Alex's inquiring glance, "I may have made a huge mistake."

I decided to leave before the main bout was over, despite the fact that it appeared as if the lions might win, and of course Alex came along. On our way back to the apartment, I reluctantly divulged what I had become certain was a grievous error, and I suppose I was holding out a faint hope that Alex would dismiss my concerns.

Instead, he agreed, "You were right. That's a huge fucking mistake." I groaned, but he was silent for a moment as he thought, then said, "First thing we need to do is to get a message to Sempronius."

"Why? So that I can tell him I ruined his perfect plan to throw suspicion away from me?"

"Basically, yes," Alex replied firmly. "He deserves to know. And," he added something I did not like hearing, "maybe he can get you some protection."

"From who?" I scoffed. "There's nobody in the Praetorians, and there's no fucking gladiator who could take me!"

Only after he gave it to me did I realize that Alex had not given me that almost pitying look that sent the message that I was being thick, when the answer was obvious and right in front of me, in some time.

However, he started out by saying, "I agree, Gnaeus, I don't think there's a single man who can face you and survive, but are you really willing to gamble your life on that? And," he pointed out, "endangering Bronwen and the baby?" I noticed that he did not mention himself, Algaia, and Iras, but they are certainly on my list of people I would do anything to protect. "Besides, remember how many men they sent after you in the Boarium? When Sejanus learns that it was you and not Fidenus, do you really think he'd just send one man?"

"No." The word came grudgingly, but it came out nonetheless. Sighing, I said, "You're right. We need to contact Sempronius."

"You might want to think about contacting Lysander as well," Alex suggested, but on this, I refused to budge.

"No, I'm not getting Germanicus involved in a mess that I made. I don't care what might happen."

By the time we reached the apartment, we had settled on a plan and made the decision that it was best to keep our women in the dark about what was going on. And, for the first and so far, the only time, I was not the one who broke, a fact that is making Alex turn a satisfying shade of red as he scribbles.

The first indication of how angry Algaia was came in the manner in which she flung the door opening without knocking, but thankfully, I was sitting at the table and not near Scrofa's blade hanging by the door, because my instinctive reaction would have been to grab it. And, if I had any doubt that she was angry, it was quickly erased when she marched directly to me, her eyes narrowed to slits and her lips tightly pressed together.

"Are you *mad*?" She did not scream, exactly, but it was loud enough that it brought Bronwen into the main room. Instead of continuing to rant at me, Algaia looked at Bronwen and demanded, "Did Gnaeus tell you? Did he tell you what he's done?"

Bronwen was understandably bewildered since I had managed to keep my mouth shut, but she became instantly alarmed, and aroused, coming to stand over me.

"What have you done, Gnaeus?" she demanded, and while she did not look angry like Algaia, I recognized the signs that she was not far off.

Truly, a part of me wanted to protest at the manner in which she had instantly accepted Algaia's word that I had done something stupid, dangerous, or both, but I managed to refrain, understanding that with my next breath I would be confirming that Algaia was correct. I also briefly entertained trying to downplay my error.

Closing my eyes, I told her, "I told a Centurion of the First Cohort who's close to Sejanus that I was the one who killed Appius and his men."

It was not her words that cut me most deeply, it was the way the blood drained from her face as her eyes went wide, and she seemed to more collapse than sit down on the bench next to me, but her whispered "Why?" was almost as bad, if only because I only had one explanation.

"I was...angry," I said, which elicited a small moan from her, just before she buried her face in her hands, and her shoulders began shaking.

This earned Algaia an irate glare from me, but she was completely uncowed and unrepentant, matching if not surpassing me in her passion.

"She deserved to know," she said, then pointed at me, "and you and your pride have put not just yourself in danger, but Bronwen and the baby!"

"You think I don't know that?" I snapped, but now my ire was aimed at myself.

We both fell silent, which meant we could hear Bronwen's sobs; when I tried to comfort her by putting an arm around my shoulder, while she did not pull away, she did not lean into me as she normally would have. Finally, she lifted her head, and while her eyes were red, they were also narrowed in what I knew was her practical side coming out.

"You need to alert Sempronius," she said, and I was happy to assure her that Alex was doing that at this very moment, making a chalk mark at the fountain across from the Temple of Isis, which Sempronius said he would check twice a day, although he never specified the time, which meant he might have already checked for the second time that day given that the sun was just going down. This was something I decided not to mention and hope for the best, and we lapsed into a silence again, which was when we heard someone climbing the stairs.

"Hand me Scrofa's blade," I commanded Algaia, who was closest, but while she moved immediately, she said, "It's probably Alex coming back."

She was right; she was just handing me the blade when he entered, although unlike Algaia, he did rap twice on the door before opening it and walking into a scene where the two women were glaring at me, while I was doing the same directly at him.

"She told you," he sighed.

"Oh, do you think so?" I shot back, indicating the pair. "What gave that away?"

"I'm sorry, Gnaeus," he apologized, in a manner of speaking, "but the more I thought about it, the more I thought it was a bad idea."

"But you're the one who suggested it!" I exclaimed, perfectly happy to drop him in the *cac* with me and get at least one pair of eyes off of me and onto him.

"Is that true?" Algaia challenged him, crossing her arms in a manner I have seen her do with Iras more than once.

Alex grimaced, and I could see he did not want to, but he is too honest a fellow, so he sighed, "Yes, I initially thought it would be better."

"This does not matter right now." Bronwen was standing up as she said this, and she began pacing, although she kept her eyes on me as she demanded, "What do you think Sempronius is likely to do?"

"I think," deciding using that word was better than using "hope," "he's going to arrange for some sort of protection for you while I'm on duty."

"What about you?"

While I was contrite, I was also unwilling to bend to that degree, but my hope that just giving her a long look would suffice was short-lived and signaled by her crossing her arms in a posture identical to Algaia's.

"I'm more than capable of taking care of myself. And," I indicated Alex, "Alex is very skilled as well. I'll be fine."

"Oh, you're fine putting my husband in danger because of your pride." Algaia's words matched the scornful expression she was giving me.

Thankfully, Alex had his own limits, because he interjected, "First, I'm standing right here, and second, Gnaeus is right. I'm no raw boy who's never seen battle, and while I don't train like Gnaeus does, I can handle myself." He paused, then added quietly to his wife, "Which is something you know better than anyone."

Given that Alex had killed for her when Gaius kidnapped her, this was not only an accurate statement, I saw that Algaia understood that by the way her shoulders slumped.

"I know," she said softly. "But I worry."

This served as a signal for both of the couples in the room, and this time when I embraced Bronwen, she pressed herself against me, while I felt relieved and horrible at the same moment.

Once more, Fortuna smiled down on me, because less than a third of a watch later, Sempronius knocked on the door. And, to my shock, and relief, once we had sent Bronwen, Algaia, and the baby down to Alex's apartment, when I explained what I had done, he only gave a barely noticeable grimace.

"It wasn't very likely that Sejanus was going to remain in the dark about Appius," he commented. Any good feeling that I had from his reaction evaporated in the time it took him to say, "I'm not sure there's much I can do, Centurion."

"Why?" This came from Alex, just beating me to it.

"Because the kind of men who are available to me are the same kind of men that the Prefect would use." He hesitated, then added carefully, "Or he might use one of the men of the First Cohort. Or more."

I do not know why I was surprised, but this wrenched a gasp from me. "He'd do that? That would never happen in the Legions!"

I could have said the words with him, because as soon as it was out of my mouth, I knew what to expect as he replied, "The Praetorians aren't the Legions, Centurion. The men of the First Cohort in particular are completely loyal to Sejanus because they all owe him in one way or another."

I know that it was not his intention, but with those words, Sempronius also explained why Cethegus had approached me about a seemingly minor matter in one Century of the Second Cohort; Sejanus was expanding his power and influence through the other Praetorian Cohorts over and above just the Centurions, most of whom he had either personally selected or arranged to be appointed by Tiberius. That was why he had been angered by my decision, because not only was it about his pride, it was about the idea that his control over the Praetorians was not absolute if one of the Centurions could defy him so openly. Suddenly, the threat became very real, because I could see a larger motive than just personal pique on the part of the Prefect. This was why I did not bother arguing the point, and instead simply asked what he suggested we do.

"Just be ready," he said grimly. I think he was sincere when he added, "I wish there was more that I could do, Centurion, I truly do."

"What about letting Tiberius know?" Alex asked.

We got the answer in the way Sempronius suddenly began studying the table, although he did say, "I don't think that would be wise."

"Why not?" I asked, not quite angry but getting close. "I know Sejanus is powerful, but surely the Princeps isn't scared of him."

That got me a glare from Sempronius, but he paused, I suppose to gather himself before he answered, "No, Pullus, the Princeps isn't scared of Sejanus." He hesitated for a moment, then spoke carefully. "The problem with telling Tiberius is a matter of access. Before he will speak with anyone who requests an audience, he has to know what the subject is about beforehand."

He stopped, but I nodded that I understood as I said, "Which means that you'd have to tell someone, and that person might work for Sejanus."

Sempronius surprised me by shaking his head, though not because he disagreed.

"It's not a question of 'might,' Centurion. I've already learned the hard way that it's a fact that Sejanus has men in Tiberius' employ who report directly to him. And," he added with what sounded like bitterness, "there are women as well."

"Do you know who they are?" Alex asked.

This earned us a hiss of frustration from Sempronius, then he said, "I know some of them, but not all of them, and until I'm certain that I've sniffed them all out, I'm not taking that risk."

That he was still refusing made me angry, and I snapped, "It's the lives of my woman and my child we're talking about, Sempronius. I'm sorry that you think taking a risk on their behalf isn't worth it."

His expression did not change much, but it was easy to see that we were now of a like mind, although his tone was calm as he said quietly, "That's who I was thinking of, Centurion. There are only three individuals who I'm not certain about, and if I choose the wrong one to tell, and they run to Sejanus, it's not going to be me that pays the price. That," he shrugged, "is one advantage that my service to the Princeps brings. Sejanus wouldn't dare touch me. So," he gave me a direct look, "are you willing to take a one in three chance on your family's life, Centurion?" It was an easy question to answer, although it was a bit harder to apologize, but Sempronius accepted it graciously. "It's completely understandable, Centurion. No apology necessary." Returning to the original subject, he started with another hissing sound. "The truth is, the real problem is that, right now, Tiberius trusts Sejanus more than anyone else, even his natural and adopted sons, so I couldn't even guarantee that the Princeps would believe what I told him." That left us in a morose silence, and I suppose it made sense that Sempronius wanted to offer some sort of consolation, which he offered as he got up to leave. "You should get a good night's sleep tonight, Centurion. Not even Sejanus is likely to move this fast. But tomorrow?" He shrugged as I opened the door. "Tomorrow I would start staying alert and watching your back."

After he left, I went with Alex downstairs, where we were met by Algaia, who told me, "She and the baby are asleep already, Titus."

I confess that my decision to let them sleep downstairs that night was more out of cowardice and an unwillingness to endure what I felt certain would be an unpleasant time as Bronwen made sure I knew her true feelings about my stupidity...I thank the gods that I did, no matter what the reason.

Before I joined the Legions, I was quite a heavy sleeper, something that my mother Giulia nagged at me about on an almost daily basis, but over time, I managed to learn how to choose how deeply I sleep. And, while I accepted Sempronius' judgment that nothing was likely to happen, I suppose somewhere in the back of my mind, I warned myself that I needed to sleep as if I was on campaign. However, it was the third step from the top of our stairs that probably saved my life. It had become something of a running jest between Bronwen and me, because almost from the first day we moved in, she had been after me to contact the owner of the building to fix it.

"Every time I step on it, it creaks so loudly that I am sure that it's about to collapse," she would complain, to which my counter was simply pointing out that if it did not collapse under my weight, it was highly unlikely to collapse under hers.

It is not only that my slumber is light enough that a sound like a creaking stair will wake me up, but that when I do wake up, I am instantly alert, and this night was no different; I doubt that by the time whoever was leading what turned out to be three men up the stairs had even reached the top step before I was up and with my *gladius* in my hand. Subsequently, it meant that by the time the first man through the door kicked it open, I was already out of the bedroom and halfway across the outer room, which he clearly did not expect judging from his cry of alarm, a cry that sounded muffled to my ears, though I would not learn why immediately. Like me, he had a *gladius* in his hand, but it was not up in a ready position since he had just kicked in the door; what killed him, though, was that the man behind him apparently shoved him forward when the first man balked at my dark shape standing less than a half-dozen paces away, which the second man could not see. Between this and the fact that I was still moving forward, the effect was that he essentially ran himself onto my blade, the point punching through just below his sternum while, because of the barely audible sound of metal striking metal and the extra tension I felt, I learned this man was wearing a *hamata* under his tunic. There was a shout, one of alarm and not pain, and not from the man I had just killed but from the man behind him; piecing it together later, it was because he either saw or sensed the point of my *gladius* burst out of his accomplice's back. To his credit, he did not hesitate, nor did he behave mercifully to his mortally wounded comrade, because I felt myself staggering backward as the second man brutally shoved the one between us from behind, directly at me. For an eyeblink, I thought I would be able to stop moving backward as my bare feet managed to get a purchase on the floor, but I believe the third man added his weight to the second's, whereupon I felt myself starting to topple backward.

"The first man who loses his feet in a fight is usually the first man to die."

It was something that had been pounded into my head by the man who, at the time, I thought of only as the Pilus Prior of my Cohort, until they became words that I found myself repeating whenever a new *Tirone* arrived to plump my Century out. However, I understood that if I let go of my *gladius* and made an attempt to twist out from under the man I had just killed, I would stay on my feet but be unarmed, yet thanks to Fortuna and the fact that the Scrofa *gladius* was hanging on a hook next to the door, I had another option. Even so, I almost did not succeed, despite not hesitating in relinquishing my grip on the *gladius* as I twisted my body out from under the first man, because I was unable to completely arrest my backward momentum. Consequently, while it was at an angle to my original movement straight back from the door, I still was moving away from it. My progress was stopped by the wall to the right of the door, and the third man came rushing at me, while the second man had to make his own escape from falling on top of his dead comrade and the part of my blade that was protruding from his back because I had managed to extricate myself. Even before I stopped at the wall, I heard the result of my escape, when the hilt of my *gladius* hit the wooden floor, forcing the rest of the blade into the man's body, followed by the sound a body makes when it collapses to a wooden floor, although the breathy moan may have just been the result of the remaining air in his lungs being forcibly expelled. It was quite dark, but since I had not had time to light a lamp, my eyes were adjusted to it, and with the door open, the light from the three-quarter moon that was hanging slightly above the rooftop, it gave me just enough light to see when the third assailant made a lunge with his own *gladius*. If it had been brighter, I probably would have been able to dodge the blow cleanly, instead of suddenly feeling as if someone had sliced into my right side with a burning stick, my sudden bellow of pain the loudest sound to that point. As I would learn later, it was also what woke up Alex, but the other thing that the pain did was enrage me to the point all thought of scrambling to the door to either escape or grab Scrofa's *gladius* left my mind. Instead, I threw myself directly at the man who had cut me, smashing into him bodily to send him reeling and hearing his blade clattering to the floor. Still intent on killing this *cunnus*, it was the movement from the second man who had gotten to his feet that changed my mind, and without turning around, I backpedaled towards the door. I have no idea if the second man saw the *gladius* or if he thought I was trying to escape, but whatever it was, he came rushing at me, seemingly racing me to the door. I could not see his *gladius* well, but I saw that his arm was up and pulled back in a classic second position as he prepared to thrust it into my throat, just as my hand grasped the hilt of the Scrofa blade. As hard as I tried later, I was unable to piece together how I not only managed to grab the blade and draw it from its scabbard, but to swing it across my body so that my blade struck his in such a way that the point of his blade buried itself in the wall immediately to the left of my head, creating a shower of small bits of plaster. To his peril, I was also now in a position to finally retaliate and I did not waste the chance. Since the pommel of my blade was essentially directly aligned with his face, I lashed out with it as if I was throwing a punch, catching him squarely in the nose, and while he gave a scream of agony, for the second time, I noticed the muffled quality to it, except this time, I realized why. They're wearing hoods! I thought, which was what prompted me to push myself away from the wall while reaching out with my left hand to snatch at it. But, while I managed to grab a handful of cloth, when I yanked, the only thing that happened was I wrenched another cry of pain from the man who, fortunately, had temporarily forgotten he still was holding his *gladius*, and I realized the hood was pinned on.

"*Gnaeus! Behind you!*"

You forgot the other man, you stupid bastard; I was sure that this would be my last thought, despite the fact that I reacted instantly, and while I never advocate swinging blindly to my men, that was exactly what I did as I spun around. It undoubtedly saved my life, the tip and first couple of inches of Scrofa's blade meeting resistance, although it was the sudden bellow of pain that was as informative because, while it was loud, it was not the kind that one learns signals a mortal wound, nor had I heard the same metal on metal sound. Most importantly, it drove all ideas of continuing the fight from this man's mind, except that rather than rush straight for the door, where Alex was standing, he quickly sidestepped to the man I had punched in the face, grabbing him by the arm before standing up straight to face us. The only sound was the harsh panting from all of us, making it extremely odd, while I stood a couple of paces from the wall, with the door on my left, and the two men standing almost the same distance as the door, but to my right directly across from the doorway.

"Alex," I broke the silence. "Stand aside."

"What?" he exclaimed. "Why would we do that?"

"Stand. Aside," I ordered.

He did so, reluctantly, but he stepped inside the door and came to my side, whereupon I pointed at the door with my *gladius*. The man with the smashed face moved, but it was to his dead comrade.

"If you touch him, we'll kill the both of you," I promised, then impulsively, I added, "Apparently, you weren't warned about what you were facing."

This got a reaction, but it was muttered, and the hoods muffled it to the point I could not have picked up the accent. What was important was that they began moving, slowly, towards the door, and when they got into the doorway, the light from the moon made the blood running down the third man's right arm glisten blackly, telling me what I had struck.

"You're going to need a tourniquet on that before you get where you're going," Alex said, earning him a puzzled glance from me, to which he responded to with a shrug, whispering, "I'm also a *medicus*. It's habit."

"Tell whoever sent you," I called out just as they stepped out onto the landing, deciding not to use a name, "this is what will happen to anyone who comes after me."

I was not surprised when they did not answer, and we heard the creaking of the third stair as they descended.

Suddenly, Alex gasped, "What if they go into my apartment?"

We went rushing out, but the only sign they had been there was the outer door hanging open, with blotches of black liquid glistening in the moonlight out in the street beyond.

"Do you recognize him?"

I shook my head to Alex's question. We had removed the dead man's hood, and Alex had lit all of the lamps, but only after we assured our women that the threat was gone. I say "we"; I sent Alex downstairs while I stayed upstairs to examine my own wound, which was bloody but not terribly serious, although it required Alex to stitch it up. Before returning upstairs, he closed the outer door to the building, then dragged a heavy bench from the atrium across the doorway. Neither of us thought that they would come back that night, nor would this do anything more than make them force the door, but it made both of us feel better. Once he tended to my wound and wrapped it, we tried to determine the identity of the man they had left behind. His hair was close-cropped, which is favored but not required for the Praetorian Guard, and he was clean-shaven, which *was* required, though it was hardly unique. If I had to guess, I would say half the men in Rome are clean-shaven, although I had been told this was going out of style with the fashionable set.

"He *looks* military," I concluded, although if Alex had forced me to describe what that meant, I could not have come up with anything definitive, but he actually nodded in agreement.

Then he turned to practical matters.

"So what do we do with him?"

I briefly thought about sending a message to Sempronius, almost immediately deciding against it; he had already cleaned up one of my messes, so I did not feel right about involving him in another.

"First thing," I decided, "we need to wrap him up in something, and clean this up." Despite the circumstances, I felt a grin cross my face. "And since I've been wounded, I guess you're going to have to do it."

"I didn't kill him!" he protested, but I just shook my head, pointing down to my bandaged side. "Wounded," I reminded him. Then I added, "Or do you want to have Algaia and Bronwen do it?"

This actually made him shudder at the idea.

"Gods, no!" he exclaimed. "Neither of us would hear the end of it." Suddenly, his voice changed, becoming higher pitched, and he perfectly mimicked Algaia's accent as he shook his finger at me. "Why do we always have to clean up the messes you men make? What do you think? The gods put us here just for that purpose?"

I do not think that I did as good a job as he did when I imitated Bronwen's Parisii accent, if only because I still sometimes did not understand her when she said an unfamiliar word, but my spirit was in it.

"I am Bronwen, daughter of Prausetauguas of the Parisii." I drew myself up and tilted my nose into the air. "I am no slave! And," I did my own finger wag, "I have just borne you a child, Gnaeus Pullus! Is this what you expect of the mother of your child, to be on her knees, scrubbing blood off the floor because *you* are the barbarian who thinks the best way to solve a problem is to kill it?"

By the time I was through, both of us were clutching our stomachs and doubled over with laughter...which was why neither of us saw the pair of them standing there in the doorway, both of them with the same identical posture of arms crossed, heads tilted to one side, lips pursed, and neither of them seemed amused in the slightest.

My wound saved me from the full wrath of my woman, while Alex worked his debt off by scrubbing the floor, and we all tried to ignore the body we had ended up wrapping in a sheet, which was difficult to do once his bowels released. I volunteered to at least carry the corpse downstairs and put him in the atrium, but Alex in his role of *medicus* had forbidden it, which was a good thing because my side had begun to hurt. It had taken twenty stitches, and Alex informed me that he had seen the bone of my lowest rib.

"Fortuna was smiling on you," he commented. "That cut was deep enough that a couple inches lower and it might have nicked your liver at the very least."

"I hope that *cunnus'* wound corrupts," I said, and I meant it.

"It's not long before dawn," Alex commented, and as usual, he had a larger reason than idle chatter. "You're going to have to report for duty shortly." He pointed to my side. "I can wrap that tightly and add another thickness of bandage so it won't bleed through, but anyone with eyes will be able to see something happened to you just by the way you move." I was not convinced of this, and I told him so. "All right," he said with a touch of impatience, "prove it. Render a salute." I did not get my arm up to my chest before I groaned, but more importantly, I felt the stitches pulling, prompting me to grumble, "You think you're so clever."

Nevertheless, he was right, and I knew it.

I showed my acknowledgment by asking, "What do you think I should do?"

As I have come to learn, he had thought this through, since he rarely if ever mentions a problem without having thought up at least one possible solution, but I was *not* expecting what he came up with.

"That's Norbanus. He's in the First of the First."

It was still a third of a watch before dawn, and Sabinus was standing in the atrium of the apartment, where we had dragged the now-identified Praetorian, and our world was instantly more dangerous. Sabinus' presence was the result of Alex slipping out and, armed with my pass, hurrying to the barracks and summoned the only man I trusted, not just in my Century, but the entire Cohort.

"Who does he associate with?" I asked. "Any idea?"

"Not really," my Optio answered, but I wondered if he was keeping his eyes on the dead man because he had not seen this sight this close before, or he was trying to avoid my gaze. Whether he sensed my suspicion or not, he did offer, "I do know that whenever I heard his name, it was usually in association with Numerius Vettus." He paused, and I understood why when he said, "He's the *Tesserarius* of the First of the First."

Alex and I glanced at each other, and I could tell our minds were running along the same lines; in all likelihood, the man who had made the decision to flee was this Vettus, acting as the commander of this trio.

Impulsively, I asked Sabinus, "What do you think I should do, Optio?"

I had used his rank on purpose, and I saw that he recognized as much.

As he rubbed his chin, I was completely unprepared to hear him say, "I think you should tell the Pilus Prior."

"*Creticus?*" I gasped. "Pluto's thorny cock, why would I tell *him?*"

"I know what you think, Centurion," Sabinus answered calmly, "but I think that you're at least partially wrong about him."

"Which part?" I asked coldly. "That he's a weakling? Or that he's the Secundus Pilus Prior in the Praetorians for a reason?"

I should not have been so blunt, but I was sufficiently rattled to let my tongue slip. To his credit, Sabinus confronted my questions squarely.

"You're right. Pilus Prior Creticus isn't a...strong man, at least not in the way we're talking about. But," he insisted, "I think you're wrong about how deep in Sejanus' purse he is. That is," he asked, "what you're referring to?"

"Yes." I nodded. "If I go to him, how do I know that he doesn't turn me over to Sejanus immediately?"

"Because Creticus hates Sejanus, probably more than you do," Sabinus answered, without hesitation. "He's been humiliated by the Prefect more times than any of us can count, and the reason for that is that Creticus has refused to be bought by the Prefect."

This sounded good, but Alex interjected, "If that's the case, why hasn't Sejanus replaced him?"

"The rumor is that Pilus Prior Creticus' father once served under Tiberius when he was a Tribune on his first campaign against the Rhaeti and Vindelici and that Creticus' father either did something for him or performed some feat that Tiberius felt obligated to repay."

I had heard this rumor, although it had come from Princeps Prior Atticus, shortly after my arrival, but it seemed to be awfully thin gruel, considering that I was in essence placing my fate in Creticus' hands.

"What do you think?"

Alex considered my question for a long moment before he finally answered, "I think it might be the only thing you can do at this point, Gnaeus."

During the time Alex was thinking about it, I had already begun leaning in that direction, not because of my mind, which was screaming at me not to be so foolish to risk everything on what was only an unsubstantiated rumor, but something else that I could not, nor can I now identify, which was why I heard the words that I agreed come out of my mouth with a fair amount of surprise. However, Alex also had something else in mind, and once he explained it, while I thought it was a good idea, I also knew there was no time to waste. I changed into my Praetorian tunic, but along with my *vitus*, I strapped on the Gallic blade, from which I had cleaned the blood of Norbanus, and while I oiled it, I fretted slightly that I did not have time to hone it again because cutting through a *hamata* always slightly dulls the blade. The one disagreement we had was when I ordered Alex to stay at the apartment, but despite vociferously arguing against it, I did not budge, so it was just Sabinus and I who left, hurrying through the streets to the barracks. My wound meant that I was not in the mood to talk, especially when I quickly learned that because of our moving at a trot, the act of breathing heavier than normal caused me to snarl at him to stop asking questions. Entering the barracks building, I hesitated, not because I had changed my mind, but something else occurred to me, which was what prompted me to change the plan.

"I'm going to wait to talk to the Pilus Prior until after morning assembly is sounded," I told Sabinus, who gasped in surprise.

"Then why did we have to run to get here before that if you were going to wait?"

It was a reasonable question, but rather than explain, I said only, "You'll see."

We entered my office, Demetrios leaping to his feet from his pallet in surprise, but when he asked me if he should prepare the morning meal, I shook my head. When he made to leave the office, however, I stopped him, asking him why.

"I need to use the latrine, Pilus Posterior," was his answer, and it was a perfectly reasonable thing, but I nonetheless pointed at the bucket in the corner.

"You're not leaving until after morning assembly is called," I told him, and he was wise not to argue, because at this moment, I was suspicious of everyone, even a clerk, though I did feel a bit badly, enough to say, "Once the *bucina* sounds the assembly and the Cohort is formed, you can go."

Sabinus and I sat in my private quarters, and he wisely did not resume the questioning he had attempted on our run across the city. I spent the time trying to ignore the throbbing in my side, which meant that it seemed much, much longer than it actually was before the *bucina* sounded the first call of the morning. The noise started immediately; the sounds of footsteps of the sections on the second floor as they leapt from their cots first, followed by slamming doors as the men dashed down to the latrines to relieve themselves, then returning to break their fast before donning their tunics and *balteae*. Normally, the call to assemble comes about a sixth part of a watch after the call to rise, and this day was no different, but when Sabinus looked at me as he got to his feet, I did not move.

"You go out and get them in formation," I said. "Once you call them to *intente*, that's when I'll come out."

I believe this was when Sabinus understood why I was doing so, or his nod may have just been acknowledging my orders; judging by the manner in which he behaved not long after, I think he had figured out my goal. Following him out into the outer office, just before he opened the door, he stopped and pointed down towards the area of my waist.

"Centurion, are you going to take that off?"

"No," I said flatly. "I'm going to be wearing my *gladius* for as long as this is going on."

It was mostly a practical precaution, but not completely; I was also determined to send a signal to whoever might be watching me that I was not going to be caught unprepared again. Sabinus did not reply, simply opening the door just widely enough to slip out without anyone seeing inside, which I appreciated. The windows were still shuttered, but I did not need to see out because my ears told me everything I needed to know, the racket created by the hobnailed soles as the men assembled, along with the talking that would cease in a few moments. I almost had a false start when I heard someone shout the order to *intente*, and my hand was on the doorknob before my mind registered that it had not come from directly outside my door, meaning that it was another Century. A half-dozen heartbeats later, I recognized Sabinus' voice, but I still hesitated, although it was only to take an unthinking deep breath that made me gasp in pain. It also cleared my mind, strengthened my resolve, and more than anything, renewed my anger so that, when I did open the door and step outside, my gaze was already on the spot where I knew my *Signifer* would be standing. As it turned out, I could have had my eyes closed because Flaccus' gasp was audible several paces away, but then I would have missed the pleasure of watching the blood drain from his face as he gaped at me, slack-jawed at the sight of what just heartbeats before he had obviously thought was a dead man. I also noticed that at least one other man, Crito of the First Section who was in the middle of the rank, reacted in much the same manner, although they were the only two I noticed. There was one oversight on my part, and that was the effort it took to return

Sabinus' salute without gasping from the pain and the certainty that I ripped at least one stitch loose in doing so. Somehow, I managed, and Sabinus executed his about turn as I stepped into my spot next to Flaccus, who was now visibly shaking, ready to receive the orders of the day from our Pilus Prior.

"Are you all right, *Signifer* Flaccus?" I asked. "You look ill." I could not resist adding, "If I believed in such things, I'd say you had just seen a *numen*."

"I...I...N-no, Pilus Posterior, I just...have something on my mind."

"It must be something very important for you to behave like this," I commented, but Creticus chose that moment to emerge from his quarters, and I called the Century to *intente*, as did the other five Centurions.

Creticus' reaction at seeing me standing in my spot actually strengthened Sabinus' argument because there was absolutely nothing close to Flaccus' expression on his face. Everything that followed was part of the routine, and while it seemed as if Creticus was moving through the ritual more slowly than normal, I knew that he was not. Then, after issuing the orders for the day, which actually included my half of the Cohort going to the stakes with the other half sparring, the first time that we would be obeying Tiberius' new training directive as an entire Cohort, Creticus dismissed us.

I was prepared for Flaccus to try and move away from me more quickly than normal as he hurried to the quarters he shared with my *Tesserarius* Spurius Dido, except this time, I could not stop the hiss of pain when I reached out with my left hand and snatched the back of his tunic, although his yelp of surprise drowned it out, and I snarled, "You're not going anywhere, Flaccus."

He almost dropped the standard as he looked over his shoulder at me, his eyes wide, protesting, "But why, Pilus Posterior? We're going to the stakes, so I need to..."

"Shut. Your. Mouth." I signaled Sabinus, who hurried over to me, and I ordered him, "Take him to the Century office, Optio, then go get Crito and bring him there as well."

"Yes, Pilus Posterior. I understand and will obey." Sabinus neither hesitated nor asked why, which told me that he had figured it out.

"Pilus Posterior," Flaccus began, but he got no further because he suddenly lost the air out of his lungs from the end of my *vitus*, which almost caused Sabinus to lose his grip on Flaccus' arm as the *Signifer* collapsed.

"What part of 'shut your mouth' was unclear, you *cunnus*?"

"Pilus Posterior Pullus!"

I turned at the sound of Creticus' voice, and this time, I was prepared for the pain of saluting, which he returned, but he walked towards me with a frown, an expression that he always seemed to be wearing when he dealt with me for anything.

"Why did you strike *Signifer* Flaccus?" he demanded, then before I could answer, his eyes dropped to my waist, noticing the *gladius* for the first time. "And why," he used his *vitus* to point at it, "are you wearing that?"

"Carry out your orders, Sabinus," I said quietly over my shoulder, then walked to Creticus, mainly to get away from the Century, most of them now standing gawking at the unusual scene and completely forgetting what they were supposed to be doing. Addressing Creticus, I kept my voice low. "Pilus Prior, what I need to tell you has to be in private."

"What now, Pullus?" He gave a weary sigh. "Who have you offended this time?"

"I'll tell you, but only in private. And," I warned, "without your clerks present."

Perhaps it was my own expression that convinced him, but whatever it was, he gave a curt nod, then said, "Follow me."

As soon as he entered the office, he dismissed the clerks, then led me into his private quarters.

"What's going on, Pullus?" he asked even as he was taking his seat, and I decided the best way to do it was to pretend it was an after-action report, just reciting the facts without any interpretation of my own.

By the time I was finished, his pallor was a match for Flaccus', while I waited to see if Sabinus had been right.

"Pluto's thorny cock," were his first words, but then he fell silent, staring at his desk, the time stretching until he looked up, and what I saw was a scared but determined man. "First thing, where is Norbanus' body?"

"It's still in the atrium at my apartment," I told him, and it was not surprising this elicited another curse.

"I'm going to have to go off books," he spoke as if to himself. Taking a tablet from the stack of blanks, he scribbled something, then set it aside. "The next thing I need to do is go to the Palatine. I usually send Diodorus with the morning report, but not always, so it won't arouse suspicion if I take it myself. I'll try and find out what I can."

"What should I do?" I asked.

"You need to stay here, at least until I find out more," he replied without hesitation.

"But what about my family?"

"I can't bring them here, Pullus," Creticus said, not unkindly, but with a tone that told me I would not persuade him. "That's out of the question."

Before I had a chance to say anything, there was a sharp rapping on the door, followed immediately by it being opened.

"Pilus Prior Creticus? Are you in your quarters?"

It took a heartbeat for me to recognize the voice, but before either of us could react, the inner door was opened and Marcus Asprenas entered, but while he looked a bit embarrassed at interrupting, he did not leave.

"Now that I'm back, I thought I'd spend some time with you to find out if anything noteworthy has happened. Like," he actually smiled as he nodded towards me, "getting a new Centurion." I suppose it was that neither of us smiled or acknowledged his lighthearted tone that alerted him to something, and his smile faded, but he sounded more puzzled than concerned. "Is there something wrong?"

Instead of addressing or even glancing at Asprenas, Creticus looked directly at me, though it took a heartbeat or two for me to understand his silent question. Yes, Asprenas and my father developed, if not a bond, then a mutual respect; yes, he had been friendly whenever we had crossed paths, and yes, he had even teased me about Latobius and offered to buy him, but this was completely different.

"My family is in danger, Tribune," I broke the silence. "Last night, there was an attempt on my life by three Praetorians from the First Cohort."

"Sejanus."

Asprenas did not ask this, he said it, but he looked at Creticus, who nodded.

Stumbling to one of the other chairs, Asprenas dropped into it, muttering, "He's getting more dangerous by the day."

While true, this was also a startling thing to hear from a Tribune, but it was Creticus who explained, "Before you arrived in the Cohort, Pullus, the Tribune and I have had several...candid conversations, and we both share the same concern, that Prefect Sejanus is accumulating power for his own ends and not in the service of the Imperator and Rome."

This got me looking at Asprenas, who nodded his confirmation.

"While that's good to hear, it doesn't do my family, or my clerk's family any good," I pointed out.

"Are you talking about Alexandros Pullus?" Asprenas asked. When I nodded, he asked, "Where is he right now?" I did not hesitate, much, but he shook his head impatiently. "I mean, specifically. Where is your apartment?" Once I told him, he asked Creticus for a tablet, while I sat there, completely bemused. Asprenas incised a few lines, then extended tablet and stylus towards me, instructing, "Put something on here that only Pullus or your wife would know so that it confirms that this is genuine."

While I took the tablet, it was not until I read what he had written that I understood, and it made me look up at him in surprise.

"You're going to have them stay at your home?"

"It's the safest place I can think of," he said as if we were discussing the weather, and he actually grinned. "The fact that it's on the Palatine..." He raised a hand as he explained, "...on the lower slope, means that *if* anyone searched, that would be the last place they would look."

What I wrote was for Bronwen, and I will not divulge what it said, but it included a few words of Parisii, written in the Latin, of course, that I had learned she used at certain moments so that it would be nonsense to anyone who intercepted this.

When I handed the tablet back to him, I asked, "How are you going to get the message to them?"

"My body slave is outside," Asprenas answered. He must have seen something in my expression, because he added, "He's been with our family since before I was born, and he's completely loyal. I trust him with my life. Which," he pointed out, "is now on the line as well."

This was true, but it also engendered me to ask bluntly, "Why are you helping me?"

Asprenas did not answer immediately, regarding me with a thoughtful gaze before he spoke.

"I could tell you that it's because of the regard that I still hold for your father, and for your family. And, that is certainly a large part of it." He took a breath before continuing, "But the truth is that Sejanus represents a threat to my family as well, along with several other high-ranking families that have been trusted by first Divus Augustus, then Tiberius. At least," his mouth twisted into a bitter grimace, "until recently. So," he finished, "it's in my interests as much as it is in yours to do what we can to thwart whatever he's planning."

Rather than being offended that Asprenas' motives were not purely because of how much he respected my father, this actually convinced me that he could be trusted, because it made sense.

Nevertheless, I meant it sincerely when I said, "Thank you, Tribune."

He got up and left the office, returning very quickly to inform us that his body slave was on his way. The next problem was Flaccus and Crito, but this did not concern Creticus, although not for a reason that made me feel any better.

"Pullus, there are more men like Flaccus and Crito in this Cohort, and one of them is a Centurion," he said disgustedly. "So there's no doubt that a little bird has already flown to the *Domus Augusti* to inform Sejanus that you showed up safe and sound this morning."

"I don't feel safe," I burst out bitterly, then pointed to my side, "and I'm certainly not sound."

"What?" Asprenas looked over at me sharply. "Were you injured?" I explained what had happened and how Alex had utilized his skills to stitch me up, my mood not helped at all by the fact that talking about it made it hurt more. Asprenas rubbed his chin, frowning down at the floor, but I learned why when he said, "I wonder if there's a way that we can use that to our advantage?"

"How so?" Creticus asked, and I was just as curious.

"I'm not sure yet, but let me think about it." He stood then, saying "I'm going to the Palatine, so I'll find out what I can." Creticus stood up and explained this was what he intended to do as well, but Asprenas correctly pointed out, "There's no need for both of us to go, and if you don't do that normally, it might make Sejanus suspicious, given that you said he probably knows that Pullus is still alive. You've managed to avoid becoming a target of Sejanus to this point; there's no need to start now."

This made eminent sense to me, and Creticus obviously agreed, because he dropped back down into his chair, while Asprenas left. Once he was gone, I returned my attention to what I still thought of as a problem.

"What about Flaccus and Crito?"

"Let's go have a talk with them," Creticus stood up with a grim smile, but I cleared my throat in a manner that told him I had something to say, and he eyed me warily, asking, "Yes, Pullus?"

"It's just that, do you *really* want to be present for that, Pilus Prior?" I asked, then added pointedly, "In the event that either of them decide to...refuse to cooperate?"

To my relief, he immediately saw the sense in this, dropping back down into his chair and saying only to inform him of what I learned, and I left his office, admonishing myself that it would do no good to let my temper get out of control, no matter how tempting.

As I had ordered, Sabinus was with Flaccus and Crito who, up until this moment, had impressed me as being one of those who had never served under the standard who I believed could have made the transition with little trouble. I was pleased, however, to see that Crito's expression matched his comrade's, both of them eyeing my entrance with the same expressions that those men in the arena wore when the lions were set loose the day before. Sabinus was standing just next to the door, and when I entered, he made as if he was leaving, but I stopped him.

"I need at least one witness for this," I told him.

He did not reply verbally, though he nodded, which was good enough for me.

"Demetrios, you can go to the latrine now," I said, "but you need to make it a long trip, do you understand me?"

"Y-yes, Pilus Posterior," he agreed, and I do not believe his eagerness to leave was due only to an urgent call of nature, although he did stop at the door to ask, "Will Alexandros be coming, Pilus Posterior?"

"Not today, so you'll need to do his reports," I told him, which he clearly did not appreciate, though he wisely said nothing as he slipped out the door.

Both men were standing, but not at *intente*, and while I thought for a moment of starting with that, I discarded the notion.

"There *is* good news for the two of you," I said pleasantly, taking a seat on the edge of the desk, enjoying the look of hope my words brought, which I took away with the next breath. "I don't intend to beat either of you to death...unless you make it necessary."

It was Crito who spoke first, or gasped, "Why would you need to beat us at all, Pilus Posterior?"

Rather than answer the question directly, I addressed Flaccus instead.

"Were you the one who gave Norbanus in the First Cohort the directions to where I lived?"

"Norbanus?" Flaccus frowned. "I don't know Numerius Norbanus, Pilus Posterior."

"Really?" I feigned surprise, then pounced on his error. "Then how do you know his *praenomen*?"

"I-I-I know *of* him," he stammered, "but I don't know him personally."

"He must be fairly well known, then," I commented casually, but before Flaccus could respond, it was Crito who spoke next.

"What do you want from us, Pilus Posterior?" he asked quietly, and I got the sense that he had decided against prolonging whatever was going to happen to them.

"I want to know why you two were so surprised to see me this morning. And," I added, somewhat cruelly, "the first of you who tells me everything I want to know will escape what's coming."

"What does that mean?"

"I'll answer your questions."

Those two things were uttered at the same moment, but it was Crito I addressed, since he beat Flaccus with a promise to cooperate. "How did Norbanus and the other two know where I lived?"

"Sextus!" Flaccus turned to look at Crito, behaving as if they were the only two there. "You know what will happen if you say anything!"

"Right now, I'm more worried about what will happen if I don't, Vibius," Crito replied evenly. Nodding his head in my direction, he reminded my *Signifer*, "You saw what he's capable of with just a *rudis*. And," now he did point to my waist, "*that's* not a *rudis*."

Even in the moment, I was struck by the thought how I never tire of hearing other men compliment my skill, though I kept any sign of that from my expression.

Flaccus, evidently persuaded, turned to address me. "I'll tell you what you want to know, Pilus Posterior! I swear it!"

"That's good to hear," I said, but then I heaved a sigh since it seemed appropriate, "but I told you that only one of you would escape punishment, and that it would be whoever talked first." Pointing at Crito, I said reasonably, "He beat you to it, Flaccus, and what kind of Centurion would I be if I suddenly went back on my promise? How would any of you be able to trust me again?"

I was doing my best to remain impassive, but Sabinus tried to cover his chuckle with a cough, and failed at it, so it was difficult. Flaccus did not seem to appreciate the irony, however, and he closed his eyes, letting out a soft moan that was gratifying to hear, but while I was pleased he was terrified, the reality was that I had very limited options with him, at least if I was to punish him officially. Setting that aside for the moment, now that Flaccus understood his situation, I returned my attention to Crito, though only with a raised eyebrow, which he interpreted correctly.

"One day about a month ago," Crito began, "we followed you home to find out where your apartment is on the Caelian." I opened my mouth to ask, but he beat me to it. "We did so on orders, Pilus Posterior. It wasn't our idea."

He did stop then, but I am certain he knew I would not be satisfied with just this, and to prod him, I pointed to Flaccus. "He said he's willing to talk as well..."

"I am!" Flaccus' expression was akin to the look a drowning man has when he sees a rope, just out of reach, but before he could say anything else, Crito continued, "We receive our orders for...things...from Numerius Vettus. He's the..."

"He's the *Tesserarius* of the First of the First; yes, I know," I cut him off, but while this was relevant and did not surprise me, my mind had latched on to something else, which was why I demanded, "When you say 'things,' what kind of things are we talking about?"

Crito did not reply immediately, except this time, all I had to do was glance at Flaccus to get him to talk.

"Things like reminding certain business owners that it's a wise policy to cooperate with the Praetorians who frequent their establishments."

I suppose I should have anticipated this, but I was caught completely by surprise when I made the connection, gasping, "Are you the ones who beat Gallus and killed two of his whores?"

I had another surprise coming when Crito shook his head, but I quickly understood when he explained, "No, we don't do anything with the businesses our Cohort frequents. So we do for the First Cohort and the First does for us. Or," he shrugged, "for the Third or Fourth."

"Every Cohort is involved?" By this moment, my head was already proverbially spinning, and his simple nod did not help, although I thought I was beginning to understand, and I could not help the bitterness in my voice. "So I suppose the same principle applies here. You *cunni* wouldn't be the ones to kill your Centurion; you'd just have someone else do it."

This elicited a reaction from both of them, and they glanced at each other, but Crito signaled that it was Flaccus who should speak for them, and my *Signifer* said passionately, "Pilus Prior, we had nothing to do with what happened last night!"

"No," I countered, and as I thought about the night before, I was growing angry, enough so that I found myself standing over Flaccus before I knew it, and I poked him in his chest with my finger to emphasize, "you didn't order it, but you knew about it!"

"We didn't know they were going to kill you, I swear on Jupiter's Stone, Centurion!"

"What did you think they were going to do?" I snarled, and again, before I realized it, I had snatched a fistful of Flaccus' tunic, the searing flash of pain from my wound actually enraging me even more, and I began shaking him like a dog with a rat as I bellowed in his face, *"What the fuck did you think that Norbanus and the other two* mentulae *were there to do? Tell my infant son a bedtime story?"*

I was both gratified and disgusted that by the time I finished, Flaccus was sobbing, although while he was talking, it was a gibberish I did not understand, so I threw him away from me with enough force that he collided with the wall right next to Sabinus, who made no attempt to catch him, and he slid to the floor, still behaving like a woman as I turned to face Crito.

Who, I will give him credit, was obviously scared, but retained enough of his wits to ask me, "Pilus Posterior, do you have any idea what would happen to us if we had warned you?"

It was, I knew, a valid point; however, I did not care, and while

I did not grab Crito, I did stand directly in front of him, managing to keep my voice calm as I asked, "Do you feel safe right now, Crito?"

He broke eye contact by closing his eyes, which was a good thing because I had just gotten an idea that I thought would neutralize the pair as a possible threat. I actually retreated back to the desk and resumed my seat, watching in disgust as Flaccus pulled himself to his feet, wiping the tears and snot off of his face with the sleeve of his tunic.

I tried to sound conversational as I informed them, "As far as what I'm going to do to the pair of you right now?" I paused, then said, "Nothing. I'm not going to enter anything into the Century diary, nor am I going to put you on any kind of punishment list." It interested me to see that Flaccus suddenly looked hopeful, but Crito was looking at me with an expression of resignation that suggested he might have an idea of where I was heading, which I explained, "But depending on how events unfold, I *will* be sure that your names are mentioned when I talk about how, thanks to a warning I received from the two of you, I was ready and waiting for Vettus and the others." Since I was making this up as I went along, it was just as I was finishing that when I had what I still believe is a divinely inspired idea, which got me standing up and walking around the desk as I explained, "In fact, here's what I'm going to do." I picked up a blank tablet as I sat down, and began writing, explaining as I did so. "This is an official report for the two of you, commending you on your bravery," I could not help applying a certain amount of scorn to the word, "in alerting me to an attempt to murder your Centurion and his family."

I did not actually finish writing since the demonstration was more important, and when I snapped it shut and looked up, the total lack of surprise and resignation on Crito's face told the story that he had at least partially comprehended what I was doing.

Flaccus, on the other hand, had gone back to crying again, and I asked disgustedly, "How did a woman like you get into the Praetorian Guard?"

He made no reply, but I did not expect it, and for the first time, I addressed Sabinus, altering my tone that told him I was acting as his superior.

"Optio," I held out the tablet, and he obediently crossed the room to take it as I said, "you will take possession of this report. If *anything* happens to me, to Alexandros Pullus and his family, or to my woman and child, I'm assuming you know what to do."

"I do, Pilus Posterior," Sabinus replied crisply, then added his own nice flourish by adding, "I understand and will obey." Thankfully, he did not salute, but I noticed that he was not looking me in the eye, and I followed his gaze to see a dark stain on my tunic, and I muttered the only thing I could think to say. "Pluto's cock." This seemed as good a moment as any to dismiss the pair, so I pointed to the door. "You two are free to go, but I don't have to tell you to keep your fucking mouths shut, do I? Or that," I indicated the tablet in Sabinus' hand, "goes to the Pilus Prior first, then on to the Prefect."

Flaccus did not run out of the office, but it was close, and while Crito followed him, it was at a slower pace. He surprised me by stopping before he exited the office, then turned to look at me directly.

"Pilus Prior," he asked quietly, "what would you have done in our position?" He held his hands out in a helpless gesture, "What choice did we have?"

"If I had been in your position," I admitted, "I probably would have done the same. *But*," I hardened my voice, "I would never have put myself in that position to begin with, Crito."

"This isn't the Legions, Pilus Posterior," Crito answered bitterly. "Sometimes even when you think you have a choice a make, you find out that the gods are using you for a good laugh."

Then, he left the office, leaving me to wonder what he meant.

Chapter 8

I changed into my last clean Praetorian tunic as I waited in my office, Sabinus taking the Century out to the stakes with the other two first line Centuries, while the second line were out in the square, the sound of men sparring penetrating the walls, making me think that this was the first time where it sounded like a real Legionary camp. This was probably why I dozed off, sitting at my desk in my private quarters, so that when the door opened, I nearly jumped out of my skin, which of course meant I gave a sharp cry of pain. Since Demetrios had returned and was busy doing Alex's work, I moved behind my desk but remained standing, my hand on the hilt of my *gladius*; I did not think that Sejanus would be so foolish, but I was still shaken from being taken by surprise the night before.

"Pilus Posterior?" Demetrios called as he rapped on the door, and I sighed with relief when he said, "Tribune Asprenas and Pilus Prior Creticus are here to see you."

Not feeling right about summoning them into my private quarters, I went into the outer office, pleased that Demetrios immediately excused himself without being asked, leaving the office for parts unknown. Any positive feeling that I may have had with their arrival lasted just long enough to see their expressions, which can only be characterized as grim.

That was reinforced when Asprenas pointed to the chair behind Alex's desk, which was the closest. "You might want to sit down, Pullus." They did the same on the opposite side, and Asprenas wasted no time. "The First Cohort is in an uproar because Cinna has reported that he has three men who have deserted." This did bring a smile to his face, a grim one as he added, "And I'll let you guess who those three are."

This was certainly interesting, but when he did not seem disposed to continue, I asked, "What does this mean?"

"It means that either Sejanus told Cinna to clean up his mess, or Cinna took it upon himself to do it before Sejanus ordered him to do it."

Given how desertion is treated in the Legions, this could be taken as a sign that these three men's fates were sealed, but I suppose I had been caught out too many times thinking that the Praetorians operated like the Legions, so I was opening my mouth to repeat my question, but Creticus must have guessed, because he spoke up, "This is the one area where the Praetorians are, if anything, even harsher than the Legions, Pullus. Deserting the Imperator is an automatic death sentence, with no right to appeal. And," he assured me, "like they do in the Legions, his comrades are the ones to beat them to death."

"One of them is already dead," I pointed out, and while I was not certain, I offered, "and it's possible that if the man I cut is Vettus, he might have bled to death already, given the blood trail."

"He'd actually be better off if that's the case," Creticus muttered.

While I understood why he said it, I did not agree, but instead I remembered something, and I addressed the Tribune.

"You said that you had an idea you wanted to think about?"

Asprenas shifted in his chair, and he seemed uncomfortable, although he did answer, "Yes, about that. I *have* thought about it, but I'm not sure it's a good idea now that I've had time to go through it."

"It can't hurt to hear it," I said, then thought it was appropriate to grin as I assured him, "and if I think it's a stupid idea, I won't say that, Tribune."

He did give a short laugh but immediately turned serious again.

"My thought was using you as bait," he began, which certainly got my attention, although I did not say anything. Taking this as a sign, I suppose, Asprenas went on, "The other thing that I learned on the Palatine is that nobody appears to know your condition."

"How could that be?" Creticus interjected with a frown. "You took the morning report there, and I have Pullus listed as present and fit."

Asprenas' expression changed, and it turned out to be one of embarrassment as he said hesitantly, "Yes, about that. I...I decided to alter the report and put him down on the sick list and being confined to quarters."

"Why would you do that?"

Creticus beat me to the question, although Asprenas explained, "I did it when I was still considering the idea I had, but while I hadn't thought it through, I had to do something in case I thought it was a good idea, and," he turned to me, "you agreed." This made sense as far as it went, but I was more interested in the details; thankfully, Creticus nodded his agreement and Asprenas continued, "So as of this moment, nobody on the Palatine knows exactly where you are, since as a Centurion in the Praetorians, if you're on the sick list, you can choose to stay here or go to your apartment, but the more important part is that, when they see your name, they're going to be certain that you're not sick at all."

"They'll be sure that I'm wounded," I said slowly, "and seriously enough that I can't report for duty."

"Exactly," Asprenas agreed, then going on, "So, if I was Cinna and knowing how unhappy Sejanus will be that you're still breathing, I wouldn't waste any time finishing the job." Pointing a finger at me, he said, "You are a major embarrassment for the Prefect right now, for a number of reasons."

"He's worried that I'll go directly to Germanicus," I said by way of agreement, but Asprenas shook his head, though not in dispute.

"It's not just that, Pullus," he assured me. "Remember, he saw Tiberius talking to you, but more than that, the fact that Sejanus failed to achieve a result he wanted will enrage him, not just because of the failure itself, but because he sees it as an embarrassment." I suppose the doubt showed on my face, causing Asprenas to lean forward, his own expression taking on an intensity that supported his words. "My family has been endangered by Sejanus for the last five years, Pullus, and I've studied the man. Under the surface, despite all of the pretensions and his lavish habits, Sejanus is just a jumped-up Equestrian provincial with aspirations towards elevating himself up into our order. Which," Asprenas' mouth twisted into a sneer, "will never happen. Even if he manages to convince Tiberius to elevate his status, he'll never be accepted by us. So," he finished, "this is a personal failure on his part as well, which means that you're still in danger."

There were so many thoughts running through my mind that it was hard for me to know where to start, but I will confess that at the forefront was my anger and indignation at Asprenas' sneering condescension towards the Equestrian Order and anyone who wanted to better the fortunes of themselves and their family, while men like Asprenas firmly believe that each of us and our place in our orders has been ordained by the gods, and to attempt to change that is either challenging or mocking them. More than anything, it reminded me of reading my great-grandfather's account that documented how nothing has changed over the last seventy years, even with two civil wars. That said, I was also honest with myself, because this was precisely how Gnaeus Volusenus had viewed those men of the Head Count like my real great-grandfather, and my true father, who aspired to qualify for the Equestrian Order.

Shoving this aside, and although I still had a bitter taste in my mouth at Asprenas' casual arrogance, I asked the more important question. "What purpose does using me as bait serve?"

"We need some bargaining power," Asprenas explained, and in the moment, I thought he was using "we" in a figurative sense, "because as long as Sejanus knows that you're breathing, you're in danger. And," he hesitated, "while your family is safe in my home right now, I can promise you that, at this very moment, Sejanus has men scouring Rome looking for them, so it's really only a matter of time before they're found."

As hard as it was to hear, I also understood he was right.

"What do you have in mind?" I asked him.

"An ambush," Asprenas answered immediately, "but we don't want to kill any more Praetorians than is absolutely necessary to survive. And it's vital that we have at least one man alive."

"But why would Sejanus hesitate to sacrifice one or two more men when Pullus threatens them?" Creticus asked, and though he did it on his own, I was every bit as interested.

This was when I learned that Asprenas had not been speaking figuratively, although he started out by saying flatly, "He wouldn't, not if Pullus still threatens him." He paused, and I had the sense that he was waiting for us to work it out, but I still was blind to where he was going. Which was why, with a hint of impatience, he explained, "But if one of his Praetorian Tribunes, especially one with more than one Consul in our family line, threatens to go to Tiberius himself, that would make Sejanus more...amenable," he offered a cruel smile, "...to a negotiation that includes an agreement that keeps you and your family safe."

He stopped then, and I certainly did not know what to say, while a glance at Creticus told me that his mind was as full of all of this and the possible outcomes as mine was.

"Why are you doing this?" I asked him in an echo of the same question I had posed earlier in the day. "It's one thing to falsify a report and snoop around on the Palatine, but this," I shook my head, "this is something else entirely." Before he could reply, something else occurred to me, "And where would this ambush happen?"

Answering my last question first, Asprenas admitted, "That's what we need to talk about. Given that you could be in one of two places while you're on the sick list, we need to decide which is the most likely."

"If they came here," Creticus spoke up, "they can at least enter the barracks building without arousing suspicion." This was true, but I did not think it likely, and I learned he agreed. "But I doubt they'll do that. There's just too many men here, and while Sejanus has men like Flaccus and Crito in your Century, and," his expression mirrored Asprenas' a moment earlier as he said bitterly, "there are four men in my Century that I'm sure are in Sejanus' purse and at least two more that I suspect. That's not going to be enough to help if things go to Hades."

"My apartment then," I sighed, "again."

"Yes." Asprenas nodded. "That's my judgment as well."

Something occurred to me, and I addressed Creticus. "You said you were going to take care of...?"

I did not finish, but I did not need to.

"That's been done," Creticus assured me. "I ordered that Norbanus be stripped of anything identifying him as a Praetorian. And," he smiled grimly, "his body has been eaten by pigs. Or maybe they're not done yet, but they will be soon."

This is hardly a secret method for disposing of a body, and in fact, something similar had been done in Arelate on behalf of myself and my family, but I was unsettled by how familiar Creticus seemed to be with it, not that I commented. The other two men looked at me, and I realized that, ultimately, this was up to me, and I also knew that time was running out to make a decision.

As much to buy time as anything, I mused aloud, "I suppose I should wait until it's dark before I leave here."

"You mean, before *we* leave here," Asprenas interjected. I suppose my expression gave me away, because he argued, "Pullus, there's no doubt that you can handle yourself, but surely you don't think that it will just be three men this time?"

I knew he was right as soon as he said it, which I signaled by asking, "How many do you think?"

"At least a half-dozen," Asprenas said immediately, although it was Creticus who put in, "It won't be much more than that. Not," he shook his head, "an entire section. Eight man rushing into one apartment would be as dangerous to them as it would be to whoever's inside."

"So that means six or seven," I mused. Reluctantly, I allowed, "If it was six men and there were two of us, that would be fine. But," I pointed down to my side, "I'm not at full strength, and twisting my body is going to be hard."

"I'll come as well," Creticus said, but Asprenas gave an emphatic shake of his head.

"No, Pilus Prior," the Tribune countered. "It will be enough of a risk that I'm going to be there, but if you're there as well, and if things go badly, this entire Cohort will be under suspicion by Sejanus."

This made sense, and Creticus signaled his agreement with a nod, so I was preparing for it to just be Asprenas and myself. However, we had been so absorbed in our own discussion that we did not notice the noise made by the three Centuries out at the stakes returning, meaning that all three of us leapt to our feet when the door was opened suddenly, while my hand was on the hilt once more.

"Am I...interrupting anything?" Sabinus asked, clearly as startled by the three of us staring at him in surprise as we were by him.

Realizing I had been holding my breath by how much it hurt to do so, I let it out and waved him in, ignoring Asprenas' look of alarm.

"Sit down, Optio." I pointed to the one empty chair. "You need to be aware of what's going on."

I was a bit surprised that neither Asprenas nor Creticus objected, although the Tribune asked me directly, "Are you sure about this, Pullus?"

"Given what he's done so far," I replied, trying to sound confident when I was not, at least not completely, "I think he deserves to know what's going on."

I explained the situation, Sabinus saying nothing to interrupt me, and when I finished, he sat there, considering.

"When do we leave for your apartment, Pilus Prior? Will I have time to get something to eat?"

Mentioning food made me hungry, and I assured him there was time, but I decided against it for myself because I did not want anyone seeing Demetrios entering with the amount of food that I consume, so I resigned myself to being hungry; only later did it occur to me that I could have simply eaten less food. Asprenas and Creticus left, the Tribune telling me that he would return shortly before dark, so without anything better to do, I lay down on my cot and tried to sleep, but I could not keep my mind still. Foremost in my mind was the plan itself, and I could not shake the thought, It's a shaky plan, and we're gambling that Creticus' logic about there not being even a full section is solid, so I spent my time trying to think of what to do in that event, but that competed with my worry about whether Bronwen, Titus, and Alex, Algaia, and Iras were safe, although Asprenas had assured me before he left that they were, and that he had stopped to check on them, which I appreciated, especially since Alex knew Asprenas and would undoubtedly tell Bronwen this. The *bucina* sounded the official end of the day, the sounds of footsteps and slamming doors as the men returned to their section quarters to prepare their evening meal, although some men preferred to hurry out into the city and buy a meat pie or a bowl of porridge from one of the establishments that surrounded the barracks. Asprenas returned, and I got up and entered the outer office, noticing that he was now wearing his *gladius*, while his cloak was fastened to hide his cuirass, although he was not wearing a helmet or greaves since that would have been too obvious. It did make me realize that I was still wearing just my tunic, so I hurried into my quarters to don my *hamata*, and without thinking, I grabbed it from the stand and lifted my arms up.

"Pilus Posterior?" Demetrios sounded alarmed. "Did you say something? Are you all right?"

I assured him that I was fine, embarrassed at my sharp cry of pain, but I gritted my teeth and slid the *hamata* down over my head and dropped it onto my shoulders. My cloak was at the apartment, and not only was my other tunic stained, it was already tight across my shoulders so that I could not put it over my armor, so I was left with just hoping that it did not attract attention. My reentry into the office coincided with the outer door opening again, but while it was Sabinus as expected, I immediately saw that he was not alone, but it was who it was that made me stare at my Optio as if he had gone mad.

Sabinus clearly saw my expression, because he held up a placating hand as he said quickly, "Please, Pilus Posterior, you need to hear this!"

He stepped aside to let Crito enter the office, and while the Optio shut the door, the ranker approached me, not shirking my stare.

"Pilus Posterior," Crito began after he came to *intente* without being told, "there's something you need to know. Actually," he amended, "there's two things. And," I saw him swallow, "I have a request."

"Tell me what it is you think I should know, Crito," I said coldly. "Then we'll see about any request."

"The first is about Flaccus," he began. "Right after dismissal, he tried to leave the barracks." Naturally, this got my attention, but before I could say anything, Crito said, "He's still here. We...detained him," he added quickly, but this did not really make me feel better.

"Who's we?" I demanded.

"Valerius," he replied, naming one of the Legion veterans and Sergeant of the Sixth Section, but he was not through, "and *Tesserarius* Dido. Actually," he explained, "it was Dido who got suspicious of the way Flaccus was behaving, and he came and got me. And," he shrugged, "I asked Valerius to help."

"What do you mean you detained him?" Asprenas broke in, which was a good question.

Crito did not hesitate to reply, "He's bound and gagged and in his and Dido's quarters right now."

"What was he going to do?" I asked. "Did he say something?"

"No," Crito admitted, "but I know him, Centurion." He hesitated, and I sensed the reluctance to say the words, but he explained, "He's my friend, sir, but he's a weak man, and he's the kind of man who goes in whatever direction the wind is blowing the strongest."

"Thank you, Crito" I said this somewhat reluctantly. "And what's the other thing?"

"Do you remember what I told you? About how one Cohort does for another?" I nodded, and he went on, "Well, it's the same in a Cohort. One Century does for another."

It took a moment for his meaning to sink in, and even then I was not certain, so I asked, "Are you saying that it won't be men from the First Century since that's who came last night?"

Nodding, he affirmed, "Yes, sir. And I'm almost certain that it will not only be the Second Century, but who will be leading them."

"Who?"

"One of Vettus' best friends is Pilus Posterior Cethegus," Crito replied. "I can almost guarantee that he'll be leading whoever's coming tonight."

"And how did you know that's what's happening?" I demanded, but I was looking directly at Sabinus, which Crito saw, and he shook his head.

"The Optio didn't say anything, Pilus Posterior," he said emphatically. "This is something I worked out on my own." Naturally, I was obviously skeptical, and he explained, "I've been a Praetorian for some time, Pilus Posterior, and I know how the Prefect thinks. You surviving his first attempt is a slap in his face, so he won't rest until you're dead."

"Knowing that," I pointed out, "why are you warning me? If Sejanus won't stop until I'm dead, anyone who helps me is likely to share the same fate."

For the first time, Crito averted his gaze from my face, staring at the floor for a moment, then as if he was talking to himself, he said, "I didn't join the Praetorians to do what I'm doing, Pilus Posterior. I thought that we'd be protecting the Imperator and defeating his enemies...but all the things we do we're doing for the Prefect, not the Imperator."

I am certain that he had no way of knowing this, but he could not have said anything better to convince me of his sincerity, and I signaled my acceptance by asking, "So, what's your request?"

He did not hesitate, and he lifted his head so that he could look me in the eye.

"Let me go with you, Pilus Posterior. Let me help you face whatever's coming. I," for the first time, he showed some emotion, "owe you that."

Before I answered, I glanced over at Asprenas and Creticus, the former shaking his head, while the latter was doing the opposite.

My objection, however, was practical in nature, and I brought it up by pointing down at his waist, "You had to check that *gladius* out from the armory. Won't that raise suspicion?"

Crito suddenly became interested in the floor, saying carefully, "This isn't from the armory, Pilus Posterior. Some of us have...extra blades in our quarters."

"Hidden away," I said coldly, since as Centurion, I conducted a weekly inspection of every section's quarters.

Crito replied with just a nod, then I realized that it did not really matter at this moment. Like everyone but me, Crito was wearing his blue Praetorian cloak, as was Sabinus, meaning that I was the one most likely to stick out since I could hide neither my *hamata* nor my *gladius*, so we waited just a bit longer, then Creticus, leading the way, opened the door to my office and took a quick look around before he stepped out of the doorway.

"Go with Fortuna, Pullus," Creticus said quietly as I walked by. "I hope this works out the way we need it to."

Biting back the retort that he was staying behind, knowing how ungracious it was, and reminding myself that Creticus was not by nature a courageous man, I simply thanked him and promised, "As soon as I can, I'll send Sabinus and Crito back."

Exiting the barracks, I had to fight the urge to walk quickly, knowing that we were already likely to attract attention from the people in the streets, even in the darkness. Since we were not wearing helmets, and I was not even carrying my Praetorian *vitus*, while we got a few glances, nothing in the reaction of the passersby indicated alarm, nor did any of them suddenly start dashing off to presumably warn whoever was coming. It was not that I disbelieved Crito about Cethegus, necessarily, but I did remember our conversation at the games about my father and my fighting prowess, and he did not strike me as the kind of man who would be eager to test himself against me. Just before we reached the corner around which the apartment was located, Asprenas tugged at my sleeve, stopping me.

"I think we might want to watch for a moment to see if they have someone watching," he suggested.

It was a good one, because I took a quick peek and saw a pair of men on the opposite side of the building, seemingly engaged in a conversation, but there was enough light to see that they were positioned in a way that they were both facing the doorway, which was unusual, since when people are truly engaged in conversation, they face each other. Pulling back, I told the others, prompting Asprenas to ask if there was another way to get into the building.

"Yes, there is." I recalled the first couple days when Alex and I explored the street on the other side of the building and found that there was an alley that separated my building from the back of the building on the parallel street, just wide enough for a wagon. Thinking a moment, I said, "We'll have to take the long way around to get to the alley from the opposite direction."

Reversing course, we went back the way we came. Reaching the alley unseen from the opposite end of the street from the apartment, I did warn them to hold their breath since, like all alleyways in every large city, it smelled of piss because they serve as an emergency latrine. The rear door was located roughly in the middle of the building, and it opened into a small room behind the atrium that at one time was the kitchen when the building was used for one family, although it was currently used as a storeroom. It was where I kept Latobius' saddle and tack, and there were some crates belonging to Alex and Algaia. The important thing was that there was a lock on the outer door, and someone had thought like a Legionary because there was a locking bar across the outside of the door that opened out onto the atrium, which meant that nobody could use this back entrance without breaking through the inner door, and would give us more than enough time to respond if whoever was coming attempted to do so. Since it was empty now, no lamps were lit, and I led them out into the atrium where there was moonlight, as I realized that while we had discussed what to do, there had been no mention of how we were going to do it.

Consequently, I broke the silence by asking Asprenas bluntly, "Since this was your idea, have you given any thought about how we're supposed to ensure we do what we need to do?"

I suspect he was happy for the dim lighting so that we could not see his face flush, but he did not hesitate to admit, "No, Pullus, I haven't. And," he added ruefully, "I should have."

Since this was immaterial, I ignored it, and thought aloud, "Maybe we should split into two teams. One," I pointed to Alex's apartment, "will be in there, and the other will be in my apartment."

I was somewhat surprised that Asprenas did not seem accepting of this because he was shaking his head, but I learned why when he pointed out, "We don't want to put them in a position where they feel trapped and their only way out is to kill all of us. We're going to have the element of surprise because they're expecting you to not only be alone, but hurt to a certain degree, but once we come out of hiding, we're also going to be coming in blind since we won't know how many men they have."

He was right, and I knew it, yet at the same time, I suppose I was thinking like a Legionary, because when Asprenas mentioned that we actually wanted to let most of them escape, I instinctively rebelled at the idea. Simply put, I didn't want to leave any of these men alive to seek vengeance for what we were about to do, however, nor could I argue with the logic; killing six or seven men with only four of us, and Crito never having seen combat of any kind, while Sabinus had been involved in a short campaign to quell a local uprising against untrained tribesmen, was no easy task. And, if I am being honest, I had doubts about just how experienced Asprenas was, but at least he had been on a battlefield more than once, so he at least knew what killing a man looks like.

"Putting us all together in one room is just as bad," I countered, pointing out, "There will be four of us, and then only the gods know how many of them, and it will be dark, so we're just as likely to stab each other as them."

Now it was time for Asprenas to nod his head in acknowledgement.

"May I make a suggestion, Pilus Posterior?"

I had almost forgotten the presence of my Optio and Crito, but I nodded to Sabinus to continue.

"They think that you're at the very least wounded to some degree," he began.

By the time he was through, I was convinced that he had come up with a good plan, and I saw that Asprenas agreed. Of course, we also forgot a saying that was quite popular under the standard that a plan only lasts long enough for Fortuna to piss all over it.

It took a bit of work to make the pile of clothing, bolsters, and whatever else we could find to create a lifelike-looking body lying in the bed Bronwen and I shared. I say lifelike; if whoever was coming lit a lamp, the ruse would be immediately discovered, but we were confident that they would work in darkness. Besides, it only had to work for an instant, and we were counting on whoever went upstairs into my apartment to raise the alarm, which would be our signal to burst out of Alex's apartment, where we would then block the stairway. In something of a compromise, only three of us would be in the downstairs apartment, as I argued that even with a locking bar, we needed someone at the back entrance. Honestly, it was more to keep Crito out of the way, and I assured him that I would keep the inner door wide open, both so that he would not be trapped in the event that one or more Praetorian showed up, but that we could more easily hear him if he shouted for help while we were still downstairs. With everything done, there was nothing to do but sit in the dark and wait, and since everything was shuttered and the door closed, the air in Alex's apartment began to get close, with that smell that I first became acquainted with as a new paid man when, under

Germanicus' command, we marched out to quell what was essentially a heavily armed war party of Tencteri and Sugambri who crossed the Rhenus. Fear sweat has a distinctively different odor, and this was what filled my nostrils, although I know I contributed to it just as much as Asprenas and Sabinus. We did not talk, even in a whisper, and I quickly lost track of time, so I do not really know how long we waited, but it was long enough for the sounds outside to die down as people returned home from the *taverna*, and the delivery wagons who begin operating after dark, which has been the law since Divus Julius made it one, began doing their business. After that, it was the normal sounds of the night of crickets and frogs, punctuated by an occasional slamming door as some couple's argument reached a climax, and the sounds of our breathing. When the noise came, while we all heard it, I for one could not identify its location, and my initial thought was that it was farther down the street. I think it was, because the next noise was definitely outside my door, and we all instantly recognized it as someone trying the latch. Yes, it was locked but, especially in a city like Rome, there are men, and women, who are skilled in defeating them within a span of a couple heartbeats, but as we listened, it was easy to determine that whoever was attempting to unlock the door was not one of those. This was confirmed when we heard what sounded like an oath, although it was not distinguishable, but then the sound stopped, followed by a barely audible squeaking of the hinges. We were all standing, and I already had my *gladius* out, holding it down by my side as I made tiny circles with the point, a habit that I picked up from my father that, while I have no idea if it translates into better performance, I still feel odd when I do not do it. Nobody outside the apartment was speaking, but just from the sound, it was clear that there were several men, and the first one began ascending the stairs. They were very careful, but just as had happened the night before, whoever was leading them up the stairs did not know about that third step from the top, because it creaked audibly enough that we could hear it, and I put my hand on the latch with my left hand. I suppose that, since I was now right next to the door, I could hear better, because I heard someone mutter "Pluto's cock," which was immediately followed by a hissed order, then all went silent. They're waiting to see if they've been heard, I thought, but whoever was leading them resumed moving, then the rattling sound of the apartment door lock being manipulated, but I noticed that the step did not creak again, which I took to mean that whoever was first had warned the others by pointing it out to them. It was impossible to tell how many there were, which prompted me to close my eyes to try and envision what was happening. My guess was that at least three and perhaps four men were now on the stairs, ready to rush inside my apartment, my logic being that since they had sent three men after me the night before and none of them had returned, they would want more men immediately available to prevent that from happening again. I also forced myself to recognize the possibility that these men knew that, while I had killed one, wounded another, and at least broken the nose of the third, there were two survivors. Add to this their belief that I was wounded, I felt somewhat confident that there would not be more than four on the stairs, leaving two men unaccounted for, and if it had been me, I would have had one man on the front door and another man sent around back to look for another way into the building. As I was thinking about this, we heard a sudden clattering of footsteps above us, the man defeating the lock opening the door and immediately rushing inside, followed by the sounds of other men pounding up the stairs to follow their leader.

"Here we go," Asprenas muttered, and I fought the urge to yank the door open then, managing to wait for what was coming next.

There was a loud bang that we knew was the door to the bedroom being kicked open, the sound of feet running across the floor...a heartbeat later, the sound of someone bellowing in frustration, and I yanked the door open, except, rather than rush out headlong, I held my blade up and out in front of me, just in the event that somehow a Praetorian had managed to move outside Alex's apartment without me hearing it. They had not, so I felt a bit foolish rushing out blindly waving my *gladius* in front of me, but from this moment, things happened so quickly, it is still difficult for me to put them in order, even after we talked about it later. The first thing I saw was a dark shape standing in the front doorway, but it was what he did that created the havoc.

"*AMBUSH! AMBUSH!*" This was followed an instant later by him shouting, "*RUN!*"

This man's attempt to warn his comrades cost him his life, because even as he was shouting this, I was racing across the seven or eight paces, my blade now pulled back in a first position. Whether he saw the glint of the blade or he just assumed that this would be what I would be coming with, a low thrust, he did get his own *gladius* up and across his body, prepared to swing his arm down and to his right in the classic block of a first position thrust when all you have is a *gladius*, but he was too slow. Oh, his blade struck mine, but a third of it was already buried in his gut, which meant he only made his death more agonizing by striking my blade, and the smell of *cac* filled the air around us, although it was his shrill scream that was actually a bigger problem, and I remember feeling a brief pang of...something at this man sacrificing himself for his comrades. This did not keep me from finishing my job of twisting the blade, and with my left hand, I shoved him with brutal force back out into the street. While I did not see him fall, I heard it, but I was already pivoting to see that, as we planned, Asprenas and Sabinus were standing at the bottom of the stairs, their blades out and ready, and since our eyes were adjusted to the darkness, I could see that there were three men huddled together on the small landing at the top. Is that all of them? I wondered, but from a completely unexpected direction, there was a shout, and while it took a fraction of a heartbeat as I turned my attention, I realized it was Crito.

"Centurion Pullus! Someone just jumped out the window on the second floor! I'm going after him!"

To Asprenas' eternal credit, he did not hesitate, shouting over his shoulder, "Go after him, Pullus! He can't get away!"

Which was a good thing, because I was already moving, sprinting down the street to the corner, turning it just in time to barely glimpse a figure dashing down the cross street. I did not hesitate, following behind as fast as my legs could work, but while my body was moving, my mind was just a half-step behind, so it took an eyeblink for it to register that, since I only saw one man running, it had to be Crito, and whoever he was pursuing was just out of visibility because of the placement of the torches that are only at each intersection. Lengthening my stride, I was actually thankful that this pursuit was more than just a matter of a hundred paces or less, because it takes me some time to build up my speed before my longer legs show their advantage, and I quickly closed on Crito. More importantly, as the street curved around, I glimpsed our quarry when I was perhaps about ten paces from catching Crito, who I could hear puffing, his arms pumping with his *gladius* in one hand, and despite everything that was going on, I found myself eyeing him as his instructor, thinking that he needed to hold his blade farther away from his body so that he did not break his rhythm and ended up slicing his leg open. We had passed two cross streets, but at the third, our quarry darted left to duck down this street, Crito following hard on his heels. When I rounded the corner, I was just in time to see the man, who I was close enough to see was wearing a hood like the men the night before, skid to a stop and spin about, his *gladius* up and in position. For a fraction of a heartbeat, I was certain that, because he was so close behind, Crito would essentially kill himself, but with admirable agility, he managed to somehow twist his body enough to avoid being impaled, although his momentum carried him past our foe. And just that quickly, the tables turned for our prey, because he now had Crito on one side, while I had enough time to slow to a stop just out of his reach where, for the first time, I became aware of the searing pain in my side caused by my lungs drawing in the air needed for a pursuit, which was of course compounded by my stitches, almost making me double over. It was the sound first, the clattering noise that metal makes when dropped on a hard surface like the paving stones of a street that sent the message that whoever this was apparently was capitulating. Before the gods, I swear that I tried to warn Crito who, having heard the same thing, moved back towards our quarry, thinking he was surrendering, but as if it was in slow motion, I saw the man spin about, and I caught the glint of metal in his hand as he thrust his *pugio* into Crito's chest. He did not cry out, but he did issue a breathy moan as his legs gave out from under him, half-falling and half-pushed backward by the man who had just killed him and who was already moving, resuming his attempt to escape.

I am afraid that I did not even give Crito a glance, although as I hopped over him, at the bottom of my vision I saw that his eyes were open and moving, watching me essentially ignore him as I opened my stride so that the pursued did not get more than twenty paces further before I was close enough to deal with him. I could have ended him, and in that moment I wanted to, but when I shoved my hand out, it was the left one, hitting him squarely in the back. As I intended, this sent him flying forward so quickly that he could not get his hands out in front of him, and as badly as I wanted to hurt him, I did wince as he smashed face first into the street then slid a couple of paces. Just as Crito had, I overran him, though only by a couple of steps, and I will credit him for his quick reaction because, as painful as it must have been to collide face first, his arms and legs immediately began scrabbling as he tried to get to his feet. He might have managed, except that my kick to his head sent him sprawling again and served to knock him temporarily senseless, thereby enabling me to stand over him and put a foot on his chest.

"You're less than a heartbeat away from death," I said, or panted, "so you need to stop squirming about or I might slip with this," I prodded the point into his chest, mainly to see if he was wearing a *hamata*, which he was.

His breathing was ragged, but he did not speak, and despite the darkness, I saw the dull glint of the *fibulae* that he had used to secure the hood to his tunic, which was over his armor. For a moment, I was unsure what to do next, so there was a silence that was only filled by the sound of us panting.

He broke the silence, and froze my blood when he asked, "How much do you want to let me go?"

Not long after this, I understood that I should not have been surprised, but in that moment, I could only gasp out his name.

"*Cethegus?*"

"I knew that we only had one chance at this with you." Even muffled by his hood, it was impossible to miss the bitterness in his voice. His head moved slightly, and I got the impression that he was trying to peer up at me through the eyeholes of his hood. "That was a good trick," he admitted. "The fake body in the bed. Although," he added, "the instant I thrust into it, I knew we had been fooled."

"Can you walk?" I asked, but rather than answer immediately, he just shrugged.

"What if I can't?"

"Then you die right here," I said coldly.

I was not prepared for him to actually chuckle at this.

"I highly doubt that you're going to kill me, Pullus."

"Why's that?" I snapped, which earned me another shrug.

"Because I'm worth nothing dead. And," despite his own circumstances, his voice hardened, "you're going to need something. Or," he amended, "*someone* to bargain with."

He was right, and he knew it, but I actually glanced back up the street at Crito, who had not moved and was still lying in the middle of the street, and that beast inside me stirred.

I removed my sword point from his body, but I placed it, not under his chin, but at his groin, and I knew that if I could hear the anger in my voice, he could as well.

"You just killed one of my men, Cethegus." I actually pressed down a bit, causing a yelp of pain. Suddenly, I had a thought. "Have you ever heard about what happens with we Pulluses when we're angry, I mean, truly enraged? What we're capable of doing?"

"N-no." His head shook wildly. "I haven't."

"You're lying," I said flatly, and I knew that he was just by his reaction. "As many stories as there are floating around the Legions, I know that you've heard about this..." I actually did try to think of the right word, "...madness that overtakes us sometimes. And do you know what makes it happen the most often?" Before he could say anything, I pressed down a bit more so that his moan became a sharp scream, which actually saved him because it startled me and made me aware that we were out in the middle of a street in Rome, but I still finished, "Losing one of the men under our command." Removing the blade from his cock, I ordered, "Now, get on your feet."

He did so, albeit carefully, then I pointed back towards Crito and motioned with my weapon for him to walk in that direction. Even in the darkness, I could see the pool of blood that meant, even if Crito was still breathing, he would not be much longer. I offered a prayer to the gods that he had already perished, but then I saw his eyes moving again as he looked up at us approaching. I was holding Cethegus by the collar, and I moved him past Crito before shoving him down to his knees so that I could attend to my fallen ranker, although I knew there was little that I could do for him. Kneeling, I saw the blood coming from his mouth, and I did not need any light to know that it would be frothy with tiny bubbles, the sign that at least one lung had been punctured.

"I...I...I'm sorry..." Crito tried to speak, but it was just a wheezy sound, and I reached down to grasp his hand, cutting him off by saying firmly, "You've nothing to apologize for, Crito, nothing at all." I looked away from him to where Cethegus was kneeling, raising my voice so that he would hear me. "It was just bad fortune that you were chasing a treacherous *cunnus* who's willing to cut down a comrade." Without thinking, I muttered, "Something like this would never happen in the Legions."

"P-Pilus Prior," Crito actually smiled, the blood covering his teeth and his mouth full of it, "the Praetorians aren't..."

Rather than let him continue, I said quietly, "I know, Crito. You told me, and I should have listened to everyone sooner."

"Will you make sure that I have the burial rites?"

"I will," I assured him. Then, feeling I owed him this much, I told him, "And, Crito, I would have been proud to have you as a man of the First of the Fourth Cohort of the 1st Legion."

He did not reply, I suppose because his mouth was too full of blood, but he did look up at me with an expression that informed me that he had heard me. Then he suddenly spasmed and took in one last gurgling breath before a long, slow rattling exhale that all men who deal with death have heard. I felt badly, because I did not want to just leave him there, but I had no choice, and I snatched the back of Cethegus' tunic, jerked him to his feet, then gave him a shove to get him moving.

Before we had gone a dozen paces, I saw Cethegus' hood moving, an indication he was looking at me, then he made the mistake of speaking. "I didn't want to kill that Praetorian, Pullus. I just didn't have any choice."

I cheerfully admit that it was counterproductive, but backhanding Cethegus and sending him reeling to collide with the wall of one of the buildings made me feel much better.

"Shut your fucking mouth," I snarled. Then I said, "And his name was Gregarius Crito." Realizing that this might be considered as an invitation for further interaction, I warned, "If you say another fucking word until we get back to the apartment, I'm going to cut two of your fingers off."

Since he did not utter another word, I think he believed me.

I approached the apartment cautiously, but I immediately noticed that the body of the Praetorian I had slain was no longer out in the street, although the dark pool of blood still shone in the faint light, and the door was closed. Shoving Cethegus face first against the wall next to the door, I used the pommel to knock, then I took a step back, preparing myself for anything. Fortuna smiled on me

334

when the door was opened immediately, by Sabinus, who stepped aside while I grabbed Cethegus and shoved him inside. Asprenas was standing over three men, two prone and one of them kneeling, his head hanging, with his hands bound behind him.

"Who's that?"

Asprenas and I asked the same question at the exact same time, each of us pointing to the other's prisoners, prompting a laugh from the both of us, but I insisted, "You go first."

"This," Asprenas gave the man a slight kick, the disgust easy to hear in his voice, "is one Gregarius Immunes Gnaeus Poplicola, Second Section of the Second Century of the First Cohort."

He looked over at me, and I gave him a grin. "I can beat that." However, rather than say anything, I grabbed a handful of Cethegus' hood, making sure to get some of his hair, and I gave a hard yank on it, ripping it from where it was pinned to his tunic, bringing with it a handful of hair along with the hood, evoking a howl of pain on the part of my prisoner. Only then did I say grandly, "May I present to you Primus Pilus Posterior Cethegus."

My reward was Asprenas' gasp of surprise, and since it was dark, the Tribune walked closer, where Cethegus was rubbing the back of his head as he glared at me, and when he pulled his hand away, I saw that it was wet, although I was not sure if it was because of the slap I had given him earlier or that I had yanked out some of his scalp along with his hair.

"*Salve*, Cethegus," Asprenas used the formal word, but there was no welcome in it. "I think we should have a talk."

Cethegus surprised me then, because he pointed to Poplicola.

"Only if you release Poplicola," he said without hesitation. "He was just following my orders."

He did not see the blow coming, mainly because I had not planned on doing it, but the flash of rage overcame me so quickly that I do not remember punching him in the face, albeit with my left hand, flattening his nose with enough force that I felt a spatter of blood hit my own, then I was standing over him, pointing my *gladius* at his throat.

"So was Crito, you *cunnus,* you...*mentula,*" I roared down at him. "And you killed him for doing his fucking duty! A fellow Praetorian!"

The words hung in the air, then Sabinus asked with obvious shock, "Crito is dead?"

I felt a pang of shame, both for the abrupt way that I had informed my Optio and because it was the first moment I thought of the ranker. Taking care to step back from Cethegus since I was still sorely tempted to end him right then, I turned to Sabinus.

"Yes, Optio," I said quietly. "But he helped me catch this *cunnus* before he died, and Cethegus tricked him by throwing down his *gladius* and pretending to surrender, then stabbed him with his *pugio*."

This reminded me of the more practical issue, and I told Sabinus where to find Crito, and that he was to bring the body back to the apartment.

He saluted me, but I did not return it, then he was gone, which was when it occurred to me to ask Asprenas, "How did he do?"

"He did well," Asprenas assured me, then answered the next question by pointing upstairs, and with a laugh, he said, "although I think you have a mess to clean up upstairs. There's another body up there, and that belongs to Sabinus."

My instinctive reaction was to curse at the thought of having to try and remove all traces that there had been a dead body before Bronwen and the baby returned, but I stifled it.

Instead, I indicated the two bodies next to Poplicola, who still had his hood on and had remained silent the entire time, asking, "Who did for them?"

I got my answer by the expression of pride on the Tribune's face, but he answered, "I did." Shrugging, he said, "It wasn't that much."

"Taking two men in a close fight like this is a rare feat, Tribune," I said honestly. Then, while some men of his class frown on it, I gave him a clap on the shoulder as I joked, "Maybe spending that time with my father helped, *neh*?"

He had been staring down at the two corpses when I did this, and he looked up at me sharply, with his eyes narrowed, prompting me to think he was indeed one of those touchy upper classmen, but he shocked me when he asked, "Are you a mind reader? I was just thinking about how I managed this, and I just remembered something your father told me during our trip about how to move so that you effectively put your immediate foe in the path of the second man. And," he continued, "how you only have one chance for it to work because they wouldn't be fooled again."

"He taught me the same thing," it was all I could think to say, but then the memory came back, and I said ruefully, "but he didn't tell me, he showed me. I had a fucking bruise on my chest for a week."

This made him laugh, then it was time to turn to more practical matters, and I began by pointing down to Poplicola. "What do we do with him?"

"Use him," Asprenas answered without hesitation, telling me that he had already thought about this. "He's going to be our messenger that we send to Cinna and tell him we have a valuable hostage."

For the first time, Cethegus reminded us of his presence; he had not gotten up off the floor, and there was a new nasal quality to his voice as he laughed without any humor.

"I might not be as valuable as you think," he said. Before speaking again, he brought himself up to a sitting position, one hand clutching his nose, and he asked, "Can I have a rag to stop the bleeding?"

Bending down, I used my *gladius* to cut a square of cloth from the tunic of one of the dead men, and I sensed Asprenas looking at me uncomfortably, but I tossed the Centurion the wad of cloth, which Cethegus immediately pressed against his face, making his words both nasal and muffled.

"Why do you say that?" Asprenas demanded, but Cethegus' initial response was a shrug.

It only took me taking a step towards him for him say hurriedly, "I failed with the task I was given. Cinna doesn't tolerate failure." He paused, then finished with obvious bitterness, "And neither does the Prefect."

"That may be true," I seemingly agreed, then pointed out, "but you also know the answers to what would be very...awkward questions that could be put to the Princeps." Thinking I was unclear, I added, "Awkward for the Prefect, I mean."

"Yes, I know what you mean."

To my ears, Cethegus sounded resigned, but when I glanced at Asprenas, he was frowning. When I started to ask him what was bothering him, he shook his head and said quietly, "Not here." Raising his voice, he continued, "First, we have to make sure that Cethegus here isn't going anywhere, and that he can't make any mischief."

Cethegus surprised me by giving a short laugh, and I learned why when he pointed to me and said, "If I tried to escape again, Pullus here will catch me, and this time, he'd kill me."

Asprenas was busy, unbuckling one of the dead men's *baltea*, then pulled it out from underneath the body and held it out for me, while I sliced through the leather to create a makeshift binding. Cethegus, seeing what was coming, actually extended his hands, wrists together, and this time, it was my turn to laugh.

"If you think that we're going to tie your arms in front of you, you're mad."

"It was worth a try," he said as he presented his arms behind him, which Asprenas bound while I watched since I had yet to sheathe my blade.

Grabbing his arm, Asprenas led Cethegus to Poplicola and the two corpses, but he shoved the Centurion down to the floor just far enough away that the two Praetorians would have to raise their voices just enough to be heard, then the Tribune beckoned me to step deeper into the atrium with him. Since he had lit one lamp, there was a bit of illumination now, but I noticed that he still turned his back to the Praetorians and kept his voice low.

"We have a decision to make," he began, but since I was not sure what he meant, I simply nodded at him to continue. "Once we send Poplicola back to Cinna, we can count on having less than a full watch left to live. If," he took a breath, "we stay here."

Instantly knowing that he was right, I felt like a fool for not seeing this immediately.

"So do we go to your house on the Palatine?" I asked, but he gave an adamant shake of his head.

"Not only is my family and yours in danger already, Pullus, that would put them in even greater danger. And," he pointed out, "it would give Sejanus the perfect pretext to destroy my family."

Again, it was difficult not to be irritated at this self-interest, while at the same time, I could not deny what he was saying was true.

"Do you have any other properties here in Rome?"

He shook his head.

"We have a few villas, but the nearest one is Alba Longa," he said in the same manner as one would order a cup of wine, with that thoughtless indifference that is so jarring on the ears of men of the lower classes. "There's not enough time, and there's too much chance of discovery. We need to find someplace where Sejanus would never think to look."

This was the moment the idea came to me, and when I explained it to Asprenas, his initial reaction was to gasp, "Are you *mad?*" But then, once the idea settled in a bit, he asked cautiously, "Do you think they would let you?"

"Yes," I answered with more confidence than I felt. "They wouldn't turn us away."

Before we could enact the plan, we had to wait for Sabinus, and he returned with Crito's body draped over his shoulder, huffing and puffing from the effort, but both because it was a mark of respect and I did not want his body anywhere near the corpses of the men who tried to kill me, I directed Sabinus to lay him in the middle of the atrium so that he could see the sky above him.

"I heard you did well," I commented, and I could see this pleased him. It was only in jest, although I kept a straight face as I said, "But you also made a mess in my apartment, Optio, and since you made it, you're going to have to clean it up before my woman sees and smells a body stinking up our rooms."

"I'll clean it up immediately, Pilus Posterior," he replied, but he turned so quickly to head to do that very thing, I could not grab his arm in time to stop him.

"Sabinus!" When he turned, I said, "Don't worry about it; I was joking. But at least drag the man out of the apartment."

While we waited for Sabinus to finish his grisly chore, Asprenas and I held a whispered council about the various possibilities that we might be facing in the near future. Our conversation was interrupted by both the sight and the sound of my Optio, holding the dead Praetorian by one heel as he dragged the corpse out onto the landing, then descended the stairs with the arms of the dead man flopping about as if he was wildly gesturing to us, although it was the sound his head made on each step that we would remember.

The sight led Asprenas to comment, "Good thing he's dead, or he'd have the worst headache in history tomorrow."

My laughter startled Sabinus to the point he paused on the steps, and his expression caused Asprenas to join me, while the Optio resumed his progress to deposit the body next to the other two. And, for the first time, Poplicola showed some emotion, although we heard it and did not see it because Asprenas had kept his hood on, the Praetorian giving a muffled sob.

"What's that about?" I muttered, but Asprenas only offered a shrug.

"We need to take his hood off before we let him loose anyway," I suggested, and when Asprenas nodded, I called to Sabinus.

The Optio was gentler than I had been, taking the time to unpin the hood and not snatching a handful of hair as he pulled it off. Even with the dim light, Poplicola blinked rapidly as his eyes adjusted to seeing through more than two eyeholes, but it was how he turned his head to look at the third body that was most instructive, because he began openly weeping.

"Who is that, Poplicola?" I asked, mostly out of idle curiosity.

At first, it appeared as if he would not answer, but then he said dully, "That's Sergeant Ahenobarbus of my section. We were..." his voice trailed off, but when he just finished with "...friends," the manner in which he said it caused Asprenas and me to exchange a glance, and I saw by his raised eyebrow our thoughts were running along the same lines.

Not that it mattered, and I ordered, "On your feet, Poplicola."

He obeyed, and I indicated to Sabinus to cut his bonds, which he did as Asprenas reminded him, "Now, what are you going to tell Pilus Prior Cinna?"

"That you have the Pilus Posterior alive," Poplicola answered. "And that you're proposing an exchange. In return for the Centurion, you require a sacred oath, stated in public in the Forum, that no harm will come to," he looked at the Tribune, "you and all of your family members, and," he turned to me, "the same for the Centurion."

Asprenas was satisfied, and I thought I was, but then what I had done with Flaccus and Crito crossed my mind.

Impulsively, I added, "And while we're waiting, the Pilus Prior and the Prefect need to know that we'll be...extracting information from Cethegus here that will be recorded, and that if any treachery occurs, we'll have these records in a safe place, and they *will* come to the attention of the Princeps."

For a moment, I was worried that Asprenas would ruin this because of the manner in which he opened his mouth, but then after the briefest of pauses, he nodded. "As Centurion Pullus says. That," he emphasized by poking Poplicola in the chest with his finger, "is probably the most important part of the message."

With this warning, we let Poplicola go. He hesitated at the door, casting a glance over his shoulder at his Sergeant, then slipped out into the night. We had mutually agreed that we would not leave immediately, on the off chance that Poplicola had sufficient iron in him to only pretend to hurry to the Palatine but stay behind to follow us. It was during this period that I remembered something, and I dashed upstairs, which was completely dark, requiring me to fumble around looking for what I wanted, which I finally found, despite the shutters hanging open to let the moonlight in. There was both something that I had to do and something that I needed, and once I was finished, I made sure to shutter the window that Cethegus had used to escape and drop the small locking bar into place, then hurried out of our bedroom. Between my haste and the darkness, I could very well have fallen on my ass when my foot slid across the floor, and while I could not see, I was sure that it was because I had slipped in a pool of blood. Despite the urgency, I admit that for a brief instant, I thought of lighting a lamp and cleaning up the mess so that Bronwen would not have to see it, but I did not. Once I was down, the four of us, with Sabinus holding Cethegus by the arm, left the apartment, pausing long enough for me to lock it. In that moment, I was struck by an odd thought that actually made me chuckle: What is the owner going to say about the mess we've made of this place?

"What's so funny?" Asprenas asked me as we began moving down the street in the direction of our destination.

"I think," I answered him, "that I'm going to owe the owners of that building a fair amount of money."

We were in a dangerous point in time, just before the earliest risers of the city began to leave their homes to those jobs that begin at dawn, and I believe Cethegus understood this, because twice we had to warn him about trying to delay us.

It finally took me asking him, "Do you really want me to punch you in your nose again?"

The first challenge was when we reached the Porta Carmentalis, but it was the wave of my *vitus* and my red Legionary tunic that earned us barely a glance from the pair of Urban Cohort men who had pulled the dead watch before dawn, while Sabinus had positioned himself so that they could not see one of our party was bound. Once out onto the Campus, we moved quickly, passing Marcellus' Theater, then Pompey's, but it was not until we were within sight of the pair of torches marking the Porta Praetoria that Cethegus understood.

"You're going to hide me in the Legion camp?" he gasped. Not surprisingly, I thought he was dismayed, but he actually chuckled. "That is brilliant, whichever one of you thought of this." When he added, "Although I'm going to be very interested to see how you enter the camp without knowing the challenge," I was thankful for the dark that he did not see me smile.

Once a man of any rank gains some experience, they learn that there is a pattern and order to everything done by the Roman army. Consequently, it becomes an ingrained habit for us, especially the

Centurions, to know upon which day it becomes the turn of our Legion to stand guard; as one might suspect, in a four Legion camp, it means that your Legion is going to be standing guard every fourth day. The only question is which Cohort, which is the standard for a peacetime camp guard shift, will be standing guard, and this was the only cause of any hesitance on my part. As much as I tried, I told myself that it was only essentially a one in three chance that the First, Second, or my own Fourth Cohort would be the ones standing guard, and while I was cordial with every other Pilus Prior, there were definitely men I preferred seeing over others. With the moment approaching, and just beyond where the men on guard duty could easily see us, we stopped.

"Wait here," I said as a command, without thinking, but if Asprenas took offense, he did not say anything. "I'm going to find out which Cohort is on guard duty."

"Which Cohort?" Cethegus interjected, and when I looked at him, I could see the kind of frown that told me he was not completely sure but had a suspicion. "Don't you mean which Legion?"

"No." I gave him a smile. "Today's the 1st's day for guard duty, so I just need to find out which Cohort is standing watch, and which Century is standing at the Porta Praetoria." I began walking away as I added cheerfully, "Maybe it will even be my own Fourth."

It was not, nor was it the Cohorts that I mentioned, but of the remaining Cohorts, I could not have been more blessed by Fortuna, because once I got close enough, and the Optio stepped into the gateway, I recognized him as the Optio of the First of the Fifth Cohort. Who, not surprisingly, was shocked to see me materialize out of the darkness, wearing my Legionary tunic and carrying my Legionary *vitus* as if I had just been out for a nighttime stroll.

"I don't know the challenge, Metellus," I called out, "but I'm guessing that you recognize me."

"Pilus...Centurion Pullus?" Metellus' expression showed a flash of chagrin, but I did not fault him for not knowing how to address me. "What brings you out to camp?"

"That," I replied pleasantly but firmly, "is none of your business, Metellus." His expression hardened, but I did not pause. "It's something I need to talk to Pilus Prior Clepsina about." He did not react immediately, and while I did not raise it, I did harden my voice. "Please send a runner to find Pilus Prior Clepsina. Tell him that it's me and that I need to see him immediately on a matter of great importance."

He did not particularly like it, but neither did he hesitate, snapping a salute that caused me to curse myself, although I managed to return it, and he snapped at one of the section on gate duty, who went at a brisk trot off into the night.

"So..." Metellus' tone was cautious, but I believe he was trying to be cordial, "how do you like the Praetorian Guard, Centurion?"

"Let's put it this way," I answered him wryly, "it's not the Legions."

"Is it true what I heard?" Metellus began, then explained, "About how the Praetorians have a different whore every night, and they get drunk every night?"

"That," I could not lie, "isn't far from the truth. Although," I held up a hand, but I was grinning as I said, "it's not *every* night. Just seven out of eight nights."

I had spoken loudly enough for the rankers standing a short distance away, and I was not a bit surprised that they were all openly envious, although judging by their grins, they were taking vicarious enjoyment.

I did not see who said it, but one of the men in the shadows called out, "Pilus Prior Pullus! If I apply for the Praetorians, would you put in a good word for me?"

We were all still laughing when I saw Clepsina emerging from the shadows, obviously surprised at seeing me, but he did not hesitate as he strode up to me, offering his arm.

"I didn't believe it," he said as he pumped my arm, while I tried not to wince at the pain it caused me. "I thought Metellus was setting me up for some sort of joke!"

"No joke," I assured him, then in a serious tone, I lowered my voice. "Can we talk?"

"Of course," he answered, then followed me when I walked a few paces away from the circle of light from the torches, so that by the time I stopped to face him, he asked soberly, "What is it, Pullus?

What's wrong?"

"I'm going to give you a choice," I told him honestly. "If you truly want to know what's happening, I'll tell you. But," I cautioned, "that will likely put you in a lot of danger." I paused, then said simply, "Or you can trust me that I know what I'm doing, and I'm doing it for the right reasons."

He did not reply immediately, and since his back was to the torches, his face was in shadow from his helmet, but I sensed that he was studying me.

I was completely unprepared for him to say, "You are your father's son, Gnaeus. And," his tone turned brisk, "that's enough for me. What do you need me to do?"

For a heartbeat, I was certain that my knees would collapse, yet somehow I managed to sound calm. "I'm bringing three men into the camp with me, all Praetorians." Suddenly, I remembered something, and I asked, "Do you remember Marcus Asprenas? The Tribune?"

"I do," Clepsina nodded, then aided my cause a great deal as he added, "and your father told me that he was one of the few Tribunes he'd met that was worth an amphora of piss."

"He's one of them," I told him.

"Pullus," Clepsina suddenly seemed hesitant, but it was not for the reason I thought, "are you in real danger here? Is there something we can do?"

It was difficult, but I maintained my composure, although I did reach out to clasp his shoulder, ignoring the pain it caused.

"Just let us into the camp. I need to talk to Marcus."

His response was a nod, and while he was confused, he followed me back towards the camp, but I stopped to stand directly under the torch and raised my *vitus*. Asprenas and Sabinus did not hesitate, materializing quickly from the darkness with Cethegus between them, and I braced myself for the Praetorian Centurion to try one last attempt to cause some form of mischief, but to my surprise, he said nothing. In fact, he did not seem willing to meet the eyes of the rankers, Metellus, or Clepsina, who watched with open curiosity. It was as we passed by Clepsina that I saw him glance down in the area of Cethegus' waist, yet despite clearly seeing that his hands were bound, he did not offer a comment.

Indeed, when I looked at him, he said with a heavy humor, "I don't want to know."

Then we were in the camp, and I led the others directly to the far side to the 1st's area next to the Tiber, going as much by smell as by sight. Reaching Macer's tent, I rapped on the wood hanging from the string. There was no stirring, and I had to knock again before I heard movement, then the flap was thrust aside and I saw, as I expected, Lucco, blinking rapidly from being roused from sleep.

"*Salve,* Lucco." I tried to sound as if it was a normal thing. "Can you tell Pilus Prior Macer that I'm here and would like to see him?"

I suppose it was more out of habit, because he only said, "Of course, Centurion Pullus." Realizing something, I reached out and grabbed his arm, "And could you tell him I have some...guests with me?"

"You're mad. It's the only explanation. Your time in Rome has rotted your brain."

This was most decidedly *not* what I wanted to hear from my best friend in the Legion and first Pilus Prior. We were alone in his private quarters, as the other three men were in the outer office, having been served wine by Lucco as they waited.

Nettled, I asked, "What would you suggest then, Marcus? We couldn't stay at my apartment. Asprenas is right, there's probably a full Century of handpicked men led by Cinna heading there right now."

Macer has a habit of rubbing the back of his neck, and he likes to pace back and forth behind his desk, but I also could see that I had made my point.

Finally, he heaved a sigh and asked, "How long do you think you'll be here in the camp?"

"We gave instructions to meet at noon in the Forum for their answer," I answered. It was with more hope than confidence that led me to say, "If all goes well, we'll be able to leave the camp immediately after that."

He considered this for a long moment, but I was not surprised when he shook his head as he pressed, "And if it doesn't? If this Cinna says no?"

"Then," I shrugged, "I have to go to Germanicus. He's the only man powerful enough to stop Sejanus."

"But that might put him on the opposite side of Tiberius," he argued, adding, "if the rumors are true that Tiberius trusts Sejanus more than any other man in Rome."

I had certainly heard the exact same thing, but in my mind was my short conversation with the Princeps, which was what prompted me to counter, "I don't think that's true. At least," I modified, "not yet. But there's no doubt it seems to be heading in that direction." Deciding to go a bit on the offensive, I challenged Macer, "What would *you* do if they turn this down?"

He did not like it, giving me an annoyed look, but he grudgingly replied, "Probably the same thing." This seemed to me to be his agreement to help us, which he confirmed when he asked, "What else do you need from me besides somewhere to hide?"

I had thought of this, but he was clearly unprepared for me to say, "I need to borrow Lucco for a bit." Naturally, Macer asked why, and I explained, "We're going to be asking Cethegus some questions that we need the answers to, and we're going to make Cethegus write them down himself, but I need Lucco to copy it because he's got such a quick hand."

I suppose that mention of Alex's friend caused Macer to remember, and he asked with obvious concern, "Where's Bronwen and the rest of them?"

"They're at Asprenas' home on the Palatine, and they're going to stay there until this is over," I explained.

"And you trust Asprenas?" Macer lowered his voice to just above a whisper. "You trust him not to sacrifice you and your family if that's the only way to save himself and *his* family?"

This had not even occurred to me, and just the suggestion made me angry, but I also knew that Macer was not only sincere in his concern, it was not without cause that he asked the question.

Regardless, I did not hesitate to say firmly, "Yes, I trust him, and no, I'm sure he won't betray me."

Whether this convinced Macer or not was impossible to say, but he replied immediately, "If you trust him, that's good enough for me." He hesitated, then said, "You know I'm going to have to speak to Sacrovir about this, don't you?"

I was certainly not happy about it, but this was not unexpected, so all I asked was, "Do you want me to go with you?"

"Yes." He nodded, and despite anticipating his answer, I could not stifle a groan, which caused Macer to grin at me. "What? You don't think the Primus Pilus will be happy to see you?"

My answer came in the form of grabbing my crotch, probably the most popular nonverbal responses under the standard.

I sighed and stood up. "Then let's get it over with."

Macer looked up at me with an expression close to horror, and he gasped, "I'm not going to go wake him up to tell him now! Have you forgotten how he is when anyone cuts his sleep short?"

The truth was that I had, albeit temporarily, but he was right, so I agreed to wait until the *bucina* call to rise.

"Do you have anything to eat?" I asked, which made him laugh.

"Why am I not surprised that you're thinking about your stomach even now?"

I was about to point out that I actually had not had anything substantial to eat for more than a day, but just thinking about it made it worse. Thankfully, he had a handful of hard cheeses and a hunk of bread that he handed me with a resigned expression.

"I was going to have that in the morning, but I know better than to keep you from food," he said sourly.

I was completely unrepentant, grinning at him as we walked back out into the outer office, and I explained what was happening.

Turning to Cethegus, I pointed to the second clerk's desk, and commanded, "Sit down. We've got some questions to ask, and you've got some writing to do."

Since it was Asprenas who knew what questions to ask, I contented myself with sitting and listening, trying to stay awake, but I was reduced to deliberately twisting my torso to make my side hurt more, which Macer noticed from where he was standing, leaning against the center pole.

His eyes narrowed, he walked over to me and asked accusingly, "Why are you doing that? What did you do this time?"

"It happened last night," I explained, then thought for a moment and amended, "Actually, I suppose it was night before last now, the first time they came for me."

"The first time!" Macer exclaimed, which was when I realized my mistake.

"Did I forget to mention that?"

"Yes, you did!" he shot back, then pointed down at my side. "And I can see that you're bandaged. So what happened?"

I told him of the events of that night, how Fortuna had smiled on me by having Bronwen and Titus fall asleep down in Alex's apartment and how we positively knew the identities of the two men who escaped because of the information Asprenas had gathered the day before when he went to the Palatine.

When I finished, his only comment was, "They were foolish enough to send only three men after you the first time?"

"Well," I chuckled at this, "they learned their lesson, but they weren't expecting me to learn mine too."

If he was going to reply, the *bucina* call to rise cut it off, and he straightened himself up, picked up his *vitus,* and headed for the tent flap.

"Let's get this over with." He grinned as he said it, no doubt making fun of me for saying the same thing earlier, and I followed him out, pausing only long enough to tell Asprenas and Sabinus that I would be back as soon as I could.

"We should have what we need by then," Asprenas assured me.

I caught up with Macer, and we moved among the men who had emerged from their tents, most of them heading for the latrines. Those men walking in the opposite direction only gave us a passing glance, a totally normal thing to do, but I was amused to see how many of them looked away, then their heads swiveled back towards us as their brain registered who was walking next to their Pilus Prior.

"You love being the center of attention," Macer grumbled, though with a smile, but I did not try to deny it.

My mouth started getting dry as it became light enough for me to see the Primus Pilus' tent, and we arrived just in time to see Menander leaving the tent to begin preparing Sacrovir's morning meal, meaning that it was his other clerk that answered our knock. I recognized him, of course, but could not recall his name, while he instantly recognized me, his jaw dropping, and Macer had to repeat himself that he was requesting an audience.

"Should...should I tell the Primus Pilus that Centurion Pullus is with you?" he asked, but I was somewhat surprised when Macer said, "Of course."

We were not left outside, nor did we have long to wait; we heard Sacrovir's oath, then he shoved through the partition in just his tunic, his gaze going immediately to me.

"Pullus?" He said my name, but he was looking at Macer, who replied, "I think we should speak in private, Primus Pilus. And," he added, "I think you'll understand why Pullus is here."

"That may be," Sacrovir surprised me, but then he pointed at my own tunic, "but why aren't you in Praetorian blue, Pullus?"

Since he was walking back into his quarters, I waited to explain the events of the previous three days until he dropped the flap. For the most part, Sacrovir listened, only interrupting a couple of times, but to ask a question that told me he was paying close attention.

Once I finished, I was completely unprepared for him to ask, "What do you need from the Legion, Pullus?"

"Just somewhere to stay until it's time to meet Cinna in the Forum," I answered.

"Done," he replied immediately, and I felt a lump form in my throat, but when I tried to thank him, Sacrovir stopped me, saying simply, "You're a man of the 1st, Pullus, you always will be. Besides," his weathered features twisted into a sneer, "I've heard more than enough about this Sejanus to know that he's a danger to not just Rome, but to Tiberius if he's allowed to go unchecked." He would get no argument from me, but it was what he said next that proved he was a man of surprises, and of a truly rare quality. He sat down, wearing a frown, which I only understood when he said, "But I'm not comfortable with the idea of just you and the Tribune going into the city and meeting in the Forum by yourselves."

"I've been thinking about that myself," Macer interjected. When Sacrovir looked to him, Macer went on, "Since we're about to leave in two days, the men aren't being allowed into the city until the duty day ends."

"Yes," Sacrovir said dryly, "I'm aware of that since I'm the one who gave the order."

This seemed odd to me, although I was aware that the last of the games and races for the Legions had been held the day before, but when I glanced at Macer, he obviously interpreted my look because he explained to me, "We've been fortunate so far without any major trouble, but the men have been getting...restless, and the Primus Pilus decided that he didn't want the boys getting started drinking early enough in the day that they were out of control by the time the sun went down." This made sense, but I stopped myself from saying as much, while Macer turned back to Sacrovir to explain, "But that rule does *not* apply to the officers, correct, Primus Pilus?"

"No," Sacrovir said slowly, though he was nodding as he spoke, "it does not." Obviously understanding, and most importantly accepting Macer's suggestion, the Primus Pilus addressed me, "Pullus, you and the Tribune are going to have an escort that accompanies you to the Forum." Addressing Macer, he asked, "What are you thinking, Marcus? Just Pili Priores?"

"I think," Macer shook his head, "that if we leave out the Fourth's Centurions, and the Optios, they won't be happy."

This was so far beyond what I had expected, I do not believe I could have said anything else if I wanted to, and I just listened as they discussed the matter a bit more.

Then Sacrovir turned back to me. "I'll handle this, Pullus. Just come back here when you and Asprenas are ready to leave, and we'll be ready as well."

There was one thing I felt it important to mention, reminding him, "You won't be able to carry your *gladii* past the *pomerium*, Primus Pilus."

"I know," Sacrovir nodded, his expression turning sober. "And, Pullus, this is more symbolic than anything. If Cinna and his men decide to take you into custody, we'll do everything in our power to convince him that that will be a bad idea, but we're not going to shed any blood." I understood this, although it was still disheartening, and I do not know if that showed in my expression, because he added grimly, "But if they try to harm you or the Tribune in some way, we're not going to just stand by and let it happen, even if we only have our *viti*."

With that, there was nothing more to say, and I left with Macer, but I remained silent on the way back to his tent, mainly because I had just had another idea.

"Do you have a toga?" I asked Macer, which understandably startled him.

"Well, yes," he said slowly, but then pointed out, "not one that would fit you, though."

"No," I shook my head, "I was thinking about Asprenas."

"Why would he need a toga?" Macer asked, a reasonable question.

"Because the Primus Pilus made me think of something," I answered. "Yes, you can't be armed inside the city. But the Tribune is a Praetorian, and so am I, and that rule doesn't apply to us."

We had reached Macer's tent, and before we walked in, I explained what I was thinking, to which he nodded and said, "That makes sense. So," he turned to reach for the flap, "yes, I'll lend him my toga."

I reached out and stopped him, because what I was about to ask for next was dangerous, not for him but for Lucco. Once I finished, I was worried that he would flatly refuse me even broaching it with the clerk.

Instead, he said curtly, "I'll leave it up to him, Gnaeus. If he says no, then that's it."

"That's fine," I assured him, then we entered.

"I'll do it," Lucco said without hesitation.

Judging from Macer's reaction, he had been expecting his clerk to decline, and to my irritation, he interjected, "Don't do this because you feel pressure from us, Lucco. This is going to be dangerous."

However, while I was irritated, Lucco was clearly angered with his Centurion, but while there are many of us who would thrash a clerk for using the tone Lucco did, Marcus Macer is not one of them.

"Alexandros Pullus is my best friend, Pilus Prior," Lucco shot back. "He's risked his life for me before, and this is my opportunity to repay the debt I owe him." He pointedly turned away from Macer, who looked both surprised and a bit abashed, to say to me, "I'll need a map, Centurion."

I immediately complied, drawing it in a tablet and starting from a landmark that Lucco knew, but while it meant a bit of a longer route than the direct one that I was about to sketch, I decided this was better.

I took the key from around my neck to hand him with the tablet, explaining as I did, "This key fits both the front and the back entrance. The back way is probably the best, but only after you watch for a bit and see if there are Praetorians there, and if there are, how many of them and where they're positioned. And," I raised a finger and admonished, "if it looks like there's the slightest possibility you might be caught, turn around and come back. This is important, but it's not worth your life, do you understand me, Lucco?"

He was obviously unimpressed judging from the grin he gave me as he assured us, "Centurion, I can promise I've gotten into tighter spots than your apartment."

Macer had been silently witnessing this, but he looked slightly worried, and he asked Lucco, "Do I want to know about these 'tighter spots,' Lucco?"

"Probably not," the clerk answered cheerfully, and he did not linger, leaving us both to stare at each other until Macer broke the silence.

"I'm sorry that I asked."

Once more, there was nothing to do except wait, but while I briefly considered walking over to the Fourth's area, I decided not to risk being seen. Instead, I sat and listened to the horn calls that signaled the next part of the official day of an army in camp. The main calls come from the *praetorium*, beginning with the signal to start the day, then the call for the Legions to have their own formations; after that, it is the Legion *Cornicen* who tells the men of that Legion what is happening, and it was soon after the formation call that Paterculus, the Legion *Cornicen,* sounded the signal for all officers, both Centurions and Optios, to attend to the Primus Pilus.

"I better make an appearance," Macer commented, picking up his *vitus*, and while he tried to sound casual, I knew him well enough to hear the tension there.

Once he left the tent, I beckoned Asprenas to follow me into Macer's private quarters, where I pointed to the toga Macer had pulled out.

"You're a bit bigger than the Pilus Prior, but I think this should fit," I said, whereupon I learned I had made a faulty assumption, because Asprenas' reaction was a frown and shake of his head.

"Why would I want to wear a toga to the Forum instead of my armor?"

"Because even if you wear your armor, if they see you're armed, that will be a problem, Tribune," I reminded him. "This way, you can be armed without anyone knowing it."

Thankfully, he understood immediately, looking a bit chagrined, and quickly unstrapped his *baltea* then picked up the toga, examining it for a moment before he shook his head.

"It's not going to be big enough for me to wear my armor underneath." He was clearly disappointed, but I saw that he was right.

"It won't fit over your cuirass," I agreed, "but let's see if you wear a *hamata* like mine if it will work." I went to Macer's stand and picked it up, but we quickly learned that, as loose as the toga is, because of their size difference, it would be obvious Asprenas was wearing armor because the toga was tighter than normal. Shedding the armor, he draped the toga as I returned the armor, but now he complained, "There's no slit in this so that I can get to my *gladius*."

I did my best to hide my impatience, and I offered a silent apology as I used my *pugio* to slice through the wool at the spot where it would allow Asprenas to reach into his, or Macer's, toga.

"There," I said. "Problem solved."

"I'll tell Macer that I'll pay for it," Asprenas assured me, his tone a bit stiff, making me think I may have wounded his pride a bit.

More to soothe any tensions than anything, I said, "Marcus won't mind. I doubt he's worn that thing more than once in his life anyway."

I was later informed by Macer that I was wrong, but it was because I had long before forgotten that Marcus Macer was an Equestrian and a paid man like me. My friend was not gone long, returning to the tent to inform us that we would be assembling in the forum of the camp.

"The Primus Pilus told everyone that this was voluntary, and that there might be trouble, so we'll see who shows up."

"Did you talk to Licinius?" I asked, and when he nodded, I asked somewhat anxiously, "And is he coming?"

"You should know better than to ask, Gnaeus," Macer said scornfully. "Of course he's coming, and so is every one of the others."

I did realize as soon as I said it that it was a shameful thing to verbalize, the idea that my comrade Licinius would not be there, but my only defense is that there is still a vestige of the Gnaeus Volusenus who showed up to this Legion as an arrogant ass who was roundly hated by his men, and it was only because of this Centurion standing before me and my father, with Macer showing a patience I did not deserve and my father teaching me what it means to wear the transverse crest that I am who I am today. We had loosened Cethegus' bindings, and he had asked for and received a cup of wine, but otherwise, he seemed to be in a bit of a daze, or perhaps he was just disinterested because he had decided that his fate would be up to the gods. I had been surprised how forthcoming he had been, especially since Asprenas had known what questions to ask, but while he had been reluctant in the beginning, I got the sense after a bit that we would have trouble shutting him up. In fact, I had the nagging sense that in some way Cethegus was unburdening his soul, as if he had been holding secrets inside himself that had steadily worn him down. Now he was sprawled on the dirt floor, staring up at the roof, seemingly oblivious to our conversation, but whereas Sabinus was similarly quiet, after a moment of observation, I thought I knew why. I asked Macer if I could use his private quarters, then called Sabinus to follow me into them. Without asking, I poured him a cup of wine, and did not water it, thrusting it at him in a manner that he correctly interpreted was not a request.

Rather than work up to it, I decided to broach the subject, asking him directly, "Is this about Crito?"

I think he tried to appear startled, but I was not fooled, although he did try weakly, "Is what about Crito?"

"Sabinus, we don't have much time before we go to the Forum, and you're going to be left alone with Cethegus. I need you to be alert and without your mind wandering because, honestly, I don't trust that bastard. He may look like he's resigned to his fate, but I don't believe that for a heartbeat, and neither should you. And," I finished, "something is clearly bothering you, and Crito and what happened to him is the most obvious cause."

It was slight, but I saw him nod before he admitted, "Yes, Pilus Posterior, it's about Crito. It should have been me going after Cethegus, not him."

"What makes you say that?" I was certain I knew, but I also knew that I needed him to articulate it.

"Because I've seen combat. Not," he allowed, "as much as you, of course, but Crito has only been in the Praetorians."

"You weren't as close to Cethegus as Crito was," I pointed out. "Remember, the bastard jumped out of the second-floor window, right above the back entrance, and that's where Crito was standing, just inside the building a few feet away."

"I know that," he said quietly, tapping his head, "up here, Pilus Posterior. But," he shook his head and touched his heart as he finished miserably, "that's not how I feel."

"Every time you lose a man under your command," I assured him, "you feel what you're feeling now. Is there something that you could have done? Why was it Crito? What if you had spent more time training him?" I ran through the questions I always ask myself. Thinking of something, I said firmly, "But that last part is *not* your fault in any way. It's because Prefect Sejanus doesn't want the Praetorians to be good at fighting. At least," I added, "not now." I saw by Sabinus' expression that I had entered dangerous territory, so I hurried on, "But that doesn't matter right now. I just wanted to tell you that what you're feeling is not only normal, but if you *didn't* feel that way, I'd be more concerned about whether you were qualified to be my Optio."

Sabinus sat there, saying nothing as he sipped from his cup with a thoughtful expression.

Finally, he asked, "Does it ever get easier?"

"Easier?" I shook my head, and I felt compelled to be honest with him. "It never gets easier. And this is as easy as it gets, I'm afraid."

"What?" He started, obviously alarmed, and I could not blame him. "You mean it can be harder than this?"

"Sabinus," I told him quietly, "you only lost one man today. But," I thought to add, "given that you're a Praetorian, it's not likely that you're going to have more than one man in your Century die in any given battle." Thinking I needed to lighten the mood, I grinned. "Unless you count getting drunk and breaking your neck falling down the stairs at a brothel battle."

He smiled briefly, but that was all, preferring to return to his study of the rest of the wine in his cup. Deciding that I had said my piece, I got up, patted him on the shoulder, and returned to the outer office. It was perhaps a sixth of a watch later when we heard running footsteps approaching the tent, then the flap was shoved aside and Lucco, panting as if Cerberus was on his heels, and carrying not just one of my togas, although he had to unwrap it to reveal what the other thing was.

"I wasn't sure, but I thought you'd need to carry this instead of the one you came with," he explained, and I could have kissed him because it was only after he had left and it was too late to go after him did I remember that I had carried my Legionary *vitus* to the camp.

"Were there Praetorians there?" Macer asked.

"No," Lucco shook his head, which surprised the both of us, but he cleared it up when he added, "but they had been there." He looked at me a little uneasily. "And, Centurion, they made a mess."

"A mess? What kind of mess?"

When he said this, my immediate thought was that they had destroyed anything breakable or valuable, but thankfully, Lucco said, "They searched your apartment and pulled all of your and your wife's clothing out and threw it on the floor, and they turned over the table and they broke a couple of chairs."

Another thought struck me, and I asked him about the presence of bodies, but he said he had seen no sign of them.

"Lucco," I said sincerely and mischievously, "whatever Macer is paying you, it's not enough. You need a pay raise."

"You don't even know what I pay him," Macer said indignantly.

"Not enough." I grinned, but I was already donning the toga, adjusting it carefully so that the hidden slit was exactly where I wanted it, which was when I remembered something. "Oh, Marcus?" He looked at me, but with a peevish expression, so I shook my head, thinking I would tell him I had ruined his toga later. "Never mind, it's not important."

Macer stepped outside to look at the sun, but while it was cloudy, he said it was time to go to the forum. This time, Asprenas ordered that Cethegus' feet be bound. Cethegus protested, but to no avail, although he was allowed to sit up and lean against the wall of the tent.

"If he makes a fucking sound that makes you think he's trying to call for help," I instructed Sabinus, "you gag him."

Asprenas was holding the tablet that we were taking to the Forum, while I picked up my Praetorian *vitus*, which would get us through the Porta Carmentalis without any questions, although we did not think it likely to be needed in any case. I should not have been surprised that as soon as we stepped out of Macer's tent, I was immediately recognized, not only by the rankers of the Second, but by the Centurions and Optios who were heading to the camp forum to assemble, including Licinius, Saloninus, Gillo, Columella, and Mus, but most surprising was seeing Gemellus, Atartinus, and the other *Signiferi* of the Fourth.

When I asked Licinius, he just grinned and said with a shrug, "They said they were coming no matter what. Besides," he joked, "none of these misbegotten bastards have actually been to the Forum. The only sights they've seen in Rome is the Circus, the games, and the brothels."

As surprising as the presence of the *Signiferi* were, it was the scene at the Forum that caused my heart to stand still, because standing there were well more than just the hundred twenty officers of the 1st Legion. Standing with Sacrovir were the other three Primi Pili, so Asprenas and I approached them, but despite my concern, they all recognized the Tribune and rendered a salute to him, then I offered mine to them.

"I thought it was just the 1st that was coming," I said to Sacrovir; the dismissive wave he offered was completely unconvincing.

"I might have mentioned that one of ours was being threatened by the Praetorians," he replied casually.

"You know I don't like you, Pullus," Nerva growled, giving me what seemed to be a furious scowl but is actually his normal expression, "but you're a man of the Legions, and you've done your duty to Rome. She owes you more than this."

"I'm just coming along to watch," was how Neratius put it, but I thought I saw a gleam in his eye that might have been a sign that he was speaking in jest.

Before either Asprenas or I could say anything, Sacrovir spoke up loudly, "All right, enough of this gossip! We're not going to be looking like a fucking rabble when we go into the city." Turning to the other three, he said, "I'll leave you to sort your boys out, and I'll do the same."

Using his bone whistle to get everyone's attention, the Primus Pilus issued his instructions, which was nothing more than a rank of three men across, with the Centurions, Optios, and in the case of the Fourth and the Second Cohort, the *Signifer* of their First Century, reminding me that Macer's *Signifer* had come to the Second with him and had served my father. There was a brief squabble between the other three about who would follow the 1st, but when Sacrovir suggested that it be in numerical order, this was too reasonable for anyone to argue, especially since it satisfied Nerva anyway, and he was the one putting up the biggest fight.

"Are they always like this?" Asprenas whispered, which made me laugh, and when I assured him that they were, he muttered, "They're no different than Senators, always squabbling about who goes first, and who gets what."

"Pullus! Tribune! We're ready and waiting anytime you are," Sacrovir called out, and we exchanged a glance as if we were schoolboys caught out, but I indicated that, being Tribune, the command should be given by him.

"Detail!" He did not hesitate, and I think only I heard the tension there in his voice. "March!"

Not surprisingly, this unusual activity had drawn a crowd, the men lining the Via Praetoria and cheering us despite having no idea what was happening. Or, so I hoped.

I suppose it was naïve to think that this impromptu procession would not draw a great deal of attention, so that by the time we crossed the Campus and rounded Marcellus' Theater, it was hard for me to tell, but it looked like we had at least three hundred people following along, while children scampered up and down the sides of our small column, shouting questions about what we were doing and receiving all sorts of answers, none of them close to the actual truth. As we approached the gate, the section of Urban Cohort men saw us coming, and we could tell they were arguing with each other, then for a brief moment, it seemed as if one of them had worked up the courage to stand in the roadway to block us. This was the moment my Praetorian *vitus* worked its magic, because no sooner did I lift it than he quickly scrambled out of the way while offering a salute as he did so.

"They're saluting you, Tribune," I said out of the side of my mouth, mainly because I did not want to raise my right arm again if I did not have to, and Asprenas returned it.

"No they weren't," he muttered, "because I'm not wearing my Praetorian Tribune's toga. They were saluting you."

"Maybe," I suggested, "it's just your overwhelming command presence. They just knew that you were the ranking officer."

He tried to scowl at me, but it did not hold, and he laughed, getting into the spirit by offering a majestic nod.

"I have often been told that I have a....what was it? Overwhelming command presence?" he joked.

It was still cloudy, but it was also early Junius; nevertheless, I knew it was not the heat that was making me sweat. I did feel better when I glanced over at Asprenas and saw beads of sweat on his forehead. Approaching the Forum on the Vicus Iugarius, it is almost impossible to see past the Forum Julia because it is always crowded, so I was not sure that I actually saw what I thought I had seen until we were much closer.

Asprenas saw it at the same moment, and while he did not stop, he did falter, expressing my thoughts with his curse. "Pluto's cock. That's the standard of the First Cohort!"

Without thinking, I thrust my hand up in the air with my fist clenched, and I heard the officers behind us crash to a stop, although not with the kind of precision that any of us would have accepted from our men. I was turning towards them when Sacrovir came trotting up, and I recognized the questioning expression on his face, but rather than say anything, I simply pointed.

"Pluto's cock," he mumbled, and despite the moment, Asprenas and I grinned at his unconscious echo of the Tribune's sentiments. Tearing his eyes away, he looked at us and asked, "What do you think it means?"

"I think it means that that *cunnus* Cinna betrayed us," I spat out. "They plan on arresting us. Or," I had to swallow before I finished, "worse."

Asprenas, however, shook his head, saying confidently, "No he's not. He wants us to *think* that's what's happening. But," he lifted the tablet, "he's not going to do anything until he knows what's on this. And," he turned to look me in the eye, "I knew what questions to ask."

"That's good enough for me," I declared, and I was largely being honest, but I was also at a point where I just wanted all of this over, so without saying anything else, I resumed walking towards the Forum.

While I expected it, hearing the tromping footsteps of my comrades still following us made me feel better. The citizens who loitered in the Forum saw us coming, scrambling out of the way in a manner that indicated they knew that something potentially dangerous was happening, which made sense when I saw all six Centuries of the First Praetorian Cohort aligned with two Centuries apiece forming a three-sided box, with the open end in the direction from which we were coming. Most importantly, and unusually, they were all in their armor in a naked show of power, which explained the nervous demeanor of the people around us.

"They knew that we'd be coming from this way," Asprenas commented, but I was now more focused on the Rostra, spotting the blue crest of a Praetorian Pilus Prior.

"Cinna is in his armor," I commented, "not a toga."

"I see that," Asprenas snapped. Using his head, he indicated the Centuries. "But I'm more worried about them." Unexpectedly, he looked up at me with a grin. "I mean, you *can* take Cinna, can't you? I," he added, "can handle the rest of this bunch."

It was such an odd and incongruous thing to say that I burst out laughing, and while I know that it was not Asprenas' intention, judging by Cinna's expression, it startled him to see us laughing given what was happening.

"Officers of the 1st! Align by Century on your Primus Pilus!"

Honestly, I had forgotten Sacrovir and the others, and neither of us were expecting that, as if they had practiced it, the officers of the four Legions, starting with the 1st Legion on the left, aligned themselves so that, in effect, they formed the fourth side of the box, facing inward. They were only in their tunics, with the Centurions holding their *viti*, but judging from the expression of the Praetorian Pilus Prior and the other Centurion commanding the second of the Centuries directly opposite us, we were the ones who were armed and armored, and they were only in their tunics. Seeing this gave me a sudden burst of not just energy but confidence, and I glanced down at Asprenas.

"Ready, Tribune?"

Just from his expression, I was certain that he was of a like mind, taking strength from this show of support. I silently ceded command to him, and he signaled he understood with a curt nod.

"Come with me, Pilus Posterior," he said, then walked towards Cinna.

At our previous meeting, I had only given Cinna a casual glance, and at that time, he had looked like one expected of a Praetorian Centurion. Of average height for the Praetorians, he was broad across the shoulders, with features that might have been chiseled from marble and with what we call a proud Roman nose, tilted to just the degree that one expects of anyone wearing the transverse crest who ostensibly protects the Imperator. Now that I was examining him more intently, however, I saw that his eyes were a bit too close together, and I *had* noticed the first time that he actually had a weak chin for which he compensated by thrusting his jaw out when he was not speaking, the effect immediately ruined the moment he opened his mouth to speak. Despite this, I reminded myself that nobody who was trusted by Prefect Sejanus and held, in effect the post of Primus Pilus, even if that was not his official title, he was not to be underestimated, as we were about to learn the hard way. I do not fault Asprenas at all; the spot in front of the Rostra Cinna had chosen to stand meant that we could not see anyone if they were around the side because the ship beaks blocked our view.

It began when we came to a stop a couple of paces away, and when Cinna did not move, Asprenas said coldly, "I believe that it's customary for a subordinate to salute his superior upon greeting them, Pilus Prior Cinna."

Cinna did not answer, nor did he try; instead, in what can only be called a deliberate insult, he turned his head to look over his shoulder. Naturally, my gaze shifted, in time to see another man wearing the uniform of a Praetorian Tribune step from around the corner of the Rostra.

"Do forgive me, Asprenas," this new actor in our drama called out as he walked with what I thought was insulting slowness up to us. "I was running late, as usual." The smile he offered was aimed at Asprenas, but I did not need to know this Tribune to see the deadly, poisonous malice in the man's eyes. As if it had never been there, the smile vanished, his voice turning cold as he said, "And I believe that it is *required* for a junior Tribune to be the one who offers a salute when his *superior* is present."

"Galba," Asprenas' voice turned flat, but I thought I detected a tremor of concern in it, "I didn't realize that you were involved in this."

"I didn't realize it either," the now-identified Tribune, who I knew was in command of the First Praetorian Cohort, replied, sounding almost cheerful. "But then I noticed my Pilus Prior ordering the entire Cohort to turn out in a manner that Prefect Sejanus doesn't care for, so I decided I had to get involved. But," his tone hardened, "I'm still waiting for the two of you to acknowledge the presence of a superior officer."

I could almost hear Asprenas' teeth grinding, although I cannot say I was any happier about what I had to do, mainly because it hurt, but we both rendered our salute, which Galba did not seem disposed to return. Finally, heaving a theatrical sigh, he did so, but then he pointed beyond us.

"What are these men doing here?" he demanded. "Do these Centurions, and," he frowned as he squinted at my comrades, "what looks like Optios and even some *Signiferi* have permission to be in the city? Aren't the Legions marching in the next day or so?"

"They're here to support me, Tribune," I spoke without thinking.

"For what?" Galba asked, and if his surprise was feigned, he did a good job of it.

Instead of answering him, I pointed at Cinna.

"Ask the Pilus Prior," I answered. I should have kept my mouth shut, but the events of the preceding two days came back to me, which meant that I was the one who said, "Men under his command have tried to kill me, not once but twice."

And, just that quickly, we learned something important, because Galba did not show a flicker of surprise.

"That is...regrettable," if Galba tried to look remorseful, he did a horrible job of it, "but I have no idea what you're talking about."

Turning to Cinna, he asked pointedly, "Do you, Pilus Prior Cinna?"

"No idea, Tribune," Cinna answered crisply and without hesitation.

I felt my jaw drop, but before I could say anything, Asprenas nudged me with his elbow, which I managed to interpret correctly so that I let him do the talking.

"If that's the case," Asprenas replied evenly, "then why did you agree to meet with us, Cinna?" He pointed to the armed Praetorians. "And why did you bring them?"

"Because you're both traitors to Rome!" Cinna snapped. "I've been ordered by Prefect Sejanus to place you under arrest, the both of you!"

Asprenas acted is if he had not heard, extracting the tablet from a fold of his toga, then waved it in the air as he said, "I think you might actually be more interested in this than in arresting us, Cinna."

I was not watching Cinna at this moment, I was watching Galba, and I saw his eyes narrow, but it was his glance at Cinna that was most telling.

"What's that?" Galba demanded.

"Oh," Asprenas replied, his tone making him sound like he was discussing a wager on one of the chariot teams instead of bargaining for our lives, "nothing much. Just the answer to some...questions that I know have been plaguing our Imperator for some time."

"Let me see that!" Galba snapped, but before I could react, Asprenas actually handed him the tablet, and I had to bite my tongue, literally, thinking that he had gone mad; now I know that I should have had more faith in the Tribune.

Galba flipped it open, and I at least had the satisfaction of watching him go pale before, without a word, he thrust it at Cinna, who took it and, while his reaction was similar, he frowned in a manner that seemed separate from the actual information.

I learned why when he looked up and demanded from Asprenas, "Whose handwriting is this?"

Rather than answer Cinna directly, Asprenas turned to me and asked, "What was that clerk's name, Pullus? Do you recall?"

"Lucco," I answered, and while I was still a bit confused, I thought I knew what was happening, which was why I added helpfully, "He actually has a very good hand."

"That he does," Asprenas agreed enthusiastically. Turning back to Cinna and Galba, however, there was no sign of levity as he informed them, "That means that I not only have your Primus Pilus Posterior's statement in his own handwriting, but I have Cethegus himself."

"That doesn't mean..." Cinna began, but he got no further.

"Shut your mouth, Pilus Prior," Galba did not raise his voice, yet there was no mistaking this was a command. Addressing Asprenas, he asked curtly, "What is it that you want, Asprenas?"

This actually surprised Asprenas, but he addressed Cinna instead.

"You didn't tell him?" he demanded, and Cinna suddenly looked as if he had somewhere better to be.

"Tell me what?" Galba snapped.

Asprenas opened his mouth, but I beat him to it, and while it was with a great deal of weariness, I was being as honest as I could be.

"Tribune Galba, neither Tribune Asprenas nor I have any desire to cause trouble. For *anyone*," I emphasized. "We just want to be able to sleep without keeping one eye open because someone is coming to try and kill us." Turning my gaze away from Galba, I not only pinned Cinna with my eyes, I took a single step towards him, the beast suddenly and without any warning threatening to come bursting out of me as I looked him in the eye. "The first time you sent three men. I killed one of them outright. His name was Norbanus, yes?" He did not answer, but I was not done, "And if Vettus is still alive, he'll never be able to hold his cock again, let alone a *gladius,* which means you need to find a new *Tesserarius.*" I was pleased to see that, while Cinna was angry, he was also worried, so I hammered on, "The second time you sent six, and we captured Cethegus and killed four more men." I did not have to try and make my tone as hard as I could make it, but while I did not like to do so, I did allow, "But I'm no fool. Sooner or later, you'll send enough men that I can't kill, I know that. But," it did not take an effort for me to sneer, "what about you? Are you going to lead them, Cinna? Do you think that you could survive a dozen heartbeats facing me? How many of your men do you think I'll kill before you finally kill me?"

"That's enough, Pullus," Asprenas said quietly, but with a tone that communicated it was an order, and the habit of obedience runs deeply. "I think you've made your point."

"What do you want?" Galba addressed his social equal, barely offering me a glance, which made me want to kill him, badly.

"We want a sacred oath, sworn by *you*," Asprenas surprised me since we had only discussed Cinna, "as the representative of the Prefect that both Pilus Posterior Pullus and I, along with every member of our family," I held my breath, "*and* those of us in our service and their family members, will not be harmed or molested in any way." Galba opened his mouth, but Asprenas held up a hand. "I'm not through," he said coldly. "Finally, there will be no adverse report made in either my record, or that of Pilus Posterior Pullus."

"In exchange for what?"

"In exchange for Pilus Posterior Cethegus, and the written answers he offered in his hand," Asprenas replied, but before Galba could reply, Asprenas addressed Cinna. "I suppose you understand why the fact that it's in Cethegus' own hand is important?"

I was baffled, but what mattered was that Cinna clearly understood, replying tersely, "Yes, Tribune. I understand."

"That's it?" Galba asked, and I had the sense that he was suspicious. "That's all that you want?"

Nevertheless, Asprenas nodded, assuring him, "That's all. Both Pullus and I are happy to continue serving in the Praetorian Guard, but as Pullus said, neither of us want to spend our time sleeping with one eye open and our awake time looking over our shoulder."

Speak for yourself, I thought sourly, but I said nothing; at this point, I was resigned to serving in the Praetorians as long as Germanicus wanted me there. Galba did not reply immediately, choosing instead to look from Asprenas to me, as the gods only know how many people were watching what was taking place, most of them having no idea what was happening, but being Romans, sensing that there was something interesting and perhaps important taking place.

It was his shrug that sent the preliminary signal of his response; aloud, he said, "I accept those terms."

Cinna pivoted on his heel to stare at the Tribune, looking at Galba as if he had lost his wits, but his tone was respectful enough as he asked, "Tribune Galba, may we speak about this in private for a moment?"

"I don't see why," Galba sniffed. "I'm in command, after all."

If it had been under different circumstances, I might have had some sympathy for Cinna, understanding the frustration that comes from professionals when dealing with men who, by a quirk of the gods, are their nominal superiors...but I did not.

"Please, Tribune," Cinna began, but this irritated Galba enough for him to snap, "Enough, Pilus Prior Cinna!" Turning to us, he asked, "You say I need to swear a sacred oath, but what guarantees do I have that if I give it, you will honor your own word?"

Before Asprenas could say anything, I turned around and raised my arm, and by doing so, I caught the attention of Sacrovir. When I beckoned to him, he did not hesitate, striding up to us, while I turned back to Galba.

"May I assume that you at least know who the Primus Pilus of the 1st Legion is?" The words were polite, but my tone was not, earning me a warning glare from Asprenas.

Galba did not like it either, but he answered, "Yes, I know who Primus Pilus Sacrovir is."

"So will you accept his assurance that we'll abide by our terms of this agreement?" I asked Galba.

This made him look uneasy, but Sacrovir, hearing what I had said, spoke up, "Wait a moment, Pullus. I think I can do better than that."

He spun about, and while he did not trot, he walked quickly back to where the assembled officers were standing.

"What's he doing?" Asprenas murmured, and I told him, "I think he's going to bring at least the Pili Priores of the 1st to stand with him."

I was wrong, which I learned when Sacrovir walked down the line of the officers of the 1st to stop where Nerva was standing, and they exchanged a few words, but Nerva nodded, then joined Sacrovir as he continued down the formation, which was when I understood.

"He's getting the Primi Pili." I took advantage of the fact that I had to turn away from Galba and Cinna to tell this to Asprenas, and his expression matched how I felt.

Very soon, the four senior Centurions of the Legions returned to us, and when I looked over at Cinna, I could see the defeat written on his face. What was more interesting, and telling, was that Galba looked unhappy, and I wondered if he had had time to think things through and was beginning to have doubts about his agreement. Seeing what Sacrovir was doing had made me feel confident that this would be soon coming to an end, but now I was the one beset by misgivings, and I could not tear my eyes from Galba.

I did not realize I had been holding my breath until Galba, assuming the pose that Romans use when making a sacred oath, began to speak, and I will give him credit that he did not falter, doing so loudly and clearly.

"I, Gaius Sulpicius Galba, Senior Tribune and commander of the First Cohort of the Praetorian Guard, take this sacred oath, swearing on the Black Stone of Jupiter Optimus Maximus, and on the honor of my illustrious ancestors, that if Tribune Asprenas and Secundus Pilus Posterior Pullus abide by the terms of our agreement, neither the lives of themselves or their families will be harmed in any way." He stopped and started to lower his arms, but whether it was Asprenas' glare or mine, he resumed in a tighter voice, "I also affirm that there will be no repercussions, or any adverse report that might damage their careers and fortunes." I nodded, and so did Asprenas, whereupon Galba finished, "I offer this vow on behalf of Praetorian Prefect Sejanus, commander of the Praetorian Guard!" He did drop his arms then, and addressed Asprenas. "I hope that was satisfactory, Asprenas?"

Before he answered, Asprenas actually glanced up at me, and taking my nod, turned back to Galba to say, "It was satisfactory, Tribune Galba."

Cinna spoke next, and we could clearly hear his displeasure as he demanded, "So, where is Cethegus and that tablet?"

"They're back in camp," Asprenas assured him. Then he turned and made a sweeping gesture in the general direction of the Campus. "If you will come with us, we can conclude this agreement."

Neither Galba nor Cinna were actually allowed to enter the camp boundaries, which irritated Galba and enraged Cinna who, according to the men on guard, spent the time pacing back and forth cursing us, presumably at the insult done to him by lowly Legionaries. When we returned to Macer's tent, Cethegus was not only still bound hand and foot, but he had a rag in his mouth as he sat there, glaring up at me, which I suppose was understandable given my broad grin at the sight.

Sabinus looked uncomfortable, but when I asked him what happened, he said with a shrug, "He wouldn't shut his mouth, Pilus Posterior. I just got tired of hearing him talk."

"I'm just glad that you didn't kill him." I laughed, but Sabinus did not even smile, giving me a direct look.

"I thought about it," he said quietly. His expression altered slightly, looking more troubled as he admitted, "I really wanted to, Pilus Posterior. He," his eyes started glimmering, "murdered Crito."

Cethegus began making emphatic noises through his gag, so I walked over and yanked it out of his mouth, triggering a coughing fit before he finally gasped out, "I tried to tell this ignorant *cunnus* that I was doing the same thing he was, following orders! That's all! I didn't want to kill Gregarius Crito!"

Rather than address Cethegus, I turned back to Sabinus.

"I can see why you'd want to kill him if he was trying to sell you that bag of *cac*." Thinking that I would brighten Sabinus up, I said, "But we're parting company with the Centurion now, and we're safe."

If he had punched me in the stomach, it would not have hurt more, although it was not his intent to do so.

"What about me, Centurion?" he asked, the anxiety written on his face. "Does that agreement include me?"

My first instinct was to lie to him, but I could not do it, and a glance at Asprenas told me that he was similarly affected, looking stricken and, frankly, ashamed, although if he was as ashamed as I was, I never asked.

"I...I'm sorry, Sabinus," I finally managed, then knowing how lame it sounded, offered, "I suppose in all the excitement of the moment, we forgot about making sure that you were included."

It would have been better if Sabinus reacted angrily, because that I completely understood, but if anything, his look of sadness and disappointment felt like a blade through my vitals.

"Nothing will happen to Optio Sabinus. I'll make sure of it."

All of us spun about from our respective spots to stare at Cethegus, who was rubbing his wrists, wearing an expression that I could not decipher.

"Why should Optio Sabinus believe you, Cethegus?"

This came from Asprenas, who was regarding the Praetorian coldly, his arms crossed, but to his credit, Cethegus did not flinch, nor did he falter, although I do not think any of us expected him to say quietly, "Because I owe him that much, Tribune. I meant it when I said that I was just following the orders given to me by a superior officer. But," he pointed at Sabinus, "so was he." He hesitated for a moment, then added, "And he was obeying orders for the right reasons, to help protect a fellow Praetorian."

I certainly had no reason to trust, or to believe Cethegus, yet I did, and when I glanced over at Sabinus, I saw that he did as well.

Breaking the silence, Sabinus said, "I appreciate your gesture, Centurion, but I can't forgive you for what you did."

"I don't expect you to, Sabinus," Cethegus assured him. "But I *am* being sincere. While I'm not certain about my fate right now, I can make sure that you don't suffer any consequences for doing what was the right thing."

I looked over at Asprenas, and I thought that he might object, judging by the way his mouth was open, but before I could interject, he gave an almost imperceptible shrug, closing it without saying anything.

371

"We don't want to keep Tribune Galba or Pilus Prior Cinna waiting," I suggested, ending the moment.

Sabinus walked to the Porta Praetoria with us, and now that it was fully daylight and the men were out and about doing whatever their Centurions had instructed them to do for the march, many of them hailed me, some of them joking about how I had become a patrician who only wore togas and things of that nature. All of which I enjoyed thoroughly, savoring the moment even as I wondered when I would be seeing any of these men again, if ever. When we got to the Porta Praetoria, at Asprenas' suggestion, I stayed back, so I could not hear what was said, but judging from the manner in which Cinna treated Cethegus, I did not think the man was long for this world.

"Should I go with them, Pilus Posterior?"

There was no mistaking the nervousness in his voice, but that was only partly the reason I shook my head and told him, "No, you're an Optio under my command, so you're going to stay with me for the time being."

I did not comment on his obvious relief. The three Praetorians turned and headed back to the city, while Asprenas returned to us. He had given Macer's toga back, which my friend took without examining it, and while I debated about telling him the damage I had done to it, in the moment, I decided it could wait.

"What now?" I asked Asprenas, although I had a very strong idea what I was going to be doing.

Asprenas actually had a better idea than mine, explaining, "I was thinking that I would go to my house and tell our families that they're safe, while you head back to your apartment so that you can straighten it up a bit before your wife and child come home." He grinned. "Remember, I'm a married man as well, Pullus. I know women like a tidy home. I'll escort them back to your apartment."

Even if I had opposed this, I probably would not have argued, and his idea did make more sense, so I agreed. Then, since he was back in uniform, I rendered him a salute, which he returned, then followed behind the Praetorians.

Macer had come with us, but when I asked him if he wanted to come with me, he said, "No, I've got things to do. Remember, we're leaving day after tomorrow."

"Will you have time to come for dinner tomorrow night?"

"I'll be there," he promised, then left Sabinus and me.

"Optio, when's the last time you used a broom?" Sabinus laughed, admitting that it had been some time, to which I replied, "I wouldn't want you forgetting how, so let's get to work. Besides," I reminded him, "you left a mess behind that needs to be cleaned up before my woman gets back, or our blood is going to be on the floor too."

All I can say is that we did our best, and at least we scrubbed out the bloodstain, the furniture had been set upright and most of the clothes strewn about put away, but when we heard the outer door open, I think that both Sabinus and I bore the same expression, which I would liken to a *Tirone* about to undergo his first inspection. A scuffle of footsteps climbing the stairs, then the door was flung open; there stood Bronwen, Titus on her hip, her eyes wide and her hair unbound, and I fell in love with her all over again. I did not have much time to savor the moment because, without so much as a glance at Sabinus, she ran across the room to fling herself into my arms, both of us temporarily forgetting everyone else, including poor Titus who ended up being squashed between us, although he instantly let us know that he did not appreciate it. It was not perfect, however, because when she threw her free arm around my side, I gave a yelp of pain, although it hurt her worse than me.

"I am *so* sorry, my love!" she gasped, but rather than say anything, I swept Titus up and, ignoring the pain and showing her I was fine, I lifted him high in the air, something that he loves even now when he is older, and his squeal of delight served as the perfect distraction.

Or so I believed, but it gave her an opportunity to survey the apartment, so that when I turned back to her, she was regarding me with a raised eyebrow, although she did not say anything.

"We weren't quite through," I mumbled, then I realized something, taking advantage of another distraction by turning to beckon Sabinus. "*Meum mel*," I gestured to him, "I would like to introduce you to my Optio, Publius Sabinus. Sabinus," I smiled down at her, "this is my woman, Bronwen of the Parisii, and this is my son, Titus."

"Lady," Sabinus surprised me greatly, because he did not behave with a trace of awkwardness, knowing to bow slightly and kiss Bronwen's hand, who had learned about what she considered a silly custom of Romans and had immediately extended her hand, "Pilus Posterior Pullus talks of your beauty, and I realize now that not only was he not exaggerating, he was being modest."

The sudden flushing of her face did not make me particularly happy, and it was only partially in jest when I growled, "I see I have to keep my eyes on my Optio now."

He looked at me uncertainly, searching my face for a sign that I was not being serious, and while I lifted one corner of my lip, judging from his expression, he got the message.

"So," Bronwen asked anxiously, "is it truly over, Gnaeus? Is what the Tribune told us true?"

"Yes," I assured her. "It's over. We don't have to worry anymore."

This appeased her, but only partially, and she pointed out, "But you still must serve in the Praetorians, yes? You must return to the barracks?"

"Yes," I admitted, not especially pleased to do so. "But at least I won't have to worry about you and the baby."

By this time, Alex and Algaia had come upstairs, and Alex reported that his apartment had not been molested for some reason. I debated about asking Sabinus to stay, but decided that the sooner he returned to the barracks the better; if I was going by the letter of the regulations, I should have gone with him, but I decided that it was worth the risk of running afoul of Creticus, although I provided a note that I would be reporting for duty in the morning as normal, which I handed to Sabinus to take, along with his own pass. I also had instructions for him, but for this, I walked out of the apartment with him.

"I want you to find out where Crito was taken," I explained. "If he hasn't been given his burial rites, then I'll make sure they're carried out tomorrow."

Once Sabinus was gone, there was still a period where our collective mood made for a tense atmosphere, until Algaia suggested to Bronwen that they work together to prepare the evening meal. As they worked, I felt myself slowly relax, and I saw that I was not alone, the other three adults also becoming easier, until before I knew it, the women were chattering away, while Iras was playing with baby Titus, leaving Alex and me sitting at the table to discuss matters.

"What next?"

It was not only a logical question, but it was really the only one, although all I could offer Alex was a shrug.

"Right this moment, I don't know," I said honestly. Understanding that I owed him more than that, I went on, "I think I'll have a much better idea in the morning when I report for duty." As soon as the words were out, I realized that I was the one who should be asking the question, which I did. "And what do *you* think, Alex?"

He did not answer immediately, seemingly more interested in turning his cup round and round as it sat on the table.

Finally, he began, "While I think that *this* is over, I also don't think it's over." Seeing my puzzled expression, he elaborated, "What I mean is that I think it's over for now, and that we're out of immediate danger. But, Gnaeus," he leaned forward so that he could lower his voice, "I talked to Asprenas' slaves while we were there." I had the sense that he heard the words out of his mouth, because he took a momentary detour. "I wanted to tell you that the Tribune, his family, and his slaves treated us with utmost courtesy and saw to our every need. And," he added, "I believe your judgment about Tribune Asprenas and his trustworthiness is sound. He's an honorable man, and a good one...for a patrician." He smiled as he said this. This made me feel better, but it did not last long once Alex returned to the original topic. "I don't have to tell you that if you want to know what's really going on, not just in a household, but even in a city as big as Rome, you talk to the people that men like Asprenas don't even notice." This was something that I had had to learn, since I was once one of those men who never noticed those who served me, nor did I give them more than a passing thought, and I nodded in recognition of this fact. Alex continued, "They are terrified of Sejanus because they believe he has eyes and ears everywhere. They're scared to even talk to their friends from other households when they meet in the market."

Although I knew that Sejanus was feared, the idea that it permeated down to the lowliest household slave baffled me, prompting me to ask, "Why is that?"

Alex lowered his voice even more as he explained, "There have been men of the upper orders who have...disappeared over the last few months, and the slaves are scared that they'll be blamed for saying something they shouldn't have about their master or mistress to someone from another household."

I cannot say that this was not perfectly understandable, given an ancient law dating back centuries that the only way the testimony of a slave is considered valid is if whatever information is extracted by torture.

Nevertheless, I was still not convinced, at least completely, which prompted me to ask, "But why do they think Sejanus is behind it?"

"Because every one of those men had some sort of connection to either Tiberius, Drusus, or Germanicus," he explained. "And while there are certainly men who would love to take advantage of a situation where Tiberius' hold on power was weakened somehow, none of them would be mad enough to risk the wrath of that entire family, no matter what the prize. So," he took a deep breath and exhaled, "after I thought about it, there's only one man in Rome I can think of who would be willing, and able, to carry out these things."

"So how do I fit in with any of this?" I asked, although I was now convinced that he was correct in his assessment.

His expression should have given me a hint that I would not like it, but I missed it.

"I think that Tribune Asprenas had it right. Coming after you wasn't political; it was about his pride and how he sees himself. It was a personal affront to him that someone like...you," he said vaguely, "could best him at anything. And," he finished, "the fact that your father publicly humiliated him just made it even more personal."

Sitting back up in a signal that he was finished, I absorbed his words along with the wine, which had suddenly taken on a bitter taste, because I believed now I fully understood what my friend was saying.

"Which is why you're saying that this might be over for now, but it's not over as far as Sejanus is concerned," I said this slowly as the thought fully formed.

What I got from Alex was a grim nod, and suddenly, I forgot how hungry I was, even as the cooking smells began drifting our way. Draining my cup, I poured another wine, thinking that perhaps I should just get drunk. That I did not was because, just as we were sitting down for our meal, there was a sharp rap on the door, and despite calming down, we all jumped at the noise to one degree or another, but I got to my feet, as did Alex.

"Who do you think it is?" he whispered, to which I answered with the first name that popped into my head.

"It's probably Sempronius." I tried to sound both confident and calm, but a glance at Bronwen told me I was fooling nobody.

Walking over to the door, instead of just placing my hand on Scrofa's *gladius*, I withdrew it from its sheath, slowly so that it did not make too much noise, before I opened the door with my left hand.

My first reaction was confusion, and it did not clear up, although I did manage to tell the others, "It's Lysander."

"May I come in, Centurion?" he asked politely, and this was when I noticed that he actually had a satchel slung over his shoulder. "I'm afraid that it's urgent, and you're my first stop, not my last."

I pulled the door open and stepped aside to let Germanicus' scribe enter, who was met by Alex before he got more than a couple more paces to the table.

"What is it, Lysander?" he beat me to asking. "Why are you here?"

Rather than answer directly, Lysander pointed to the table, saying quietly, "May I sit down? There's much to discuss and not much time."

Chapter 9

"What? *What?* This is real?"

Pointing to the seal that he had just broken, I assured Creticus, "Yes, Pilus Prior. It's very real, and it bears the seal of Germanicus, as you can see."

Creticus had been seated when I reported to him the next morning and handed him the scroll, then leapt to his feet in astonishment and, from what I saw, a bit of fear, before collapsing back into his chair.

He was still holding the scroll, which he waved feebly, and his tone sounded plaintive when he asked me, "But...why?"

Why, indeed? This was what had been running through my head most of the night after Lysander left our apartment, upending my life, although probably saving it in the process. By the time I had tossed and turned through the night, then Alex and I had walked to the barracks, I thought I had a good idea, but the question was how much of it to share with Creticus.

In something of a compromise with myself, I answered him quietly, "I think you know why, Pilus Prior. It's not...safe for me here in Rome." The words coming out of my mouth tasted bitter, and a part of me hated myself for what Gnaeus Volusenus would have seen as an act of cowardice in refusing to stand and fight, but Gnaeus Volusenianus Pullus is a veteran, and he is a father, although I still found myself adding what is ultimately the most important factor. "Nor is it safe for my family."

Somewhat surprisingly, Creticus did not disagree, and in fact, he gave a slow nod.

"You're right, Pullus. It's not safe for you. But this," he waved the scroll again, "is...unexpected."

This was such a monumental understatement that before I could stop myself, I began laughing, hard. I suppose something about my reaction must have been infectious, because within a couple of heartbeats, Creticus had joined in, and we shared a moment that, looking back, I know was as much about a way to release the tension of the previous days as it was from any real humor.

Waving me to sit down, Creticus' face was as red and his eyes were as shining as I suspect mine were, and he finally managed to gasp, "By the *gods*, I needed that, Pullus. I needed a reason to laugh." Once we subsided, Creticus wiped a tear away, and his expression turned sober as he regarded me for a long moment. Clearing his throat, he said with obvious awkwardness, "Pullus, I know that we've had our differences, and I know you don't think much of me, but I just want you to know that I hold you in high regard. And," he gave a wan smile, "you brought something to this Cohort that it's needed for some time. Something," he sighed, "I don't know how to give."

I knew that I was obligated to say something kind, and I had resigned myself to the idea that I would have to offer some platitude, yet to my utter surprise, I realized I was being honest when I said, "Pilus Prior, while I may not have always shown it, I do respect you. You are in a..." I searched for the right word, coming up with, "...delicate position. But I've seen that you have the best interest of your men at heart, and that you're doing the best possible job under impossible circumstances." I suddenly laughed as the thought hit me. "I used to think there was too much politics in the Legions, but I will *never* say that again."

I could see that he was pleased, and he did chuckle. Turning back to practical matters, his countenance turned grave, and I understood why when he began, "About Gregarius Crito, Pullus, I just want to say that I mourn his loss. And," his voice hardened, "more than that, I mourn the fact that it was at the hands of Pilus Posterior Cethegus." The mention of his name prompted me to open my mouth to ask about him, but Creticus was not done. "But as much as it shames me to tell you this, when Optio Sabinus came to me last night about securing Crito's remains and I sent a runner to the First Cohort, I got a message back from Pilus Prior Cinna that his body had been," his lips twisted into something that was a cross between a sneer and a grimace, "disposed of already and couldn't be recovered."

I experienced a sudden rumbling inside me, the beast stirring, which I shoved down ruthlessly, but I could still hear the anger in my voice as I asked, "And what about Cethegus? Is there any word about what will happen to him?"

"No," Creticus admitted, then he brightened a bit, "but in Cinna's message to me, there was a...commendation of sorts about your Optio."

"A commendation?" I did not understand, but Creticus was a Praetorian, so he did comprehend the arcane language that they share.

"That's Cinna's assurance that Sabinus has no reason to worry."

This was reassuring, but the thought of the Optio made me eager to begin what would be my last day in the Praetorian Guard.

Consequently, I asked, "May I be excused, Pilus Prior? I'd like to spend as much time with my Century as possible."

"Of course." He stood up, but when I began to render a salute, he thrust his arm out, which I naturally accepted. "I wasn't lying about what I said, Pullus," he said quietly.

"Neither was I," I assured him. "Under different circumstances, I think you'd find a home in the Legions, Pilus Prior."

I could see this pleased him, and I decided to leave it at that, hoping the gods would forgive me for my small lie, because I was, and am convinced that, while he was a good man, Marcus Silanus Creticus did not possess the qualities needed to wear the transverse crest in anything other than the Praetorians or Urban Cohorts.

"Germanicus can't protect you if you stay in Rome."

This was how Lysander opened the conversation the night before. Naturally, this made Bronwen, and Algaia, quite upset, and they began talking at once. Such was their agitation that they both lapsed into their original tongue, each of them glaring at their men, while I scowled at Lysander for his inartful way of opening a conversation.

Either he interpreted my look correctly, or he simply wanted to stop the noise, because he raised his voice to say, "That's why you're marching back to Ubiorum with the 1st." If his intention was to cease our chatter, it worked wonderfully, all of us staring at him as he sat there, sipping from his cup as if this was just a pause in normal conversation. It was the way one corner of his lip curled up that told me he was enjoying himself, but I was still trying to absorb the meaning of this. Seeing that he had our attention, he reached into his satchel to extract a scroll, "This is an order from the *Propraetor* Germanicus Julius Caesar, detaching you from your duty with the Praetorian Guard and returning you to the 1st Legion, effective immediately so that you can return with them to Ubiorum day after tomorrow."

My head was spinning, but I latched on to what I considered the most important part.

"So I'm returning as Quartus Pilus Prior? I'm going back to the Fourth?"

Lysander shook his head, sending my soaring heart plummeting back down, which seemed confirmed when he began, "No, Pullus, you're not returning to the Fourth." Seeing my expression, and probably fearing my wrath, he added hurriedly, "What I mean to say is that Germanicus is leaving it up to Primus Pilus Sacrovir where to place you in the 1st, that's all, Pullus."

It was not ideal, but I also knew I had no right to argue or complain, so setting that aside, I turned to the larger issue.

"You said that Germanicus can't protect me, Lysander." I shook my head. "I don't believe that Sejanus is more powerful than Germanicus."

"He's not," Lysander answered immediately in seeming agreement. He hesitated for a moment, and I got the sense he was having an internal debate, which was confirmed by him saying, "Since you're leaving day after tomorrow, I don't suppose it can do any harm. The reason Germanicus can't protect you is that he's not going to be in Rome either."

"*What?*" Alex exclaimed, but before I could say anything, he turned to ask Lysander excitedly, "Does that mean he's going to be coming back to the Rhenus with us?" He glanced over at me, but he was still addressing Lysander, and I felt a stab of guilt because I realized it was my fault that Alex asked, "Are we going to finish Arminius once and for all? *Finally?*"

"No." It was not Lysander who answered but me, since I

actually knew where Germanicus was going, although I had momentarily forgotten, and because he had sworn me to secrecy, it was one of the only times I had not confided in Alex. Before I went on, I glanced over at Lysander, and I assumed that Germanicus had told the clerk that he had spoken to me, because he gave a faint nod, and I explained, "The Princeps is sending him on a diplomatic mission to the East."

"The East?" Alex echoed, then guessed, "Where? Pontus?" I nodded, but he sensed there was more, guessing, "Syria?"

I nodded again, but rather than drag this out, I said, "And Parthia."

"*Parthia?*"

This time, Alex was joined by Algaia, while Bronwen looked more bemused than provoked, reminding me that she had still not learned everything about Rome's enemies and how they ranked in terms of our enmity towards each other, and what followed was a brief explanation on my part to Bronwen that I hoped partially explained the vehemence of Alex and Algaia's response, while I tried to ignore Alex's gaze and dreading the conversation I was sure was coming, although it never came.

Once we had settled down a bit, Lysander went on, "Since he won't be here in Rome, he doesn't feel comfortable leaving you here, since he was the one who asked you to come to Rome on his behalf."

Now, I do not recall being asked, but I was not about to say as much; besides, I was struck by something else that concerned me.

"What about Asprenas?" I asked, and while I did not need to, I still reminded him, "He was just as much a part of...whatever this was with Sejanus as I was."

"Which is why Tribune Asprenas is back on the *Propraetor*'s staff." Now Lysander did smile, I suppose because his master had thought of everything, or perhaps because it was Lysander who had. "He'll be accompanying Germanicus on his mission."

Naturally, it was Alex whose mind was on more than just our own immediate fates, and a sign that he is as devoted to Rome as any man in uniform under the standard.

"So who's going to be here to stop Sejanus?"

This made Lysander's smile evaporate as if it had never been there, although it was not because he was angry but clearly worried, and he admitted, "That's a good question, Alex, it truly is." He made a helpless gesture, "For some reason, the Princeps has begun entrusting him with more duties and responsibilities, but worst of all, it's clear that he trusts Sejanus far more than he should."

It should not be surprising that the next thought that crossed my mind was what Tiberius' reaction would be, albeit through Sempronius, which prompted me to ask Lysander that very thing.

"What about Tiberius? Do you know if he's aware of any of this?"

"Not directly, no," Lysander admitted, suddenly looking uncomfortable, making me wonder why. We learned the reason when he said, "But I met with Sempronius early this morning and told him of Germanicus' plans regarding you and the Tribune, and I met with him again just before I came here, and the Princeps has no objections to the decision."

I did not try and hide my relief, although it was not exactly what I wanted to hear; saying that Tiberius did not object was a bit vague, but I would settle for it.

"I thought you hated Sempronius," Alex commented, and now Lysander looked even more uncomfortable.

With obvious reluctance, he admitted, "Sempronius and I had a...falling out several years ago. But," he refused to look at any of us as he shrugged, "I suppose what they say about time healing all wounds is true." With that, he drained his cup and stood up, bowing in the direction of Bronwen and Algaia. "And with that, I'm afraid I must go. I still have to talk to Tribune Asprenas and inform him of his new orders."

Mention of Asprenas reminded me of where he was going and with whom, which prompted me to ask, "When is Germanicus leaving, Lysander?"

"The day after you begin your march back to the Rhenus," he informed us, then opened the door and left the apartment, leaving us still slightly stunned.

It was Alex who broke the silence with the understatement,

"We have a lot to do and not much time to do it."

"That is why I love you," Algaia said dryly. "You have such a way with words."

My last day with the Second Century of the Second Praetorian Cohort was partially spent at the stakes, mainly because I was too sore to spar, but I took the opportunity to speak to each of the men of my Century, most of whom I had barely gotten to know. Regardless, I came away with a strong sense that most of them were disappointed to see me leave, and perhaps Valerius summed up the reason why.

"We finally started being treated and trained like a Roman man should, Pilus Posterior," he told me as he waited his turn at their section's stake. "I know the boys complained about it, but that's a soldier's right given to us by Mars and Bellona, isn't it?" He grinned, and I returned it, since this is an oft repeated belief of men under the standard. The grin did not last, turning into a bitter grimace. "Now we have to worry about who's going to replace you and if he puts us back to polishing and buffing and standing around looking pretty."

Since I did not have the heart to tell him that I viewed this as an absolute certainty, and that whoever was selected, it would not be with Creticus' input and solely Sejanus' decision, I settled for giving him a pat on the shoulder as I moved along. Initially, I had thought I would be looking forward to spending a moment with Flaccus, but he was so clearly grief-stricken and remorseful, I lost the taste for what I had wanted to say, and do, to him.

Still, I did not expect to hear myself saying, "I know you and Crito were close, Flaccus, and I grieve with you over his loss. He was a good man."

Even more surprising was Flaccus' reply. "He was a better man than I'll ever be, Pilus Posterior." His eyes had been on the ground, but he chose to look me in the eye as he said quietly, "I know what you think of me, Centurion. And," his chin began quivering, "you're not wrong. I am a weak man, I know that. And," he sighed, "it's why my father purchased this posting for me in the Praetorians. He hoped that it would make me stronger and tougher." His expression transformed into an unconscious match to what I had seen with Valerius as he said bitterly, "My father is a good man, but he's also something of a fool for thinking that the Praetorians would teach me anything worth knowing."

Part of me hated myself for the sympathy I felt for Flaccus. After all, he had given *Tesserarius* Vettus the location of my apartment and had not only put my life in danger, but that of my woman and child. Despite this, if I have to describe how I felt as I listened and watched a man come face to face with their true character and realize that it is lacking in the characteristics that are expected in a Roman man, and one in the military at that, I was more sad than anything else. Could Vibius Flaccus have become a different man if he had been under a Legion standard rather than a Praetorian one? Only the gods know, but what *I* knew in that moment was that I had lost my taste for tormenting Flaccus, but neither could I bring myself to be very sympathetic.

"Flaccus, I don't know what the gods have in store for you any more than I know what they have in store for me, but I do know this," I said. "Only you have control over what kind of man you are, nobody else."

With that, I walked away from Flaccus, we concluded the training for the day, then I marched them back to the barracks. It was as we were marching that the idea came to me, one that I knew if I gave it more thought I would abandon, so that when we entered the barracks, I turned the Century over to Sabinus. I went to my quarters, and before I could talk myself out of it, I put on my *baltea* and donned my toga, my thought being that what I was doing was foolhardy enough and going unarmed could be suicidal. Slipping out of my quarters, I took the long way out of the barracks so that I did not have to pass by the Cohort office, and I set a quick pace through the streets towards my destination. As I had at the barracks, I chose to take the longer route up onto the Palatine so that I could approach Germanicus' house without passing by the *Domus Augusti*, although I knew that it was still possible to encounter trouble, either in the form of Pilus Prior Cinna, or even worse, Sejanus himself. As always, there were a pair of Praetorians in their tunics standing watch outside the entrance, but while I did not recognize them, their reaction at seeing me approach told me they knew exactly who I was, causing me to curse under my breath as I watched one of them turn his head to call over his shoulder.

An Optio that I did not recognize either emerged, and as tense as I was, I had to suppress a grin at the manner in which his eyes went wide, though he did snap to *intente* to salute, which I returned as I said, "I'm Secundus Pilus Posterior..."

"I know who you are, Pilus Posterior," he assured me, and while being cut off irritated me, I was determined to maintain my composure. His tone was polite enough as he asked, "Are you coming at the request of the *Propraetor*?"

"No," I had to admit, "he's not expecting me."

I suppose I should have felt grateful that he tried to look regretful as he informed me, "I'm sorry, Pilus Posterior, but we've been given orders that only those whose presence has been requested by the *Propraetor* be allowed inside," but it was the wording that caught my attention, and I did not hesitate.

"Who gave these orders, Optio?" I asked, trying to sound as if I was only mildly interested.

"Sir?" He shifted on his feet, looking uneasy. "I'm not sure I understand."

"Ah," I lied, "that's my fault, of course. I apologize for not putting it correctly. Did," I hardened my tone fractionally, "those orders come from the *Propraetor* or anyone on his staff?"

"Well, no," he answered uncomfortably, but I was not done.

"Did they come from the Princeps?"

"No, Pilus Posterior," he admitted, "they did not."

I had run out of patience at this point, so instead of answering, I gently moved the ranker standing in my path out of the way, and I was already between the Praetorians and the doorway when the Optio gave what sounded like a squawk of alarm, then he called out, "Pilus Posterior, I'm afraid I can't allow you to pass!" His tone turned pleading as I spun about to face him. "I have my orders! Surely you understand that!"

Rather than answer him directly and more to throw him off balance, I commented, "I thought you said you know who I am."

"I do," he assured me, and given where we were standing, I could see the two rankers standing behind him eyeing each other, and it was clear to see they were silently debating with each other how far they were willing to go to support their Optio, which made me smile, which made the Optio even more uneasy.

To keep him on the back foot, I seemingly switched subjects, asking, "What Century and Cohort are you with, Optio?"

"The Third of the Third," he answered automatically.

"Ah," I nodded, "I see." I paused, then asked, "Do you know many men in the First Cohort, by any chance?"

"Some of them," he answered cautiously, and I could see him trying to decipher where this was going. "Some I know personally, others I know by name."

"Like *Tesserarius* Vettus? And Gregarius Immunes Norbanus?"

Perhaps if I had lightly slapped him, he would have reacted more strongly, going pale with his mouth dropping open, but it was his men's reaction that was the most telling that conveyed to me they knew why I was bringing it up.

"I...I...knew *Tesserarius* Vettus," the Optio stammered, and his use of the past tense also informed me of his fate, "but not Norbanus, or Servilius."

Ah, that was the third man's name, I thought; aloud, I asked, "If they couldn't stop me, why do you think you could?"

I did not wait for him to answer, and while I listened, I did not hear any footsteps as I entered the courtyard and walked to the door into the house itself, the Optio following me inside into the vestibule.

"Pilus Posterior Pullus! I'm afraid I must insist..."

The Optio did not get any farther because a closed door on the left side of the house opened, but while nobody stepped out, I could see them peering through the opening.

I recognized him as one of Germanicus' clerks, except I did not know his name, and I called out to him, "Go find Lysander, and tell him that Centurion Pullus is here, and that it's an urgent matter."

He did not say anything, but he did close the door, and I turned to face the Optio, immediately noticing that he was alone, his men apparently deciding not to follow him into the house.

"You were saying?" I asked genially. "Something about you insisting that I do something?"

I did not bear this Optio any malice, and I did feel sympathetic about the position I had put him in, but not enough to feel guilty about it.

"Pilus Posterior, I'm just trying to follow the orders I was given," he said, looking thoroughly miserable.

Before I could commiserate with him, from behind me I heard the door opening, followed by a gasp of surprise.

"Pullus? What are you doing here?"

Turning to address Lysander, who looked almost as unhappy as the Optio, I told him, "I'm requesting an audience with the *Propraetor*, Lysander. There's something I need to see him about. It's something...urgent and important," I hoped that my tone would convey enough information that it would preclude me having to say it aloud in front of the Optio.

My hopes were dashed when Lysander shook his head.

"That's not enough information, Pullus. As you can imagine, he is *very* busy."

Recognizing that I had no choice, I still tried to veil my purpose by saying, "It concerns one of the men under my command...my current command."

At first, I was afraid that this was not enough, because Lysander looked more confused than anything else, but then I saw the change in his expression as his mind worked out what the subject of my visit was.

Nevertheless, he only said, "I'll go ask him, Pullus, but I can't promise anything."

He closed the door, leaving me and the Optio alone again, although this time, neither of us were disposed to talk. As we stood there, I realized that I stank; I had been at the stakes, then thrown on this toga and hurried across the city, and was now standing in a stuffy vestibule, which did not make me feel particularly worthy of an audience with Germanicus. It was probably no more than five hundred heartbeats when the door opened, and Lysander beckoned to me.

I tried to hide a triumphant smile from the Optio, but when I reached the door, Lysander said sharply, "This had better be for a good reason, Pullus. He's not in a good mood as it is, and he's got a lot of things that he has to do that talking to you takes his time away from."

When put that way, I could only say, "I believe that it is, Lysander, or I wouldn't be here."

My first thought when I saw him, as usual behind a desk, although this time he was standing and dressed in a tunic with the purple stripe, was, Has it really only been a week since his triumph? He was talking to one clerk while, without looking, he extended a hand to take a scroll another one was presenting him as I marched to stand in front of his desk.

He finished with the clerk just as I arrived, but when I began a salute, he stopped me with a wave, saying curtly, "I don't have time for that right now, Pullus." I cannot say that he was unfriendly, but there was a coolness in his demeanor that I had never been subjected to, which did not help my stomach any, nor did him asking, "Why are you here?"

As briefly as I could, I explained my purpose, and while it was not by much, I could see his features soften a bit, and when I finished, he said, "But I was informed by Lysander that he's not in any danger, that the Centurion..." His voice trailed off, and I supplied the name, which he acknowledged with a nod as he continued, "...Cethegus personally vouched for him and that he wouldn't be harmed."

"He did, sir," I agreed, but then brought up the real cause for my concern. "But I'm not particularly inclined to accept the word of a Praetorian, given all that's happened." His features hardened again, so I hurried on to add, "I do believe that Cethegus was sincere, sir. But," I shook my head, "I don't think Pilus Prior Cinna cares all that much about supporting Cethegus right now, given what Cethegus said when he was in our custody."

Germanicus did not reply immediately, although he gave a slight nod that could have meant almost anything.

Finally, he asked, "And have you spoken to your Optio about this?"

"No, sir," I told him, which seemed to surprise him, and he asked, "Why not?"

"Because I didn't want to offer him something without knowing if I had the permission to do so," I answered honestly.

I was completely unprepared for his reaction, which was to laugh, and for a brief moment, I saw the Germanicus that I had come to know, and I learned why when he said with obvious amusement, "I believe this is a first, a Pullus who actually asks permission beforehand and not just goes ahead and does it then hope the gods smile on him. Like," he pointed at me, but he was still smiling, "a certain Pilus Prior moving his Cohort without orders at the Battle of Idistaviso." This made me grin, but he was not through, and his expression altered slightly, "Or that Pilus Prior's father when he made Servius Metellus a Pilus Prior instead of the man I had chosen in the Legio Germanicus." His smile faded then, and I thought that perhaps this memory made him angry, but it was for an entirely different reason, as he added soberly, "And that man went on to sacrifice himself and his Century so that their bumbling boy Legate and the rest of the men inside Raetinium didn't burn to death." He lapsed into silence, and I noticed that the men around us had also momentarily paused, I suppose because they were aware that their master's mood had altered in some way, and they were watching for a sign of some sort that might indicate what it was. Germanicus was staring down at his desk, the smile replaced with a frown, and while I believe he was talking to himself, I heard him say in a near whisper, "I made *so* many mistakes on that campaign." Lifting his gaze up, he glanced at me, but his eyes roamed the room, and I learned why when he called out, "Lysander, I want you to draft up an order that transfers Optio Sabinus from the Second of the Second Praetorian Cohort to the 1st Legion for my signature." I thought he was finished, so I began to speak, but he anticipated what I was going to ask, adding, "And that he is *not* guaranteed to remain in the Optionate, and that it will be entirely up to Primus Pilus Sacrovir."

"Thank you, sir," I said sincerely, but he only answered with another wave and pointedly turned back to one of his clerks, resuming their conversation, leaving me to stand there.

It did not take long for Lysander to do as he was ordered, using a fresh sheet of vellum that he brought to Germanicus' desk, who barely glanced at what it said before he signed it, then handed it back to Lysander to finish putting on the spool, then sealed it with fresh blob of wax before pressing Germanicus' signet into it. However, contrary to my belief, Germanicus was not done with me, not completely.

When Lysander came to me and handed me the scroll, Germanicus instructed me, "Pullus, in the event that Optio Sabinus decides to stay in the Praetorian Guard, you are to burn this order and never speak of its existence, is that clear?"

"Yes, sir," I assured him, and this time when I saluted, he returned it. I had every intention of executing an about turn, but before I could, I blurted out, "I'm going to make an offering to Fortuna for your safe voyage and success of your mission, *Propraetor.*" I thought I was finished, but then I added, "And I'm sorry I was unable to help you with..." I did not finish, not only because I did not want to say "Sejanus," but I saw by his expression he understood, and he proved it by saying, "No apology is necessary, Pullus. Believe it or not, you confirmed several things that I suspected, and that wouldn't have happened without you. And," he finished, "I'll offer the same prayer for you and your family as well. Besides," he grinned suddenly, "on the way back to Ubiorum, you can spoil Latobius again."

I have not seen Germanicus since, and only the gods know if I will ever see him again, so I think it is appropriate that, if we do never meet again, being teased about my love for my father's horse is not a bad last memory.

"I have to decide by tomorrow, don't I?"

"At the latest," I told Sabinus.

I had returned to the barracks and summoned him to my quarters with the offer to transfer into the 1ˢᵗ from the Praetorians which, while not unheard of, was certainly unusual since most rankers in the Legions yearn to be in the Praetorians, based in their belief that all they do is drink and whore and escape onerous duties...and they are right, for the most part. While I had not expected Sabinus to leap at the offer, there was a hesitance that I did not understand, but he offered a partial explanation.

"I worry about the men, Pilus Posterior," he said. Proving that he shared the same concerns I did, he went on, "We both know that whoever replaces you will be Sejanus' man. He couldn't do anything about your appointment, but he never makes the same mistake twice."

"I won't deny that it's a valid concern," I agreed, then pointed out, "but what kind of position does that put you in, Sabinus?"

"Not a good one," Sabinus admitted. Heaving a sigh, his tone turned wry. "But it's not just that. I'm afraid duty in the Praetorians has made me soft and fat."

Sabinus was not fat in any real sense, but I understood what he meant, and I adopted a cheerful tone as I reminded him, "We're going to have a nice, long march back to Ubiorum to work that all off, Optio!"

As I hoped, this made him laugh, but while I was hoping that he would commit right then, he stood and said, "I'll make my decision by tomorrow, Pilus Posterior."

I tried to hide my disappointment, and I reminded myself that this was a truly momentous decision Sabinus was making, so I contented myself with simply nodding and seeing him out. Alex had already packed up what few of his belongings he had brought to the office, and he helped me pack my things.

Suddenly, he pointed to the pile of togas and blue Praetorian tunics. "What are you going to do with those?"

It was a simple question, and understandable, but for some reason, it hit me harder than I expected.

"I'm taking them with me," I finally decided, "to remind me how much I never want to wear that *cac* again."

"I knew you'd say that," Alex grumbled, but he stuffed them into the chest.

I had thought of shedding the toga I was wearing, then decided against it so that I could wear my *gladius* and not have my hands as full. Nevertheless, we were both huffing and puffing from climbing the hill, with Alex balancing a small box on one shoulder, while holding the rope handle of my large chest on one side as I held the other on the opposite side.

"We should have used some slaves for this," he gasped.

I was only partly joking when I growled at him, "You're just thinking of this now?"

We were still bickering as we reached the apartment to find that we were not alone in our disagreement, as Bronwen and Algaia were quarreling in the atrium about something. However, when Alex and I inquired into the cause, they were unanimous in their insistence that it was none of our business. I have no idea if they were aware of this, but both Alex and I were perfectly happy to obey our respective women; we also agreed to leave the baggage on the ground floor. Deciding that this was an opportune moment, both Alex and I excused ourselves and headed to the public bath three blocks from the apartment, while Alex brought along a fresh bandage and wrapping for my side, which had settled into a dull ache that only flared into something sharper when I made a sudden movement or lifted my arm up above my chest. Since it was late in the day, the bath was crowded, but while I had shed the toga, I had decided to keep wearing the Praetorian tunic, mainly because it moved us to the head of the line, just another of the privileges that come with wearing it. I ignored the hostile stares and the muttered curses, mainly because I would have done the same in their situation now that I had experienced the manner in which the Praetorians treated the average citizen, but when we entered the *apodyterium* to disrobe, there was no way to avoid being the object of scrutiny, although this time, it was as much the bloody bandage that was revealed when I shed the tunic as it was my size and musculature.

Ignoring my carping about how roughly he was handling me, Alex unwrapped the bandage, giving us both the first look at it since he had stitched me up, but while I could see it, Alex had a better view, and he frowned as he said, "That's pretty red, Gnaeus. And," he pointed at my side while he looked at me reprovingly, "you tore two stitches loose."

"I didn't do it on purpose," I protested, but I was more worried about the color. Ignoring the sudden crowd of onlookers in various states of undress drawn to the sight of my wound, I tried to hide the concern. "How red is it?"

"It's not corrupted," he answered immediately and confidently. "I just expected that it would be a bit less red by this time."

"It's only been two days," I pointed out, which caused him to jerk in surprise.

"Pluto's cock, you're right." He laughed. "It seems like it happened a week ago!"

I did not try to hide my relief and joined him in laughing.

"Praetorian!" Turning, I saw an older, bald man with a pot belly clad only in his *subligaculum*, giving me an obsequious smile, while just behind him were three other men about the same age, although they were still wearing tunics, peering over his shoulder at me. "May I just say that I'm going to be sleeping better tonight now that I've seen what kind of man is protecting our Imperator!" Three heads bobbed in unison behind him as the man who had either been selected or volunteered to speak for them exclaimed, "And the only men I've ever seen who might match you in size are on the sand! Have you ever thought of being a gladiator?"

Now he was still smiling, but the manner in which he was looking at me expectantly made me believe he was actually serious, although I answered with a laugh, "Gods no, Citizen. Why would I ever do that?" I winked and added, "That's dangerous work. Not like the Praetorians."

This seemed to satisfy him to a degree, but then he pointed to the wound. "It can't be that safe, Praetorian. How did that happen?"

I was tiring of this, but I decided to have some fun.

Widening my eyes, I asked, "You mean you haven't heard, Citizen?"

I felt a bit badly at the way he eagerly snapped up the bait, while at the same time it reminded me that of the things Romans love, especially of the lower orders; they love gossip, the more lurid the better, especially if it concerns members of the upper orders.

"Arminius sent a group of Germans to murder the Imperator in his sleep," I said with a straight face, prompting gasps of horror and curses, not just from the four men, but from seemingly everyone else in hearing distance, making me aware that there were more people listening than I thought. This, I thought, is getting out of hand, so I believed I could end it by shrugging. "But they were all caught before they even made it onto the Palatine and were killed to the last man." Before I could stop myself, I added, "Every one of them was my size or bigger, and I personally slew three of them myself."

"You're a hero of Rome!" someone shouted, but he was immediately drowned out with cries and shouts of agreement, then I found myself suddenly surrounded by men slapping me on the back or offering their arms, which I demurred, pointing to my side and since I could not have been heard, mimicked wincing.

"You need to come to Aphrodite's Lair so that we can stand you for drinks and a whore!"

"*Gerrae*! Aphrodite's Lair is a *cac* pit! Come with me to the Den of Venus! The women there will make you forget every woman you've ever fucked before!"

I was trying to be polite, but being surrounded by partially clothed and fully naked men who seemed to want to touch me was making me uncomfortable, so I began pushing my way through them to get to the *tepidarium*. When they moved to follow me, I finally had to bellow at them to leave me alone, while flexing my arms, wearing the expression I used when I wanted my men to think I was enraged. The matter in which they scrambled back into the *apodyterium* was quite satisfying, but when I turned around and grinned, Alex was glaring at me.

"You just can't help yourself, can you?"

"What? I was just having some fun," I protested, but his snort told me that he was not buying it.

"You know this might spread across the city," he warned.

"So?" I shrugged, and I refused to stop grinning. "We'll be gone."

As it tends to do, a full bath served to revive and refresh the both of us, although the instant we walked through the door, there were two women who had patched up their differences, ready to issue orders about what needed to be done.

"I need to get you a slave to order around," I grumbled. "This is unbecoming of a Roman man."

This made Bronwen laugh, and her tone was gently mocking.

"Parisii men say the same thing," she assured me, which did not make me feel any better.

"What time is Marcus coming?" she asked me, and I stopped

what I was doing, suddenly realizing that he was in for a surprise.

Thinking for a moment as I recalled the routine, I ventured, "Probably at the beginning of first night watch."

"That soon?" Her eyes widened. "That's not enough time! We've been busy packing and I haven't even begun to prepare the meal yet!"

Hoping to soothe her, I assured Bronwen, "Marcus isn't going to mind if the meal isn't ready when he gets here."

I could instantly see this had no effect whatsoever, and she muttered things I had learned that I did not want to know the meaning of in her native tongue as she fled out of the apartment to go down to the kitchen, but when I looked to Alex for support, he offered a mute shake of his head.

When the knock came, while I was certain that it was Macer, I still glanced at Scrofa's blade before I opened the door, but it was indeed Macer, dressed in his Legionary tunic, while in one hand he carried his *vitus* and in the other a stoppered jug.

By way of greeting, he said, "I can't guarantee that it's the quality that you Praetorians are accustomed to, but I hope it doesn't make you gag."

Stepping aside, I let Macer enter, but Iras, having heard the commotion, came out of her apartment carrying Titus, and they were following closely behind my former Pilus Prior, who was clearly amused.

"When I came into the atrium, whatever is cooking smells wonderful."

"Be sure and tell Bronwen that," I responded in answer to Macer's comment, then pointed to the jug. "But that's not doing any good in the jug, is it?"

I went to the cupboard where the cups were stored, retrieving three of them before returning to the table. Just one glance at Alex told me that he was waiting for me to spring the news, but I decided to be gentle, and perhaps a bit mischievous.

"So, are you ready to march?" I asked innocently, which earned me a chuckle.

"It depends on who you ask," Macer countered. "As far as the men are concerned, we're evil bastards who are tearing them away from the wonders of Rome. In fact," he informed me with relish, "I've had more than one man come to me to complain that they haven't had the chance to visit the Forum and make offerings at the temples. It's," he changed his voice to mimic Publius, the name we use for a non-specific ranker, "a sacrilege that good Roman men aren't allowed to make the proper obeisance to the gods before a long march!"

This did make me laugh, but I was not satisfied, although I tried to sound casual. "Aside from that, did you hear anything else?"

Macer was sipping from his cup, but stopped in mid-sip, his eyes searching mine, and I recognized the sudden plunge of his eyebrows that was the signal that he understood there was something going on about which he was not fully informed.

Setting his cup down, he asked, "About what?"

"Oh," I shrugged, "I don't know." I paused, letting the silence draw out, but when Macer was opening his mouth, I said, "Maybe about you adding someone to the ranks of the 1st for your march back to Ubiorum?"

I was supremely satisfied that, while Macer clearly understood something was afoot, he was clearly mystified, and curious.

"What are you talking about?" Macer demanded. "I haven't heard anything that sounds like what you're saying."

Rather than address Macer, I turned to Alex, asking, "Should we tell him?"

"I don't see why not." He grinned. "The Primus Pilus will have gotten the orders by now, so when he goes back to camp, he'll find out anyway."

While it was not exactly how I envisioned it, I decided to inform Macer, "It turns out I'm not a Praetorian anymore. Now," I grinned, "I'm just a Centurion looking for a Cohort to command."

Despite my belief that I had not milked this for its entire value, I was rewarded by the look on Macer's face, his mouth dropping open as he stared at me, although I was not surprised that he immediately looked to Alex as he gasped, "*Gerrae!*"

"It's true," I assured him, then went on to explain without going into any detail the circumstances that led to me returning to the 1st.

"Does Sacrovir know?"

"If he doesn't know already, he'll know very shortly," Alex answered for me, but Macer's reaction was, while certainly not unhappy, not what I expected.

"I'm sure he'll be very pleased," Macer said in a neutral tone that could have meant anything.

"When you say it that way, it doesn't sound like it," I said, trying to keep my tone light.

Setting the cup back down, Macer pursed his lips, another mannerism that anyone who knew him meant that there was potentially troubling information coming.

"Gnaeus," he finally spoke in a quiet voice, "I don't think that you're going to be given the Fourth Cohort."

Perhaps if he had punched me, I would have reacted more strongly, but it would have been close.

Nevertheless, I tried to sound calm as I asked, "Any idea why?"

Before he could reply, Bronwen and Algaia appeared with our food, and I believe that Macer stuffing a hunk of hot bread into his mouth was done deliberately to stall for time, which only increased my anxiety. I suppose from the expectant looks he was getting, since I informed Bronwen of what had been said up to that moment, he realized that he could not put it off, but when he answered, I recognized his careful tone that told me he was choosing his words.

"It's just that there are some...changes being made with the front line Cohorts," he explained.

"What kind of changes?"

Macer shot Alex an annoyed look, but he should have expected it, if not from Alex then from me.

"Primus Hastatus Prior Varo is retiring, for one thing," he explained. "And you know Sacrovir's policy."

"That any First Cohort Centurion has to have been a Pilus

Prior?"

Macer nodded. "Yes, so that means that he's making some decisions. And," he hesitated, "I know that one of them is that Licinius remains in command of the Fourth."

"But he doesn't know that Gnaeus isn't with the Praetorians anymore," Alex pointed out.

"That's true," Macer allowed, then shrugged. "I suppose we'll all learn soon enough." Pointedly changing the subject, Macer turned to Bronwen. "How do you feel about leaving Rome?"

She did not hesitate, almost spitting out the words. "It is a nest of vipers here! It is unsafe, and it is so dirty and crowded. Although," she softened slightly, "there are so many things to see, and there are more people from other countries and kingdoms here than what we saw even in Alexandria. Still," she looked at me as she pronounced, "while I am happy that I have seen and lived in Rome, I am also ready to leave."

This reminded me of all that there was to do, but Alex was thinking along the same lines because he beat me to it, saying, "We need to rent a wagon first thing tomorrow, and hire someone to help me pack while you go to camp with your orders."

"I also need to get an answer from Sabinus," I said, more to myself.

"Sabinus?" Macer asked, and I gave him a brief explanation of what I was doing.

I was not altogether surprised when he said doubtfully, "I don't know how Sacrovir will feel about a former Praetorian in the ranks."

"I'm now a former Praetorian." I grinned, which he returned, but said, "And you're a different case."

"That," Alex murmured, "is one way to put it."

This amused everyone at the table, save one, but even I could not help from laughing, and we quickly moved on to other matters as we ate. Both Alex and I were relieved to see whatever disagreement had occurred between our women was clearly forgotten, and the evening meal passed very pleasantly. Seeing Macer to the door, it felt strange to say that I would be seeing him the next day but no longer as a visitor to the camp, but I am afraid I was also preoccupied by the news that Macer was sure that I was not returning to the Fourth. I had also resigned myself to not hearing from Sabinus until the last possible moment, but I was in for a pleasant surprise because, about a third of a watch before we retired, there was a knock on the door. Alex, Algaia, and Iras were back in their apartment downstairs, and Bronwen was closest to the door, but when she walked over to open it, I grabbed her sleeve and shook my head, still unwilling to fully believe that the danger was over. Opening the door and seeing it was Sabinus, I greeted him more warmly than I would have normally because I was relieved to see him.

"*Meum mel*," I made sure I turned so that Sabinus could not see my expression, "would you excuse us for a moment? The Optio and I have an important matter to discuss."

Fortunately, Bronwen interpreted my countenance perfectly, because she did not betray that she knew the topic in any way.

"Of course, my love." She smiled at Sabinus again, and just as she had comprehended my intentions, I knew that she was teasing me, or probably reminding me that other men find her desirable, something I assure her she has no need to do, but I believe she enjoys it. "I will go rock Titus. He gets fussy sometimes after he has been asleep for a while."

Sabinus started to watch her leave the room, but he caught my glare and looked at the floor, then once Bronwen shut the door, he said quietly, "I've come to tell you my decision, Pilus Post...Centurion," he corrected himself, though there was no need.

When he did not utter it immediately, I got impatient.

"Well? What is it?"

"I've decided that the Praetorian Guard isn't what I thought it would be, and I don't like what it is," he replied, using the same quiet tone, but with a firmness that put me at ease that he had indeed made up his mind. "I can't say I like the idea of starting all over as a Gregarius," he confessed, adding, "and I hope that that's not what happens, but I think things are going to get worse for any of us in the Guard who don't want to be in Sejanus' coin purse. And," he concluded, "I think it's going to be more dangerous as well."

"All I can promise," I answered honestly, "is that I'll do my best to make sure that at the very least you lead a section, and that it will be under my command, or if not, that I'll talk to a couple Pili Priores I consider friends to make that happen."

I could see he was a bit disappointed, but he also nodded and said he understood.

Offering my arm, I told him, "Come back here at noon tomorrow, and if I can't be here, I'll make sure Alex is here and one of us will tell you what's on offer."

"Thank you, Centurion." He accepted my arm with a bit of surprise. After he stepped outside, he paused for a moment, and I got the sense he was deciding something. Apparently, he was, because he turned to face me to say, "I consider myself blessed by Fortuna that we met, Centurion. You reminded me of what it means to be under the standard." It was not there long, but there was no mistaking the sudden look of angry contempt. "I mean, a *real* standard."

He headed down the stairs before I could respond, and I walked out onto the landing to watch him leave through the outer door, then I went down and bolted it before retiring, a habit that I had developed over the previous days.

While I had already worn my Legionary tunic for the triumph, it felt distinctly different this time, and I am afraid that my tossing and turning kept Bronwen from getting a good night's sleep since Titus had begun sleeping through the night. On that note, I confess that when I heard other men comment on how important a babe that sleeps through the night is for both parents, I did not really understand it, but now I do. Nevertheless, I essentially launched myself out of bed at the first crow of one of the cocks that are kept in coops all over the city in a state that is hard to describe. Excited, certainly, at the thought of returning to where I knew I belonged, but not knowing exactly where I was headed added an element of anxiety that, while not as potent as the feeling before going into battle, was nonetheless unsettling. Gobbling down some cold stew and a half loaf from the night before, I drank straight water, wanting a clear head, then kissed Bronwen and baby Titus, although he was still asleep and did not stir when his Tata kissed him, bounding down the stairs and momentarily forgetting that when I do that it shakes the staircase, something that had earned me a rebuke by both women. The streets were just beginning to fill up, but I was not excessively delayed in reaching the city gate. Once out onto the Campus, the traffic lightened considerably, but while most of the people I encountered were heading into the city from the suburbs, I spotted a few men, and while it was still a bit too dark to make out colors, it was light enough to see they were all carrying a *vitus* like I was, the sign that my fellow Centurions had found a warm bed somewhere in the city. That this was the case solved a problem for me, because the Optio standing at the Porta Praetoria did not stop any of the Centurions ahead of me, and while he did give me more attention, it was of the normal sort. The camp was awake, with men either heading to or returning from the latrines, the stench of it now that the army had been here for several weeks almost overpowering, especially as I reached the 1st's area. I did have to pause outside the Legion office to take a breath, bracing myself for whatever Sacrovir had decided, including the possibility that he had yet to reach a decision. He had, actually, but never in my wildest imaginings would I have guessed what lay in my future. Menander pushed aside the flap at my knock, and I could tell that he had been expecting me.

"It looks as if the Primus Pilus received the message from the *Propraetor*," I said jokingly.

I was not encouraged by the manner in which Menander replied, with a curt, "Yes he did, Centurion. And he's expecting you. Although," his tone turned disapproving and I think he wanted to wag a finger at me, "not quite this early, so you may have to wait."

"I thought I'd get an early start," I replied with a bit of chagrin, which was why I felt compelled to add, "I'm just happy to be back with the 1st."

Menander did not reply immediately, seemingly considering what to say for a moment, then he surprised me a great deal.

Taking a quick glance over his shoulder at the flap that served as the door to the Primus Pilus' private quarters, he dropped to a whisper to say, "I doubt he's going to show it, Centurion Pullus, but trust me. Primus Pilus Sacrovir is happy as well. I think," he looked back at the flap, "you've made a decision much easier for him."

Pluto's cock, what does *that* mean? I managed to keep this inside my skull, while aloud I could only offer, "I'm happy to help him and the Legion in any way that I can."

We both heard a stirring from Sacrovir's quarters, and if he had suddenly stepped out into the office, I think that we would have both reacted like guilty schoolboys, but thankfully, all he did was call for Menander to attend to him. Telling me to have a seat, Menander disappeared, leaving me to ignore the surreptitious glances of the other two clerks who were seated behind their desks, although they were consuming their morning meal. Even with a watch candle disabusing me, I would have sworn that it was not actually melting the wax, but the *bucina* had not sounded the call to assembly yet when Menander returned and beckoned to me. With my heart in my mouth, I entered to find Sacrovir sitting behind his desk, seeing the scroll from Germanicus in front of him, and he returned my salute immediately, then regarded me with an impassive expression.

"Well, Pullus," he said finally, "I'll admit that I've gotten accustomed to anyone with the Pullus name doing things in an...unusual manner, but I don't know that I've ever heard of a man going from the Praetorians to the Legions. It's always the other way around."

It was more the manner in which he said it than the words that told me he was joking with me, which was why I answered with a shrug and a grin, "I suppose it's in the blood, Primus Pilus."

He offered a slight smile as he gestured to the stool in front of the desk, and I complied by dropping onto it.

Before I could ask, he informed me, "Pilus Prior Macer stopped by last night after having the evening meal with you, and he told me that he informed you that you won't be going back to the Fourth Cohort." Since he did not seem upset, I confirmed this, but then he surprised me by saying, "That actually makes this a bit easier, because he also told me he informed you about the changes that I'm making now that Varo has decided to retire." I only nodded this time, studying his expression for some clue what was coming, but when he spoke next, I was so shocked that he suddenly looked concerned. "Pullus, did you hear what I said?" I could not even seem to make my head move, and he snapped impatiently, "Have you suddenly lost your wits?"

Since this was a question I could answer, I did so, although all I could manage was, "No, Primus Pilus."

"Then what did I say?"

"That you're naming me the Primus Hastatus Prior," I managed, and this was the first moment where it began to hit me. Suddenly, though, another thought crossed my mind, and before I could stop myself, I voiced it. "But you only consider Pili Priores for any slot in the First Cohort, Primus Pilus."

Sacrovir actually looked concerned, which was understandable since he reminded me, "You *were* a Pilus Prior, Pullus."

This was certainly true, yet for some reason, I could not fight the feeling there was something more going on, which was why I asked him, "You only found out that I was coming back to the Legion late yesterday, so I couldn't have been your first choice. May I ask who was?"

For the first time during this conversation, and one of the few times I had ever witnessed, Sacrovir suddenly did not seem willing to meet my eyes, dropping them to his desk instead as he fiddled with Germanicus' order with one hand.

Finally, he broke the increasingly strained silence, informing me, "I offered it to Pilus Prior Macer first."

As soon as the name was out of his mouth, I realized that I had already begun to suspect this from the moment Sacrovir looked uncomfortable, but I still could not stop myself from gasping aloud.

My stomach clenched in a tight knot, but I had to ask, "Have you already informed him that you rescinded the offer?"

Sacrovir reacted strongly, but confusingly to me, he was obviously surprised.

"I didn't rescind the offer, Pullus," he assured me. "He turned it down last night."

"But...why?" I could only shake my head, utterly confused. "Did he give a reason?"

Rather than answer me directly, Sacrovir suggested in a kindly tone, yet another first, "Why don't you go talk to Marcus, Gnaeus? Let him explain it to you."

"It's not that I didn't want it," Macer told me after I had essentially stormed into the Cohort office, and he was completely unsurprised at my appearance. "But," unlike Sacrovir, Macer did look me in the eye as he said quietly, "you're a better choice, Gnaeus."

"I'm too young," I argued, part of me not really believing what I was hearing come out of my mouth.

"Sacrovir didn't think so," Macer countered, then hesitated for a heartbeat. Leaning across his desk, he gave me an intense look, matched by his words. "I'm willing to tell you something, but only if you swear that you will *never* let Sacrovir know I told you."

"I swear it," I promised, but while I expected him to demand more than this, he seemed satisfied.

"Varo told Sacrovir on the march that he was retiring when we got back to Ubiorum," Macer explained. "I was with the Primus Pilus when Varo told him. After Varo left, Sacrovir was...upset, so asked me to stay and he drank more than he should have..."

"He?" I interrupted with a grin, and Macer gave me a mock glare as he countered, "Who's telling this story, eh?" He chuckled as he admitted, "And I *may* have matched him cup for cup." He turned serious again as he went on, "But at one point, he said something like, 'It's a shame that Pullus still isn't with the Legion, because I think he'd be perfect for the First.' And," he sat back up, "I actually agreed with him then, and I agree now. So," he finished, "rather than put the Primus Pilus in an awkward position by forcing him to choose between rescinding his offer to me when his original first choice became available again, I told him last night I was withdrawing my name from consideration."

What does one say to that? I was not certain then, and I still do not really know now, other than to confess, "I...I don't know what to say, Marcus."

"By the gods, I hope you said yes," he said jokingly, but I could also see that he thought it was a possibility that I had not, but despite everything he had just told me, I did feel a pang of guilt when I assured him that I had in fact accepted the offer. Macer obviously decided to change the subject by asking, "What did Sacrovir say about your Optio?"

"Pluto's cock," I groaned. "I forgot."

I got up to leave to go back to Sacrovir immediately, but then the *bucina* sounded the call for morning formation, and I walked with Macer towards the forum, except that I stopped at the Legion office. Sacrovir was already gone, so I occupied myself by interrogating Menander about the current state of the Legion, particularly the Fifth of the First, which was about to become my new command.

Before he answered, Menander turned to the other two clerks and commanded, "Both of you go to the *praetorium* with the daily report while I talk to the Centurion."

I noticed that one of them, who I personally thought had eyes that seemed to perpetually dart about as if he was expecting some trouble to materialize, was clearly disappointed, while the other gave me no hint of his thoughts.

Once they left, I observed, "One of your clerks seemed upset that he couldn't stay behind."

"That's Arcadius." Menander grimaced. "He's a devious little bastard who likes to know more than he's supposed to. In fact," I could hear the anger in his voice, and I understood why when he said, "I'm almost certain that he's in Nerva's purse and selling him bits of gossip about the Primus Pilus."

"Why don't you have him flogged, then dismiss him?"

"Because it's just a suspicion, Centurion, and I'm not willing to have the man striped until I'm certain, even if he is a slave. Besides," he shrugged, "Arcadius is a master at sums. He can do them in his head and supply the answer before any of us have even written it out."

This was certainly a good asset to have; it always surprises citizens who have never served under the standard exactly how much record keeping and paperwork that anyone in the Centurionate does on a daily basis. Divus Augustus was famous for his attention to details that, while seemingly trivial, are actually crucial to keeping a Legion ready to march on short notice. There was a joke that he knew exactly how many hobnails were on the sole of a *caliga* and how many chickpeas are in a bowl of soldier's porridge, so it made sense that this slave had value. On the other hand, if you cannot trust a man to keep Legion business, particularly when it pertains to the Primus Pilus, within the Legion, I found it hard to see how the value outweighed the liability.

While a vexing problem for Menander, it was not my concern, so I asked him bluntly, "What do I need to know, Menander? What's the state of the Fifth?"

Menander sighed before he spoke, a portent of what was coming when he told me, "Morale is lower in the Fifth than any other Century in the Cohort. And," he allowed, "it may be the worst in the Legion."

"Any idea why?"

Menander hesitated, but he did answer me eventually, "Hastatus Prior Varo lost his wife to a fever while we were in Germania, and his son was on a ship like yours. Except," his expression turned grim, "unlike your ship, none of the men on his were ever seen again. Since then," he shrugged, "Varo's been a *numen*. His Optio has been running the Century, and while he's capable enough, it *is* a First Cohort Century, which means..."

"Twice the men, twice the problems," I finished for him. Although this was not ideal, I also thought it could have been worse, like Varo was a striper, or he was one of those Centurions who viewed their men as nothing more than a source of money. "What's the Optio's name?"

"Quintus Bibaculus," he answered. "He was promoted by Varo three years ago."

I had heard the name but did not remember anything that stuck in my memory, so I set that aside for the time. Just then, there was a dull roar from the forum, the tent and distance muffling the sound of thousands of men shouting in what I could at least tell was approbation or appreciation.

When I glanced at Menander with a raised eyebrow, he chuckled. "I believe the men just learned they're going to be allowed to go into the city tonight."

"The night before we march?" I gasped. "Whose idea was that?"

"From the *Domus Augusti*," he replied, but when I pressed him, he shook his head. "That's all I'm saying." Pausing a beat, he said, "Now, if you should happen to *guess* correctly, I can't stop you."

I thought for a moment.

"You said it came from the *Domus Augusti*, and Germanicus has his own residence down the street," I began. "And I don't see Tiberius thinking it would be a good idea, because from everything I've heard, most of the city is ready to see the army leave by now." What came to me next made even less sense. "I can't see why Sejanus would do it...unless he's hoping for some sort of trouble between the Praetorians and the Legions."

Menander coughed, and I looked up sharply, but while he did not say anything, he offered an almost imperceptible shrug that, frankly, could have meant anything. Naturally, this was the moment the Primus Pilus returned, and I leapt to my feet.

"I talked to Macer," I began, but he stopped me with a wave of his hand.

"Yes, I talked to him just now and he told me. He also told me that you have a...request?"

While it was not exactly how I planned it, I explained to him about Sabinus, watching Sacrovir carefully as I talked, yet there was not a hint I could glean from his expression of his thoughts on the matter.

He waited until I finished before he spoke, and it was to ask, "And you think that he's in danger if he stays with the Praetorians?"

"It's hard to say, sir," I replied honestly. "I think that it's certainly possible because the one man who can and would protect him is leaving the day after we march tomorrow with the *Propraetor*. And," I pointed out, "the *Propraetor* is taking Tribune Asprenas with him to keep the Tribune safe from Sejanus."

"He's a patrician," Sacrovir pointed out, clearly unmoved by my argument. "Asprenas matters, this Sabinus isn't important enough."

This was true enough, but I still had a feeling, and I did try to explain it. Slightly inspired, I said, "Prefect Sejanus considers himself the cleverest man in a room at any given moment. And, he's vindictive. I've witnessed that firsthand. Sabinus isn't important in and of himself, but he's a symbol of Sejanus' failure, and I think that, while Sejanus won't move immediately, Sabinus' presence is going to remind him of the time he failed to make things happen to his benefit. Then one day," I shrugged, "I think that the Prefect will have something done to Sabinus. Maybe it will just be a bad beating. Or it might be worse."

"Do you trust him?" Sacrovir asked once I was finished, and I assured him, "With my life, Primus Pilus."

"It will be late to go through the transfer process," Menander spoke up, but I was already reaching into the bag slung over my shoulder, although I had to fumble for it a bit before I pulled out the scroll.

"This is from the *Propraetor*, authorizing Sabinus' transfer from the Praetorians. And," I added quickly as I handed it to him, "he gives you complete authority to place Sabinus wherever you see fit."

Sacrovir seemed to be torn between being irritated and amused, which he explained as he cracked the seal and unrolled the scroll. "I suppose I should have known that you had used your relationship with Germanicus and that I wouldn't have any choice."

I was tempted to argue by pointing out that I had not talked to Sabinus before I spoke with Germanicus but decided it might make things contentious.

After scanning the order, Sacrovir handed the scroll to Menander as he addressed me. "As of now, I'm willing to put this Sabinus onto the books, as a Gregarius *Immunes* only, and in your Century." I would not say he became evasive, but Sacrovir sounded vague when he said, "There may be some other changes coming once we're back at Ubiorum, and depending on what they are, we'll see then if he can be fit into at least a Sergeant slot."

With that concluded, I asked to be excused so that I could return to help with what packing was left.

Sacrovir surprised me by asking, "How is your woman taking this moving about? She's been traveling all over the world ever since you met her."

I instantly realized this was true, but I felt confident in assuring him, "She's ready to be gone from Rome, Primus Pilus."

"Well," Sacrovir sighed, "I know that we're going to have a tail on the way back. There's not one Centurion in the Legion who hasn't informed me that one of their rankers is bringing a woman back with him. And some," he grinned at me and gave me a wink, "are bringing back more than one."

"Thank the gods Algaia is with us," I said fervently. "She'll be able to warn Bronwen what to expect."

"We'll see about that," Sacrovir countered, still with a smile. "Until she's seen two women rolling round on the ground trying to claw each other's eyes out, that's only when she'll understand."

This was certainly true, but I still reminded myself to speak with Algaia.

I arrived back at the apartment before Sabinus did, and Alex had brought the wagon with a slave from the stable where Latobius was kept, unhitching the team and leaving the wagon behind for us to load. It was not that large, but it did have a canvas cover that would provide some protection if the weather turned bad, although we were going to be marching in Junius, and it would not be completely full, so Alex and I arranged the baggage in a way that left room for Titus' cradle, right behind the driver's seat, along with some room for Bronwen and Iras as well.

"You know that we're going to have to have someone stand watch tonight," Alex reminded me. "If we leave this wagon alone even to piss, we'll come back and it will be stripped clean."

This was certainly true, and we had repeatedly been warned to never leave anything valuable unattended, even if it was behind locked doors. We had heeded this warning; there was always at least one person in our apartments at all times, but honestly, I do not believe that Romans who live in the city are any more honest or dishonest than places like Mediolanum, I just believe that when you jam a million people into a small area, there are more of those who are thieves by nature or by circumstance. Fortunately, Alex had spoken to the owner of the stable, who also owned the wagon, and he had promised to send a trustworthy slave to stand watch during the night. Sabinus showed up precisely at noon, carrying his Optio's pack, which is designed to be carried by a mule that is shared between the three junior officers and the *Cornicen*, which I had Alex put into the wagon while I spoke with Sabinus down in the atrium.

"As of this moment, you're going to be drawing the pay of a Gregarius *Immune* in my Century, the Fifth of the First," I began, which seemed to alarm him.

"But I don't have a skill, Centurion," he protested.

"That doesn't matter right now; it's just that the pay is a bit more than a Gregarius," I assured him. Choosing my words carefully, I explained, "Primus Pilus Sacrovir isn't the type to make promises he can't keep, so he was very careful in what he said, but there may be other...opportunities opening up when we get back to Ubiorum. While we're on the march, I'll introduce you to Pilus Prior Macer, Licinius, and Clepsina, and if they like what they see and hear, they might be able to find you a spot in their Cohort."

"I appreciate that, Centurion." He tried not to look disappointed.

Feeling badly, I invited him to stay for the evening meal, but he shook his head, then with a grin, he explained, "The boys are seeing me off in style, Centurion. We're meeting at Isis' Grotto, and Pilus Prior Creticus is standing for the first round."

"How did he take you leaving?" I asked him, which wiped the grin off his face, though not for the reason I thought, that Creticus was angry at the fact that one of his Centuries was leaderless.

"He said that I made a wise choice, and he wished me well," Sabinus said soberly.

"I thought he'd be upset because the Second is down two officers," I commented.

This earned me a look of amused bitterness from Sabinus.

"Oh, I don't think that's a concern. The Second can survive a day without us." Seeing I did not grasp his meaning, he explained, "Your replacement is reporting to the Cohort tomorrow."

"That didn't take long," I commented, but Sabinus was not done.

"That's because of who it is," he replied. "It's Cinna's Optio.

Or," he corrected himself, "former Optio."

"And I suppose it's safe to assume that this Optio..."

"Publius Vitellius Rufio," Sabinus supplied, and understanding where I was going, he assured me, "and yes, he's one of Sejanus'. Although," he added in an afterthought, "I think he's actually loyal to Cinna, who promoted him, but since Cinna is the Praetorian Sejanus trusts the most, then it's safe to say that Rufio will be every bit as loyal to Sejanus as he is to Cinna."

"Well, it's no longer either of our problems." It was all I could think to say, and Sabinus left immediately after, although I warned him, "I don't want to have to go searching the gutter for you in the middle of the night, Sabinus. I'm trusting that you'll come back here in time for us to leave. Who knows?" I gave him a grin, "If you're hungover and I'm feeling generous, I may let you sleep it off in the wagon."

"I'll try to behave, Centurion," he said, laughing.

Once he left, with the bulk of the packing done, there was not much to do, so I went down to the stable to give Latobius his daily apple and let him know that, finally, we would get to go riding more than just the twice a week I had managed as a Praetorian, then I stopped at the bath, returning just before dark to the smell of cooking, though not just any cooking. My mouth began to water as I entered the building, where I was met by Bronwen, who had chosen to wear one of the two green silk stolae she had had made here in Rome from the cloth we brought back from Alexandria, although at the moment, it was covered by an apron.

"Is that beef I smell?"

"Yes." She smiled at me. "I decided to make your favorite. We're having a feast on our last night in Rome!"

During my time with the Parisii, while I cannot say I ate better, their diet was far more conducive to my tastes than what I normally ate, because most of their wealth comes from cattle, much like the tribes in Germania. But, more than the type of meat, the Parisii prepare it in a way that, if I had my way, I would eat every day, but that is not possible both under the standard and at home because I would have a rebellion on my hands in both places. While the women worked, I relieved Alex from watching the wagon, which we had pushed into the alley behind the building to make it less conspicuous, and he hurried off to the baths, leaving me sitting on the wagon seat reading a scroll, although I had to light a lamp fairly soon after I took over. I had just grabbed one from the box, and it turned out to be one by the Prefect where he described marching in the four triumphs under Caesar. While I am loath to ascribe such a thing to the gods and prefer to think of it as more of a happy accident, I found myself smiling as I read about the songs that they sang about Divus Julius, back when he was a mortal man. It also gave me an even stronger sense of connection to the Prefect, but I also felt a sense of sadness at the thought that, while my great-grandfather and grandfather, neither of whom I ever knew, had been afforded the opportunity that men under the standard dream about, marching through the sacred precincts of the city that bears the name by which the entire Empire is known, just as I had done a few days earlier, my father had not gotten to enjoy that. So absorbed was I that when young Iras, sent by Algaia to inform me that the meal was ready called my name, I jumped so obviously that it made her giggle.

"You're as sneaky as a German," I complained before sweeping her up and throwing her over my shoulder as she shrieked with laughter and ascended the stairs.

Alex had returned from the baths and was in my apartment, but he immediately went down to wait for the slave, who was due to arrive at any moment, while my stomach was making insistent demands, fueled by the sight and smell of the large joint of beef on a wooden platter, still sizzling and dripping from the fire.

"That," I said it without thinking, "is the most beautiful sight my eyes have ever seen."

"Oh? Is that so?" Bronwen crossed her arms, one eyebrow arched, but while her mouth was set in the kind of firm line that sent the message that she was being serious, I saw the truth in her merrily dancing eyes. "Let us see if you feel that way later tonight!"

By this time, I had learned to recognize when I was defeated; besides, my stomach was making so much noise that Iras, still slung over my shoulder so that her ear was pressed to my stomach, was howling with laughter, which in turn made Titus give a big, slobbery grin with just the nubs of two bottom and two top teeth showing, something that Bronwen informed me was quite painful, although she was laughing with all of us. Honestly, there was not much talking, or if there was, I was so concerned with shoving slices of meat into my mouth that I did not hear it. I cannot honestly say how much I ate; Bronwen would slice a slab of beef, pink and glistening from the juices, and I would devour it, but gradually, I became aware that the conversation by the others had died down until, finally, I looked up from my plate to see all eyes on me, and I include Titus in that, sitting in his mother's lap, watching me with widened eyes.

"That," Alex broke the silence, "is something I will never forget." Turning from me, he asked Algaia, seemingly serious, "Have you ever seen anyone eat that much?"

"No." She shook her head solemnly. "I have not."

"Cogibdunus' slaves told anyone who would listen that Gnaeus ate more than any man they had ever seen," Bronwen told the others, but while she had said this before, I suppose that the others seeing it firsthand had an impact.

"I can't help it!" I protested, and I knew I sounded defensive as I said it. "I just eat until I'm not hungry anymore."

"If every Legionary throughout Rome's history ate like you did, they'd still be a village."

Even I had to laugh at Alex's remark, but that does not mean I stopped eating. Finally, once I was sated, I had to let my *baltea* out a bit, and I patted my stomach, just when there was a sudden hammering on the outer door.

"Tymon!" Alex leapt up, saying the name of the slave the owner of the stable had sent to watch the wagon, and I was right behind him as we rushed out of the apartment and ran down the stairs.

It was not Tymon, it was Sabinus, who was gasping for breath as he bent over and put his hands on his knees, just managing to get out, "Centurion! I need you! There's trouble at Isis' Grotto!"

I did not understand him, my first thought being, I'm not the Pilus Posterior of the Second Praetorian anymore, but in an instant, everything changed.

"Some men from the Fourth Cohort of the 1st showed up, and there's trouble!"

Before we were halfway there, I was certain that I would throw up, yet somehow I managed to avoid it, but I was also having a hard time keeping up with Sabinus, who weaved in and around the people out in the streets with an ease that spoke of long practice. I had ordered Alex to stay behind, not wanting to leave the women alone with just the slave Tymon guarding the wagon in case someone decided to try their hand anyway. Climbing the Esquiline was torture, and we heard the brawl even before we turned the corner, yet despite the urgency, I had to gasp at Sabinus to stop when we were still down the street so that I could catch at least part of my breath.

"They weren't out in the street when I left," he panted, pointing to a pair of men who were rolling in the middle of the street and barely illuminated by the pair of lamps that hung above the sign over the doorway, but I could not make out anything other than that one men was wearing red, and one was wearing blue.

Even as we watched the first pair, another man shot out into the street from inside Isis' Grotto as if he had been launched from a *ballista*, reeling backward and wind-milling his arms as he tried to regain his balance. Before he could recover, another man appeared, but while he was sprinting, he was under control and bent over at the waist so that he could slam his shoulder directly into the first man. This time, however, I could see not just the color of the charging man's tunic, but I recognized him.

"Cotta!"

I bellowed the name of one of my former rankers, a brawler from the Second Section who had been with us in Britannia as I started to move towards him, though not in time to keep him from smashing into the Praetorian and take him off his feet, driving his body down onto the paving stones, and even with all the yelling, I heard the whooshing sound of the air being driven from the man's lungs. Then, I was within reach and, without thinking, I began swinging my *vitus,* striking Cotta on the back even as he was pummeling the Praetorian, who was now covering his face with both arms so that I could not recognize him at the moment. Cotta yelped in pain, but when he craned his neck and saw me standing there, his mouth dropped open, one fist stopping in mid-punch, his face suddenly splitting into a grin.

415

"Pilus Prior!" he shouted, and completely forgetting his victim, leapt to his feet, then offered a weaving salute. "It's fucking good to see you, sir! The boys inside will be..."

While I was certainly happy to see Cotta, and that he was happy to see me, his mention of what sounded like an all-out melee caused me to snap, "There's no time for old home day, Cotta! What the *fuck* is going on in there?"

I did not wait for him to answer and went striding to the door, which had partially shut again, opening it with a kick then pausing for a heartbeat in case someone responded by throwing something at whoever would be coming in. I was rewarded by a cup shattering against the door with enough force that I was sprayed by shards of clay, one of them cutting my cheek, and while my roar was more from the surprise than the pain, it also got me moving and I stepped inside, my eye instantly catching movement to my right that was heading right at me, and I spun about to face whoever it was attacking me. Honestly, it was the eyepatch that I recognized rather than his features, and it was obvious that he recognized me as well as he tried to slide to a stop, although his fist was still pulled back.

"*Saloninus?*"

Like Cotta, my former Optio and now the Quartus Pilus Posterior grinned, although he was weaving in a similar manner as he dropped his fist and I saw his eye go wide. I had just enough time to see that he was looking behind me, and I was just starting to turn when I was struck by what turned out to be a chair that sent me reeling into Saloninus; this time when I bellowed, it was because I was hurt...but I was also angry. The Praetorian who struck me made a crucial error by not pressing his attack, although part of his problem was that the chair had shattered, albeit against my body, which I think astonished the man, given how he was staring down at the remnants of the back of the chair in his hands while I was still upright and, as he was about to learn, more angry than hurt. I did not recognize him, which meant that I did not hesitate, dropping my *vitus* to grasp his tunic with my left hand to lift him off the floor before delivering a straight punch to his chin that snapped his head back, while I was able to tell by the way his weight became dead in my hand that he was out cold, so I dropped him to the floor. This was when I noticed that the sound level had dropped down quite a bit, so that when I looked up from the unconscious man, it was as if everyone in the *taverna* had turned to stone like I was Medusa, to the point that men still had their fist raised, while their foe had hold of the man's tunic.

"Would someone care to explain what the fuck is going on here?"

While my instinct had been to use my lungs to shock the combatants into ceasing their battling, it felt somewhat silly to do it since they had already done it, except that rather than answer, men glared at their opponent as if challenging them to be the one to answer. To my utter shock, it was actually *Signifer* Flaccus who, stepping into my line of view, spoke up, despite the fact that blood was running down his nose.

"Er, nothing, Pilus Posterior," he answered, somewhat shakily. I suppose he realized how absurd that sounded, because he added quickly, "I mean, nothing serious, really. It was just a..."

"A soldier's disagreement, Pilus Prior," Saloninus broke in. "Nothing more than that."

This was met by a ragged but seemingly heartfelt chorus of agreement by both Praetorian and Legionaries, men suddenly united as brothers in arms, and if I were to just go by the way heads were nodding in unison, with each man wearing an expression that was as solemn and holy as a Vestal, I might have believed them. From the back, Gallus emerged from behind the counter and hurried towards me, a smile on his face that I thought was probably the only time he was being genuine.

"Pilus Posterior Pullus," his relief was palpable, "thank the gods you're here!"

"Who started what?" I asked him, and suddenly, he did not look quite so happy, but again, I was in for a surprise.

"We did, Pilus Posterior," Flaccus said quietly. "We were...upset."

Thinking I understood, I nodded.

"These men," I jerked a thumb over to where Saloninus, who had been joined by the other Fourth men as the two parties separated, was standing, "showed up. Is that it?"

Rather than look at me, Flaccus glanced over at, of all people,

Saloninus, and it was my former second in command who answered, "Not exactly. I mean," he elaborated, "yes, we came here, but it wasn't to start trouble. We were hoping we'd find you here."

"We didn't get much chance to talk, and we're leaving tomorrow."

I had not seen Gemellus, who was standing towards the rear of the group, but rather than informing me, I was even more baffled, so I returned my attention back to Flaccus.

"So if that's true, how did the brawl start?"

Flaccus did not answer, but only because Valerius beat him to it.

"I wouldn't say we started it, Pilus Posterior," he began, yet before he could go on, I stopped him because I was so distracted by something.

"All right, before you keep going, I'm not your Pilus Posterior anymore," I explained, then turned and addressed my old Fourth men, "but I'm not your Pilus Prior anymore, so let's just use Centurion, eh?"

"Er, right," Valerius agreed, but as I was about to learn, I had inadvertently cut to the heart of the matter. "You see, Centurion, the thing is, that we just learned today that you're leaving us. And," he looked away from me and shrugged, "we were upset about it."

Flaccus resumed the tale that was, frankly, making me more confused than it was enlightening me. "So these boys showed up looking for you..."

"And *we* didn't know that you were coming back to the 1st," Saloninus interjected, and I heard the anger, and the accusation, there, "so we had to hear it from these bas...men."

Honestly, I did not know whether to laugh or cry. The idea that these idiots were bashing each other because they were angry about me, with the men of the Second of the Second Praetorian upset because I was leaving, while the men of the First of the Fourth were angry because they had not known that I was returning to the Legion, is one that I am still trying to understand.

Sighing, I said loudly enough for everyone to hear, "Well, if you bastards are going to try and kill each other over me, I might as well stand you for a round of drinks."

I was not surprised in the slightest that this was unanimously accepted as a wonderful idea, but there were two more surprises waiting for me; the first was when I told Gallus that I would have to return to my apartment to get the money, and he refused.

"Centurion, you've already done enough with Cethegus," he assured me. "He won't be bothering me again."

I thanked him, but then the Praetorian I had not recognized who had hit me with the chair and was still lying at my feet began to stir, moaning as he came back to consciousness.

"Flaccus," I called him to me, then pointed down, "who is that?"

Flaccus suddenly began shifting from one foot to another, which I had learned was the sign that he was distressed, although he did not hesitate in answering, "That's our new Pilus Posterior, Centurion. Meet Publius Vitellius Rufio."

By the time the midnight watch started, not only was every man in Isis' Grotto, no matter what color tunic they wore, roaring drunk, they were all the fastest of friends and lifelong boon comrades...and I was every bit as drunk as any of them. In the back of my mind, I knew that I would be paying for this, and not just in the form of a roaring hangover. And, as I anticipated, when I came staggering into the apartment, I was met by a very, very angry woman who had changed out of her green stola, and while she did not say a word, pointed to the couch in the outer room before turning and entering our bedroom, again without another word. The only man who was clearly unhappy was Rufio, or so I assumed because, once he came to, he left the Grotto without saying a word. I did have to endure the men of the Fourth swapping stories about me with the Praetorians, and of course, given my longer association with them, they had many more to tell. Actually, the Praetorians had more to say about Sabinus, yet to my surprise, they did not seem all that bitter about the fact that he was leaving them as well, and it was Flaccus of all people who seemed to sum up the sentiment of the Century.

"If I had somewhere to go, I'd do the same." His words were

slurred, but he seemed sincere, and he was sober enough to see the surprise on my face; suddenly, his eyes filled with tears. "Crito was my best friend, Centurion, and he was murdered by our own comrades. That's not right!"

"No, it's not," I agreed quietly. "And Crito was a good man, Flaccus. Never forget that he was trying to do the right thing."

"It's only going to be getting worse," the *Signifer* said morosely, but then he brightened a bit, grinning at me. "But it was worth it watching you knock that *cunnus* Rufio out."

"He'll never live that down." Valerius chuckled from his spot next to Flaccus. Addressing Sabinus, the Sergeant said, "In case you haven't heard, the rumor is that Paperna is going to be your replacement."

I was not familiar with the name, but Sabinus was, as were the others, and he groaned, "Not *that* thieving bastard! I thought that once he got demoted, he was never going to be an Optio again!" Seeing the reaction of me, Saloninus, and Gemellus, who were sitting on my side of the table, Sabinus explained, "He was Optio in the Fifth of the First when he got caught squeezing his men, but he kept all the money himself and didn't kick any up to his Centurion."

"That," Saloninus laughed, "doesn't sound all that different from the Legions."

"He must have promised to give Rufio an even bigger cut," Valerius said sourly. "Which means that bastard is going to be squeezing us even more."

"That's rough," Gemellus said sympathetically. Then, he added something that I know men under the standard believe. "But at least you're getting paid a lot more than we are."

The Praetorians at the table exchanged glances of bitter amusement, while I felt compelled to point something out that I had learned during my time in Rome.

"It's true that they're paid more," I told my Legion comrades, "but their deductions are almost twice what ours are."

"*Gerrae!*" Gemellus exclaimed, though not in a doubting manner, while Valerius nodded, assuring my former *Signifer,* "It's true. We're charged for our tunics because blue dye is more expensive."

"We use twice as much varnish as you do in the Legions," Flaccus said, and when my Legion comrades glanced at me, I nodded in confirmation.

And, I confess, I was starting to feel a bit guilty about how I had shut down their practice of refusing to pay, although I think that this was due more to the wine and the sudden wave of sentiment I was feeling. These men, I had come to realize, were not bad men, at least most of them, yet the same could be said for the Legions as well. For the most part, they were decent enough, and they were trying to do their duty; it is just that what that duty is now seems to be exclusive loyalty to Prefect Sejanus and not to the Imperator that is the real problem, and I mean not just for the Imperator, but for Rome. It is a truism I first learned from my father, and I also read in the Prefect's account, that there are no bad Centuries, only bad Centurions, but I had come to realize that, in the Praetorians, it is not that simple. Specifically, I thought about Pilus Prior Creticus, and while I had not quite yet reached the conclusion and belief I have now, that night in Isis' Grotto I was already leaning in that direction. I had simply thought of him as a weak leader, one who was taking the path of least resistance, but if he had tried to take a stand and led the Second Praetorian Cohort in the manner it should have been led, he would have faced the same threat that I had just survived, and I am not boasting when I say that he was nowhere near as skilled as I am, yet I was almost killed nonetheless. Consequently, it was not just the wine that, just before I left, found me standing up on the table, prompting Sabinus to shout at the men to shut up. From my vantage point, I could see that at every table there was an almost equal mixture of red and blue tunics, and I was caught by surprise at the sudden lump in my throat at the sight.

"I just wanted to say," I began, "to the men of the Second of the Second Praetorian, it was an honor to be your Centurion. And," I admitted, "I hope that you learned from me as much as I learned from you. The challenges of being a Praetorian may not be exactly the same as they are under the standard, but what I learned is that they're not any less difficult, they're just...different." Raising my cup, I finished, "To the Second Century of the Second Praetorian Cohort, I salute you!"

I was pleased to see that the men of the Fourth stood as well, and this time, the roaring made the dust sift down from the rafters. I needed help climbing down from the table, but I made sure to speak to every Praetorian before I left Isis' Grotto to stagger back to the apartment, telling Saloninus and the others I would see them at camp the next morning.

I was awakened by Alex before dawn, although only because Bronwen refused to have anything to do with me. She was already dressed in her traveling robe, and while she did drop a half-loaf of bread and some cold pork on the table, it was without a word. Naturally, I was miserable, but I knew better than to utter a peep, so I picked at the bread as she finished packing up the baby's things then carried them down to the wagon. After waking me, Alex had gone to the stable, and as much to get away from my woman, I carried the remnant of my meal and hurried down the stairs, meeting Alex on the way back with the pair of mules for the wagon.

"I'll saddle Latobius and Lightning and bring them back to the apartment on my way to camp," I told Alex. "And I'll make sure to find out where your spot will be in the baggage train."

"She'll get over it," he said by way of answer, then after a pause, he added with a grin, "I just don't know how long it will be."

"I'm just glad that I'm riding and not marching," I replied, then we went our separate ways.

I realized I forgot to bring Latobius his apple when he reminded me by nipping at my tunic and "accidentally" grabbing some skin with it, and I more or less resigned myself to being miserable for the foreseeable future, although I was prepared for him to arch his back when I swung into the saddle, followed by a hop or two that rattled my spine. Then we moved at a trot with Lightning in tow, dropping him off just as Alex was finishing hitching the mules. The women and children were already in the wagon, but I was ignored again, which elicited a curse that I barely managed to stifle before I kicked Latobius into a trot. The army was in the process of forming up, and there was actually a crowd of a few thousand people standing nearby, and I wondered if they were happy or sorry to see us leaving. It was not quite light yet, so I had some difficulty finding the 1st's eagle, although I actually found it when I recognized Primus Pilus Sacrovir bellowing at his Century for taking their sweet time falling into formation. I dismounted and led Latobius over to where the Primus

Pilus was standing next to Calpurnius, and it was actually the *Aquilifer* who saw me first, alerting Sacrovir, who turned as I approached.

He returned my salute readily enough, but then he surprised me by saying, "So I suppose I should thank you for whatever it was that you did at Isis' Grotto last night."

"You know about that?" I asked in surprise, which earned me a mocking laugh.

"Of course I know about it," he snapped. "I got a late night visit from your former Pilus Prior Creticus. He came to sing your praises and ask that we keep it between ourselves. Of course," he added sourly, "I *didn't* know about it before then. And believe me, I intend to talk to Saloninus about it." He surprised me further by asking, "Is your woman happy to be leaving Rome?"

"You," I assured him fervently, "have no idea, sir."

This made him laugh, but he was also ready to finish the conversation, and he pointed to Latobius. "Since you don't have an official posting right now, you have my permission to ride with your family. I assume you have a wagon?"

That reminded me, and I replied, "I do, but I don't know where we're supposed to be in the baggage train."

"You might as well add yourself to the 1st's wagons." He shrugged, then said in an obvious dismissal, "Right, I need to get these misbegotten bastards sorted, Pullus."

I saluted, and he returned it, then I led Latobius away but rather than head immediately to the rear of the long column, I walked down the column to the Second Cohort, finding Macer doing essentially the same thing as Sacrovir, bellowing at the men to get into their spots.

"I heard about last night," he began, then teased, "Who knew you were such a peacemaker?"

"I certainly didn't," I admitted ruefully. "But I'm paying for it now."

"Yes, Saloninus told me that you were in rare form with your drinking." He laughed. Pointing to Latobius, he added, "Good thing you can ride today."

I agreed, then told him, "I'm going to have to endure the silent treatment from Bronwen all day. Although," I grinned, "maybe that's not such a bad thing given this fucking headache."

"Well, if you revive somewhat, come see me when we stop."

I told him I would, then mounted Latobius and headed for the rear of the column. The sun was just coming up when the Legate's *Bucinator* sounded the preparatory call, paused, then played the command to begin the march. Naturally, back in the rear with the baggage, it meant that we had to wait for some time before we could begin moving, which meant that I sat next to my wagon as Bronwen studiously ignored me from her spot right behind the bench, while Algaia, sitting next to Alex, glared at me. It was, I thought, going to be a long day. Still, as happy as I was to be leaving Rome, I found myself turning in the saddle as we marched north from the Campus, the walls now visible.

"I am happy that we came here," Bronwen said quietly. Then she leaned out from the wagon and held out her hand, while I bent down, took it, and kissed it as she smiled, and finished, "but I hope I never see Rome again."

And, so far, we have not. That, however, is all I have time for, because we are about to embark on campaign against Marobdunus, and I am back where I belong, wearing the color of the Legions that protect Rome from all of our foreign enemies, but I will never forget my time as a Praetorian, and I have a new appreciation for the challenges the men of the ranks, and those officers who are loyal to the one man in Rome who is our rightful ruler, and not an overambitious, grasping man like Lucius Aelius Sejanus. Unfortunately, I am also convinced that we'll be hearing his name out here on the frontier for some time to come.

Made in the USA
Middletown, DE
31 October 2021

51395292R00257